WITH EVERY BREATH

BY MAYA BANKS

Slow Burn Series

KEEP ME SAFE
IN HIS KEEPING
SAFE AT LAST
WITH EVERY BREATH

Surrender Trilogy

LETTING GO
GIVING IN
TAKING IT ALL

Breathless Trilogy

RUSH
FEVER
BURN

The KGI Series

THE DARKEST HOUR
NO PLACE TO RUN
HIDDEN AWAY
WHISPERS IN THE DARK
ECHOES AT DAWN
SOFTLY AT SUNRISE
SHADES OF GRAY
FORGED IN STEELE
AFTER THE STORM
WHEN THE DAY BREAKS

WITH EVERY BREATH

A Slow Burn Novel

MAYA BANKS

A V O N

An Imprint of HarperCollins*Publishers*

WITH EVERY BREATH. Copyright © 2016 by Maya Banks. All rights reserved. Printed in the United States of America. No part of this book may be used or reproduced in any manner whatsoever without written permission except in the case of brief quotations embodied in critical articles and reviews. For information, address HarperCollins Publishers, 195 Broadway, New York, NY 10007.

HarperCollins books may be purchased for educational, business, or sales promotional use. For information, please email the Special Markets Department at SPsales@harpercollins.com.

FIRST EDITION

Library of Congress Cataloging-in-Publication Data has been applied for.

ISBN 978-0-06-241016-0 (paperback)
ISBN 978-0-06-246648-8 (hardcover library edition)

16 17 18 19 20   DIX/RRD   10 9 8 7 6 5 4 3 2 1

WITH EVERY BREATH

ELIZA came awake with none of her usual crispness and ready-to-take-on-the-world attitude. She felt as though she'd been hit by a truck and her first instinct was to roll over and pull the covers over her head and sleep for several more hours. Even as she knew she wouldn't do any such thing, it was still a nice thought. Still, she thought she could give herself another five minutes before stumbling out of bed and into the shower.

For once, things were slow at Devereaux Security Services after a veritable shit storm of activity over the last several months. She only hoped something popped up when she went into the office today, otherwise it was going to be another boring-ass day at work.

Just as she roused herself from her laziness and threw her legs over the side of the bed to stand, the landline on her nightstand rang. She glanced down at it, frowning. If it was Dane or anyone else from DSS, surely they'd call her cell. A quick look told her that her cell phone was on the nightstand charging and a glance at it also told her she hadn't missed any calls. If this was a telemarketer calling her at oh-dark-thirty so help her she was going to hunt them down and shove her foot as far up their ass as she could.

If it weren't for the fact that it *could* be one of her coworkers she would have simply ignored the ringing all together. With a sigh, she yanked up the phone and barked an unwelcome hello into the receiver.

There was a short pause and then the clearing of a throat. "Miss Caldwell? Melissa Caldwell?"

Eliza froze, her blood turning to ice in her veins. She hadn't heard that name in ten years. Hadn't been that person in ten years. And in two seconds flat, her past had slammed into her present like a speeding train.

"What do you want?" she asked in a dull voice.

"This is Clyde Barksdale, district attorney for Keerney County, Oregon."

She knew damn well who Clyde Barksdale was. Like she'd forget that it was him she'd worked with to put Thomas Harrington away?

"I take it this isn't a social call," she said acidly.

"You'd be correct." The DA emitted an exhausted sounding sigh. "Look, there's no easy way to say this but Thomas Harrington won an appeal to overturn his conviction and he'll be set free in three weeks' time."

Eliza's knees folded and she landed with a hard bounce on the bed. She was utterly numb with shock, and she shook her head in an effort to dispel the fog and confusion surrounding her. Was this some fucked-up dream—nightmare—she was trapped in?

"*What?*" she whispered in horror. "What the fuck? What do you *mean* his conviction was overturned? Is this some kind of twisted *joke?*"

"He must have gotten to one of the cops who worked his case," the DA said in a furious voice. "It's the only explanation. The cop admitted under oath to tampering with evidence in order to make the case against Harrington a slam dunk. As if we goddamn needed the evidence when we had your testimony. But with his admission, and the fact that you were painted as a scorned child, angry and humiliated by the rejection of an older man, the court had no choice but to exonerate him."

Eliza was speechless. She was absolutely paralyzed and awash with a multitude of differing emotions. Sweat beaded her forehead and nausea swirled in her gut. She was going to be sick. This couldn't be happening. They couldn't let such a dangerous sociopathic monster free! Ever!

"When?" she managed to croak out.

Oh dear God, she was going to be sick. She clamped a hand over her mouth and sucked in mouthfuls of air in a desperate effort not to heave up the contents of her stomach.

"Three weeks," the DA said grimly. "I've thrown everything at the courts that I can. I've tried everything in my power to pull together enough evidence to nail him with something—anything—that would prevent him walking out of prison a free man and my hands are goddamn tied! He can't be tried for murder again and we can't hope to press rape charges because we don't have any viable evidence. It would be your word against his. All that can be done at this point is for one of his victims, the only surviving victim—you—to file a civil suit and that does jack."

"Oh dear God," Eliza breathed, her voice muffled by the

hand still held tightly over her mouth. "He'll kill again. He thinks he's invincible, that he's God, and him beating the system just proves his superiority in his mind."

"He'll want revenge, Miss Caldwell," the DA said quietly. "He'll come after you. I had to call and warn you."

"I hope to hell he does," she said savagely.

But even as she spoke, she shook her head, her thoughts in chaos as she attempted to sort through her horror. No. Fuck that. To hell with running, hiding, all the things Thomas would expect her to do. He'd expect to find that same sixteen-year-old timid girl so desperate for love and acceptance.

No, she wasn't running. She would go after *him*. She would make it damn easy for him to find her because she would be waiting when he was released in prison. And then she'd take him down and send him to hell where he belonged.

Alarm sounded in the DA's voice. "Miss Caldwell, don't do anything you'll regret. I called you because you had the right to know and so you could take protective measures and heed caution."

"I can assure you, Mr. Barksdale, my *only* regret is that I didn't take him out the first time," she said in an ice-cold tone. Steely determination gripped her. She was infused with purpose. A goal. One she would not fail in.

As she quietly disconnected the call, her nostrils flared and she embraced the frigid chill that had invaded her limbs the second the DA had announced the reason for his call. She had to lock down her rioting emotions or she'd go insane with grief—and guilt.

Her eyes closed and her head lowered, so much anguish threatening to overwhelm her. She shook her head vehemently, refusing to give in to despair. The justice system had utterly failed Thomas Harrington's victims. It had failed her.

No one knew Thomas like she did. No one knew of his enormous power and how so very easily he could enthrall his victims. There was nothing left but for *her* to seek justice and to protect the only people in the world who mattered to her. The only people she had allowed herself to get close to in the ten years since she'd put the man she'd loved with all the innocence of a teenaged girl away for what she thought had been for good.

Only now he would be set free, and it was up to her to ensure that he would claim no further victims. Even if it meant being consigned to hell right along with him.

She should have killed him, but she'd naïvely believed in the system and that he would pay for his crimes. Now, she knew better, and unless she stopped him, he'd kill and keep killing.

TWO

"ALL set?" Wade Sterling asked his good friend, perhaps his only friend, Anna-Grace Covington.

Wade the quintessential lone wolf. He shunned personal relationships of any kind and he had little time for friends. Having a friend meant a level of trust he simply wasn't able to give another person. Blind faith wasn't what had made him the ruthless, successful businessman he'd become.

But his own self-imposed rules had simply disappeared when he'd met Anna-Grace. True, at first, he'd been interested in her on a more personal level, but he'd quickly discovered that the vulnerable, fragile woman had suffered unimaginable tragedy and a relationship—any kind of romantic or sexual relationship— with a man was the last thing she needed or wanted.

As a result, surprised by the true affection he'd felt for her, they'd instead become close friends, and he had become her only confidant.

Anna-Grace, or Gracie as most people called her, though

Wade had always known—and addressed—her by her full name until recent months, stared anxiously at the array of paintings that were displayed to their best advantage.

Wade slipped an arm around her shoulders and gave her a reassuring squeeze. "Everyone is going to love you." Then, to distract her from her panic, he asked, "Did Cheryl arrange everything to your liking?"

Gracie nodded though she still pensively studied her artwork and she looked very much like she wanted to vomit. Wade sighed. He turned to Gracie and collected her hands in his.

"Honey, do you think I would display just anyone in my gallery? I know you think the studio is a side interest of mine that I pay little or no attention to, but I have a great deal of time and money invested in this place and before you suggest that our friendship is why I'm holding an exhibition for you, may I remind you that we only became friends *because* of your art? I was interested in your *work* and could see the potential in you as an artist before I knew anything about you. Our friendship was the result of your talent, and furthermore, friend or not, and you of all people should know how ruthless I am when it comes to business, I wouldn't sink this kind of capital into launching you if I wasn't one hundred percent certain that I was making a sound investment."

True, Joie de Vivre was one of many things Wade dabbled in. One of his many legitimate business interests. But he hadn't lied. He did enjoy art. Good art. And Gracie was a very talented artist.

The two had met when he'd seen a sample of her work when she had come in, looking for the world like someone who had lost her way a long time before. Perhaps he'd seen a kindred spirit. They'd both known pain and disillusionment. Gracie's story, however, was worse than most.

He'd sought to protect her when the source of her anguish had stormed back into her life, but over time, he'd come to realize that Zack Covington, her husband, had been just as betrayed as Gracie. Zack had mourned the loss of his childhood sweetheart for over a decade and had never stopped in his search for her. The two had overcome insurmountable odds and even their reunion was fraught with peril. But finally, the two were happily married, and the art exhibit that Wade had planned for Gracie before things had gone straight to hell was back on the schedule with just a few days left until the big day.

"It must seem like I'm fishing for compliments and want you to kiss my ass," Gracie said with an unhappy sigh.

Wade put a finger over her lips to hush her before she could continue.

"You are one of the most humble, genuine people I know, Gracie. No one would ever think you were fishing for compliments. Now, if the paintings are arranged to your liking, perhaps you can give me a list of your guests for the big night? It will be open to the public, of course, but I am extending personal invitations to several potential buyers I believe will love your work, and anyone you'd like to attend, I will also send a personal invitation to.

"Cheryl has been working with a publicity firm and we have an extensive marketing campaign already launched, with newspaper, magazine, internet and television advertising. I dare say you're going to make quite a splash in the art world, sweetheart."

Her lips rounded to an *O* and her eyes widened as she stared back at Wade. Then her nose wrinkled, her expression becoming one of doubt and dismay.

"That sounds awfully expensive, Wade! I could never afford anything like that."

He shook his head and sighed. "It's called an investment, Gracie. One I think will net me rather large returns considering I'll demand exclusivity on your work and will receive commission on every painting sold. See? If I were doing this out of friendship or charity, then I wouldn't be such a bastard by demanding exclusivity and commission. The way I see it, you're going to make us both a lot of money."

She laughed, some of the tension easing from her rigid stance. "Maybe you should be my manager as well. Lord knows I don't know a thing about arranging, well . . . anything. If I am even moderately successful I won't have the first clue how to handle my own affairs."

"Which is why you have me," he said. "You paint. I do everything else. I think we will have a mutually beneficial arrangement. Now, all I need from you is your guest list and you're done. I'll expect you to go home and practice that gorgeous smile. You're going to be an absolute hit, and I'll get credit for having discovered the next big thing in modern art."

She donned a pensive look. "I don't have many. Everyone at DSS. Oh and especially Eliza." Wade stiffened at both the mention of Eliza's name *and* the instant anxiety that was reflected in Gracie's features. "Do you think she'll come, Wade? Everyone is so concerned about her. She needs to get out more."

"What's wrong with Eliza?" Wade demanded, though he disagreed that she needed to get out more. If anything the fool woman needed to stay in for once. Rest. Recover. Process the horrifying ordeal she'd experienced. None of which she'd done. Hadn't had time to do because she was too busy saving the rest of the world. Everyone but her own pretty ass.

Gracie looked even unhappier. "No one knows but they're all worried. She isn't herself. Hasn't been for some time but especially over the past several days. Everyone has been on tiptoe around her but you know Eliza. She's very private and extremely tight-lipped."

"What the hell do they expect?" Wade snapped in a louder voice than he'd intended.

Damn it. She didn't even have to be anywhere in the vicinity and she still managed to rattle his iron composure. He needed to get laid. Work her out of his system and damn sure out of his every waking thought. The problem was, when he looked at other women with sex on his mind, all he saw was . . . *her*. And that pissed him off.

Gracie recoiled at the fury in his voice, her eyes widening in surprise at his vehemence.

Wade's jaw ticked with irritation and he held up his hand, ticking off points one by one on his fingers.

"Let's see. She gets kidnapped, tortured and fucking waterboarded. She came this close to dying," he snapped, pausing to lift his hand and hold his thumb and first finger an inch apart before resuming once more. "And she doesn't even take a goddamn day off to rest and recover before she's back on the job and we go after the fuckers that hurt her, *you* and Ari. She damn near gets killed *again*, but I took the bullet meant for her. If I hadn't been there? She'd be in the ground right now. Does she take any down time *then*? Fuck no. She's back at work like nothing ever happened and *now* suddenly everyone is worried about her?"

He shook his head, his anger simmering like a cauldron.

"Is she sleeping at all?" he demanded.

Gracie blinked. "I-I don't know, Wade. How would I?"

"You can read her damn mind, can't you?"

Gracie flushed and Wade immediately felt guilty.

"I'm sorry, Gracie," Wade said in a low voice. "That was un-called for and a shitty thing to say. Damn it! That woman infuri-ates me."

"I could read her mind if I ever *saw* her," Gracie said quietly. "I think . . ."

"What?" Wade said sharply.

"I think she's avoiding me for that very reason," she said with a frown. "It's like if I run into her or I go to the office to see Zack and she's there, she immediately finds a reason to disappear. What else am I supposed to think?"

Wade swore viciously under his breath. Oh yeah. The little hellcat likely did have something—a lot—to hide. Like the fact that she was probably running on empty and barely existing on fumes. He wanted to track her down and beat some sense into her, and he *would* if it weren't likely she'd kick *his* ass. Or at the very least rearrange his nuts for him. And well, he was finished with the little vixen. She was trouble with a capital T. If it were all the same, Wade was done with her and DSS and anything to do with them or their missions. He had enough on his plate without trailing after a brazen woman who was bent on saving the world while he had the unfortunate task of saving *her*.

Ungrateful heifer. She'd spit on him before ever acknowledg-ing that he'd saved her snarly ass. Not even a thank-you. A fuck off, yeah. Thank you? No. Instead, all the thanks he'd gotten was that he couldn't look at another woman and see anyone but her.

Couldn't imagine having sex with anyone but a petite, snarly-mouthed, sassy, short-tempered blonde. He snorted, causing Gracie to look at him with an odd expression on her face.

"Eliza is a coward," Wade said. "She won't want to set foot in a place owned and run by me. After I took a bullet for her, she conveniently finds a reason to be elsewhere if I'm anywhere around."

"Join the crowd," Gracie said, a hint of hurt to her voice.

That settled it for Wade. Eliza could get over whatever was up her ass. No matter what the little spitfire was afraid Gracie would pick up from her thoughts, she would attend. He wasn't going to let anything or anyone ruin Gracie's night to shine.

"She'll be here," Wade said grimly. "If I have to haul her here over my shoulder, she'll be here."

Gracie immediately looked alarmed. "Uh, Wade, never mind. Really. Maybe we should just back off and give Eliza her space."

"Don't worry," Wade said silkily. "I won't really haul her to your exhibit over my shoulder." *Liar.* "I just plan to have a perfectly civil conversation with Eliza when I *personally* issue the invitation to her."

Or rather his ultimatum. For the first time when thinking of an impending confrontation with Eliza, he wasn't seized by annoyance. No, he was looking forward to pissing her off. And the best part? He might annoy the ever-loving hell out of her—the feeling was entirely mutual—but she damn well knew he didn't bluff. So she'd have no choice but to come of her own volition. Or suffer the indignity of being hauled to the event by Wade.

THREE

ELIZA knew she'd been scarce ever since she'd received the call from the DA. She also knew she'd been avoiding her coworkers, which wasn't the smartest thing in the world if she didn't want them thinking, or rather knowing, what she was planning, what she must do at all costs. But the simple truth was she couldn't bear to face them. Shame was a living, breathing presence that encompassed her heart and soul.

The people she worked for epitomized all that was good. No, they didn't always do everything by the book. They broke the rules, but in the end, justice was served, and wasn't that all that mattered?

One of her bosses disarmed a monster who posed no further threat, but then that hadn't been true either. The bastard's psychic ability and the fact he'd created a link to both Caleb and his now wife, Ramie, meant that even behind bars, he could exert his will and control, making the couple's lives hell. He'd already used Caleb to hurt Ramie in a horrifying manner. The memory still sickened Eliza every time it came to mind. The only way to sever that irrevocable tie binding them to him was for Caleb to kill him. And he had. By putting a bullet through his evil, twisted brain.

Oh, they'd wiped down the scene. Made damn sure it had appeared as though Caleb shot in self-defense, planting a gun with no other prints into a madman's hand, finger on the trigger. It may not have been the *legal* or *moral* thing to do. But it had been righteous.

Just as her mission was righteous. Maybe not to the public, the police, the justice system. But to the women he'd tortured and killed? To their families? To Eliza herself? Yeah, it was righteous. She doubted the families cared how he paid, just as long as he did. People couldn't possibly understand or conceive the monster behind the polished, charming façade. But Eliza was acquainted with it better than anyone. Only she truly knew the depths of his evilness and it was only she who could end it all. Maybe that made her just as sick and twisted as Thomas was. Or perhaps it took evil to hunt evil.

Right now, the families of the victims had no doubt been told, just as she had been, that Thomas Harrington was being freed in a very short time. They were likely feeling every single emotion Eliza had felt—was still feeling. Betrayal. Rage. Sorrow. Grief. A deep sense of injustice. They had likely lost all faith in the justice system sworn to uphold the law and sworn to punish those who broke it. But they were helpless to do anything about it. They would dream of revenge and retribution. Of justice. But Eliza would serve it cold.

And this was where Eliza differed from the others who might entertain unholy thoughts of making Thomas suffer a long and painful death. She *could* do something about it. She *would* do something about it even if it meant her own death. In many ways she'd died ten years ago when she'd realized just how stupid and very naïve she'd been. So very gullible. She was as guilty and complicit in the murder of those women as Thomas himself and she'd never forgive herself for the atrocities committed. Yes, she had died and been reborn another woman. Eliza Cummings. She'd become Eliza and had embraced a new chance. The opportunity to start over. To make a difference. To help protect those who needed protection. To seek justice for those who couldn't. And somehow she'd managed to buy into her new-but-not-real new identity. What a fool she'd been to ever think she could atone for her sins and outrun her past. Death could only be delayed, not avoided.

In some ways ... She stopped, frozen by the thought as it floated through her mind before she could call it back. Her heart pounded and her palms grew sweaty as she tried to open the door to her car. But she realized that thought had been there since the morning of the phone call. In the instant she'd made her decision, it had been there, only she'd ignored it, refusing to give voice to it. Refusing to acknowledge it because it made her weak, something she'd sworn never to be again.

But she had *deserved* to die with Thomas. And now, she was fully prepared for her death. It was her punishment. Justice being served, finally, to the fullest. Thomas had been the only one who had paid when he'd been sentenced to life in prison. *She* hadn't. But she'd deserved the same punishment and now that she'd sentenced him to death by her own sense of justice, not only was it likely she'd die taking him down, it was no less than she deserved. She embraced it with calm resolution. Didn't fear it. No longer would she try so hard to avoid the inevitable. Maybe then she would have a semblance of peace and maybe God would grant mercy on her soul for the sins she'd committed when she'd been little more than a child, powerless against the manipulation of an older more experienced man. No, not man. Psychopath. Monster. The kind that only existed in nightmares and horror movies.

The very face of evil.

Only he wasn't a nightmare. He wasn't fiction, some book or movie. He was very real.

She yanked open her car door and threw herself inside, backing from her parking spot at the DSS building just as she saw Dane exit the building. She made certain she didn't make eye contact with him, but she watched from the corner of her eye as he waved in a motion for her to stop. At least by not overtly glancing in his direction, she could plead ignorance when he asked her—and he would—why the hell she'd ignored him.

Oh hell no she wasn't stopping. When she faced Dane, she had to have her shit together and her best game face on. She accelerated a little too sharply, her tires barking in protest as she barreled from the parking garage. No doubt her esteemed leader, partner—Dane filled many roles at DSS—wanted to interrogate her and that was the last thing she needed. She had seen the looks Dane and the rest of her coworkers cast her way when they thought she wasn't looking. They were all filled with concern, making her cringe and guilt wash through her all over again. They all knew something was up and that she wasn't herself, but Dane would know better than anyone. She and Dane had worked together far too long and Dane never missed a goddamn thing.

The man had a way of making a person squirm with a look. No words were necessary. All he'd have to do is stare at her and she'd be blurting her confession with no prompting whatsoever and then he'd lock her up if he had to. No way he'd let her fulfill what she now considered her sacred mission. Her last mission. A mission that was more important than any other she'd ever undertaken.

She chanced a glance in her rearview mirror and grimaced as she saw Dane standing in the middle of the traffic lane to the parking garage, a frown on his face as he stared broodingly after her.

She couldn't avoid him forever but until she was ready, until she was composed enough to carry off the biggest—only—lie she'd ever told her most trusted friend, she would continue to brush him and the others off and run like a bat out of hell anytime one of them had the opportunity to get her alone.

Just a few more days, she promised herself. A few more days to pull the rest of her plan together, to gather everything she needed and give her carefully orchestrated lie to Dane and then she'd be on her way.

Sorrow gripped her and she briefly closed her eyes before pulling into traffic. It would be the last time she saw any of them, which is why she'd approach Dane after the "state of the union" meeting given the first of every month by either Caleb Devereaux or his brother, Beau, in the offices of DSS.

It would give her one last opportunity to see the people who'd grown so important to her. Her family. People she would and did go to the wall for each and every day. People who did the same for her. Her only regret was that she wouldn't see the Devereaux wives and Zack's wife, Gracie, before she left.

She inwardly flinched because she knew she'd hurt Gracie's feelings more than once by avoiding her every time Gracie had been around Eliza. Eliza had promptly fled when Gracie appeared, and it had been obvious to the other woman, and the last thing in the world Eliza ever wanted to do was hurt Gracie.

Gracie was the epitome of sweet, and she'd already been hurt so much in her young life. She was shy and still struggling with her confidence. Eliza was so very happy that Gracie and Zack had found their way back to one another after over a decade of misery for both of them, but especially Gracie. Eliza dearly loved all the wives. Ramie, Ari and Gracie. And Tori Devereaux, Caleb's, Beau's and Quinn's baby sister, who like the other women had suffered greatly at the hands of a madman. She had been brutalized by a serial killer and was still recovering from the horrific attack. Perhaps she'd never fully recover but then Eliza could hardly blame her.

If it hadn't been for Caleb hunting down Ramie, a gifted young psychic, and giving her no choice but to aid in his search for his sister, they wouldn't have rescued Tori in time and she would have died.

All the women were gifted with extraordinary powers. Tori had dreams of future events, though of all the women, her gift was not as fully developed or focused as the others. Her gift was more of a curse, giving her glimpses, but without enough knowledge revealed, she was helpless to prevent the events or even warn anyone they were in danger, and it was a source of great torment to her. Ramie could track the same kind of monster Eliza now found herself about to track. But Eliza would never pit Ramie against a man who was likely every bit as psychically gifted as Ramie was herself. Ari had enormous power, a lot that hadn't even been tapped into yet. She grew more powerful all the time and as she learned to control it, she would be an unstoppable force. And Gracie . . . Eliza winced again, because it wasn't the other two she avoided like the plague. Only Gracie because Gracie could read minds and Eliza couldn't chance being in close proximity to her because if she read Eliza's mind, it would be all over and Eliza wouldn't allow that to happen.

Eliza aimlessly drove in the direction of her apartment, stopping at a drive-thru to get lunch though her heart wasn't into eating, but she had to keep her strength up. She couldn't be weak when she faced off against Thomas. Weak physically or emotionally.

Her lunch laying unopened in the bag in the passenger seat, she pulled into her parking spot and when she saw the vehicle next to her and the man standing arrogantly in front of the expensive car, leaning against the hood, her mood went from bad to worse.

What the hell was Wade Sterling doing here?

Her lunch forgotten, she climbed out of her car and slammed the door with unnecessary force, a scowl already forming on her face. To her further annoyance, Wade only smirked, his eyes gleaming with amusement as he took in her reaction to his presence.

Deciding that acknowledging him would be far worse than asking him what he was doing here, she clutched her keys and stalked around to the front of her vehicle and started to walk by him without a word. Her "welcoming" expression could do the talking for her.

To her utter shock, as she was nearly past him, a hand suddenly gripped her elbow, stopping her in her tracks. She narrowed her eyes, pasting her most ferocious snarl on her lips, and rounded furiously on him.

"What the fuck is your problem, Sterling? Take your hand off me. *Now.*"

"Is that any way to express gratitude to the man who saved your life?" he drawled.

She wanted to scream. No one and she meant *no one* knew how to push her buttons like this man did. But then his mere *presence* was a huge button. Anytime he opened his mouth, instant push of her many buttons. And the arrogant pull of his lips, all that alpha superiority and smugness? Every single button she had was pushed simultaneously.

She actually *growled* at him. Or rather it was a combination of a vicious sounding snarl and a throaty growl of frustration. She was tempted to do something incredibly childish and decidedly un-Eliza like, such as stomp her foot, pull her hair out by the roots or throw the mother of all hissy fits. God, she didn't have time for this bullshit today! They had successfully—and mutually—avoided each other ever since the incident he'd just referred to, one that Eliza would prefer to just forget all together. Saved her life, her ass! If he hadn't been there, and if she hadn't been so goddamn busy trying to make sure *his* dumb civilian ass didn't get shot then she would have never nearly taken a fatal bullet. One that he'd taken for her instead, and it chapped her ass that apparently he thought she should be on her knees in gratitude for taking a bullet that was his own goddamn fault! Mutual avoidance had been working just fine, so what the hell was he doing at *her* apartment. And why?

Sure there had been a few times when being in the same room had been unavoidable. Zack and Gracie's wedding for one. And on those few occasions, Sterling had goaded her mercilessly. First he'd called her a coward and accused her of hiding from him. Then he had pissed her off to no end by "claiming" a dance with her at the reception, and since she had just so happened to have been giving Zack and Gracie her well wishes in preparation of fleeing the way too happy, gushy, *mushy* lovefest involving more than the "just married" couple it was in honor of, she couldn't gracefully—or ungracefully—get out of it. Gracie had seemed delighted and had told Eliza that *of course* she just *had* to dance with Wade, after all they were two of her most favorite people in the world.

Eliza had groaned, knowing she'd been royally set up by the bastard. He'd planned it meticulously and had approached her when he damn well *knew* she couldn't tell him what to do with his invitation to dance along with a few other choice words that would have singed the hair of most people and embarrassed the radiant bride. It hadn't, however, stopped her from purposely baiting *him* the entire time they danced. But he hadn't responded to her sarcasm, insults or her attempts to get a rise out of him. Instead he'd simply stared at her with smug amusement, those dark eyes peeling back every layer of skin on her. To add insult to injury, he'd held her far closer than necessary, making it appear like they were glued to each other and practically fucking on the dance floor. The only way she'd managed to get through it was by imagining at least a dozen different scenarios in which she separated his balls from his anatomy.

In the end, she'd fled as if the hounds of hell were after her, and damn it, but his laughter had followed her the entire way out. As had his last words: "Little coward." Something he'd become increasingly in the habit of calling her and the second time he'd hurled it at her that night.

And now as they stood in an apparent standoff, her glaring

holes through him and him looking as though he found her hilarious, those images of bodily dismemberment she'd entertained during their dance were even more appealing.

Sterling didn't even attempt to hide his smile at her growl. His eyes twinkled and then his lips broadened into an honest-to-goodness real smile. She stared at him, momentarily forgetting just how furious she was with him. She was completely flabbergasted by the change to his features. He *never* smiled. Not really. He'd always done this half smile thing that came out more as a smirk and sometimes as a grimace, depending on his mood. But he'd never, at least not in her sight, actually smiled a broad, teeth-flashing smile that extended all the way up to his eyes. Sweet Jesus but it made him look . . . delicious. She nearly groaned at that betraying thought. *Delicious?* She needed her head examined. But she couldn't stop her perusal to save her life.

She continued to stare in equal parts bewilderment and feminine fascination, riveted by how freaking gorgeous he was with that million megawatt smile. Holy hell, now she could understand why he never lacked for female company. Gracie had told her, after it was established that a romantic relationship between her and Sterling was never going to happen and the two settled on being just friends, that she lost count of the women who sailed in and out of his life.

At first Eliza had misunderstood, thinking that he was such an ogre that he couldn't keep a woman. That idea had appealed immensely to her and she'd warmed to it immediately. Until Gracie burst that bubble by telling her that *he* never kept a woman more than a few dates before moving on to the next one. Figures. Apparently he was a complete player out for only one thing. But, a man with his looks and money could be as picky and selective as he wanted. Women flocked to that badass, bad boy, darker edge persona and the danger that seemed to swirl in his eyes and fit him like a second skin. Eliza scoffed at that.

The man was nebulous at best. She'd done some checking into him when he'd contacted DSS about a potential job and nothing in her research led her to believe he was completely on the up and up. Dirty, she'd suspected and had told Zack as much. The problem was, she had no solid proof. Only discrepancies and her own suspicions. And her gut, which she never ignored.

But that likely appealed to the section of the female population who were shorter on brains and superficial enough not to care about anything beyond good looks, lots of money—that was likely the biggest attraction—and the aura of dark and dangerous that cloaked him at all times. Who cared if he killed puppies, kittens or people as long as he was rich, handsome and good in the sack? She nearly bared her teeth in irritation but instead returned to getting the handsome, rich *asshole* out of her space.

"Do tell, what do you find so amusing?" Eliza asked snidely. She'd never in a million years admit or confide to anyone *how* flustered she'd been over that smile. Or that for a moment she'd entertained a few naked fantasies about him.

Though disappointment was keen when the smile was replaced by the more common mocking twist of his lips, which told her he was about to start firing back the same insults and resort to the same ribbing and cut downs she routinely gave him. Oh well, it would hardly be fun if he *didn't* fire back. She would have been disappointed if he acted like she'd hurt his little feelings or his masculine pride. Goading him was the only fun she had these days. Besides, when he was being a dick, it was too easy to despise him and then at least she wouldn't become a damn *girl* and start thinking about licking those delectable lips.

And then she remembered that she didn't have time for fun or for juvenile fantasies. Hadn't that been what had got her in the mess she'd become so firmly entrenched in years ago? How could she have even thought about *anything* else when all her focus, her concentration and her training should be on preparation for the single most important mission of her life?

Suddenly Sterling's eyes narrowed, and his hand was curled around her chin before she even registered it was there. He turned her to face him, his sharp gaze boring into hers, studying her, probing deeply until she felt stripped bare and utterly vulnerable before him.

"What the hell were you just thinking about?" he demanded. "And don't make this about me, Eliza. I'll call bullshit and you know it. You enjoy taunting me, hurling insults and doing your damnedest to make me believe you want no part of me, which we *both* know is untrue. Whatever it was that just crossed your mind was *not* a source of enjoyment. You went *pale* and your eyes went from fiery and spitting sparks at me to dull and shadowed and your shoulders sagged and you are *nothing* if not confident. Your back is always up, shoulders straight and you don't lower your head to fucking *anyone* and yet you just did all of those things. What the *fuck* is going on with you?"

She stared at him in astonishment, not knowing which of his absurd statements to refute first. In his own way, he'd just complimented her. As much of a compliment as Sterling ever gave anyone. At least she *thought* he was complimenting her. He hadn't listed her attributes with a distasteful look nor did he seem disapproving. He was just . . . matter-of-fact.

She went backward through all the other crap he'd said, and it *was* crap. Then her cheeks blazed with a mixture of fury and abject embarrassment when she got to the most important, most errant assumption the arrogant little prick had made.

She got into his face and jabbed her finger into his chest, causing him to take one step backward before steadying himself. He simply brushed her finger away and then folded his very muscled arms over his very muscled chest and stared down at her, his lips pressed together as if . . .

"Don't you dare laugh!" she shouted. "And as for me not wanting any part of you? Get a clue, Sterling. A woman who wants a part of you doesn't tell you to fuck off every time she sees you. She doesn't constantly insult you. Nor does she avoid you because you annoy the ever-loving fuck out of her. Get it into your head. I want *nothing* to do with you. In fact, I don't want you here right now. Which begs the question, why *are* you? Our avoiding each other is *mutual*. I avoid you. You avoid me. I think it's established that neither of us can stand the sight of the other. Neither of us wants to be in the same room together. It's an arrangement that suits me just fine. So don't tell me that we both know it isn't true that I want nothing to do with you!"

She jabbed her finger just above his overlapped arms so that it met the solid wall of his chest, accentuating every word with another jab.

"I." *Poke.* "Don't." *Poke.* "Ever." *Jab.* "Want." *Jab.* "To." *Poke.* "See." *Poke.* "You ever, ever, *ever* again!" She balled her fist and punched him as she said the last.

He threw back his head and laughed. It took every bit of her discipline not to let her mouth drop open and stare shamelessly at the sight. Because Sterling actually smiling, as in a real honest-to-God smile, was a sight enough in itself, but him laughing? Holy hell but him smiling *and* laughing was a very beautiful thing indeed. *He* was beautiful.

"Keep telling yourself that, Eliza," he said, his eyes still sparking with laughter. "If you tell yourself often enough you might even start believing your lies."

"Oh for fuck's sake," she muttered, turning on her heel to stalk past him so she could be rid of him.

But once again he caught her arm, though his grasp was gentle. Gentle, but no less confining. His thumb stroked gently over her upper arm, softly caressing the bare skin under the short sleeve of her T-shirt, and it did funny, ridiculous things to her pulse. She tried to yank away, but his grip only tightened, again, not a bruising manhandling-type grip, but one that prevented her from freeing herself, nonetheless.

She glared at him in silence and then looked pointedly down at her arm. He either didn't get that particular message or refused to acknowledge it.

"Gracie's opening is tonight. I trust you'll be there."

It wasn't a question. In no way was it a question or even a polite *request*. It was an order and Eliza did not take orders very well at all. Even Dane didn't order her around and he was her partner and boss of sorts.

"As a matter of fact, I have other plans," she said sweetly. "Important plans that I can't cancel. Job related. I'm sure Gracie will understand."

Sterling's presence would be enough to make her cry off the exhibit but throw in the fact that Gracie could read her mind? No way in hell she'd be caught dead in attendance.

Sterling's face suddenly became rock hard, his eyes turning

glacial, all hint of amusement and laughter gone, as was his smile. "Let there be no mistake, Eliza. You *will* be there tonight even if I have to throw you over my shoulder and carry you cursing and making threats against humanity the entire way. This means everything to Gracie and all she wants is the support of the people she cares about and *thinks* care about her. Whatever your issue with Gracie is I suggest you do your best to ensure she knows nothing about it. It will hurt her if you refuse to come and I won't allow Gracie to ever be hurt by anyone again. Are we understood?"

Eliza looked at him in shock. "I don't have anything against Gracie! I love her dearly. Where on earth would you get the idea that I have a problem with her? Just because I can't make it to her opening doesn't mean I don't like her. I'm not going because I can't. I have something important to do tonight. Something I can't postpone."

Sterling shrugged. "I suggest you find a way to do just that. You can't hide from me, Eliza. And if you think I was making an idle threat, one I have no intention of following through on, you should know me better than that by now. I *will* find you and I *will* bring you to the exhibit no matter how you're dressed. My advice? Dress appropriately and be there promptly when it begins and paste a smile on that pretty face of yours and at least act like you're enjoying yourself and that you're supporting the woman who calls you her friend."

"What gives you the right to rearrange my life to suit your wants?" she snapped. "I'm not one of your little bimbos who flutters her eyelashes and gives in to your every whim and allows you all the control."

He barked out a laugh. "As if. A man would be a fool to ever think you'd be a simpering, timid, submissive woman without a mind and will of her own. But, Eliza, do not test me on this," he said, his voice growing somber and gravely serious. His eyes bore intently into hers and the unsettled feeling in her stomach grew until all her insides were knotted with panic.

"Good God, you mean it," she whispered, horrified.

"Bet your pretty little ass I do," he said, his eyes narrowing. "Have I ever bluffed, Eliza? Have I ever stood down from any promise I've made? Veered from the course I've sworn to follow? Not followed through on any action I've decided on?"

"No," she said faintly, a sinking feeling of doom clenching her stomach.

She just wanted to run and hide in her apartment, and she was not someone who ever hid from anything. She confronted her problems, her fears, and she never backed down. But Wade Sterling was a problem unlike any she'd ever encountered and if she knew one thing at all about this infuriating, pain-in-the-ass man, was that he wouldn't simply go away. No wasn't an answer he was accustomed to nor was it a word in his vocabulary unless he was the one using it.

Which meant that if she didn't want a very ugly, very embarrassing, humiliating scene tonight, she was going to have to find a dress and appropriate shoes, neither of which she owned. Fast.

Further proof that the man was a mind reader in his own right, either that or extremely intuitive, he suddenly did that half smirk, half grin thing she was far more accustomed to than the full on, teeth-baring smile she'd witnessed earlier.

"I took the liberty of having an appropriate dress, shoes and all of the accessories delivered to your apartment. Expect them within the hour. And may I say, Eliza, you are going to look stunning in what I picked out."

FOUR

ONLY because she didn't want *more* speculation among her co-workers that something was definitely up with her, something she wasn't sharing—and planned to keep it that way—did Eliza grudgingly put on the dress, shoes and accessories Sterling had delivered to her apartment as she got ready for what she already considered a night in hell. Or so she told herself, knowing that her feminine ego had been just a little stroked by the fact Sterling had told her with none of his typical, arrogant smugness that she would look fantastic in what he'd picked out for her. No, his gaze had smoldered, and he'd been completely serious and worse, he'd also looked as though he was *interested* in and couldn't *wait* to see the results of his handiwork. And so, like a damn girl, even though she despised the man, she'd seen definite male appreciation in his sexy gaze, and it appealed to her feminine ego to further tempt the beast with what he'd never have a shot at, so she'd not only worn the gorgeous, ridiculously expensive dress—sans bra because she was in a particularly wicked mood—but she'd also taken extra effort with her hair and makeup, which disgusted her because she didn't want it to be blatantly obvious she wanted to look good. For *him*. Because she did not give one fuck when it came to her looks nor did she have a clue what looked good on her, something apparently Sterling felt *he* knew. And since he'd taken the liberty of choosing her wardrobe, he would hardly be able to find fault with her appearance tonight. She just hoped to hell she could avoid him *and* Gracie, make an appearance and then exit as gracefully and as unnoticed as possible.

Jesus, but she was the worst sort of idiot for even contemplating knocking Wade Sterling down a few notches and making him swallow his sharp tongue. She didn't have time for making cute, being a tease with no intention of following through on the promise this damn dress offered not only to Sterling, but to any man. Gah! She hadn't even considered the "other men" in the equation. Not that she had to worry about the guys she worked for. To them, she was one of them. But whoever else was in attendance wouldn't be able to look at her sexy vamp look and remotely think, *oh yeah, she's one of the guys.*

A prickle irritated her nape and she frowned at the sudden, unwelcome thought that for once, just one night, she didn't want to be one of the guys. She was a woman even if she'd refused to give in to most parts of her femininity after the disaster that was Thomas. And now, when he was about to become a free man, unleashed on hapless women he would victimize, she suddenly wanted to reclaim everything he'd stolen from her? She had to be out of her goddamn mind.

She should have gotten laid a long time ago and gotten it done with. But Thomas Harrington controlled her from behind bars every bit as much as he had when he was a free man, and that fact disgusted her most of all.

Eliza pulled up to Joie de Vivre in the "swanky" part of Westheimer, as she termed it. Everything about the businesses, and even buildings, looked so new and shiny to practically scream wealth, power, influence. In other words, *swank*. And it was definitely a place she didn't belong.

Reluctantly, she got out of her car, opting to have parked a block away rather than use the valet service Sterling had installed for the occasion. When it was time for her to ditch the event and get the hell out before drawing undue notice, the last thing she wanted was to have to wait in line for her car. Kind of defeated the purpose of fleeing in the first place.

She glanced critically down her body, biting her lips in vexation. Oh the dress fit. Even her heels fit, and they were the likes of which she'd never be caught dead in, but she'd fallen in love with them the moment she'd pulled them reverently from the elegant box they'd arrived in. Apparently it was get-in-touch-with-Eliza's-feminine-side night.

She shimmered in silver from head to toe. Even her shoes sparkled and twinkled when they caught the light just so. The dressed was extremely formfitting, and yet somehow seemed to give the illusion of flowing motion when she moved, sending a glittery flash that enchanted her.

The thin material cupped her breasts lovingly in a seeming caress. Much like a man's palms gently cupping and molding her breasts.

Now where the hell had that thought come from? And why the fuck had the hands in question belonged to Sterling?

Her cheeks were blazing and she subconsciously ducked her

head in case she ran in to anyone she knew on the walk to the studio.

The dress was modest—again, when it wasn't on her! By most standards. Anyone looking at only the dress on a hanger would likely think the dress plain, dull even, that it covered far too much. Not sexy enough. Too simple.

Eliza had thought the same and had been oddly grateful to Sterling for not having her outfitted like a tramp. That thought quickly evaporated when she'd put on the dress to get ready tonight. On the right person, the dress turned into a study in seduction. It outlined in stunning clarity just how large her breasts were, their shape, size. She prayed it wouldn't be cold inside the gallery because if her nipples puckered, she was walking out and when she got home she'd burn the damn dress. Hell, she was burning it after tonight anyway.

In another time, under different circumstances, if she'd had such an opportunity to wear such a beautiful, provocative dress, she would have embraced and gloried in it. She would have had fun with it and enjoyed herself. Maybe even done a little flirting. But then, she thought she would forever be free of Thomas, free of her humiliating past, and she'd been more than ready to finally embrace her present, was even looking forward to a future, something she would have never contemplated having. Firmly ensconced in her new life with a wealth of good friends and coworkers—the very best kind of people—she'd relaxed, become complacent and allowed herself the luxury of thinking that maybe, just *maybe*, she could leave Thomas and everything associated with him in the past, get the fuck over it, move forward and finally step into the sun.

How stupid and naïve she continued to be when those were

the very things she'd sworn never to be a victim of again. What was the saying? You could never outrun your past because it inevitably caught up to you when you least expected it. And there was no such thing as absolution. Not for the wrongs *she'd* committed, had been complicit in. There was always a price to pay for the mistakes you made. She could delay them but never escape them.

Oh well, one more night to get through and then tomorrow . . . A wave of grief consumed her. Tomorrow was the big staff meeting at DSS. Her plans were completed. Arrangements made. Everything she needed, weapons and intel she'd meticulously gathered, careful to ensure no one, *especially* Dane, ever discovered all the things she'd so carefully collected starting the morning she'd received the call from the DA.

At least she'd get to see Ari, Ramie and Tori—provided Tori hadn't opted out of the evening—say goodbye, even if she didn't voice that farewell. She'd see them, commit their faces, their love, loyalty and friendship to memory. Pain surged as she crossed the street, drawing closer to the gallery. Except Gracie. She had to avoid Gracie at all costs. Simply seeing her from afar would have to suffice. Later. When she had made her escape, she would send Gracie a letter and say goodbye.

Then tomorrow morning, she'd see everyone she'd worked with the past several years, including being introduced to the new recruits, proof of DSS's—and Caleb, Beau and Dane's—commitment to hiring only the best and as many of the best as they could pull into the expanding security system.

She paused at the gallery door, noticing that it was already a packed house. Deciding to be "fashionably late" had been a good idea after all. Less chance of being cornered by too many friends all giving her the stare down she'd grown accustomed to over the past week. Her nerves were so frayed that there was no way she'd be able to withstand a full-scale assault from all the people who mattered to her. Just like she mattered to them.

She eased inside, not wanting to draw any undue attention to her entrance.

No such luck.

As she did a quick survey of the room, her gaze unerringly settled on Sterling and she froze when she saw his eyes solidly fixed on her. He'd evidently clocked her the moment she'd walked in the door as if he'd been waiting for her—had he? And he stared at her with those piercing dark eyes that never missed a damn thing and when she thought things couldn't get worse than the fact he'd obviously been keeping an eye out for her arrival, he began shoving through the crowd not even caring that he was being rude and pushing people out of his way. And he was making a beeline for *her*.

Damn his arrogant, smug ass straight to hell. She was here. So why was he so intent on making a scene when he'd been the one so adamant that things be perfect for Gracie's debut, had been pissed that Gracie's feelings would be hurt if *all* her friends weren't here.

She glanced left and right looking for an escape route, any escape route so she could melt into the crowd and not be there when Sterling shoved into her space. Or maybe she could fake a sudden onset of the flu or some wicked stomach virus. Food poisoning! But then she hadn't eaten her forgotten takeout in her car because the damn man had forced a confrontation on her turf and well, after that, her appetite had fled.

A waiter bearing a tray full of champagne glasses brushed by her and she lunged for one of the glasses and then on impulse grabbed another one. If this wasn't a double-fisted drinking occasion she didn't know what was. She gulped down the contents before the waiter had time to move on and she plunked the empty down with a thud and quickly nabbed another two. The waiter gave her a wary glance and hastily went on to the next patron.

Too bad they were serving smaltzy alcohol and not something more fitting. Like vodka or tequila. Preferably in a solo cup instead of a tiny-ass shot glass. She needed all the liquid courage she could muster for what she could only describe as the night from hell.

Avoiding one person was difficult enough, though God knew she'd had plenty of practice avoiding Sterling. Hell, she'd become an expert. But having to avoid not only a knuckles-dragging-the-ground Neanderthal but also a woman she considered a friend, who just happened to have the ability to read minds, stretched even Eliza's impressive set of skills.

Knowing that Sterling was the lesser of the two evils because he could *think* what he wanted, she resigned herself to having to grind her teeth and somehow get through the next hour without getting close enough to Gracie to be busted. At least *he* couldn't see into her head and *know* everything she was thinking.

The damn bastard's eyes were full of laughter though his lips and expression reflected none of the humor in his gaze.

"You came," he drawled.

She sent him an acid look that normally withered the recipient but Sterling didn't even flinch.

"Wow, your powers of observation are astounding," she mocked sweetly, giving him her most saccharine smile. "And you stating the obvious is ever so intelligent. I find smart men *soooo* attractive. Too bad you're lacking in the IQ department."

"I *must* be stupid," he said, his words laced with sarcasm and a bite she'd become all too acquainted with.

She lifted an eyebrow, shocked to hear those words coming out of his mouth. If he was nothing else, he was decidedly sure of himself. Confident. Arrogant. Cocky. No one could ever call him humble.

"If I had half a brain, then I'd stay the hell away from you," he growled.

Only because she lifted one of the two champagne glasses she held to her lips was she able to prevent her mouth from falling open. What the hell was that supposed to mean?

"Then use the other half and do what the missing half would if it were present," she said sweetly. "Because apparently common sense left with the missing half as well. Stay the hell away from me, Sterling, and make us *both* happy."

And then it happened again. He smiled, teeth flashing, and he threw back his head and issued a throaty laugh that gave her actual goose bumps. His smile and that laugh were so devastatingly sexy they should be outlawed. Jesus, no wonder he had a veritable parade of women in and out of his bedroom.

His gaze drifted down to the two champagne flutes she had a death grip on and his eyes continued to twinkle with silent laughter. Even forced to be in his company for a short time was worth hearing him laugh and seeing that breathtaking smile. Twice she'd seen it now. In the same day. Surely the world was ending.

Or at least hers was.

Her thoughts quickly sobered because once again, for just

a few seconds, she forgot herself. Forgot that this was her last night to see Ramie and Ari. Grief overwhelmed her because she wouldn't *get* to say goodbye to Gracie. And in the morning she'd say a silent farewell, a permanent farewell to the people she worked with. Her family. And, God, Dane.

Sterling's eyes narrowed, losing the amusement so prevalent just seconds before. His lips became a thin line and his jaw bulged, his cheekbones more defined as he stared piercingly at her.

"What the hell is going on with you, Eliza?" he asked quietly.

She lifted her glass and drained the contents, glancing frantically around for one of the servers, though she still had one full glass left. Seeing no one, she raised her last glass to her lips, or rather was in the process when Sterling intercepted it, wresting it from her grasp.

"What are you doing?" Eliza demanded. "That was my drink!"

"Your third," he said dryly. "Is this the only way you can work up the courage to face me? By getting shit-faced as soon as you walk through the door?"

She fought the heat and betraying flush that crept slowly up her neck. She never blushed. Nothing embarrassed her. Pissed her off? Yeah. And she tended to get red in the face then, so she would have no problem passing off her embarrassment as rage.

"Sorry to have offended your prudish sensibilities," she said snidely. "Or maybe there is a drink limit I wasn't aware of? You getting cheap, Sterling? Can't afford free booze so you expect everyone to limit their intake?"

He shook his head, the half grin, half grimace back in place.

Well, at least he was no longer prying or trying to pry into her thoughts.

"You are so full of shit, Eliza," he said in what sounded like an exasperated tone but nothing seemed to fluster the man. Not that she'd ever witnessed. "Now, what were you thinking about a minute ago? Care to share?"

So much for him no longer being nosy.

"No, I don't care to share," she said in a frosty voice. "I don't care to share anything with you, Sterling. Not your company, not your presence. I don't want to share the same space or even the same air you do so *get out of my way and leave me alone.*"

He didn't respond, instead turning as if to walk away. Oh God, please let her prayer be answered. Just when she thought her fervent prayer had been granted, Sterling snagged her elbow and deftly escorted her through the crowd.

Apparently God was occupied with far more important things than indulging in her cowardice. She could hardly blame him. After all, she'd rather save her prayers for when she really needed them, and she would need them soon.

"What do you think you're doing?" she hissed.

He shot her a pissed off look—a look she was intimately acquainted with, having been the recipient of it every time their paths crossed.

"Taking you to your posse," he said in a tone that matched his expression.

That brightened her considerably until she looked to the group they were approaching and saw that Gracie was in the middle of them looking stunning. Shy and overwhelmed but drop-dead gorgeous and deliriously happy. Her heart ached just to see the group of people she worked with, called friends, people she loved and people who had one hundred and ten percent of her loyalty.

Inwardly she cringed because her thought had been in the present tense. She had been loyal to them. Until now. She'd never lied to them. Until now. And she'd never deceived them. Until fucking now.

"Gracie will be thrilled you're here," Sterling murmured.

Thank God Gracie hadn't looked away from her husband to see Eliza yet. Eliza stopped in her tracks, nearly tripping because Sterling was still in the process of his long-legged stride and well, her legs were considerably shorter.

He frowned, rounding on her, purposely positioning himself between her and the DSS group, something she was grateful for even though she knew he hadn't done it for her. He'd done it so Gracie wouldn't see Eliza and realize that Eliza had no intention of speaking to her.

"What the fuck is wrong with you?" Sterling snapped, his eyes blazing with anger and judgment. Oh yeah, he'd judged her and found her lacking all right. He thought her the worst sort of person and an even worse friend.

Eliza closed her eyes, so miserable she wanted to do something that appalled her. She wanted to cry.

"It's not what you think," she choked out, her mind churning to come up with a plausible excuse.

"What I think is that you're being a selfish bitch and shitting all over someone who risked her life to save you. Someone who took a fucking knife and was slashed because she was trying to get to you, to do whatever she could to protect you when you were helpless."

"Don't you think I know that?" she yelled, thanking the

heavens that the music and the huge group of people mingling and conversing drowned out her passionate outburst. "Don't you think I relive that moment every fucking night? Every goddamn *day* for that matter. Do you think I would have *ever* wanted Gracie, Ramie or Ari to risk themselves the way they did to help *me*? I would give my *life* for them. *All* of them," she raged, gesturing to where the rest of the DSS group was standing.

Sterling looked genuinely perplexed as he studied her. Almost as if he had some built-in "Eliza truth detector" able to ferret out what was truth and what was lie. Then sudden realization dawned on his features. She could practically see the "aha" moment in his eyes and on his face. His eyes became sharp and piercing, examining every inch of her face as if he could see behind her outer mask.

Fuck this. Only one man had been able to do that and she'd spent years finding ways of mentally strengthening her natural shields and barriers. She'd taken every class on psychic abilities available. She'd read countless books on the subject matter. Dug through thousands of articles. She would love the chance to try her blocking abilities with Gracie, but she hadn't thought she'd ever need that ability until that damn phone call and now she couldn't take the chance. She couldn't risk not being able to block Gracie from her mind and, besides, if she couldn't block Gracie she would be defenseless against Thomas. And right now, all she had was *hope* that she would be successful. If she knew she would fail, then her already flagging confidence and courage would vanish and she'd be spilling the entire story to Dane, begging for his help or running in the opposite direction as Thomas instead of straight to him. As far from his reach as she possibly could, even if it meant landing halfway across the world. But even there, he'd find her. She knew he would and that made her feel even more helpless.

"What is it you don't want Gracie knowing, Eliza?" Sterling asked so softly that she almost didn't hear him above the surrounding noise.

Eliza froze. She had to act fast. She'd always been good on her feet and quick-witted—when she *had* her wits about her. In other circumstances she would be smug and triumphant at how easily she thought of a way to throw Sterling off her trail, but right now she just felt desperate and scared to death he'd see right through her lie. Well part of it was a lie. Part of it was truth. Just the *details* were muggy.

Her face fell, a carefully orchestrated act as if she'd been caught out and wasn't happy about it. She even managed a convincing glare from underneath her eyelashes, one that told him what she thought of his intrusion into her privacy.

"I've been planning a surprise for her," Eliza said grudgingly, making sure she sounded her normal pissed off self any time she came face-to-face with Sterling, which until yesterday hadn't been often. Why he suddenly popped up on her radar after so long of mutual avoidance she had no clue. But whatever the reason he could just slink back to whatever rock he lived under and get the hell out of her life.

"A surprise?"

There was no disguising the outright disbelief in his voice or expression. His eyes narrowed dangerously, and it was clear his Eliza-truth radar was beeping nonstop. He looked as though he wanted to wrap his hands around her neck and throttle her. Given his really large hands, she doubted he'd have any difficulty.

"Wade," she said in a pleading voice, giving him her best

big-eyed totally girl plea. It wasn't a look she could remember using in a very long time. It was rare for her to dip into her feminine arsenal when a snarl, a threat or an ass-kicking would achieve the same results. But she could do none of those things with a roomful of people surrounding her and worse, every single person she worked with was halfway across the room and they'd certainly notice.

He looked shocked, his eyes widening and he stared at her like he didn't know whether to throttle her, kiss her—oh God!— or take her to the hospital for psychiatric evaluation.

"That's the first time you've ever said my name," he said in a low husky voice that made her knees go weak and tremble. A voice and expression that said he liked it. A *lot*. His eyes were soft, a slight crinkle at the corners as he studied her, and for some reason her gaze was drawn to his lips that weren't contorted into his usual Eliza scowl of exasperation. In fact, the ends were curled upward slightly, not a smile. Something altogether different. Something she wasn't about to analyze or figure out because his entire body language had changed and, worse, his hold on her had tightened so an air of intimacy shrouded them. *Now* she realized she should have gone with the snarl, threats and ass-kicking. *Fuck!*

She nearly groaned out loud and had to physically restrain herself from banging her head on the nearest possible place, which happened to be his shoulder. He was right. She never called him Wade. And what was worse was that it hadn't been intentional. It hadn't been part of her trying to worm her way out of a disastrous situation, though so far it seemed to be working. It had just slipped out. If he didn't have her so rattled and off her game, she would have never called him by his first name.

She'd called him plenty of things but never that because, damn it, it was too personal. Friends, family, people she liked, those were the people she was on a first name basis with. Sterling was none of those things.

He stared at her a long moment, something shifting in his gaze. Something dangerous that made a light shiver work up her spine. It was as if something huge had changed in that moment and she did not want to know what that was because she had the distinct feeling it had everything to do with her. Then he shook his head as if dispelling cobwebs and just as quickly that intense scowl was back and the moment was gone. Thank God.

"So this surprise," he drawled. "Do tell. You avoid a woman who considers you her friend thus making her believe you're *angry* with her, which causes her untold grief, and if I had to guess makes her husband and *your* coworker not very happy with you, and now you're telling me you've been hurting her feelings and making her feel like shit because you have a *surprise* for her?"

He ended with a snort of pure disbelief. Eliza winced at hearing the words "hurt feelings" and "feel like shit." Then, mentally, she thought back, trying to remember if Zack had treated her any differently. Truth be told, she hadn't even considered the consequences. She'd been too focused on her mission. Then she winced again, because yeah, she could remember Zack shooting her searching looks, laced with anger in his eyes and a tight jaw, though he'd never approached her and that surprised her because he and Eliza were tight after all the shit that went down when he and Gracie had their thing.

Eliza didn't have to pretend agitation or fake regret when she glanced back up at Sterling. She stared at him with stricken eyes, allowing all her regret and sorrow to show, evidenced by his look of surprise. At least she was keeping him as off balance as he was her.

"I was planning it, have been planning it for over a week," she said quietly. That wasn't a lie. She *had* been planning. Sterling would just assume she'd been planning Gracie's surprise. "I couldn't be around her when it was all I was thinking about and preparing for," she continued. "She would have known instantly and then it would no longer be a surprise. But I never meant to make her think I was angry with her. I didn't think." She closed her eyes against the sudden sting of tears. No way in hell she'd cry in front of Sterling. Even if it would go a long way in convincing him of her lie.

He studied her a long moment, and she got the distinct impression he didn't miss the shine of tears, gone almost before they'd even appeared. His scrutiny was unbearable and it made her squirm. Her palms itched and she had to control the urge to curl her fingers into tight fists because that would betray her supreme agitation and Sterling was someone who picked up on subtle clues. He never missed a goddamn thing.

"And just what is this surprise," Sterling asked, eyes narrowed, suspicion still heavy in his voice.

"I can't tell you! Are you crazy? You're around Gracie all the time. If you knew, then she'd know too."

"Then give me a goddamn clue," he bit out impatiently.

It was clear he still wasn't buying it. Damn it!

"All I can say is that it has to do with her school," Eliza said softly, referring to Gracie's plan to open her own place to teach free art classes to promising students who couldn't afford lessons otherwise.

Until recently Gracie had used a small building—owned by

Sterling of course—but now there were too many students and it broke Gracie's tender heart to have to turn anyone away because there wasn't enough space.

Her dream was to find a bigger place, which Sterling of course would provide, but Gracie needed donations to pay for supplies and at least one full-time assistant. Volunteers couldn't always be counted on to be available and that many children needed more supervision and attention than Gracie could give them alone. Not to mention Zack was heavily opposed to anything that took too much of his new wife's time. They'd been separated for twelve years by horrific circumstances and Zack was making the most of every single day now that they'd found one another again.

"And so help me, Sterling, if you even *think* about Gracie's school and or me at the same time when you're around Gracie, swear to God, I'll have your nuts."

His expression became sly and a look entered his eyes she did not like. It made her want to tuck tail and run like the coward he accused her of being.

"I don't even want to know," she muttered. "Can I leave now?"

Noticing that Sterling had loosened his grip on her arm, she took swift advantage and turned to stalk away but he was faster, reasserting his hold on her.

"I'll gladly give you my balls, Eliza. Just say the word. But you'll get a whole hell of a lot more than my nuts. That I can guarantee."

Horrified by the heat that instantly flared to life, curling in her groin and licking up her spine, she tried to jerk away from him again.

"Make you a deal," Sterling said in a silky, bone-shivering, sexy voice. "Give me one dance and I'll make your excuses to Gracie and you can leave with your secret intact. She'll just be happy you came. I doubt she's noticed much more than her new husband anyway," he added wryly.

"No one is dancing!" she protested. "You don't think Gracie"—not to mention every single one of her coworkers— "and the others wouldn't see us and know I was here, never said hi or made my presence known and then, oh gee, I had to leave. You're out of your damn mind."

He shrugged. "Suit yourself. Come on. I'll take you to Gracie then, so you can offer your hellos to your *team* and congratulations to Gracie."

She went rigid. "You little blackmailing bastard."

He shrugged again, making her want to scream. Did nothing ever ruffle him? What did it take to *really* piss off a man who rarely looked anything beyond mildly annoyed or more commonly like he didn't give a fuck?

"I gave you options," he pointed out. "That's hardly blackmail. The choice is yours. I thought I was doing you a favor but since you don't seem inclined to accept my offer then we'll carry on and you can remain until the bitter end. But fair warning, word is after the showing your posse is having a post exhibit celebratory dinner and if you're here you'll be expected to attend."

She couldn't control the panicked, deer-in-the-headlights look she knew flashed on her face and it only served to further annoy the fuck out of her that he could always get a rise out of her when her emotions and reactions were always tightly under control. They had to be in her line of work.

"I'm taking that as a yes to the dance," Sterling said with smug satisfaction.

"Asshole," she muttered.

In a show of unexpected—and rare—consideration, he propelled her to the far end of the room where the band was playing and there she found she was incorrect about no one else dancing. Why that relieved her she wasn't sure but then she hardly wanted all eyes on her and Sterling if they were the only ones dancing.

Wordlessly he pulled her into his arms and though she attempted to keep him at arm's length so their dance was entirely casual, he ignored that just like he ignored everything else about her unless it suited his purposes.

She found herself locked against a very hard, very aggressive, *aroused* male.

Ignoring that particular fact, although that was kind of difficult when she could feel the imprint of his cock, the heat and urgency through his slacks and the sheer material of her dress. It throbbed against her belly and freaked the hell out of her. Wade Sterling turned on by her? Or because of her. Or with her. Whatever the hell it was. Maybe he was one of those guys who thrived on adversity and got turned on at inappropriate times. Or maybe it had nothing to do with her at all. Maybe any female would do or maybe he just hadn't got laid in a while. And then she nearly snorted at that idea. This was a man who only had to crook his finger to have his choice of pussy.

Swallowing the knot that had formed in her throat, wishing she could wipe at the sheen of perspiration at her forehead, she fixed her gaze on Sterling's shoulder, refusing to meet his eyes.

She did not want to see whatever was reflected there. She was sure she wouldn't like it.

"So do tell, if you couldn't come up with a good enough excuse to give Gracie that I couldn't come at all without hurting her feelings, how are you going to *not* hurt her feelings by telling her I was here but had to leave?" she asked skeptically.

"Look at me, Eliza."

The words rumbled out of his chest, vibrating over her skin until she shivered. It was a command. No doubt he was accustomed to issuing commands and having them heeded.

She shook her head, mutely, refusing to be one of his mindless minions who took orders and obeyed without question.

Instead of making the demand again, he moved one of his arms from around her and cupped her chin with his hand and forced it in his direction, tilting it upward so he could see into her eyes and vice versa. Still refusing, she lowered her lids, staring downward even though her head was angled upward and her chin was still in his firm grip.

He chuckled. Bastard obviously found her funny. She almost forgot about not looking at him and nearly sliced her eyes upward so she could cut him to ribbons with a look and words.

He rubbed his thumb in an up and down motion that surprisingly felt more like a caress. His hand was gentle, though she had no doubt he wouldn't allow her to slip away from him.

"Why even make me endure this farce?" she hissed. "It's obvious you aren't too worried about Gracie's feelings or you wouldn't have offered to let me dance with you in exchange for not being up close and personal with Gracie."

"Maybe *I* wanted you to come," he said blandly.

"Bullshit," she snorted. "You have no more desire to be in the same room with me than I do you. Remember? According to you, I got you shot, and you said *never* would be too soon to see me again."

He chuckled again. "I was pissed at the time, and face it, Eliza, you're trouble with a capital T."

Her mouth opened to let him have it with both barrels but the music ended and suddenly she was free of Sterling's grasp and oddly bereft of the warmth that had surrounded her these last minutes.

"I suggest you go now and act like you're sick and in a hurry," he said in a low voice filled with mockery. "I'll make your excuses to the others."

She wanted to glare or do something childish and grind her heel into his foot, but he was offering her an escape, and she'd be a damned fool to hesitate. The cretin could change his mind in the next second, just as yet another way to torture her. So she turned, prepared to make a very hasty exit, when Sterling's hand shot out, his fingers curling firmly around her elbow, effectively halting her. She refused to give him the satisfaction of turning to face him, but his low voice reached her ears again.

"If I find out you lied about surprising Gracie with something regarding her school, you'll answer to me," he said calmly, though there was a distinct edge of threat in his voice. "I'll be watching you, Eliza."

She bit her lip and bolted, wasting no more time in her bid to be rid of the entire place. Gracie's gift of ferreting out one's deepest, innermost thoughts. But most of all *him*.

Because him keeping an eye on her was exactly what she feared the most. Thank God, in a little over twenty-four hours, she'd be in the wind. Away from the people she cared most about. Her friends. Partners. People she risked her life for every damn day and who did the same for her.

And, most of all, she'd be forever and permanently beyond Sterling's very long and encompassing reach.

FIVE

ELIZA was on edge, trying not to let it affect the unflappable composure she'd perfected and was known for, as she waited for the latest "state of the union" meeting to commence so she could tackle the most difficult task she'd set her mind to today.

Lying to Dane and hoping to hell she was convincing enough to escape his legendary bullshit detector. Technically he was her boss, and to everyone except the Devereaux brothers—Caleb, Beau and Quinn—he was. But to Eliza he wasn't as much her boss as he was her partner.

Everyone at DSS had someone they gravitated toward, worked well together with, and partnerships developed. It hadn't been long after Eliza had been hired that Dane had tagged her as his partner, which had surprised the hell out of her and pleased her enormously.

Dane ran the show. He was the leader even if he wasn't the one signing everyone's paychecks. DSS was run by the Devereaux family, primarily the two oldest brothers, Caleb and

Beau, while Quinn had been dubbed the geek and tech whiz who knew and ran all things computer and technology related. This was something that irritated and insulted Quinn to no end, but only Eliza knew this bit of personal information. Like the rest of the Devereaux clan, he was tight-lipped, extremely private and not one to share his feelings with anyone. None of them ever made public anything that would make them vulnerable, especially now that the elder Devereaux brothers had wives they loved and who were their heart and soul.

In an unexpected move, Quinn had approached Eliza—privately of course—and after swearing her to absolute secrecy, threatening to fire her—as if!—had she revealed his mysterious request. He knew and accepted with resentment that he wasn't considered the ultimate badass alpha male his older brothers were, though he was several years younger and already exhibiting that annoying trait, even if he hadn't yet recognized it. And he had asked Eliza to become his personal trainer. He knew her reputation. That she wouldn't go easy on him and wouldn't offer him platitudes because she worked, in a roundabout fashion, for him, or rather his family. And so on certain days, Eliza's regular days off unless shit was going down, Quinn always found something that had to be done and would start spouting tech language none of the others could hope to understand, which meant they avoided him like the plague for the rest of the day, leaving him free for Eliza to put him through the paces.

And she had no mercy. Quinn would have been pissed, embarrassed and insulted if she had. He was often bruised, sore and limping when she finished with him, but she could see the fire of satisfaction in his eyes, even with the sweat, obvious fatigue and the fact that he'd just gotten his ass handed to him by a girl. And to his credit, he was improving. Quickly.

He worked hard, not just during his workouts with Eliza, but on his own time as well. And he never missed a session with her. Never made an excuse. She would miss those times between them, but she would ensure Dane would take over Quinn's training when she left. Dane would never betray Quinn's confidence and while Eliza was good—more than good—Dane was the best. There were no better hands for her to leave Quinn in.

Yeah, it suited Dane for Caleb and Beau to officially run the show even if everyone, Caleb and Beau included, damn well knew that it was Dane who called the majority of the shots. Dane was . . . well, he was a badass through and through. He had a persona that was impenetrable. Icy. No one could see past his carefully constructed guard unless he chose to let you in, and well, that was rare. She'd gotten a few glimpses, usually when women, or rather the women the men of DSS had claimed, had been endangered, nearly killed, certainly harmed.

She nearly laughed. Claimed was such an old-world, outdated term, not in keeping with her modern sensibilities, but then not so very long ago, she would have proudly and without shame used that term for a monster who had certainly claimed her. She'd reveled in that sense of ownership. The idea that she belonged. That she mattered and was important to someone in the world after a lifetime of mattering to no one. Now it was only a source of never-ending shame because the claim Thomas had on her was sick, twisted and it was not love. Nothing like the claim Caleb, Beau and Zack had on their women. *That* was love. It was pure, beautiful and magical and it was the epitome of everything she'd once wanted more than she wanted to breathe and would have died for it. She nearly had.

She'd even caught a crack in Dane's icy veneer when she herself had been the one in danger on their last mission. He'd come close to completely losing all vestiges of that legendary composure when she'd lain there so still after enduring unspeakable torture and it wasn't known whether she lived or had died.

Until that Neanderthal Wade Sterling had inserted himself into a situation he clearly didn't belong in. She scowled at the memory of just how he'd taken over. He'd picked her up, had held her, cradled her, actual concern dark in those mesmerizing eyes as though she had mattered to him.

She caught herself before she did something stupid like shake her head vehemently in denial of such a crazy, unwanted thought. But a nagging voice inside her, one she wanted to bitch slap and banish forever, innocently asked if she was so certain she didn't matter to Sterling.

To get her mind off Sterling and to delay, for now, the overwhelming grief and dread of her impending meeting with Dane, she turned just enough so she could see Zack in her periphery, but made certain it wasn't obvious she was watching him. The voice of Caleb droned on and on and she could see she wasn't the only one impatient for the meeting to be done. Several of the people she worked with had bored, impatient expressions and the eyes of others were glazed over, obviously having tuned out the endless drone completely.

Her gaze slowly settled back on Zack and she went still, remembering to bring and adopt the same bored expression the rest of the team wore when he looked in her direction. Her heart plummeted because it wasn't a friendly look. Not remotely. His expression was black and brooding. Yeah, he was pissed. But then she couldn't blame him considering how protective he was of Gracie and then there was the fact that before that fucking phone call, she had been tight with Gracie. She'd been tight with all the wives. But especially Gracie, with whom she'd formed a special bond after all the shit that had gone down.

Unable to bear the anger and, worse, the disappointment in Zack's expression she averted her gaze, shutting him out. She glanced in Dane's direction, not feeling any better about the deception she was perpetrating. Guilt flooded her.

She shuddered, tears stinging her eyelids and she blinked them back, furious at her lack of control. And she should have known that if no one else would pick up on that nearly imperceptible slip up, Dane would.

He eyed her sharply, his gaze flickering over her as if revealing every secret she ever held, every thought she'd locked down permanently, never to escape and see the light of day again.

He moved closer with casualness that had her blinking because he made it seem unplanned, like he was growing weary of the prolonged meeting and was merely shifting his weight. He donned an impatient look, one he was famous for, one that said, "Are we done now?"

The others caught on and Caleb and Beau began the wrap-up and for a moment Eliza thought she was safe from Dane's scrutiny. Years working for this man and she still made a rookie mistake by underestimating him.

"What's wrong, Lizzie?" he asked in a low enough voice not to be overheard. "Is everything okay?"

She smiled brightly and if it was too bright, oh well, she was hanging on by a thread here and anything she could do in order to survive the coming private conversation with Dane once the others had dispersed, she'd latch on to with both hands and hold on to for dear life.

"Just wondering when the fuck our esteemed leaders became so goddamn long-winded," she muttered, because it was *such* an Eliza thing to say.

To cover the brightness of her smile, she bared her teeth in a barely noticeable snarl, because that too was so *her*. "Don't they have wives to go home to and make cutesy eyes at instead of wasting our time by covering shit we could recite in our sleep?"

Dane gave a light chuckle, relief flaring in his eyes, and she did a mental fist pump in victory. Getting *anything* over on Dane was cause for self-congratulation because the man did not miss a goddamn thing. He always had his eyes on every single person, his ears glued to every conversation, attuned to the slightest differences in tone, body language. If she didn't know better, she'd swear the man was psychic because his powers were superhuman.

And it wasn't as though DSS wasn't accustomed to dealing with some pretty freaky shit. Pain flashed through her chest, temporarily robbing her of breath. The women that had married the men of DSS all had kickass powers. Powers that defied scientific explanation. But then Eliza had no problem believing in the extraordinary. Because the man who'd once held her in his thrall was *nothing* like *these* women. They used their powers for good. *They* were good. They were everything that was right in a fucked-up world, filled with monsters who preyed on the innocent. And Eliza had allowed this man in her life, had allowed him to give her all the things she'd wanted, craved, had never had in her young life and that made her every bit as guilty as he.

"Lizzie?" Dane murmured, so the others wouldn't hear.

"What the fuck is wrong and swear to God if you tell me nothing, I'll wring your pretty neck."

Oh well, it was now or never, and it wasn't as if she had any plans of disappearing without a damn good cover story and telling the man she directly reported to that she planned a long vacation. He just didn't have to know the *reason* behind her leave of absence.

He'd likely be relieved. None of them, especially Wade Sterling—just thinking of the overbearing ass made her teeth clench and put her in a foul mood—had wanted her involved in the sting operation to take down the last of the people hunting DSS, and in particular Ramie, Ari and Gracie. A request for vacation to recover from her "injuries" would probably be met with relief and an order for her to take as long as she wanted and not to hurry back to work.

She felt a moment's guilt for deceiving Dane. She was leaving the comforting camaraderie that her position at DSS offered. The first true home she'd ever had. The justice system had failed her. It had failed the countless women Thomas Harrington raped and tortured and murdered. She still heard their screams at night when she closed her eyes. Many nights she couldn't sleep for the sounds of torture playing over and over in her broken heart and in the shattered pieces of her soul. Knowing it was her fault. She had done this to so many women because she'd been weak and needy and too stupid to know that behind the face of kindness— of love—lurked a monster with abilities of unlimited power and a sick, twisted mind to utilize every psychic tool in his arsenal.

She quickly yanked herself from the past, knowing Dane was studying her, growing more pissed and agitated and worried by the minute. It was the last she was most concerned about because if he got worried and *then* she fed him a line about needing vacation, he'd never believe her. He'd put her under lock and key and suffer no remorse whatsoever until he found out exactly what was going on in her mind, and he wasn't above using Gracie or any of the other women to ferret out any information he felt would keep Eliza from harm.

And she knew the women would gladly offer their help because they felt they owed Eliza. She'd been there when each of them had needed help. She'd risked her life to save them and would do so again without a single hesitation. They didn't owe her a goddamn thing for doing her job even if they weren't a job to her, but people she loved.

Damn it. She had to talk her way out of this fast.

She sighed and gave him her best "busted" look.

"I just wish they'd hurry the hell up," she grumbled. "There's something I wanted to talk to you about after this come-to-Jesus meeting. Preferably in private."

Left unsaid, but understood by Dane, judging by the softness that suddenly transformed his features from that piercing, concerned look to one more of simple question, he well knew that while Caleb and Beau owned and ran DSS and signed all their paychecks, Eliza was his. His team, his partner. The two were the closest of any two of the operatives who worked within the group, not as partners, though Beau and Zack shared a similar relationship, preferring to rely on each other rather than the larger group as a whole.

Which made what she had to do all the more painful because she was, in effect, betraying Dane. She was repaying all the faith he'd displayed in her, his respect of her, the fact that he treated her as an equal, a partner—with treachery and lying.

She tried to console herself with the fact that at the end of the day she'd rather have him alive and well, pissed, angry and never able to trust her again and for her to be out of a job than to confide everything to him and have him end up dead.

Because Dane wouldn't back off. It wouldn't be a matter of trusting her, or trusting her to know what she was talking about and believing the very real danger they were all in. But he would never leave her to face a monster alone. Never in a million years. Even if it meant going against every single member of DSS and quitting so Eliza wouldn't face the danger alone. Dane would do it without a single regret.

He'd be at her side, taking her back, just like so many times before, and they'd either triumph together or die together. And Dane *would* die.

A wave of grief consumed Eliza. Because of a bullshit legal technicality and a smooth-talking lawyer, Thomas's sentence had been reduced to ten fucking years.

Eliza wanted to scream until her voice simply broke. But she held it in stoically, knowing she was on borrowed time, and that when Thomas got out, and he would be getting out in a week, she wasn't going to bring him down like she had the first time, counting on the justice system to protect her, to protect those women and seek justice for those he'd destroyed.

No, she was going after him and fuck the legal system and doing it the right way. This mission wasn't righteous. It wasn't even revenge. It was cold-blooded murder.

And that was why she couldn't have DSS remotely involved. They couldn't know. They could never know until it was all over.

Because once her mission was done, she wouldn't resist. She

wouldn't run. She wouldn't even hire a lawyer because she would be guilty.

She was going to kill Thomas Harrington and leave nothing to chance. She'd stand over his body until his body became cold and lifeless and then and only then would she call it in, allow herself to be taken into custody and she'd give a full confession to the murder of a man who'd taken so much from her. She was Thomas's only surviving victim, the only one able to seek justice for all the women who couldn't.

They were all dead. No one left, but her, to ensure their killer would never act out his depravities on another defenseless woman.

For the first time she realized that her surviving had a purpose. She'd lived while so many hadn't. It had taken her a while to understand. To sort through her grief, guilt, shock and anger to realize that she'd lived for a reason.

And that reason was to seek justice for all the women who couldn't.

She was fully aware of the consequences of her actions. The betrayal her team would feel as she turned away from the creed they upheld, followed, seekers of justice. That she would be branded a murderer, outcast. Her sentence would be swift. She wouldn't plead not guilty. She wouldn't cut a deal. She wanted the maximum allowable sentence for the crime she planned to commit. Not only planned but would see through to the bitter end.

Because even a lifetime in jail wouldn't be long enough for her to atone for her many sins against so many beautiful, young, innocent women. Women whose lives had been traded for Eliza's so that Eliza could live in her fantasy world of being a pampered, loved-and-adored beyond measure princess by a sadistic monster who wouldn't know the meaning of love. A word—and the true meaning of the word—now that Eliza was acquainted with it, she was willing to do anything to protect, go to hell and back for. Never let evil taint the people she loved or let *her* love ever become a twisted macabre thing used to control and manipulate helpless, gullible people.

God save her soul. She winced even as she thought it. Because she had none. There was nothing to save. She was damned forever in the eyes of God and soon she'd be damned to the rest of the world, but worse, she'd be damned to the only people she'd ever allowed herself to truly care about. Their disappointment in her could very well do the one thing Thomas had tried to do—God, he'd tried—but she'd been too strong, too determined and fought every step of the way not to allow him to win. To break her.

This, the loss of the people she loved, would irrevocably break her when nothing else in her young life had been able to manage such a seemingly impossible feat.

"Before we wrap up, I'm introducing you all to the newest DSS recruits," Caleb announced, yanking Eliza from her macabre thoughts.

Caleb made a sign and Beau opened the door of the meeting room and made a motion for the others to enter.

Eliza's eyes widened when the group of four men ambled through the door. They were the epitome of badass and if she weren't so deeply ensconced in worry and stressed out of her mind over her impending come to Jesus with Dane, her feminine appreciation would have kicked in full gear.

These were not your average guys off the street. They were

legit. Professionals. Either ex-military or they had careers in cracking people's heads with a healthy dose of intimidation to boot. In other words, they were fucking perfect additions to DSS. And if they'd already been hired, then Dane would have tested their skills and they'd met his requirements, which meant they were the real deal. Big, muscled, mean looking men who could handle themselves in any situation.

Beau took over then, gesturing toward a really tall, bald African American man, muscled with not one inch of spare flesh on his body, dressed in fatigues and a very tight fitting t-shirt that looked as though it was painted on.

"This is Dex," he said, not including a last name or if Dex was a shortened version of his given name.

But Dex was seriously hot with intense eyes that studied as his gaze swept the room. Her girly parts sighed and purred, ignoring the order to stand down and not react, but who was she kidding? The room was already filled with hot guys and enough testosterone to float a barge, but with the addition of four mouthwatering specimens of pure alpha male? She was *swimming* in it.

He remained silent, merely offering a lift of his chin to indicate his acknowledgment of the already existing members of DSS. Beau wasted no time going down the line.

"This is Zeke."

Once again, feminine appreciation fully intact, she took in Zeke's appearance, noting that he wasn't as tall as Dex, but then Dex was taller than all of them, including the current members of DSS. She put Dex around six-six but Zeke was only a couple of inches shorter, which still made him much taller than the average male.

His hair was black as midnight and hung loosely to his shoulders in an unruly style that said he didn't bother with it and furthermore didn't give a fuck. It had a shine that made it appear blue-black, like a raven, and coupled with bronze skin and features that hinted of Native American ancestry convinced her that he shared at least some of the blood of his ancestors. But his eyes were a startling crystal blue, a sharp contrast that made him a work of art that someone couldn't help but stare at and appreciate.

He was a bit stockier than Dex, not quite as lean but no less muscled. He was just thicker and more solid, ropes of muscles over every body part visible. It didn't escape her notice that he bore scars and likely more on parts that were covered by his faded jeans, combat boots and black T that was a little looser fitting than Dex's.

It was hard to drag her gaze from Dex and Zeke because damn . . . But then Beau continued on.

"This is Shadow," Beau said, indicating a man about Zeke's height, maybe an inch shorter. He had a quiet look about him and his features were solemn, giving nothing away. He had tats spiraling up both arms and she wondered whether he had tats in other places as well.

His hair was shortly cropped, military style, though a bit longer than regulation. Spiked on top, the color of chestnut. His eyes were green, lighter than Zack's, but he had a piercing gaze that pinned each of the DSS operatives as his attention moved to each in turn. When he got to Eliza, he stared what she thought was a longer time than he'd spent studying the others, but then she was paranoid. It wasn't as if he knew anything about her or rather only what Dane or Beau might have said and neither were indiscreet so their conversations had likely been confined to her skills and capabilities when it came to the job and she knew Dane had her back and would have made it clear she could handle herself.

But still, she wouldn't want to be a bad guy on the receiving end of that stare pinning them solidly in place. One that would likely have Shadow's prey tripping over themselves to spill whatever it was Shadow wanted to know.

He sported a tan but was obviously Caucasian, and like the others, he obviously had a strict workout regimen because there was nothing to indicate he was anything but in top form and shape. What was it Beau had said his name was? Shadow?

For some unknown reason she found herself opening her mouth before she thought better of it.

"Your name is Shadow?" she asked, lips pursed, one eyebrow lifted in question.

Then he grinned and it was one of those lazy, I-don't-give-a-fuck smiles that plainly said he wasn't used to explaining himself, but his eyes filled with amusement and Eliza sucked in her breath, because damn, her girly parts weren't just perked up and paying attention. They were fluttering wildly and screaming at her about her neglect of them.

"Forget I asked," Eliza muttered.

"You have me at a disadvantage, darlin'," he drawled. "You know my name but I haven't been introduced to you."

Her eyes narrowed because it was also obvious he was fucking with her. As if Dane wouldn't have gone over all the names of the DSS operatives and he most certainly would have given him her name and since she was the only female working at DSS aside from the receptionist, he knew damn well what her name was.

She let her displeasure show and bared her teeth, which served two purposes. One because she was genuinely annoyed but two, it would further allay Dane's worry since this was typical Eliza-like behavior and if she hadn't reacted this way he would have known she didn't have her shit together.

"Since you've been hired, you've been briefed, which means you know who everyone in this room is. So my suggestion is to not play fucking games, which are not only a waste of my time but of everyone else's too."

Shadow's grin became broader, flashing a row of perfectly straight, perfectly white teeth and his eyes twinkled with ill-concealed amusement.

"Didn't say I didn't know your name. Said I hadn't been introduced to you. Call me old-fashioned but when it comes to the people I work with, people it's my job to protect and have their back and people I trust to watch mine, I'd rather the introduction be a little more personal."

Damn. In a fucked-up way, he sort of made sense. Not dropping her glare, she relented.

"Eliza," she said shortly. "Not that you didn't know," she muttered under her breath.

Beside her, Dane shook silently, meaning he'd heard the last part.

"Shadow," he returned politely. "But unless I missed my guess, seeing as how you were told my name, you weren't asking *if* Shadow was my name but rather if it was my real name and if not you wanna know how I came to be called it."

Eliza gave a clipped nod because she so didn't have time for this even if she had enjoyed the show. Hello? Four mouthwateringly gorgeous hunks in the same room? Too bad she'd never have a chance to work with them, get to know them, decide how compatible they were as a team and if she could ever count on them or trust them in the way she did the men she already worked with.

"It's because that's what I am," Shadow said in a serious tone, all amusement gone, replaced by a hardness you earned by doing bad shit, dangerous shit, and seeing bad shit that most people didn't even realize existed. "It was either Ghost or Shadow and seein' as how I didn't get a choice in having a nickname, I put a stop to Ghost for obvious reasons because I don't have any desire to die anytime soon, and I went with Shadow."

Eliza continued to meet his gaze steadily, though she'd relaxed because something told her this guy was solid and again, had seen and experienced shit, and he carried more baggage and had more demons than most.

"If I don't want you to know I'm around, you won't," he said matter-of-factly. There was no arrogance. He wasn't bragging or boasting. He was just stating the truth and she believed him. "My specialty is getting into places most people can't, collecting intel or retrieving something that needs retrieving and then disappearing with no one ever knowin' I was there."

"We could use that," Eliza murmured.

Shadow grinned again. "Yeah, seein' as I'm here, guess you do."

Beau cleared his throat and went on to the last man. "This is Knight."

Eliza's gaze left Shadow and settled on the last man Beau had introduced. Her first thought was that his was likely not a nickname or at least not in the sense he was considered a knight

in shining armor, because there was nothing about him that resembled a romance novel hero or even a hero period.

His features were stony, giving nothing away. He was the
shortest one of the group, but considering the others well ex-
ceeded six feet, Knight was likely about an inch over that. His
hair was long, as in it obviously hadn't been cut in years and it
was a look he'd cultivated a very long time. He had it pulled back
and secured with a leather tie.

Dark but not as dark as Zeke's midnight hair, but darker
than the chestnut brown of Shadow's short hair. He had eyes
to match, so dark it was hard to distinguish his pupils from the
irises. It gave him a menacing air, which wasn't aided by the
couldn't-crack-a-stone-on-his-face set to his features. She wondered if he ever smiled but then decided probably not since it
might well fracture the rest of his face.

He barely acknowledged the people he was being introduced
to. His gaze quickly passed over each in turn before returning his
attention to Beau.

Eliza wondered what his specialty was, but then other than
Shadow, none of the others had been forthcoming in what it was
they did, but DSS needed men who could handle themselves in
any situation and be prepared and trained for anything. From all
appearances Dane had chosen well.

It was Dane's job to vet, interview and see what all prospec-
tive new hires were made of. He was good at it. The Devereauxs
never questioned his choices. If they passed muster with Dane,
they were hired. Period.

"Now that introductions are over, if everyone will sit back, we
have a few other things to go over before we adjourn," Beau said.

There were a few unsuppressed groans and likely twice as many suppressed groans because the hope had been the introduction of the new operatives would end the boring-as-fuck meeting.

For once, Eliza was grateful it wasn't over just yet. She needed a few more precious minutes to prepare herself to face her partner, a man she considered her closest friend and her only confidant. And then lie through her teeth to him.

SIX

DANE bit his tongue and stifled his impatience. He was every bit as eager to get bullshit over with as everyone else was. Yeah, he got that his new recruits needed to be introduced and integrated into the fold, but now was not the time when everyone was bored as fuck, impatient and ready to blow this joint. The others hadn't exactly rolled out the welcome mat for Dex, Zeke, Shadow and Knight. Not that the men would give a fuck. But still, mentally he arranged a better time to meet up with the newest operatives so everyone could receive their assignments and who each of the new guys would be assigned to during training he didn't expect to last more than a few weeks at most.

He'd hired guys who were smart, knew their shit, didn't have egos and had what it took to get the job done. He hadn't hired men who needed hand-holding and an A to Z instructional manual. He needed men who could learn under fire, adapt and overcome any obstacle. And he'd chosen well. They'd all passed a series of very rigorous, intense tests, not only determining their physical skills but also their intelligence. Their ability to make split-second decisions, the ability to think quick on their feet, and how they reacted to the unexpected. He'd been impressed, and he wasn't a man who was easily impressed. He had no doubt the men he'd hired would fit in seamlessly into DSS with no dick sizing or pissing matches, because just as he hadn't hired men with egos and something to prove, neither did anyone currently working with him suffer any such issue. All of the men—and Eliza—were confident without being too confident and had no problem calling in backup when they knew they were in over their heads or were outmatched or outnumbered.

They needed the extra muscle and manpower but that wasn't all they needed. They needed men who were not new to the game, and it was obvious after reading the extensive background checks he'd performed that the new recruits were anything but rookies. They had more than proven themselves capable in all situations Dane had thrown at them. He hadn't been easy. He'd been brutal, pushing them to their very limits, putting them through countless scenarios, many of which he hoped to fuck they never encountered with DSS, but he couldn't afford to assume anything. Not with all the shit that had gone down over the last year. And he'd made it abundantly clear to the new guys, that while, yes, they worked for DSS and they would be taking missions that DSS took on, their first and most important priority was keeping the women DSS claimed as their own safe. At all costs.

He was really fucking tired of their women—Tori, Ramie, Ari, Gracie and yes, even Eliza, though she'd have his balls for including her—being targeted, threatened, at risk and being fucking tormented and brutalized by goddamn animals. Every single woman had suffered. Each of them bore the scars, some you could see and some you couldn't but existed nonetheless, and yet they came out alive, not unscathed, but alive and they were all fierce. Not many women could survive what their women had survived with their sanity intact, and not only survive but kick ass while carrying on. He admired and respected every single one, but Eliza most of all.

And right now, she had more of his attention and focus than the other four women. Ramie, Ari and Gracie each had a husband who was more than capable of protecting them, helping them work through their demons and soothe the nightmares they endured. Tori had not only her three older brothers but every single member of DSS who'd die before ever allowing her to fall into the hands of a brutal monster again. She was so much more fragile than the other women, but then she had reason to be. Yes, they'd all suffered, but Tori the most of all.

Eliza had no one except the people she worked with. But every night she went home alone to deal with her demons in private. God knows he'd pushed as hard as possible without pushing her away to confide in him, to let him help her, but he'd hit a fucking brick wall, as had anyone else who'd attempted to get Eliza to talk about the hell she'd endured. At the mere *suggestion* she might need someone, she'd take your goddamn head off, not to mention your balls. But that didn't mean he didn't worry. He worried every fucking day, and instead of that concern diminishing over time, it only got worse when she showed no sign of ever allowing anyone inside her carefully constructed barriers.

She was more than someone he worked with. More than someone who reported to him. She was *his*. All the DSS operatives were his, but Eliza more so. He worked more closely with her than anyone else. She was his partner. His equal. He counted on her judgment, her gut. He sought her out on more than one occasion to bounce ideas off her, to get her opinions, because not only was she solid, she was smart as hell, with a mind like a computer. She called it like she saw it, never held back when he asked her opinion or what her gut was screaming. And in addition to being smart and thinking fast and well on her feet, she was tough and could kick ass as well as the rest of his operatives and better than most.

Her advantage was in being underestimated, a mistake someone made only once before learning they'd been a stupid fuck not to take a small but fierce-as-fuck pretty blonde as anything more than a blonde airhead with nothing between her ears. Dane would never admit it, but he thoroughly enjoyed watching what happened when someone overlooked Eliza or disrespected her. Or worse, didn't consider her the threat she was.

He watched as Caleb got wound up again, talking and saying shit that he said every goddamn meeting, shit that as Eliza had so eloquently put, they could recite in their sleep. He had to stifle a smile over the "state of the union" because the name had been coined by Eliza, ever the irreverent one of the bunch, and, well, he had to agree. It was a pointless meeting that in no way required every man to be pulled from their jobs to assemble in the DSS offices to give report and status on past, current and potential jobs that DSS may or may not take.

But Caleb was an anal bastard, and even if he'd for the most part turned the day-to-day running of DSS to his younger brother, Beau, he still kept his finger solidly on the pulse of everything going on. Every mission, every request for help.

Dane glanced sideways at Zack Covington, who made no

attempt to disguise his scowl, or the fact he'd checked his watch every three minutes for the last twenty and Dane had to look at Eliza or risk bursting into laughter that would likely have the rest of DSS thinking he'd lost his mind.

He didn't *have* a sense of humor. Or at least to the rest of their knowledge. Eliza knew, but Dane was closer to Lizzie than to the others. She made him feel at ease, comfortable. She didn't have a chip on her shoulder because she was a woman in a predominately male profession and she didn't get involved in pissing matches. He knew she looked to him as her team leader, though Caleb and Beau ran the operation. But then no one argued with Dane. Ever. Not even Caleb, and he could be one cold, ruthless, mean-as-a-rattlesnake son of a bitch. Especially when it came to his wife, Ramie, and her protection. With good reason. Her psychic abilities made her extremely vulnerable and they also made her a target for everyone who had a missing or kidnapped loved one. Ramie had eerily accurate abilities to track and find victims by connecting to them—and the killer. It was a sickness that pervaded her soul, made her feel foul and unclean and every time she did it, it took another piece of her with it and Caleb was determined there would be no more.

Dane didn't blame him a bit. Although he was damn glad Ramie had defied Caleb and helped locate Eliza when she'd gone missing. Hell, Ari and Gracie had said to hell with them all, determined to give back to a woman who'd risked her life time and time again for them. Without them, Lizzie would be dead.

His fists curled into tight balls and he had to control the betraying quiver of his nostrils at the thought of just how close they'd come to losing someone so important to DSS. To *him*.

He nearly missed Eliza's stifled grin or her shared commis-eration, even turning to include Zack, which meant she too had been aware of his impending departure whether the meeting was declared officially over or not.

Zack sent a look in Dane's direction. Though it was more of a scowl, Dane could see it for what it really was. A plea. Because once Dane declared a meeting over, it just was. It didn't matter if the Devereauxs had more to add. Everyone deferred to Dane. And as Zack had only just returned from his honeymoon with Gracie, he must be itching with impatience to get back to her.

Dane allowed a small smile, all he would give away on his otherwise deadpan poker face, but Zack got the message and closed his eyes, mouthing, "Thank you God" behind the backs of the others.

But Eliza, damn her hide, who'd been clued in from the very start of the exchange, suddenly suffered a coughing fit, covering her laughter, so it sounded more like a cat trying to hack up a fur ball and cupped a hand over her mouth, pretending she had indeed gotten something caught in her throat.

His glare promised retribution, but she stuck out her tongue at him and the deep intuitive alarm inside him he hadn't even realized was screaming relaxed and settled. And his internal alarm was rarely wrong, and it had alternated screaming alarm and false alarm all fucking morning when it came to Eliza. Zack too had uncanny knacks or hunches as his teammates grumbled. They swore his gut had made a deal with the devil because it had gained so much respect that if he so much as muttered that his gut said something was off, the mission was immediately halted.

Dane had been convinced something was wrong and it

had everything to do with Eliza. But in that one moment of irreverence—as if he expected anything less from her—she set his world to rights and he got to the matter at hand. Damn it, but his hands were shaking! He hadn't realized just how fucking terrified he'd been over Eliza's weird behavior earlier. He had the odd sensation of her thinning in front of him, like a ghost or apparition, going from solid form to insubstantial light and shadow, slipping away from him like sand in a breeze. DSS would never be the same without Eliza and he had a lot of people to thank for the fact she was alive, healthy and still very much part of DSS.

But it was Wade Sterling he was most grateful to—*twice*—for his help in ensuring Eliza was rescued and safe. He'd taken a bullet for her that would have killed her in seconds. She didn't know that. How close she came to death or the fact that if Wade hadn't stepped in front of her she would have died. Or maybe she did and refused to acknowledge the other man in any way. There was some serious antagonism between Eliza and Wade and Dane knew it was because Wade was still firmly stuck in the Middle Ages.

"Okay, we've been repeating ourselves for the last fifteen minutes," Dane said, interjecting himself for the first time. Zack was tired of waiting for Dane's intervention and was about two seconds from walking out. And despite his earlier moment of relief, his gut still nagged him that all wasn't right with Eliza. He wanted this shit done now so he and Eliza could talk about what the fuck was on her mind—and had been on her mind for the last week.

Caleb looked slightly annoyed but Beau flashed him a grateful look as did the other operatives gathered—Isaac, Capshaw,

Eric and Brent. The new recruits hadn't endured the meeting in its entirety so they weren't being obvious with their gratitude.

"Everyone has a job to do," Dane continued. "Though one of us is still on his honeymoon and I doubt he appreciated being dragged out of a warm bed next to an equally warm but much softer woman just to hear us spout the same shit we spout every month in these state of the union addresses." He directed his gaze toward Beau and Zack, which would likely annoy Caleb, but Caleb had backed off while Beau and Zack were very much on top of things. "You two take the new recruits, show them the ropes, put each with a team and go over our current caseload, divide them up and get to work."

The initial laughter over the first of Dane's remarks died and a more serious mood quickly replaced the amusement. Dane turned and sent Eliza a mocking smile and silently told her he never got mad. He got even. And then he proceeded to throw her under the bus. Precisely what she would do given the opportunity.

"You can thank Lizzie for the name she's dubbed our monthly meetings," Dane said in a smug tone that surprised some, while others snickered—those who understood Dane better and were privy to the unique relationship he and Eliza shared.

"I'm sure she meant it with the utmost respect, though," Dane said in a solemn voice that would have worked were it not for the sarcasm dripping like syrup from his lips.

Normally Eliza would be fuming and already plotting her revenge on Dane. Some days it was the only entertainment she enjoyed. Instead she found herself walking toward Dane's office with leaden feet, her heart heavy because she knew how much she'd miss this. The camaraderie. The ease in which they operated together. Like one mind, a well-oiled machine where everyone was so familiar with their co-operatives that they could predict their next movement before it was made.

She purposely quickened her step, shaking off the feeling of dread and hastily pulled herself together or Dane would know something was wrong. She already knew he was suspicious because while others would have seen nothing but him paying strict attention to the meeting, she'd caught the glances he'd thrown her way. Looks infused with worry and concern.

She entered his office and plopped into the chair in front of his desk, purposely sprawling in a casual pose as if this were just another conversation, like the many others they'd had in the past.

When she heard him enter his office and quietly shut the door behind him, she turned, a smile on her face, her eyes glinting with promise of retribution. That more than anything would allay any concerns he may have because Eliza was nothing if not cunning and ruthless when plotting her revenge.

But Dane didn't return her smile. Shit. Instead he regarded her with that steady gaze that missed nothing. She had the mortifying thought that she needed to cover herself because he had a way of seeing past a front—anyone's front—and making them feel naked and vulnerable with those all-knowing eyes.

"Don't think I won't get even for that, you traitor," she accused, injecting a note of laughter and amusement she definitely didn't feel into her voice.

Still, he didn't smile or even acknowledge her threat with a drawled one of his own. Oh yeah, she was in trouble, and this was going to take the act of her life to convince him that what she was requesting was nothing out of the ordinary. Even if it made her appear vulnerable in front of him, something she'd die before ever allowing any of the men she worked with to see. The hell of it was, appearing vulnerable wouldn't require any acting whatsoever. She *was* vulnerable. And it was the worst, goddamn weakest feeling in the world.

He slid into the chair behind his desk and leaned back, still studying her, his stare probing intently like he could see every single secret she was trying so desperately to hide.

"What's going on, Lizzie?" he asked quietly.

She sighed and threw up her hands. "Only you would make me feel guilty for requesting vacation time."

His eyes widened in surprise and if it weren't for the pain slicing through the region of her heart, she would have taken great satisfaction in throwing him off his game for those few seconds.

"Vacation?" he asked incredulously. "*That's* what this is all about? For fuck's sake, Lizzie. You scared the shit out of me. You haven't been yourself lately and then this morning. You checked out. I doubt you even remember a goddamn thing that was said during that meeting."

She rolled her eyes. "You mean the same thing said in every single one of those pointless meetings where we're all reminded of the job we do—jobs we're damn good at by the way. Dane, I know them by heart. Pardon me for already mentally planning a few weeks on a beach somewhere soaking up as much sun and sand as possible, maybe hooking up with a single hunk and blowing off some steam."

Dane scowled and Eliza rolled her eyes. "Cut the big brother act, Dane. I don't lecture you when you're out fucking women. So far your only redeeming quality is that you don't have a double standard when it comes to men and women. Don't ruin it for me now."

Dane sighed. "You know I have no problem with you taking vacation, Lizzie. God knows I've been after you to take some time off for years. But why now? What's going on with you? And swear to God, if you tell me nothing, I'll handcuff you to the bed in the guestroom of my house and then I'll sic Ramie, Ari and Gracie on you. Especially Gracie since she'll know *exactly* what that devious mind of yours is plotting."

It didn't take as much effort as Eliza had thought to allow her aching vulnerability to show. The pain of the last weeks and that of the weeks to come. Dane must have seen the shadows of remembrance in her eyes because he suddenly cursed and rubbed a hand over his face.

"Christ I'm an asshole. You're still having a hard time aren't you, Lizzie?" he asked softly.

She shrugged. And then sighed, allowing the truth to blend with the untruths, or rather the truths of the past, things that even Dane and his ability to find information on anyone no matter how deeply hidden wouldn't have uncovered.

"I'm tired, Dane," she said quietly. "I can't sleep at night. And when I do, I relive every terror-filled moment of what they did. Of what I feared they would do to you. To Ramie, Ari and Gracie. The rest of my team. My family," she said, grief heavily laced in her voice.

But she'd be damned if she let him see her cry. No one would ever see her cry again. She wasn't that weak, helpless, idealistic sixteen-year-old girl who believed in fairy tales, princes and happily ever afters.

To her shock, Dane was on his feet and around the desk

before she could take a breath and he pulled her to her feet, enfolding her into his tight embrace, hugging her fiercely. Any other time she would be horrified. She'd have a sarcastic, caustic remark about acting like a bunch of fucking wussies and then punch him in the gut. But God, his hug felt good. It felt solid when nothing else in her life was solid. He was strong and just for a moment she allowed herself to lean on him and to be strong for her. She closed her eyes.

"*I know*," he said, fury in his voice. "Because I can't sleep either, Lizzie. Because for the worst minutes of my life I thought we were too late. That I had failed you. That we hadn't made it in time and that you were *dead*. You endured unspeakable torture and you still managed to kick ass doing it. In case I haven't told you lately or often enough, there is no one I'd rather have at my back than you."

In a rare moment, she didn't resist, didn't avoid or pull away from the close contact with cocky words meant to diffuse an awkward, emotional moment. Instead she rested her temple against Dane's chest and closed her eyes.

"I just need to get away for a while," she whispered. "They *took* something from me, Dane. As much as I hate it, hate admitting it, hate allowing those bastards to have taken any piece of me, they did, and I have to get it *back*. I don't expect you to understand. But if I'm going to continue doing my job, and I have no intention of letting those assholes ruin the one good thing in my life, then I just need some time to pull myself back together so I can come back whole again. Because right now I'm a liability. You know it. I know it. Caleb and Beau and the others know it too. And I could never live with myself if I got one of the people I care about hurt or killed because my head wasn't where it should have been."

Dane frowned, but as she'd known, he hadn't argued. She knew she was fragile and it had nothing to do with the assholes who'd abducted her and tortured her. But it suited her purposes for Dane and all the rest to believe just that because then they'd look no further than the surface. She'd never asked for vacation time in all the years she'd worked for DSS. Since its inception, and even before, she and Dane had worked together in a much smaller personal security agency, taking jobs on a much smaller scale.

When Dane had been recruited by Caleb and Beau, he'd accepted with one condition. He brought Eliza with him. No negotiation. And so they'd made the move together and continued to work together, strengthening their already very strong bond.

It was why they had such a close working relationship. They could predict the other's thoughts, movements . . . She choked back the suffocating, vile thoughts because she'd been about to compare her friendship with Dane, the only true thing she had in this world, to her relationship with Thomas, a man who had known her every thought, fantasy and deepest longing, and used them to manipulate her and make it so easy for her to fall into his lap with no resistance from her whatsoever. Never would she defile and disrespect Dane in that manner. He deserved so much better than the depraved, broken monster she'd become, still was, to guard his back. She just prayed her replacement would take that responsibility to heart and recognize how truly great a man Dane Elliot was and that they, like her, would be willing to lay down their life for him.

"How long?" Dane asked, momentarily confusing her because she'd been so caught up in her own thoughts.

She recovered quickly and glanced nervously at him, hoping he didn't read too much into the length of her request. Then she shrugged as if she hadn't put that much thought into it at all. "A month. Maybe six weeks. Provided y'all can do without me that long. Things are quiet right now but we all knows how that goes," she said with a grin. "I don't really have a plan. I just want to go where the wind takes me and enjoy the downtime."

Dane studied her a long time as if determining the veracity of her statement. Just about the time her iron discipline was about to desert her and she started to squirm under his scrutiny, he once again struck her speechless.

"You managed to hide it well, Lizzie. Even from me . . . until recently," he said in a painful tone that sounded almost hurt. As if the thought of her holding out on him had never once crossed his mind. "But they hurt you and not just physically though those sons of bitches inflicted plenty of damage. They damn near *killed* you. Far too close for my peace of mind. I still can't forget that moment, Lizzie. When I thought we'd been too late. Goddamn it!"

His voice was thick with emotion, features blackening with rage and his eyes went as dark as obsidian, glittering with menace and so much pain and regret that it took her breath away.

"Swear to God, I wish to hell Gracie hadn't been able to identify them or read their fucking thoughts so I could have killed them on the spot. And it wouldn't have been slow, Lizzie. I would have repaid them for every mark they put on you. For every thought of terror they drove into your mind. And for making you doubt even for a moment that the people who care most about you wouldn't make it to save you in time."

"Dane," she choked out, reaching up to touch his arm. "Do you honestly think I would have lasted as long as I did if I hadn't known you'd come? You know what I went through and you know most people would have given up. Accepted the inevitable. Even *prayed* for the end so they could escape. I stayed alive because I *knew* you and the others would come, that you would have never given up, and I knew we would make every last one of them pay, not just for what they did to me. But for what they did to the other women. Never for a minute think I lost faith in you."

He shook his head as if rejecting her absolute belief, her unwavering faith in *him*.

"Still, I should have seen how this affected you. I should have fucking sat on you and insisted you stand down when we took them out. Instead you were nearly killed and swear to God, my heart fucking stopped. I thought I was having a heart attack and if it's all the same, I don't ever want to go through that again."

Her eyes narrowed because now she was getting pissed. She was asking for vacation, not for an analysis of her mental state— or lack thereof.

"Am I or am I not cleared for vacation?" she snapped. "Or do I need to remind you that I haven't had so much as a day off in the entire time I've worked for you."

Slowly he smiled and the worry and fear dispersed like fog being melted away by the sun's rays. "Consider yourself on vacation as of five minutes ago. And Eliza? If I so much as see your ass within a mile of the office or poking your nose in one of our cases for at least six weeks, I'll suspend you and double your vacation time to three months and I'll have Isaac sit on you and, trust me, after you nearly getting yourself killed twice? No one would have to twist his arm to get him to take that job. He'd take great delight in being allowed to boss you around."

Then he grinned slyly. "If that's not enough incentive for you, I'd be more than happy, as part of their training of course, to have one or more of the new recruits keep you under lock and key."

She made a face and rolled her eyes. "You're all a bunch of Neanderthals. *You* just hide it under that smooth, polished preppy look you've got going on."

He frowned and then outright scowled at her.

She threw up her hands in surrender. "Hey, vacation was my idea, remember? I have no intention of doing anything remotely work related." Okay, it wasn't a lie. What she had to do in no way involved DSS or anyone involved with DSS.

"I plan to find a nice beach house somewhere private where they have nice cabana boys who will bring me fruity, girly cocktails with little umbrellas in them, work on my tan and hopefully the scars will fade and by the time I come back to work, you'll all be so sick of me and my attitude, you'll promptly wish I had taken three months instead of half that," she teased.

His scowl darkened further at the mention of her scars and she wished she'd kept her mouth shut.

"Dane," she said, a hint of impatience but gentle understanding in her voice. "I'll be fine okay? I'm not so stubborn that I can't or won't admit I need a break. It's been . . . hard."

She nearly choked on the words, on the admission that she was struggling and needed time to put herself back together. God, she hated this, putting doubt in Dane's mind that she was no longer capable of pulling her own weight in a job she loved.

But then it wasn't as if she had a job to come back to, so what did it really matter? Dane's expression immediately softened and his hand went to her shoulder and squeezed.

"I have no doubt you'll be fine, Lizzie. I won't have it any other way. Now get out of my office, go get packed, if you aren't already. But do me a favor please? Would you check in every once in a while just for my peace of mind? I . . . worry about you. You have my word that no one will call you and I'm not asking you to check in with the others. This is purely off the record. Friend to friend. Just let me know how you're doing and that you're okay."

She smiled, a genuine smile and one she hadn't been able to pull off no matter how hard she tried since her life had irrevocably changed course.

If she hadn't been so relieved to have gotten past Dane without him being astute enough to know something was definitely going on, other than her sudden desire for an impulsive vacation, she would have remembered that nothing ever got by Dane. And she was an idiot for thinking so.

Not five minutes after she left and Dane lifted one of the slats of the blinds covering his office windows to ensure her vehicle was gone, he then went back to his desk and sat down, punching in a phone number that only served to further blacken his mood.

Never in a million favors would he ask the favor he was about to request from the man he was about to ask it of. He'd never considered any situation where he'd humble himself enough to ask for help from a man who set his teeth on edge. But for Eliza, he had no pride. For Eliza, her safety and ensuring she remained safe, he'd do the unthinkable.

"Wade Sterling," Dane nearly growled into the phone. "Tell him Dane Elliot is calling about . . . Eliza Cummings."

If there was one man Eliza couldn't steamroll, it was Wade, a man who'd taken a bullet for her when he went up against every single member of DSS and told them what flaming dumbasses they were for allowing an injured, tortured woman who hadn't had sufficient time to recover from participating in the takedown of the men who'd hurt her so horrifically.

And when it became a battle of wills, with Eliza showing more fire and determination than Dane had ever seen from his usually unflappable partner, and her refusing to back down under Wade's intimidating, ferocious decree, he'd simply honed in on the mission, insisting on going along even though he in no way worked for DSS; and furthermore he was a man who lived cloaked in shadows and Dane didn't trust him as far as he could throw him.

Only, he'd stepped in front of a bullet that Lizzie's vest wouldn't have protected her from. It would have struck the vulnerable flesh of her neck and killed her instantly. Instead, Wade's much taller frame had caused the bullet to lodge into his arm and even then, the bullet used had been an armor-piercing bullet and had torn through the flesh of his arm, missing bone, thank God; and because Eliza had time to turn, the bullet had gone through Wade's arm and had wedged itself into Eliza's protective vest as Wade had taken her down, covering her body with his own.

Yes, if anyone could find out what Eliza was up to and the source of so much pain and shadows in her eyes, and worst of all the fear Dane had seen clearly reflected in a tenth of an unguarded second before she'd visibly collected herself, it was Wade Sterling.

Dane may not like the man, but he owed him a hell of a lot, and he wasn't stupid. Wade had made a claim on Eliza that any man in a ten-mile radius could recognize. Eliza, on the other hand, was oblivious, but then she was clueless as to her effect on the male population. Always had been.

He could almost feel sorry for Eliza because Dane was effectively throwing her to the wolves—or rather wolf. One large, surly lone wolf. But even losing her trust, friendship and loyalty was worth it if the end result was her safety, and one thing Dane had learned in very short order was that what Wade Sterling considered his, he protected with his every breath.

Eliza couldn't be in safer hands. Even if she didn't yet realize it.

SEVEN

WADE Sterling stood inside the open gate to Eliza's small court-yard which was surrounded by a privacy fence to give her seclu-sion not only in the front of the homey end unit but all the way around the townhome, encompassing the slightly larger backyard where she'd obviously spent a lot of time landscaping and mak-ing it into her escape from the rest of the world. He'd made sure he blended with the shadows so his presence wasn't detected until he was ready to reveal himself.

Not that he'd ever been invited *inside* her private domain. The few times he'd approached her in the parking lot in front of her building, she'd made it clear there would be no invitation into her inner sanctum. Her apartment looked like all the oth-ers in the complex—on the outside. Wade would bet everything he owned that the inside likely resembled the control room of the CIA or FBI. The image amused him. Hell, *she* amused him, and, he'd grudgingly—finally—admitted that not only was she a source of rare entertainment for him, but she intrigued and fascinated him. It wasn't a feeling he was accustomed to when it came to women.

He wouldn't go as far as to say he was an expert on females. Who in the hell in their right mind would ever make, much less convince others to believe, such an absurd statement. Women, especially their moods and temperaments, changed with the wind.

Except Eliza Cummings. He found that interesting indeed, because he was certain there were a multitude of things buried deep inside. Feelings, emotions, reactions she never allowed to surface because of training and rigid self-discipline that enabled her to suppress them, control them and never allow them their freedom.

He wondered just what it would take to unleash tightly controlled emotions. Then he shook his head in disgust. While he was skulking around her apartment building, not paying attention to his primary objective, she could have easily given him the slip and he wouldn't have known until it was too late.

As it was, Eliza would be pissed and likely shoot him on sight if she knew he was this close to her *and* that she was so completely unaware of his presence. Something that pissed *him* off.

A woman who made her living in security, protecting others, but, most importantly, keeping her own hide from being kidnapped, tortured or riddled with bullets just as she'd been a few short months ago should damn well have better instincts than this. And leaving her door wide open in the middle of the night without once doing a perimeter sweep set his teeth on edge. Was she just *trying* to get herself killed? Did she have some sort of morbid death wish and that was why she was an unstoppable force for DSS, always taking assignments even if she'd just come off of one after three days of no sleep? She needed a damn keeper, something he'd voiced to her before, and *that* hadn't gone over too well. Not that it was a huge surprise. But she couldn't continue her current pace. Even if her coworkers couldn't see it, Wade could see the shadows in her eyes that seemed to slowly grow deeper. She had a burned-out look that said if she didn't have her shit sorted in short order, it was only a matter of time before she got killed on a job. And for reasons he refused to examine or dwell on, that bothered him. It bothered him a hell of a lot. Hell, bothered was too mild of a term. It pissed him right the fuck off.

Observing her with her barriers down, when she thought no one was watching her, made him understand now why Dane Elliot had called him. He hadn't quite known what to make of the phone call or the fact that a man who had obvious animosity toward him had basically humbled himself by asking for help. He'd never admit it in a million years, but he'd already planned an impromptu visit to Eliza's apartment with every intention of finishing or at least going a hell of a lot further than the last two times they'd met. He was tired of dancing around. Dane's call had just caused him to make his move in haste instead of executing a well thought out plan of attack. One that sealed any possible escape routes.

The idea that *now* one of Eliza's team members was concerned after her two horrifying near-death experiences just pissed him the fuck off, and he rubbed at his chest to alleviate the sudden discomfort. What the fuck was he doing here as Dane fucking Elliot's puppet? Wade could check up on Eliza in his own time. His way. His terms. And he sure as hell wouldn't answer to anyone else like some hired lackey.

Why hadn't he told Dane that his babysitting stint was over with and that if he was so goddamn concerned about Eliza to put a team on her? The little time he'd spent with DSS, he respected and admired them and their work. He secretly approved of their tactics and the fact they didn't always do things by the book. Sometimes justice was best served by old-fashioned revenge.

He wasn't in the habit of lying to himself, but neither was he willing to admit the truth to anyone else. He'd already made up his mind to keep a very close eye on Eliza Cummings and insert himself into her life in ways she would not be happy about when Dane Elliot had called. It just gave him the excuse to do what he was already going to do without admitting to his own reasons for doing so.

And so here he was, spying on a woman who hated the very sight of him. She was hastily packing and not paying any damn attention to anything else. He supposed he could at least give her a small semblance of credit for not having the lights on because that meant no one could see into the house.

And so it was in the dark that she worked with quick efficiency to pack her belongings and the alarm system wasn't even on for fuck's sake. He wanted to wrap his hands around her neck and throttle her for upending his well-ordered life from the moment she barreled into it and got in his face. He'd been fascinated. No, he'd been fucking obsessed from that moment forward. She'd dressed him up one side and down the other and despite her very real fury and loyalty to her teammates, Wade had never felt so compelled to kiss a woman in his life.

He almost *had*. But they'd had one clusterfuck of a situation going on and he'd had Gracie to protect, not to mention if he had so much as touched Eliza, she would have laid his ass out. Also, Dane would be on him before he could even push Eliza off and, well, then the rest of DSS would take great satisfaction in kicking his ass. Especially Zack, who had the most reason to harbor resentment.

Admittedly, the lights being off would prevent people from being able to see into her home, but the silent cloak of night didn't hinder him in any way. His eyes, well accustomed to the dark and seeing what most others couldn't make out in the shadows, could see her hurrying from room to room, tossing several suitcases on the couch in the living room and hurriedly stuffing clothing into them.

Hardly the actions of a woman who merely wanted a leisurely vacation and was in no hurry, had no worries, only where the wind blew her and taking some much-needed R&R. It looked to him as though after her "request" for vacation, she was getting out of town as fast as possible before any of her coworkers, or Dane, decided to pay her a visit to say their goodbyes. Odd behavior for a woman who treated the people she worked with as family, and if she truly was just taking some downtime, wouldn't she want to say her farewells?

His eyes narrowed as he continued to watch from his post. Eliza was definitely packing for an extended trip. But not a single item of clothing was remotely suitable for a vacation at the beach or any other place of leisure. In fact, other than jeans, shirts, underwear, socks and a pair of tennis shoes, the rest were fatigues, lots of camo. Face paint. And, Jesus, lethal-looking knives that took up one entire side of one of the suitcases.

He was astonished, and he had never been a man who was

easily surprised. He'd learned his lessons young and had taught himself to always expect the worst and never be caught off guard or surprised by anything.

Shit. There went that rule . . . *again*. Fuck!

Her latest addition to her suitcase was several flashbang grenades but what really worried him was the addition of very real grenades and, Jesus, a stash of definitely illegal C-4 of the likes no average civilian would ever be able to get their hands on; and if that wasn't bad enough, there was also a shit ton of items one could use to build a bomb. Hell, she could probably build a nuclear missile. All she lacked was uranium. For all he knew, she had a stash of that somewhere as well. She certainly didn't lack for anything in her armory. She was better stocked than most third world military units. Was she planning to go to fucking war?

That idea froze his blood and he felt the stirrings of something he wasn't at all familiar with, having never experienced it, certainly not to this degree, but it felt like fear. And fear was not a weakness he ever allowed himself. Until now. Until *her*, goddamn it.

Most people either packed well ahead of time and lined their luggage by the door, got a good night's sleep and then embarked on an early flight the next morning. Or they procrastinated and packed last minute, getting to the airport barely on time. And just how the hell did she think she was going to get on a plane with a large enough arsenal to build an entire army? She wasn't dumb, so flying was out unless she had a private jet lined up. He'd looked into her finances and while she could live well on the generous salary DSS paid, she couldn't afford shit like private

jets. For that matter she couldn't afford all the shit she was packing, even on the black market, which begged the question, how
the fuck had she gotten her hands on this shit?

He didn't disagree that the fool woman needed a lengthy
vacation that included plenty of rest and recovery. He'd wanted
to shake some sense into her stubborn head when she'd insisted
on accompanying her team on the takedown of the remaining
fanatics whose only objective was to take the women of DSS
alive and subject them to unspeakable experiments and tests;
even animals were afforded kinder treatment.

But his built-in alarm system was beating like a mother
fucker because, despite the fact it would infuriate Eliza that her
privacy wasn't quite as carefully guarded as she liked to think, he
knew a hell of a lot more about her impromptu vacation than
even her overprotective watchdog/partner, Dane Elliot. Because
right now? Along with that alarm system cutting into his every
breath, his vision was hazy with fury and heat scorched over his
body as he curled and uncurled his fists.

Vacation my ass. If this was Eliza's idea of vacation—being a
Rambo beach bunny—then the local economy of wherever she
went would suffer because she'd scare the fuck out of everyone.

Although he had to hand it to Dane because the moment
Eliza had breezed out of his office as if she hadn't a care in the
world, Dane had been on the phone with Wade and crisply outlined the situation to him.

Wade's curiosity was instantly aroused—after he'd gotten
over his rage of her blowing off steam with a fucking cabana
boy—because Dane simply didn't give a fuck and he was a bare
bones man of few words. It was his show. He ran the business.
But apparently, when something really mattered to Dane—

which Eliza clearly did—he didn't give a shit about putting it out there. And to Dane's credit, when he, like Wade—now that he'd seen her—had observed whatever fucked-up excuse she'd given—he hadn't bought her spontaneous, out-of-the-blue request for extended vacation time. Dane was in a very delicate situation, hence the phone call to Wade, which must have pained him to no end, because if he interfered either as a friend or employer, he'd lose Eliza's trust and he knew her too well. She'd leave. She'd never stay and work under people who'd betrayed her. Even for her own good.

Hell, Wade hadn't known Eliza a fraction of the time Dane had and even he knew that much about her. It would figure that after Wade had vowed to never cross paths with DSS again, that the cause of his injury—the reason for so many sleepless nights because he couldn't stop thinking about her—would be the thing that brought him right back into their crosshairs. Or so he had tried convincing himself of. He was such a liar.

He wasn't clueless when it came to women, and he knew damn well Eliza Cummings was every bit as much under his skin as the bullet he'd shielded her from. Yet another thing she'd been highly pissed about. Like he was any happier? His life would sure be a hell of a lot easier if he'd never met the blasted woman. He smiled ruefully to himself. Since when had he ever liked things easy?

As signals went, that one was pretty clear. Death was evidently preferable to having Wade anywhere in the vicinity.

But Eliza and Dane? As more than partners, and apparently close friends? Wade was very good at reading people and he'd never seen anything that hinted of Dane and Eliza having a romantic relationship. No sign that Dane was overprotective of her in the way a lover would lock her up if he had to—like Wade would if she were his—in order to keep her safe. The fact that Dane treated her like any other teammate, allowing her to assume the same risks as the others, told him that in no way Dane considered Eliza his woman. All he'd witnessed was a deep camaraderie, a sense of loyalty that was deeply ingrained in all of them. Each and every one of them would give his or her life for one of their family.

Family. That was what he hadn't been able to put his finger on but what had niggled at his brain. It resembled jealousy, which was stupid because a man his age didn't lower himself to the indignity of juvenile feelings like envy.

But DSS was family in every sense of the word. He'd seen them in action. Had gone into battle with them. And even if he had no desire to ever get mixed up in their crazy-ass missions, he could admit to being impressed by their expertise.

Shaking his head to focus back on Eliza, he shoved aside his dour thoughts about Dane's role in Eliza's life. He'd have plenty of time to find out everything that made Eliza who she was when he managed to crack the hardened shell that disguised the sweetest, most tender and understanding heart of anyone he knew.

As quietly as if he walked on panther's feet, he inched closer so he had an even better view of just what the hell she was up to. Eliza was bent over her suitcase, arranging the boxes of ammo she'd carried out after the knives, grenades and C-4. Good God. Was it going to get worse? He shut down that train of thought as well because it could *always* get worse.

He found himself drifting off again, something that was not characteristic of him. It was that damn, infuriating woman's fault. And yet the night he'd taken a bullet for her, he'd known that now she belonged to him. Or maybe he belonged to her. Did it really matter? They were connected on a completely different plane, something most people wouldn't experience their entire life. Most people chased, waited and, with every growing day, grew more despondent until finally they simply settled because they didn't want to spend the rest of their lives alone. Except Eliza, apparently. She was too self-assured and he could never see her settling for anything. It would take a strong man to take her on and it infuriated him that he positively itched with non-issued challenge. *Come and get me.*

They had at least that in common. He would never settle and he had no desire to marry until he found someone he couldn't run over and make a meek mouse out of. He knew how rough around the edges he was. That he frowned far more than smiled. He had a temper and when sparked, it got ugly because he didn't back down from a fight. Ever. That didn't leave him too many options for marriage material. And he sure as hell didn't want a damn trophy wife who was more interested in the size of his bank account than the size of his dick.

He and Eliza would *never* work. They'd be at each other's throats constantly. She in his face. Toe to toe. Every goddamn thing would turn into a battle of wills. Yeah, he wanted to fuck her about a dozen times just to get her out of his head so he could stop thinking and worrying about her every goddamn day. She was too independent, too rash, too confident. Confidence was a trait he admired and respected and Eliza had it in spades. They were just too much alike. They were both control freaks and neither were people to ever be dictated to, and Wade was honest enough with himself to know that for the right woman, he could make small concessions. But when it came to her safety? All bets were off and he would do whatever he had to, even tying her to his damn bed if it kept her out of harm's way.

And that was the other alarm screeching like hell in his head. Yeah, no secret Eliza wasn't taking vacation. Not unusual for her to pack her gear and arsenal, because she never went anywhere unprepared, but this . . . this was different.

She was in a huge hurry and he could hear the soft curses under her breath as she tried to close the bulging suitcase. She'd never even be able to get it to her car. It weighed more than she did.

But he recognized that determination radiating from her. She'd never let a suitcase zipper defeat her because if it did, Wade was going to take great delight in tormenting her every chance he got that a zipper had kicked her ass.

Finally, her task was completed and then she took only a few moments to pull her long hair back into a ponytail, to Wade's disappointment, because he had some serious fantasies about all that glorious, silken hair. No, they weren't in the least bit compatible. They were all wrong for each other, and yet . . . Good things never came easy. They shouldn't. Anything worth having was worth fighting for. He'd never be happy with a fucking doormat. A woman who was little more than a robot programmed to comply with his demands. Was that really what he wanted? Because right now he was thinking his life would be a lot more interesting if the woman he chose challenged him at every turn. Shit would definitely never get boring. He was used to winning. He expected to win. Always. But sometimes conceding victory was a victory in itself because the reward was all the more sweeter.

Jesus, but he was losing his ever-loving fucking mind. He forced his attention back to Eliza and what she was doing.

She collected her oversize purse—armed with even more weapons if he had to guess. Then she tilted both suitcases, holding on to the two handles, and began dragging them toward the door, strain evident on her face.

He swore softly again. Stupid fucking stubborn woman. Why did he have to be drawn to her and worse actually *like* and *respect* her. If he only wanted sex, then he'd go get laid and never even think of the woman again. But once he had a taste of Eliza, he knew once would never be enough, and she deserved better than a quick fuck from a heartless bastard.

He pulled up on that thought, because if he ever got between her legs, there would be nothing *quick* about him fucking her. If he thought a dozen times inside her would ever be enough to get her out of his system, then he was out of his fucking mind. Eliza wasn't a woman a man could ever fuck and walk away from, and if they did, they were damn fools.

His breath paused and he melted farther back into the shadows as Eliza's door opened and she lugged the two large suitcases to her trunk. Then she went back inside but this time when she returned, Wade's jaw actually dropped. Hell, she could take out an entire city with the contents she very carefully arranged on the floorboard and then wrapped almost lovingly with a soft quilt.

No way in hell he was letting her leave without explaining to him exactly what the fuck had inspired this sudden need for "downtime." Because she sure as shit wasn't planning a vacation and the fact that she hadn't confided in her team, people she was intensely loyal to and trusted implicitly, made his gut tighten with dread because whatever had prompted this was bad. Very bad. And no way was he going to let Eliza shoulder it alone.

He tensed, waited a brief moment for her to be positioned

so he wouldn't be spotted when he made his move, and then he slipped silently to her SUV so when she slammed the trunk she would see him. No gap in the range of sight could prevent her from sensing his presence. Thank God she hadn't completely lost all vestige of common sense and the instincts that made her so damn good at her job. The minute she knew she wasn't alone, the trunk slammed with enough force to shatter the back glass and he found himself staring down the barrel of a pistol that looked far too big for such a small hand.

"Funny way to greet someone who saved your life," he said, heavy sarcasm lacing his voice.

He wanted her to think he was here just to piss her off and fuck with her because then it would be less obvious that he was studying her expression, her eyes and body language for anything else that set his what-the-fuck-o-meter off even more than it already was.

She looked . . . *relieved*?

What the fuck? This was getting more jacked by the minute. But her reaction was gone almost as quickly as it registered, leaving him to wonder if he was losing his mind.

He could swear she sagged the slightest bit. It registered as little more than a twitch, but he'd spent more time than he had liked studying her and getting to know her body language. What the hell was wrong with her? Why wasn't she in his face threatening to hand him his balls? For that matter, why the fuck was she so pale, despite the brief relief she hadn't been able to control that had flickered just once in her eyes. Eyes that moved swiftly beyond him, around him, everywhere *but* him, her chin lifting, almost like an animal scenting prey.

Or a predator. Or a person?

Evidently satisfied that whatever she was looking for was either there or not there—who knew with her—she lowered her gun and then gave him a scowl that lacked its usual authenticity.

"Don't you ever fucking do that again," she snarled. "What the hell are you doing here? Are you just trying to get shot? Jesus, Sterling, one would think I would be the last person you'd want to see again and yet you just keep turning up, and let me say, you're about as welcome as a swarm of mosquitos."

He stared directly into her eyes, noting that where before she'd never had a problem staring him down with defiance that aroused the hell out of him, she wouldn't meet his gaze. She glanced at his shoulder, his forehead, his ear and evidently his chin because she wouldn't be looking at his mouth. He wasn't that lucky.

He didn't like this. This whole fucked-up, middle of the night meet and greet in front of Eliza's apartment standing two feet away from a vehicle that could arm a small country. She wasn't even giving him lip. Because the watered down version of "fuck off" he'd just received was pretty damn pathetic and hardly worthy of someone who ran as hot and fierce so deeply as Eliza.

He purposely assumed an insolent pose, crossing his arms over his chest and staring right at her, despite the fact she was so obviously avoiding his eyes.

"Don't ever fucking do what again?" he asked calmly. "Check in on you to make sure you're taking care of yourself, since we both know you don't. And that you're safe and that you don't wake up every night with nightmares? You forget I've been up close and personal with you twice in the last two days, Eliza. I've *seen* you. I've seen what you're trying and miserably failing at hiding. The people you work with may be blind fools, but I'm not."

He made a show of checking his watch just to make his point that most people were in bed, asleep and not in their driveway about to go to war. He had to bite his lip to ask how long it had been since she'd been one of those people who were in bed, asleep, because she looked like she hadn't slept in weeks and his blood ran hot with fury all over again. *How* had Dane not seen this? Or Caleb, Beau, Zack, anyone! Why had she been the one to request vacation time instead of one of her *partners* stuffing her in a safe house somewhere and then sitting on her ass, making damn sure she ate, slept and didn't battle her nightmares alone. Partners his ass. A partner would have her back and not give a shit if her feelings got hurt or whether her pride got ruffled because her partner demanded she stand down.

Finally, her eyes flickered to his, the prolonged silence obviously making her uneasy. For that matter it was making *him* damn uneasy. He'd all but insulted the entire precious organization she worked for, and she'd usually defend them with her dying breath, and yet she'd acted as though she hadn't even heard his scathing criticism. As the saying went, however, never look a gift horse in the mouth, so he took advantage and pounced, pinning her with his stare.

"Just how low are your reserves right now, Eliza? Fumes aren't going to get you very far and that's all you're running on right now. I'd be surprised if you could make it down the block. If your goddamn agency is so *sacred*, then why the hell aren't they taking better care of you?"

He almost wished she hadn't looked at him. Almost. Because he was bombarded by so many conflicting emotions that it unsteadied him and he had to shift his weight to his other foot to cover his reaction.

Grief, fury, sorrow, guilt and . . . What the fuck? He wanted to roar it! What the ever loving *fuck*?

He swore long, hard and viciously in his mind. Rage hurtled through his veins and this time, he couldn't control the flex of his fingers into tight fists, knotted over his chest. Red. He could swear he was seeing red. His jaw clenched, and he wanted nothing more than to go knock Dane on his fucking ass. And the rest of his pissant agency as well.

Fear. He saw fucking *fear* in this female warrior's eyes. And a hell of a lot more. But fear was the one that clenched his gut and squeezed mercilessly. *Fucking fear* in *Eliza's* eyes.

That more than anything decided the matter for him. He had come out of curiosity after Dane's unexpected request and, well, because he'd been determined to follow up on the bullshit story she'd given him about Gracie's supposed surprise—both excuses. He damn well knew it because he hated admitting how much he thought about her and he really hated the fact he'd grasp any excuse to see her . . . but Dane's bizarre request gave Wade a *solid* excuse to run Eliza to ground. Since he hadn't expected *any* of what he'd witnessed tonight, he'd firmly planned to call Dane the next morning and tell him to go to hell. Now? Oh *hell* no.

Fuck Dane. Fuck DSS. Fuck playing babysitter and shadowing Eliza only to report in to Dane because *Dane* was "worried." This was his situation now because he was making it his. Eliza's protection, needs and especially making goddamn sure she had nothing to be afraid of was, as of now, his sole objective. And Dane and his requests for check-ins could go to hell.

She was *his*. Not Dane's. Not DSS's and damn sure not someone's teammate. Had *no* one been able to see, cared enough to see what this fierce survivor had suffered—was *still* suffering? And did they not realize that if Eliza was fucking scared, then it was bad? Not just bad. The worst.

He was so goddamn mad that he was precariously close to losing his shit right in the middle of her driveway. He wanted every last one of those bastards' blood, especially Dane's. Dane, her partner—no, *family*—according to Eliza's words. Words still ringing in his ears. Dane had wimped out and sent Wade like an errand boy knowing how she looked and admitting he was "worried." For something this precious and important, Dane was too worried over making his "friend" mad when he should have been more worried about having her at all.

The entire episode, his sudden insight and decision had taken no more than a tenth of a second. A hell of a short time for the course of his life to alter. And in just that nanosecond, Eliza recovered and her face became icy, chill radiating from her eyes.

She looked cool, unflappable, like the Eliza he *thought* he'd known. The one everyone *else* was *supposed* to know. But in the time a blink of an eye took, Wade saw something he was certain no one had ever seen or bothered to notice.

She holstered her gun and took a step forward until she was a mere twelve inches from him. She notched her chin up, defiance and fire glinting in her eyes. Too bad for her. That tenth of a second had meant the difference between him letting her walk away and him sticking to her like glue.

"You don't know *anything* about me, Sterling," she said in a cool voice. "Don't ever make the mistake of thinking you do. *As-*

sumptions get people killed. Readiness, preparation, working to become the best. Those are what save not only your life but the lives of your teammates as well. We aren't in this as every man for himself. We're a unit. We're . . . family."

Something cracked in her voice at those last words and he had the strangest compulsion to simply wrap his arms around her and do nothing but comfort her and bury his face in her sweet smelling hair. The instincts he always relied on told him she was barely hanging on by a thread and would likely fall apart.

He reined himself in before she panicked and tried to kick his ass. *Tried* being the operative word. Right now he wished she would try to kick his ass because then at least he'd be familiar with this Eliza and not this kicked puppy version.

"I know a lot more about you than you think I do," he said, his features going hard.

The lie rolled easily off his tongue, because he wanted to do something *more* to widen the crack he'd witnessed just moments before. It made him a complete bastard, but he'd never have this opportunity when her defenses were up and she'd shaken off whatever the hell haunted those soulful eyes. And it wasn't like he couldn't get the information he already claimed to have. He just hadn't had a solid reason beyond his annoying preoccupation with her to intrude on her privacy in such an underhanded way.

His code or rather sense of justice may seem twisted or even criminal by others, but if it got the job done and the desired effect achieved, then he didn't waste much time over useless emotions like remorse. And if it helped him get to the bottom of whatever the hell was making Eliza run like a scared rabbit, he'd hound her night and day until she conceded and let him in.

Because while he was raging about Eliza fearing anything, it infuriated him in equal measure that he was every bit as damn afraid, and this was *not* a familiar emotion for him. Cold. Methodical. Heartless. He'd heard them all and did not give one fuck. But Eliza had cheated death not once, but twice. Actually who knows how many other times he hadn't been there to witness just how many brushes with mortality she'd experienced.

She was highly trained, determined, dedicated and wasn't afraid to call or wait for back up. Her IQ very likely rivaled his, possibly even surpassed it, even if recent events had him muttering things like "fool woman" or "stupid female."

Death would only be cheated so many times before claiming ultimate victory and Wade would be damned if it claimed Eliza as one of its victims.

If possible, after Wade's casually tossed out statement, Eliza went even paler and she swayed on her feet, though she brushed his hand away when he reached to steady her. She took a hasty step back, slipping her slender but well-toned arms around her body in a defensive, protective measure.

This time she either didn't have the forethought to steel her emotions and not react to his words, or maybe she simply wasn't capable, because her eyes widened and once more fear chased through her eyes, leaving deep, unfathomable shadows in their wake, almost as if they were a permanent part of her, hidden by years of rigid training and only visible under extreme duress.

Goddamn it! Twice now he'd seen actual fear and . . . vulnerability. *Twice!* And he sure as hell hadn't imagined them. He was too attuned to others, and even more so to Eliza, to his disgruntlement, always watching, studying and observing. Always looking for weaknesses.

His eyes narrowed as did his scrutiny because now he had one more shocking revelation to process.

Trepidation.

She was trembling. Barely discernible, but she balled her fingers into fists to control the slight jitter. Wade was going through his own gamut of firsts. Worry knotted his insides, and he was driven by a sensation he'd never experienced when it came to a woman. To simply haul her over his shoulder and do what came naturally to him. Take control. Take charge. And do whatever it took to get Eliza to confide in him, trust him, but most importantly to protect her from whatever the hell had her running in secrecy without telling any of her coworkers what the fuck was going on.

"I've got to go," she whispered, darting quickly away and around to the driver's seat. To Wade's chagrin the passenger side door was already locked.

He pounded on the glass, marveling that he didn't break it.

"What the fuck is going on with you, Eliza? You're goddamn *running* and you've never had the damn sense to run from anything! Why are you so willing to fight for everyone else, at great risk to yourself, but not allow others to fight for *you*?"

She cranked the engine and he knew he was fucked. If he'd had more time, a quicker heads-up, hadn't fucked around for so long before deciding to move in and stake his claim, she wouldn't be packed and ready to run like a scared rabbit to God knows where. She would be solidly under his protection, in his bed, with no way of escaping. As it was, his options were down to two. Play chicken and hope she flinched ... or she flattened him when she reversed from her parking spot.

He hurled himself across the hood and plastered himself

against her windshield so they were face-to-face, so she could damn well see his fury as he roared at her.

"What. The. Fuck. Is. Going. On!"

She cracked her window just enough so she could be heard without allowing him any way of accessing the vehicle.

"I don't owe you an explanation for my whereabouts at any time," she shouted back. "You aren't my boss, so back off. No one else has a problem with me taking downtime so why the hell should you? God knows you were all about having someone sit on me and not let me out of the damn hospital bed and then you had to interfere in a mission that DSS had well in hand. My team believes in me. They trust me. Can you say the same?"

"Get this through your head, Eliza," he said in a menacing voice. "This has nothing to do with me having lack of faith in you. We both know you've more than proven your skills, your loyalty and the fact that you're willing to die for every member of your team. It has everything to do with the fact that while you're so busy saving the world, covering your partners' asses and taking out assholes who don't deserve to breathe the same oxygen as the majority of the population, that no one is *caring for you*. No one has *your back* and I know damn well you've backed off your team and have been doing your job by rote. Being reckless, taking stupid chances almost as if you *want* to die. Here's a newsflash for you. You can't run from *me*. I have resources beyond your wildest imagination, and I'll turn the fucking world over until you're back where you belong. Alive. Well. And not in pieces. You got me?"

His face was plastered against the windshield and he was looking at her as fiercely as he'd ever looked at anyone before—man or woman. There was no mistaking his determination and that he meant every word he'd shouted. Even with her window partially opened, he wanted every single word to sink in to this beautiful, infuriating and stubborn as hell woman. One who inspired both respect and absolute terror in him despite his irritation over both.

She paled and swallowed hard, as if her throat were knotted and she could barely breathe around it.

"Eliza," he said harshly, no longer even attempting to leash his temper or the bite in his voice. "Where the hell are you going and what the hell are you running from?"

She closed her eyes but not before he saw grief simmering into the liquid pools. She was unnaturally pale and one would think she would be showing signs of recovery after her ordeal, but all she looked was scared, vulnerable and unsure of herself. Three things no one would ever associate with Eliza, much less ever give voice to them. Jesus! How the hell could no one else see what he was seeing right now?

Then she leaned her head tiredly on the steering wheel where her hands still tightly gripped it. "I can't tell you, Wade," she said quietly, catching him off guard with her use of his first name. She'd made it a practice to put distance between them by calling him by his last name, as did most of the other DSS agents. And now, in the space of twenty-four hours, she'd used his name twice. He doubted she'd even realized it either time.

She lifted her head, resolve rigid in her eyes as she visibly composed herself. She stared at him with enough frost in her gaze to freeze a desert.

"I can't . . . w-won't tell you anything. Now *get off my car!*"

She emphasized her statement by pounding on the steering wheel so hard that he inwardly winced. Hell, she may have broken it, though he wasn't sure if it was the steering wheel or her hand that wouldn't have held up. If she thought to infuse strength into her statement, it was an epic fail, because all it did was make her sound and appear even more vulnerable and . . . lost. Fuck it all, she looked lost and forlorn. Like she had no options. No choices. As though her path had been decided a lifetime ago and every year had been spent in preparation for here and now.

But he'd caught her slip in speech and knew she was as aware of it as he was. She had said *can't*, only to hastily amend it to *won't*. Was the almighty Dane, the man she gave her unwavering loyalty to, fucking blind? Because if Eliza had stood in his office as Dane had said she'd done, and Dane saw what Wade was seeing now, hearing what Wade heard, then Dane should have cuffed her and sat on her until he pried the truth from her. It wasn't as if DSS didn't have invaluable resources in the wives of some of the DSS members. Especially Anna-Grace. Let Eliza weasel her way out of *that*.

"What *won't* you tell me, Eliza?" he seethed. "You don't have the goddamn sense to ask for help. You're too busy trying to save the world without thought of protecting your own ass, and it's obvious you're scared and even more obvious you aren't safe. Because you don't back down. *Ever*. And any brainless twit could see that you *know* you aren't safe."

She erupted, her eyes blazing, hands in tight fists as if it took everything she had not to punch right through the window of the car door.

"It's not me who isn't safe!" she yelled.

For a moment he was dumbfounded. Eliza was calm and cool under pressure. He'd never seen her this rattled even when those sons of bitches had tormented her and waterboarded her like the inhuman savages they were.

She was furious. He got that.

She hurt. He understood that too.

She wanted vengeance. He could see it in her eyes. God, he wanted vengeance as well, and not the kind the judicial system did—or rather didn't—dole out. But whether or not they lined up on the same side, she was damn well going to be behind him where she would be protected.

So what the fuck was going on here? She was definitely leaving town. But it sure as hell wasn't on vacation.

They stared at each other several long seconds, his thoughts formulating in meticulous fashion as he quickly assimilated all the pieces of the puzzle. His gut clenched, puzzling him, and he played it off as natural concern for any woman as courageous as Eliza.

But was she even planning to come back? Because she was definitely running, and if she was to be believed, the fear that had glittered in her eyes in those brief, unguarded moments wasn't for herself.

Realization made him swear violently. No, she wasn't afraid for herself. She was deathly afraid of anyone close to her being harmed and that pissed him the hell off.

She must have sensed his blinding rage and the fact he was about to punch right through her windshield to prevent her leaving because her expression became pleading, another jolt to his system, because his Eliza didn't beg for anything.

"Please, Wade. Just *go*. I have to get as far away from here and the people I care about before it's too late. I'm running out of time. If I don't leave soon enough, he'll find me and he'll kill every single person I love, care about, did something nice for or even just smiled at."

Wade was a writhing mass of fury and confusion because he had been one hundred percent right in his conclusion as to why she was leaving as fast as possible. He wanted answers and he wanted them now, but most of all, he wanted to know who the fuck had put such terror and panic into this fierce woman, and why she was so certain this asshole would find her and kill everyone of importance to her. Did she have so little confidence in the people she worked with? The people she trusted with her life? Or was this every bit as bad as his gut was screaming it was.

Because with the arsenal of weapons she was packing, she had no intention of simply going into hiding and luring whatever psychopath away from the people she cared about. She was going hunting and not the recreational kind.

She sent him one last determined look, or perhaps it was a warning, because he suddenly found himself on her concrete drive as she hit reverse, screeching into the street. He barely had time to lift his head before he saw her taillights fade into the distance.

He should have been pissed. He should be wiping his hands of the entire situation he'd unwillingly been dragged into. And he damn sure never fucking took orders—however politely formed as requests—from anyone. *Especially* Dane Elliot.

But he wasn't any of those things. A peculiar sensation fluttered through his chest and settled like a sinking stone in his gut. He closed and reopened his eyes in rapid succession but nothing he did could rid himself of the utter despair in Eliza's face.

Not many things scared Wade. If pressed, it was doubtful he could even come up with one. But seeing Eliza tonight and the desperation fueling her actions and emotions?

Scared the fuck out of him.

EIGHT

ELIZA wrapped the thin jacket more firmly around her, hugging her arms in an unconscious gesture of protection as a shiver worked its way up her spine. She stared woodenly at the redbrick courthouse with quaint white columns that had been repainted in recent years.

She could feel the malevolent stares from passersby, those who'd lived here years ago when their quiet, peaceful town had been thrust into the national spotlight, but then Eliza had made certain she was seen upon her arrival. It hadn't been easy. God, it had been so hard to walk the sidewalks, revisiting her old stomping grounds and even venturing into the diner she used to work in for breakfast, making certain to take her time so as many people as possible saw her and word spread like wildfire.

Barney still owned and operated the diner and he'd stood to the side of the woman at the counter where orders were placed, beefy arms crossed firmly over his chest and glaring openly at

Eliza, his distaste written all over his face, his expression one of having tasted or smelled something foul.

Ever since leaving the diner and wandering aimlessly through the town's center, the stares had increased as more people than normal were out and about. Whispers abounded. Pointed stares. Some didn't even try to disguise their disgust and had hurled insults loud enough to be heard for three blocks.

Inwardly she'd winced, each barb finding its target with pinpoint accuracy, but she'd be damned if she ever let anyone see her weak and vulnerable. She'd donned a cool, unaffected, even bored expression as though she were just passing her time until . . .

She shuddered, revolted by the mere thought that she'd purposely set out to make these people think that she was here because Thomas would be released in mere days. That she couldn't stay away. That she was still firmly under his spell. It was an act, but it hadn't always been and that was what hurt the most.

She'd sworn to leave this place and never return. She'd walked out of the courthouse relieved, yet so full of shame, shoving her way through the crowd of reporters, refusing to say a single word. Not even "no comment." What was there to say? She'd already aired her sins in front of God, judge and jury and she wasn't rehashing it again. Ever.

Except by a cruel twist of fate—No. Fate couldn't be blamed. The blame lay solely at Thomas's feet. He'd engineered his release. But whatever the case, that long ago vow of putting Thomas, this town, everything behind her and never rehashing it, had been shattered and now she stood in the middle of town in front of the courthouse, long-suppressed images surfacing with vicious clarity.

That day she'd carried only a duffel bag containing everything she owned, what little money she possessed shoved into her pocket. She'd walked and she'd kept walking, never once looking back. Not at the diner where it had all begun. Not when she'd wearily passed the city limit sign. She'd only looked forward, no definitive destination in mind. Her only goal had been to get as far away as possible, as quickly as possible and try like hell to put everything that town represented behind her. Try to forget. And to forgive . . . herself. She'd been unable to do either. *Especially* now.

She'd walked for days, the days fading to night and then slowly bleeding to light once more. Despite her efforts to blank her mind and shut out the recitation of the atrocities Thomas had committed, it had sounded as if the jury foreman had screamed the sentence for every single crime, each one more horrifying than the last. She *still* heard that voice in her nightmares echoing over and over. It sickened her now every bit as much as it had sickened her then, but far worse than living with never-ending nightmares was the knowledge that she was *not* the victim she'd been portrayed in court. The true victims were the women Thomas had defiled, degraded, violated and murdered in a gruesome, inhuman manner, and it was *they* who deserved justice. Not Eliza. She'd deserved the same punishment handed down to Thomas. She should, even now, be in prison consigned to a lifetime behind bars.

Because she was guilty of the worst crime of all. Stupidity. Naïveté. Willful ignorance. And an aching need for love and acceptance, as only a vulnerable young girl could fantasize about the things she'd never been gifted with. Things she craved far more than the truth. She didn't *want* reality. Her reality was dismal and without hope, love or acceptance. Things Thomas had offered and she'd latched on to with fervent desperation. She'd been absolute in her belief that he was a good man and was being wrongfully questioned and investigated. She'd been determined to do *anything* to prove his innocence because if he wasn't then she lost the fantasy world she'd plunged so recklessly into. Rooting herself so deeply in denial that she'd convinced herself none of it was real. Except Thomas's love for her. She'd clung to that and only that, refusing to see what was so pathetically obvious to everyone *except* her. Because she *chose* denial. Refused to return to reality. Her crime was that choice, because deep down she knew it wasn't real and she hadn't cared. And her denial and selfish desperation for love had condemned innocent women to death.

Thomas hadn't loved her. He wasn't *capable* of something so beautiful and selfless. It had taken her witnessing the depraved things he'd done to an innocent woman before she was forced to acknowledge what an utter, gullible fool she'd been. God, how so very ignorant of love she'd been then—a lifetime ago. But she'd witnessed the real deal now. And finally understood. Knew it for what it *truly* was and not the twisted, manipulative and sick perversion she'd once been immersed in. A nightmarish, unending source of shame that she'd never escape. But back *then* he'd tapped into her young mind and pulled every longing, every wish, her every dream and desire and then he'd given her precisely what her unrealistic fantasies had manifested themselves into. She'd been an easy mark and Thomas hadn't had to exert any effort whatsoever to bend her to his will.

She shivered, pulling at the sleeves of her windbreaker and finally pulling the hood to cover her head as chilly spring rain began to gently fall. There was no longer any need to ensure she was noticed and recognized. In a few hours' time, the entire town would know of her arrival. And Thomas too would be aware that she was here.

Tears welled and for once she didn't call them back and refuse to let them free. They merely mixed with the rain, disguised by the now more pronounced sprinkle that had begun just seconds ago. She wasn't breaking her vow never to let anyone see her cry ever again. Because there was no way to distinguish her tears from the rain, and she could no longer bear the horrific burden without having an outlet.

"I'm so sorry," she whispered. "I didn't know. It's no excuse. *I should have known*. I should have been smarter. If I had, none of you would be dead. But I swear to you on my life, that I won't fail you like the justice system failed you . . . and me."

She knew well how the rest would play out now that she'd made her move. Speculation would run rampant—was already rippling through the town. She'd continue to face the same scorn and ridicule she'd already been subjected to and be treated like a leper.

None of that mattered. The only thing that mattered was that *Thomas* got wind that she was here and as soon as he was a free man, not only would he know she'd come, he'd know how to find her. It wasn't as if she was going to make it hard.

Until then, she'd be treated with no better regard than Thomas himself, only the people here would be even more bitter toward her because *she* had never paid for her crimes. She'd gone free while so many other women had paid the price for her freedom.

It was nothing more than she deserved. She deserved far worse.

It mattered little what they thought of her. But soon . . . soon they would know that justice had finally been served when not only Thomas Harrington took his last breath and Eliza either died taking him out, or she spent the rest of her life in prison.

She'd only had a short time to prepare herself, and she *was* prepared. She'd trained and been trained by the best, and she didn't fear death if it meant Thomas could never hurt another woman. But she hadn't expected to feel so painfully empty, soulless and *already* dead on the inside.

And so lonely, she ached.

Knowing she was merely delaying the inevitable, she turned away from the steps of the courthouse, recalling another image of when she'd left the courtroom after the sentencing and had been swarmed by reporters, cameras and microphones. All of which she'd ignored, desperate to be away from a place that had caused her so much shame, anguish and heartrending guilt.

It, like so many other dreams, haunted her at night. Never the same one in a row. But each one eating away at her little by little, night by night, taking a piece of her soul until there was barely any left. When the nightmares became too much to bear, she simply didn't sleep and instead, remained awake, drinking coffee on autopilot as she went back over her mission, absorbing every detail, no matter how minor, and planning for every conceivable scenario.

It was ingrained in her memory. There would be no forgetting it. She could recount it verbatim down to the most minute detail. But she studied her notes, and there were stacks, as a way of atonement. A reminder to all those women that they hadn't been forgotten. Not by her. Never by her.

She knew each of their names. Whether they were married,

single, had families, or like her, had no one at all to even notice she was gone and to grieve for the loss of her. She already had personally drafted letters to each of the victims' families or loved ones ready to be mailed. Anyone she could find that a once vibrant, beautiful woman belonged to. And she would explain that justice was finally being served and apologize for her part in Thomas's madness. At least the victims' families would have confirmation instead of bitter resentment that he was alive and free while their loved one was dead.

Those letters would be mailed right before she took Thomas down in case she wasn't alive to do it after. Then and only then would she carry out her crusade, and she would *not* fail, no matter the cost, no matter if she went down with him. In the deepest, darkest recesses of what remained of her soul, she *wanted* final rest and freedom from the oppressive burden she'd carried for so many years.

Dragging her jacket more firmly around her to shield her from the now much colder drizzle, she walked slowly back by the diner, her work done for today. Now, she waited. And anticipated the feeling of redemption when Thomas Harrington ceased to exist.

At the end of the street was a mail drop. A sharp stab of pain slashed through her chest at the reminder of the letter she'd mailed to Gracie. She'd mailed it from Kansas, taking an indirect route to Oregon so no one could track her, her purpose to send anyone coming after her in the opposite direction. And they would come. But while they were chasing dead ends in the Midwest, she would be in Oregon doing what she should have done long ago.

It wasn't the smart thing to do, but she couldn't drop off the face of the earth having Gracie thinking Eliza was angry with her. She owed her this much for saving her life. And she hadn't lied to Sterling about the surprise involving Gracie's school for impoverished children. She'd gifted her entire savings to Gracie's cause because Eliza would have no use for it since she'd either be dead or in jail.

Her letter had been a goodbye and not a very subtle one. She'd asked Gracie to tell Tori, Ari and Ramie she loved them and considered them her dearest and only girlfriends and she'd made only one request in regard to her male coworkers. She'd asked Gracie to tell them she was sorry for letting them down, for failing them. But for Dane, she'd included a smaller sealed envelope and simply asked for Gracie to personally deliver it to her partner and the best friend she'd ever had.

She closed her eyes and hunched down, shielding her face from the rain as she began the half mile walk to the house she'd rented. A hotel wasn't an option and the town only sported an aging bed and breakfast and a motel that she wasn't surprised to see was still likely being used for the nightly hookups and drug binges, where dealers and buyers met and, for a price, the management looked the other way. And since it was owned by the chief of police's brother-in-law, there wasn't much to worry about as far as it being raided.

Once, after a late shift at the diner, she'd left at two in the morning to walk to the home of the elderly woman she sat for during the day and had been blocked by two potheads, high as a kite and looking to score with an easy target. They'd already reserved a room at the seedy motel and had been waiting in the shadows for her to cross their path.

Thomas, who'd been courting Eliza for several weeks, had materialized out of nowhere and quickly put the fear of God in the two drug addicts, threatening to tear them apart if they so much as looked at Eliza again.

Thomas had a mild manner about him. He didn't appear to be a badass capable of taking down one, much less two, drug users strung out on God only knew what, but there was something in the way he carried himself, the absolute confidence and determination that made others steer clear of him. The men that is.

Women were utterly charmed by him, and Eliza had been no exception. She'd found it wildly romantic and sweet that he would defend her so veraciously and then sweep her into his protection, vowing that no harm would ever come to her. And so he'd eaten supper at the diner most nights and sat in the corner until Eliza got off and then he'd walk her back to the house of the woman she sat for, with stern instructions to rest and be careful.

Oh how easy a target she'd been. Even without his psychic abilities, he would have manipulated her with ease. It wasn't difficult for a young girl who had nothing and came from nothing to be overwhelmed by a handsome older man who genuinely seemed to care about her and respect her. He embodied everything she'd never had, never hoped to have, but wanted with everything in her young romantic heart.

He'd been the consummate gentleman, never acting inappropriately, but then he had the benefit of knowing her thoughts, her cynicism and her doubts and so he knew exactly what not to do in order not to lose her faith in him. She'd never had a chance once he'd targeted her. Every action, movement, thought or gesture carefully orchestrated by plucking what she feared most and longed for most right out of her head.

If only she'd known then that when it seemed too good to be true, too perfect, then it very likely was. The woman she was now would never be so coerced or manipulated. She'd call bullshit before a man like Thomas even opened his mouth.

She despised smooth, polished men as a result and avoided them above all else. It was why it had taken her considerable time—and effort—to let her guard down with Dane and allow herself to trust someone—a man—again. Because for all his brusque mannerisms and abrupt speech and nature, Dane screamed wealth, power and polish. And an air of confidence that was tangible to anyone around him.

Just like . . . *Wade Sterling*. Goddamn it, she had to stop allowing him into her thoughts! Her lip curled just thinking of the cretin and his blatant blackmail and then the stunt he'd pulled at her apartment. Pretending he gave a damn. For one infinitesimal moment she'd actually been convinced that he *was* concerned about her and that he *was* furious at her for not taking better care of herself.

She snorted. Never again was she falling for that crap. Some lessons were simply learned only to be forgotten. Others were branded so deep that they were etched on your soul, never to be dismissed and damn sure never to be repeated.

She didn't doubt he was attracted to her or at least had a healthy dose of lust but maybe he got off on being turned down flat. Who the hell knew with a man like him. But sex and actual caring were not even in the same stratosphere.

Like Dane, Sterling exuded the same wealth, power and polish, only with a . . . rougher edge. She'd never been able to put her finger on it until right now, but she realized it wasn't practiced polish. He simply didn't give a fuck. He was just that confident, and so much arrogance made Eliza want to stab something. Preferably him. Dane was similar in attitude as far as not giving a fuck about what people thought about him, but he'd go to the wall for the few people he cared about. She had no idea what Sterling's agenda was nor did she care to find out.

Both men were dangerous and anyone would be a fool to ever think otherwise. Her brow furrowed because in all honesty, they were, in fact, very similar.

So why the hell did she trust Dane with her life, love him like a brother and have his back, no questions asked—ever—and yet the mere sight of Sterling immediately got her hackles up?

In the beginning, she'd found irritating him a great source of amusement but then he'd started turning it back around on her and she couldn't back off quickly enough. She'd questioned herself a thousand times. Had she unwittingly encouraged him? Did he think that hurling insults and taking him down a notch or two was her way of flirting? Did he think she was coming on to him? Worse, did he think she was interested because of his wealth and obvious connections?

The last thing she wanted was to become involved with a man. Especially a man like Wade. She'd been no match for Thomas and time and distance had given her a lot of perspective and it wasn't that Thomas was that skilled. She'd just been lonely and starved for human contact. She'd wanted love. Were it not for Thomas's psychic abilities, he would have been an epic failure at seducing her—or so she insisted, as a way to console herself. And if she was walking, drenched in the rain, admitting that she had been no match for Thomas, then what the hell did that say about her chances against Sterling?

He'd eat her alive and spit her out in pieces, with or without psychic abilities. He'd certainly called her out on a hell of a lot during his tantrum days earlier, so the man was intuitive and underestimating him would be the height of stupidity. But those weren't things she hadn't already known. She'd just made it a regular practice to never be in the same vicinity as him so she could exist in blissful ignorance. Wow, apparently some lessons *weren't* learned.

She shook her head, pissed that even now, thousands of miles away, Sterling was fucking with her head every bit as much as Thomas had. Obviously men weren't the problem. *She* was. She was a head case around them and clearly she must have a neon stamp on her forehead that flashed *gullible* in bold letters, because she always attracted the deviants and assholes, Sterling fitting the latter description. Or maybe the former too. How the hell would she know? It was already established her taste in men was deplorable.

As she neared the small, one-bedroom house where downtown faded to nothing but county roads, open fields and houses and trailers scattered haphazardly across the landscape, her stomach cramped and she automatically rubbed her hand over her chest in an effort to quell the panic and anxiety that screamed to be let loose and had become harder each day to keep restrained as she neared the beginning of the end.

She'd purposely turned off her cell phone for two reasons. One, she wasn't stupid, and just because the Devereauxs or Dane didn't announce that the cell phones provided by the company were equipped with sophisticated tracking devices, didn't mean they weren't, and if she used it, she may as well stand in the town square with a bullhorn and announce to the world she was here.

The second was that once Gracie received Eliza's letter—if she hadn't already—all bets were off and her phone would be blowing the hell up around the clock. Dane's request to stay in touch with only him bought her the necessary few days to make her escape before Gracie got the letter. In the meantime, she was supposed to be getting herself back together.

She almost laughed, an incongruous feeling when her heart literally felt like it was splintering apart because she'd *never* been together. She was who she was out of necessity and because of that promise she'd made all those years ago. She lived with that reminder every single day. Not a night went by that she didn't think about taking Thomas out for good, but she always stopped there, because what happened afterward was out of her control and all that mattered was that the world would be rid of one more monster.

She trudged up to the dilapidated cottage the owner had been only too happy to rent to Eliza by the week. At most, two weeks was all she needed because she was now only two days from Thomas's release, and he'd come for her.

As she unlocked her door to quietly slip inside, a sound snapped her from the oppressive weight of her thoughts and she reacted sluggishly, acknowledging helplessly that she was useless like this. She possessed none of the skills and instincts she'd spent years honing to perfection. How could she expect to face Thomas and ruthlessly kill him in cold blood when she was a walking zombie?

She reached for the knife tucked inside the sleeve of her jacket. It was the only weapon she could take into the small downtown area without drawing attention to herself and that wasn't on the agenda . . . yet.

Before she had it opened and assumed a defensive stance, familiar strong arms wrapped around her body, effectively rendering her immobile.

Sterling?

His strength was a thing of awe. She wasn't huge in stature, but she was strong for her size and she was quick—usually. But power coiled and simmered from his large frame, as did the seething heat of his fury.

And then the unthinkable registered, creeping through the sluggish mush of her mind. Sterling. Here. In Calvary. Not just in the town, but in the house she'd rented. *Seen* and *associated* with her.

A low moan of anguish tore from her throat because now, if she failed, one more person would be added to the list of those Thomas would kill for the unpardonable sin of being in Eliza's life, regardless of the capacity.

Her knees buckled and she plunged downward only to be hauled up and held firmly against the muscled wall of his chest. She pressed her hands over her face, feeling the hot tears already leaking from her eyes. No, no, no! She couldn't lose it now. She couldn't break. Not when she was so close to the end game. She had to keep it together!

"You have to go," she said, grief heavy in her voice. "*Hurry!* Get out before anyone knows you've been here and then he'll never know you have any connection to me."

She looked him straight in the eyes, lifting her chin, uncaring of her obvious vulnerability or the humiliation of tears flooding her eyes and this time she was fully aware of the name she used.

"God, *please*, Wade. I'm begging you. Save yourself and *get out!*"

NINE

WADE was so stunned that all he could do was haul Eliza's shaking body against his own, anchoring himself so they both didn't end up on the floor. Any and all thoughts of giving her a blistering outburst of just what he thought of her disappearance instantly fled, because she looked as though she was on the verge of completely shattering.

If she hadn't already. And judging by what he'd just witnessed, he'd say she was already beyond *shattered*. She was *broken*. Something painful and vicious twisted in his gut, tightening his chest as fury rolled over him like a tidal wave. Not at her but at whatever the fuck had done this to the strongest, most infuriating, solid, *selfless* woman he'd ever known.

Sudden guilt—another unfamiliar emotion—hit him hard as he remembered hurling accusations at Eliza. Selfish. Bitch. Ungrateful. Hurting Gracie by distancing herself. He should have known—he had known—that she wasn't capable of those things.

He should have known that her acting so out of character meant something was *very* wrong.

She was huddled in his arms curling into the smallest possible ball, as if she wanted to disappear all together, but what threatened to totally unhinge him was the fact that tears were streaking down her face as her body heaved with violent, silent sobs. She was shaking so hard that it took all his strength just to maintain his already rock hard hold on her.

He thought he'd been prepared this time. After the shock of their last meeting when he'd seen panic and vulnerability and lastly *fear* in her eyes, he hadn't thought it could get any worse. But Eliza curled into his arms, her fragility broadcasting in intense waves and tears running in never-ending streams, soaking his shirt, depriving him of all rational thought. Even his pulse stuttered, pain shooting through his chest as he witnessed the heartbreaking sight of this beautiful, strong woman in fragmented shards of utter despair.

Nostrils flaring, his head came up, his eyes narrowed in rage. He kicked the door shut and then swept Eliza into the only room in the house that didn't have a window. He needed to get her to a secure location immediately, but his first priority had to be . . .

Fuck! He'd never felt so helpless in his life. He couldn't deny that he'd savored the thought of, and had fantasized about how it would feel, when she was finally in his arms, her softness melded to his body, but never at this high a price. Not this way.

Broken. Fucking broken and in so many pieces that he feared he couldn't put her back together.

Eyes so dull and a look of hopelessness he'd never imagined seeing on Eliza's face.

He wanted her in his goddamn arms because she *wanted* to be there and because the fierce battle of wills between them erupted and desire they *both* felt was acted on. *Not* because there was nowhere else for her to go and because he happened to be present at the precise moment she fell apart.

In no way could he remain aloof and purposely antagonize her and act the part he'd played for the last months. He sank down on the small sofa that lined an inside wall and tenderly enfolded her once more into his embrace, but even taking care to be gentle, his grip was fierce and unyielding, giving her no choice of escaping.

"Shhh, Eliza," he whispered, his lips pressed to her hair. "It's okay. You're safe now. I've got you. I won't let anything hurt you. If you believe nothing else, know that I'll never let anyone hurt you."

She clenched his shirt, balling it along with her fingers into a fist and buried her face in his neck, the heated moisture of her tears wet against his skin. It was as though months, years, a *lifetime* of fear, stress, pressure had broken free after being so tightly restrained. She shuddered, her entire body violently shaking with the force of her sobs, and yet the silence was so eerie that it unnerved him. Her tears were wet against his neck where her face was still firmly planted, her hold on him as fierce as his was on her.

It was obvious she'd disciplined herself to hold it back, to never allow anyone to see beyond her meticulously constructed barriers, that even in grief, the strength of her self-imposed will refused to allow her to make a sound. Worse was the thought of her never having anyone to lean on, because he couldn't imagine her ever exposing so much of herself even to her teammates.

People she *trusted*. And obviously not even Dane, because Dane was merely "worried" and had no fucking clue just how serious the situation was.

He trailed his lips over the top of her hair until they touched her clammy forehead and he nuzzled to her temple, murmuring soothing sounds because he was helpless as to what else to do other than let her know she wasn't alone. And her tears. God, her tears cut into him like a knife and twisted his heart in a way he'd never experienced.

"Baby, you're breaking my heart," he whispered against her skin.

And she was. His heart felt as though it were about to burst out of his chest. He felt every single sob to the depths of his soul. Each time her shoulders heaved, it was like a fist to his gut.

He tensed when she lifted her head, fearing she'd try to bolt, but she slowly leaned back so her troubled gaze met his. He flinched at the raw grief reflected in her eyes. Jesus. What the hell had she been living with and for how *long*? Did this have anything to do with her abduction and torture? No, his gut told him this went much deeper, went much further back, which meant she'd carried her burden for God only knew how long. And that made the hole in his heart even larger.

She closed her eyes and a fresh trail of tears slipped down her cheeks that cut him to the bone. He maneuvered his body so that she was still in his arms but so he could frame her face, his palms brushing over wet skin.

"Eliza, talk to me. It's obvious you won't talk to the people you love and trust, so talk to someone who *doesn't* matter. Talk to *me*. But for God's sake you have to let go of whatever poison is festering inside you or it's going to consume you for good."

"It already has," she whispered.

He almost didn't hear her faint response and when it registered, his pulse stuttered. Sweat broke out on his forehead at the finality and defeat in her words. Eliza wasn't prone to dramatics or overreactions. She called it like she saw it and she wasn't a whiner or a complainer. Hell, he'd never met a woman in his life who was as determined as she was to demonstrate no weakness whatsoever, which is why this outburst was scaring the shit out of him, because she'd die before ever allowing that whispered admission to pass her lips.

And the resignation in her voice when she'd finally spoken?

A chill snaked down his spine, an odd contrast to the sweat on his brow. Because Eliza's subdued, dull tone was the sound of someone who'd *already* given up. Had accepted the inevitable—whatever that was for her. And he'd already figured out that she'd run like hell from Houston, not because she didn't trust her partners, but because she was protecting the people she loved, which meant whatever the hell was going on was serious trouble. The kind of trouble she was willing to sacrifice herself for to protect the people who mattered to her.

DSS had dismantled the entire organization that had done so much damage to so many lives, particularly to the women who belonged to DSS. *And* Wade, damn it. The game was over. He was staking his claim—had already staked it. Eliza was *his* and he'd take on the devil himself before ever allowing her to be hurt again. So if the bastards who'd tortured and then nearly killed her in the raid had been taken down and no longer posed a threat, then who the fuck was threatening her now? And if those twisted, sadistic motherfuckers hadn't scared her and made her back down then whatever was going on *now* wasn't good. It was the absolute worst kind of bad. Because this went way back if his instincts were right, and his gut never led him wrong. Eliza was fearless. Too fearless for her own damn good, and nothing scared or intimidated her. Until now.

If those fuckheads hadn't managed to intimidate Eliza and she'd gone after them like a ferocious guard dog after being tortured and fucking *waterboarded*, then what the *hell* could be worse that terrified her to this degree?

Eliza sagged and she was still trembling. Lines of fatigue etched her face, causing him to wonder if she'd even slept since the last time he'd seen her. For that matter it was likely she hadn't slept *before* the last time he'd seen her. She felt fragile in his arms and she was *not* a fragile woman. He doubted she'd even eaten because he could feel the weight she'd lost. Her fatigue beat at him. It was evident in her eyes, her face, her body.

This worried him and he was not a worrier. He didn't fear anything and had long ago accepted that what will be will be, but the cold hand of terror gripped him by the throat and he realized he wasn't just afraid. He was fucking terrified. He couldn't fight what he couldn't see, touch or know and, by God, he was going to find out what the fuck had Eliza scared out of her mind before the day was over.

"We're getting the hell out of here," Wade said firmly. "And after we get the fuck out of this shithole where I can be assured you're safe, you're going to tell me what the hell is going on, and I mean everything, Eliza. And during this conversation, you're going to eat even if I have to hold you down and force it down your throat. Then you're going to get some rest because it's obvious you haven't slept in weeks."

Her chin went up but the gesture lacked its usual tenacity.

"*You're* leaving, Wade," she said dully. "Not me. I *won't* be responsible for another death. Never again. I have so much blood on my hands that they'll never come clean and I'll be damned if I'll add yours. You have to leave and forget I even exist. You don't know me. You've never met me. You forget *everything* about me."

His temper flared and he was furious that she was so damned determined to protect him. What the hell? There were so many what-the-fuck parts of her impassioned statement, he didn't even know where to start. Blood on her hands? Only because he feared pushing her completely over the edge did he bite his tongue and not tear into her right then and there and demand answers to the dozens of questions festering in his mind. Reasoning wasn't going to work with her. That was obvious even *before* her falling apart moments ago. He'd seen her lack of rationale when she'd sped away from her apartment, leaving him sprawled on her concrete drive.

He didn't have time to take it slow and treat her with the soft touch he wanted so badly, and after hearing the fucked-up shit she'd just spouted, he had a lot of fucking questions he wanted answers to, but his first and only priority at the moment was ensuring her safety. So he did what it was he did best. He took matters into his own hands.

Before she could say or do anything further, he tightened his arms around her and abruptly stood and strode toward the front door.

"What the hell!" she yelled, slamming her fist into his chest.

Thank *God*. This was the Eliza he recognized. She wasn't too far gone. Yet. And he had to bear that in mind and handle her with care even while giving her no choice in anything.

"Shut up," he clipped out. "You're going with me and if I have to handcuff your wrist to mine, swear to God, I'll do it."

Her gaze turned pleading and that *really* pissed him off because she didn't ever ask for anything. And she damn sure didn't beg and everything about her expression, her eyes, was begging and he was so goddamn furious he wanted to put his fist through a wall.

"Wade, please," she said, her tone turning urgent. Desperation fired in her eyes. And panic. He could literally see the wheels turning in her mind as she scrambled to figure her way out of the situation.

Four times. Four times now she'd used his name and he liked it a hell of a lot but not under the circumstances she'd used it. He wanted her to call him Wade because they were on more intimate terms, not because she was desperate, scared and falling apart. Let her try to figure a way out of him inserting himself into her situation. She was stubborn but he was more so. She could rack her brains all she wanted.

Too bad. He could still be gentle. A gentle *asshole* and get to the bottom of this mess. She could hate him all she wanted just as long as she was alive to do it.

"You have no idea what you're getting into," she said in a terrified voice that only served to add fuel to an already raging inferno within him. "He'll kill you, Wade. You should have *never* come here! If you had just stayed in Houston, he would never have known you had any association with me. I can't let any more people die because of me. I *can't*."

Her despair gutted him and he had to steady himself, be the jerk and run over her when she was at rock bottom when all he really wanted was just to hold her and comfort her. Treat her with the delicate touch she deserved, a touch he craved to render. But not at the expense of her life and no fucking *way* would she sacrifice herself for him. Did she honest to God think for one fucking minute that he'd hide behind her and let her take the fall for him? She didn't know him very well if that was the case, but he was going to remedy that in short order.

He clenched his teeth and lowered her feet to the ground beside the vehicle he'd parked in the back so she wouldn't see it right away. Without saying a word, he shackled one of her wrists with a firm grip while he opened the passenger door with his other hand.

When she began to struggle, he hauled her up against his tall frame, his arms a steel band around her slim waist.

"Don't fight me, Eliza," he said tersely. "You won't win, and I'm not backing down. Someone has to protect you because *you* sure as hell aren't. And if you think I'm going to allow you to be a sacrificial lamb led meekly to slaughter in order to protect everyone else, get over it quick because it ain't going to happen. Now, what *is* going to happen, is that I'm taking you some place safe and you're going to eat and then you and I are going to have a long talk after which you're going to get some fucking sleep. I'll sedate your ass if I have to, so don't push me because I'm hanging on to my temper by a *very* thin thread."

She opened her mouth and he promptly clamped his hand over it and proceeded to shove her into the vehicle. Using his arm across her body to hold her in place, he reached with his other hand into the glove compartment and pulled out a pair of handcuffs.

Her mouth fell open and her eyes widened in dismay.

"Surely you didn't think I was bluffing, Eliza. Come on. You should know me better than that. When have I ever made hollow threats?"

He secured one cuff to her left wrist and then attached it to the center console. Then he withdrew, leaving her looking shell-shocked and so damn defeated that it took everything he had not to lose his shit right then and there. He stalked around to the driver's side sucking in deep breaths, trying to pull himself together as he slid into the driver's seat.

He wasted no time putting as much distance between the place she'd been staying and where he was taking her. To his surprise, she said nothing. She was completely still, her gaze rigidly fixed forward, her jaw clenched tight.

A sigh of relief nearly escaped him. At least she was no longer crying. He could deal with surly, pissed off Eliza. He had no idea what to do with fragile as an eggshell Eliza. A tearful, vulnerable, scared out of her mind Eliza. He was furious, not at her, or at least mostly not at her, but with what or who had put such fear in her eyes, who had broken one of the strongest women he'd ever known.

Taking advantage of her momentary silence, and to try to calm his murderous thoughts, he picked up his cell and punched the contact already brought up and waiting.

"This is Sterling," he bit out. "We're coming in hot and I have no fucking idea what we're dealing with yet, so make damn sure the safe house is secure and I want extra security on around-the-clock surveillance. No one and I mean no one gets within a mile without us knowing, and any threat is to be dealt with immediately."

"You got it," Derek said shortly and then the line went dead.

Wade's men, like himself, were short on words and big on results.

Out of the corner of his eye he saw her staring at him, a mixture of bewilderment and a complete what-the-fuck look on her face. He nearly smiled. *That* had gotten her attention.

"Who the hell are *you?*" Eliza whispered.

"The man who's going to keep your ass alive and make damn sure no one so much as touches a hair on your head. Except me."

She yanked her cuffed wrist angrily, her cheeks puffing outward as she blew out her rage. Good. He needed her pissed off. Alive. Fighting. Anything but the defeated, resigned to her fate woman who'd fallen apart on him.

Then she banged the back of her head against the headrest and closed her eyes, letting out another long sigh.

"God, why do you even *care?*" she hissed. "Why are you here? You've made it very clear that I rate lower than scum in your estimation, so why the sudden concern?"

"It's a habit I seem to have gotten into," he said mildly. "Saving your ass. At the rate you're going, it's going to be a full-time job."

She whipped her head around and glared at him. "Get it through your head, Sterling. I am none of your business. What I do or don't do isn't any of your business. You have no right to hold me against my will."

He shrugged. So it was back to Sterling. Good, in the manner that for the moment she'd regained the fire he was so well acquainted with. Bad, because he liked the sound of his first name on her lips. He liked it a lot. He'd like it even better when they were in bed and he was deep inside her.

"I don't really give a fuck what you think, Eliza. Get *that* through *your* head. You're not getting rid of me, so get over it. Maybe we should call Dane and get his opinion. What do you think? I'm sure he'd be interested in your choice of vacation destination."

The color leeched from her face and for a moment he thought she was going to pass out. *Fuck.* Yeah, this was as bad as it got. He'd been ninety-nine percent sure that Dane had no fucking clue what was going on with Eliza, and with that reaction, the one percent still out for jury made it unanimous.

"You can't," she whispered. "Wade, *please.* You don't understand. He will kill every single one of them. Are you hearing what I'm saying? Because I'm *not* making this shit up. I'm not exaggerating nor am I overreacting. Anyone and I mean *anyone* I care about, anyone who has had *any* part of my life in the last ten years will *die.* I am the *only* one who can stop that from happening. You have no *idea* what he's capable of. If you call Dane, then they'll *all* rush up here and go straight to their graves. But it won't end there. He'll go after Ramie, Ari *and* Gracie. And I'll die before I let that happen. Do *you* want Gracie to die because you're being an interfering asshole?"

Wade laughed. He couldn't help it. "Have you lost your mind? Do you honestly think this asshole, whoever he is, has a chance against *Ari?* She'd kick his candy ass to hell and back. That's provided he ever got past me and the rest of DSS."

Why the fuck was Eliza so goddamn afraid of one man? She kept saying "he." Over and over. Like he was God, an unstoppable force. Invincible. Untouchable. And why did Dane or any of the others not *know* anything about someone who was a threat to everyone Eliza cared about? He was seriously starting to consider that Eliza had been more emotionally traumatized by her ordeal than anyone—even Wade—realized, because this—she—the whole damn *story* just sounded ... *crazy*. And Eliza was anything but crazy. She was smart, could take care of herself and her teammates and she had confidence in spades.

Or at least she did.

But now, the Eliza he thought he knew, was *nothing* like the woman staring at him with grief, sorrow and fucking *fear* in her eyes that gutted him every time he witnessed it. And he realized he didn't know her at all. It was also apparent that none of the people she worked with, trusted, risked her life to protect and had their back no matter the risk to herself, didn't know fuck all about her either. They only saw what she wanted them to see.

She had secrets, deep secrets she'd never shared with anyone, and worse she had demons she also had never shared with another living soul. And if it was the last thing he did, he was going to ferret out every single one of those secrets *and* demons and then he was going to do whatever it took to remove the fear and the shadows so evident in her eyes and he'd personally take care of the demons that haunted her and he didn't give a damn whether she liked it or not.

TEN

GRACIE pulled into the parking garage of the downtown building that housed the offices of DSS and recklessly slammed on her brakes, opening her door before she'd even got her car into park. Clutching the envelope in clammy hands, she bolted out and headed for the stairwell at a dead run, leaving her keys, purse, everything behind in her car.

She knew everyone was in the office this afternoon to discuss a new case they were taking on, which was good since she wouldn't have to wait for everyone to filter in but bad for the new case because Eliza took priority. Nothing was more important than saving her.

Anxiety took firm hold on her as she entered the elevator, making her fingers fumble and hit the button for the wrong floor, which thankfully was above the DSS offices so she quickly hit the right one and sucked in a deep breath, battling the sting of tears as the elevator began its ascent.

When she burst into the reception area, Zack was waiting,

a grim, intense expression on his face. Not surprising since he would have tagged her arrival on the security cams and seen she was in distress.

"What's wrong?" he demanded, pulling her into his arms, his entire body rigid, his hands and eyes roving over her body as if searching for a sign of injury.

"Where are the others?" she asked, ignoring his question.

His look became puzzled. "In the conference room."

"Let's go," she said firmly, pushing her way past him.

"Gracie."

She ignored him, struggling to keep it together.

"In the conference room!" she shrieked, her entire body shaking uncontrollably.

His earlier look of worry and confusion turned to a look that would scare even the baddest-ass person alive. He gave her a clipped nod but tucked her hand gently into his and followed her toward the conference room.

When they entered, everyone was there and standing, alert, concerned and wary. Angry. Not at her but at whatever had caused her upset. Four of the men she didn't even recognize, though she vaguely recalled Zack mentioning new hires.

Her gaze found Dane's and his expression gentled though his eyes were full of worry.

"It's Eliza," she blurted. Thrusting the letter in his direction, she said, "She's on a suicide mission!"

And then she burst into tears, no longer able to maintain any semblance of her composure.

Even so, she didn't miss the initial shock reflected on an entire room full of men's faces rapidly dissipate to cold fury nor the fact that a tangible sensation of a dozen pissed off, worried, ultimate alpha warriors sizzled and crackled as if an actual flame had been lit.

And oddly, Dane paled, guilt flickering in his eyes and he looked as though someone had just punched him in the stomach. He looked absolutely sick. As sick as Gracie was when she wondered if she was too late and Eliza had already been taken from the people who considered her family.

Dane took the wrinkled envelope from Gracie's shaking hand, dread filling his entire soul. Flashes of the way Eliza had been acting prior to her asking for downtime—a vacation he *knew* was bullshit—repeated over and over in his mind. Their last conversation echoing in his ears and him knowing—fucking *knowing*—that Eliza wasn't telling him everything and the helplessness that had gripped him, remembering the sensation of her slipping through his fingers, knowing she was pulling away—had been pulling away for days leading up to her official sit-down with him in his office.

His gut never steered him wrong and he'd known something was wrong but had also known his hands were tied because he couldn't overtly act on that knowledge or he'd lose her. They'd all lose her. Calling Wade Sterling so at least someone would be looking out for her. All of that subterfuge because he'd feared losing her and if Gracie's reaction, her bald statement, was true then he'd lost her anyway.

Goddamn it! He'd made an emotional decision and he never made emotional decisions. But with Lizzie, he had and he'd fucked up. He stared frozen at the envelope, terrified to open it but time was of the essence and he had to know what they were up against. Had to know if it was too late to rectify the biggest mistake of his life.

He fumbled with the paper, his hands shaking so badly it took several tries before he managed to get the letter out of the envelope and unfold it so he could read it. Everyone was tense, alert and expectant. Impatient. All staring at him and waiting, all fearing the worst.

He quickly scanned over Eliza's handwriting, usually neat, elegant and feminine. What he saw now was barely legible, hastily scrawled words that he had to read multiple times to make sense of and, worse, in several places, the ink was smeared and what looked to be a tiny stain to the paper indicating that she'd been crying when she wrote it.

But when he forced himself to look beyond the evidence of her upset and sorted through the first several rambling paragraphs, *what* she wrote set in and his blood fucking froze. And then it unfroze because he felt it leave his body, draining as if he'd suffered a massive injury that sucked away his life's blood.

His knees locked then unlocked and his legs shook. So badly that he sank into the chair he'd vacated when Gracie had burst into the conference room with a panicked, scared out of her mind expression that never looked good on any woman.

He vaguely noted his men's reactions, a mixture of shock because Dane never lost his cool and was always steady under pressure. A rock. Unbreakable. And the other part of that mixture on the others' faces was the gut-wrenching fear and worry that was rocking him to the very core, paralyzing all rational thought.

And then the room erupted into a chorus of what the fuck's and yells and demands to know what the hell was going on. Worse, the one question he couldn't answer. *Is Eliza okay?*

"Jesus," Dane whispered. The only word he could manage.

Then he held up his hand for quiet and the room went silent, all eyes to him, expectant, angry, worried and pissed. Eliza was his, yes. But she was also theirs. She was his partner. Closer to him than anyone else at DSS. The only person he'd allowed that close. He'd hired her. Trained her personally, though her skills were already impressive. He'd just honed them and made them better.

But she also belonged to every other man assembled. Even Dex, Zeke, Shadow and Knight, though they'd only had the opportunity to meet her once before she'd taken leave. Judging by their expressions, she'd made an impression and they weren't any happier about being in the dark than the rest.

Caleb and Beau bristled with fury, edging toward Dane, jaws clenched, eyes stormy.

"What the fuck is going on with Eliza?" Beau demanded, cutting off whatever his brother had been about to say because Caleb's mouth opened and then promptly shut when Beau made his outburst.

"Eliza's supposed to be on vacation," Caleb said, opening his mouth again. "Or did you fill us in wrong?"

The insinuation that Dane had lied to them about Eliza's leave of absence pissed him off and any other time he'd be letting Caleb know exactly what he thought of that insinuation, but each second wasted on bullshit was a second they weren't getting to Eliza.

"I told you what she told me," Dane said shortly, refusing to rehash the entire story. Especially now that it appeared none of it was true.

"It's a goodbye letter," Gracie said tearfully from where she stood wrapped solidly in Zack's arms. "Oh God, Dane. She's not coming back is she?"

Her words were a knife to his heart. He couldn't imagine work—life—without Lizzie.

Gracie plunged forward, not waiting for the answer she already knew. Emotion thick in her voice, an obvious knot forming in her throat, she said to no one specifically, "She sent a check with the letter. Everything. Her savings. Told me to use it for my school, that she wouldn't need it where she was going."

Though he'd read the words, multiple times, they still punched a hole in his soul and for a moment, he couldn't speak. Even if he wanted to. Had no idea what to say.

The others sucked in their breaths and unease lay heavy over the room at the ominous meaning of those words.

"And where is she going?" Zack asked gently, concern heavy in his features and in his tone. He too was maintaining a tenuous grasp on his composure but for his wife's sake, he was handling her with care.

"I don't *know*," Gracie said desperately. "The postmark is Kansas. She talked of sins, and of blood. So much blood on her hands that they'd never be clean. That she had no hope of redemption but she vowed vengeance and she also swore that she'd never lead *him* to us, meaning she was leaving Houston and would never return. Said he could never know of us, that if he did, we'd all die and that *she* would die before ever allowing that to happen. She said she was as guilty as he was, had committed unpardonable sins and that the justice system had failed the victims, had failed her and she said she wouldn't—couldn't—allow him to go free. She . . ."

Gracie's voice wavered and a fresh torrent of tears streaked down her wan face. She closed her eyes, her next words uttered so painfully that they were felt by every single person in the room.

"She asked me to tell all of you that she loved you. That we were the only family she'd ever had. That we were the only people who'd ever loved *her* and that she was going to make sure he never hurt any of us or any other living soul."

She briefly covered her face as a sob escaped and then she looked up at Dane, her eyes red and swollen and so filled with grief that it was as if Eliza was already dead. Like Gracie suspected she was—or soon would be.

"Who is *he*, Dane?" she whispered.

"We have to find her. Now," Beau said flatly.

Isaac and Capshaw firmly nodded their agreement. The others were quick to add their vehement vow to do whatever it took to bring Eliza home. Alive.

"I have a man on her," Dane said, and prayed he wasn't lying. Prayed his instincts about Wade Sterling hadn't steered him wrong and that the very thin line between black and white that Sterling skated allowed him liberties those who stuck to the book didn't take. And that even now he was shadowing her every moment. God, let Sterling be on her.

"What?"

He couldn't tell who said it because it came from all directions. There were looks of confusion, accusation and relief.

"I knew it was all wrong," Dane muttered to himself. "Goddamn it, I *knew* it wasn't good. I just never thought it was *this* bad. Had to protect her but couldn't let her know that because I'd lose her trust. We'd lose her and, *fuck*, that's exactly what may happen anyway!"

"But we're all here," Zack asked with obvious bewilderment. "What man did you put on her if we're all standing here?"

Next to Dane, Zack was closest to Eliza and it was clear he

was not only confused but angry that he wouldn't have been apprised of anything going down with Eliza, any cause for worry and certainly Dane putting a man on her. If not Zack himself.

"Why the fuck didn't you assign me to shadow her?" Isaac demanded in a pissed-off tone. "I don't have a wife or other obligation. Eliza is important to us all and you put someone outside of DSS on her? What were you thinking?"

Isaac tended to be quiet, but he was downright surly when it came to the protection of the women who belonged to DSS, Eliza included. He had a protective streak a mile wide and at the moment, his face was mottled with fury—and worry. The big man was private and didn't divulge much of himself but he was absolute in his loyalty to the people he'd pledged his allegiance to.

"Wade Sterling," Dane said grimly.

"What the *fuck*?" Isaac and Beau both bellowed.

The room exploded again, anger vibrating the walls. Except Gracie looked relieved and for the first time a glimmer of hope flickered in her eyes.

"I gotta make a call. *Now*," Dane bit out, reaching for his cell as he spoke.

And he silently prayed the entire time as he brought up Sterling's contact and then put the phone to his ear.

He should have done what his gut had told him to do and sit on her and never let her out of his or DSS's sight. He never should have been so goddamn afraid of losing Eliza's trust, loyalty and friendship—her love—by backing off and calling in Sterling. Because even if she was pissed, quit and never spoke to him again, at least she'd be alive to hate him.

ELEVEN

WADE was never so relieved to see Eliza's mutinous, belligerent glare as she stared at him from across the small breakfast table in a safe house two hours from Calvary. Her wrist was cuffed to one leg of the table, which meant she was scooted toward the edge instead of being seated in the middle and since he was, they were at a slight angle to one another.

"Eat," he ordered in a tone he knew would piss her off.

If he kept her pissed off, then maybe the chances of her losing it again and crying were less and it would keep her focused on him instead of whatever private hell she was dealing with. Furthermore, if she fell apart and started crying again, he couldn't be assured he wouldn't completely lose it himself. And now, more than ever, he had to keep it together because he was not losing the fierce yet infinitely fragile woman currently giving him the death stare.

"You're delaying the inevitable, Eliza," he said with exasperation he didn't even attempt to hide. "If you want to sit here and have a stare down all goddamn night, I have all the time in the world but you're going to eat and we are going to talk and then you're going to get some fucking sleep."

She glanced down at the mound of food on the plate he'd put in front of her and he could see the hunger beating at her. Damn stubborn woman. Still, it was better than the alternative. Her in his arms sobbing with heart-wrenching despair he'd never before witnessed in anyone, much less her.

"You have thirty seconds to dig in before I take over and feed you myself. Your choice."

Fury blazed in her eyes but not the good kind of fury that told him she was on her game. It was helpless, hopeless fury and he hated doing this to her. She despised losing her formerly impenetrable control. He hated being forced to take it from her. Hated having to take her choices from her because the result was a subdued, beaten down Eliza and not the fiery, kickass, fearless woman who could hold her own in any situation.

She likely thought he got off on it. Enjoyed it. Was probably humiliated beyond measure that he had the upper hand and she was vulnerable. She couldn't be more wrong. He felt like the worst sort of bastard by mowing over her as he'd done. He liked her spirit, her fire, her confidence and her strength. He liked it a hell of a lot.

She sent him a final, blistering scowl and then picked up her fork with her free hand and began to eat. A dull flush worked its way up her neck as she stared down at the meat he'd cut into bite-size portions so she could eat one-handed. Then she lifted her chin and he didn't like what he saw in her eyes at all.

"Are you enjoying this?" she asked quietly. "The opportunity to take me down a notch. Show me who's boss."

His response was automatic and explosive. "Fuck no!"

He swore again and gripped his nape with his hand and rubbed wearily. She wasn't the only one who needed rest. He hadn't slept since the night she dumped him on his ass in her driveway before roaring off like a bat out of hell.

"You think I enjoy seeing you cry, Eliza? You think I enjoy imagining you hurt, tortured or dead? You think I've enjoyed being worried out of my fucking mind because I couldn't find you and was worried I'd get here too late? You think I like seeing you fall apart when you're the strongest fucking woman I've ever known?"

Faint shock registered in her eyes. Her hand froze, midway from the plate to her mouth, the bite slipping off and hitting the table.

"Eat," he growled. "We have a lot to talk about but we aren't doing it until you clean that entire plate."

Surprisingly she complied, suddenly concentrating on the food and once she started eating, his suspicions were confirmed that it had been way too fucking long since she'd had a decent meal. She ate quickly and hungrily but what bothered him was that not once did she meet his gaze again.

She was nearly finished with the plate that was prepared with enough food for three meals when she slowly put her fork down and then just as slowly lifted her eyes to his for the first time since his outburst.

"I want to know something," she said in a voice that lacked anger, scorn or fear. Her gaze was inquisitive as she studied him. Like she was trying to get a read on him or figure out some big mystery.

Despite his decree that they wouldn't be talking yet he returned her look. "What?"

"If you're so concerned about my well-being then why the hell would you haul me here, without my stuff, leaving me defenseless and without the means to protect you or myself?"

His lips thinned and his eyes narrowed. He reined his temper in, the anger and frustration that had sparked the moment she started talking about protecting him again.

"First, your stuff is here," he said, taking in the sudden arch of her eyebrows and the wrinkling of her forehead as her expression became perplexed. "Second and listen up, Eliza, because you need to get this and you need to get it now. You aren't protecting me. You aren't putting yourself in front of me. You aren't taking any hits for me. I'm the one protecting you. I'm the one who's going to keep you safe."

For a moment he could swear he saw the tiniest flicker of relief and an almost imperceptible sag of her shoulders as if for that one second she pondered the veracity of his words and considered the thought of having his protection—and *liking* it. But it was gone too quickly for him to be sure and he was also aware that it could have been a major case of wishful thinking on his part. He hadn't indulged in wishful thinking since he was four fucking years old and had wished for what every other normal kid had. Things like food on a regular basis and not week-old stale potato chips found in a trash can. Clothing with no stipulations. Not clothing that fit or seasonal clothing. Any clothing would have been welcome instead of having to resort to stealing clothing that even Goodwill stores or charity centers deemed unfit to hand out and ended up in their trash. And mostly parents who gave a fuck or no parents at all, and since he'd had no hope of his ever giving a fuck, he'd wished for the latter.

A brief flicker of amusement, unbidden and not pertinent to any of the shit he was dealing with right now, popped into his head. It was likely the remembrance of wishing for two things most others took for granted, food and clothing, that sparked his current thought.

Eliza thought he was an arrogant asshole and well, she wasn't wrong, but he wasn't the heartless bastard she likely thought. With her overactive imagination, she likely pictured him eating children or drinking their blood. He wondered what she'd think if she knew he had a number of pet charities, the majority of which provided for children with shit parents and shit lives the things he himself had been deprived of.

He brought himself back to the matter at hand and the fact that Eliza was still looking at him with fatigue-clouded confused eyes.

"Let me get this straight," she said in a softer voice than she'd ever used with him in an actual conversation that didn't include her vulnerable, falling apart or crying. "You hauled me out of the place I was staying in handcuffs. But you brought my weapons—"

"Your arsenal you mean," he cut in dryly.

She held up her free hand, still staring at him with the same questing look.

"You brought my weapons. But you have no intention of letting me use them, thus leaving me—and you—defenseless. You state I'm the strongest woman you've ever known, yet in the next breath tell me I am never protecting you, I'll never be in front of you, will never take anything for you and that you'll be the one protecting me and all this while I'm once again handcuffed, unarmed, we're the only two people in whatever place this is and you aren't armed. Now given those facts, why on earth would I believe a single word you're saying when nothing I've seen lends any credibility to your statements?"

She visibly braced. He saw her stiffen in preparation because she thought she'd pissed him off. But then she'd had enough practice at it so he supposed he couldn't fault her errant assumption this time.

He'd done more talking in the last hour than he sometimes spoke for days and it was obvious nothing he was saying was getting through. He picked up his phone, punched a button and then said, "Leave two on point. The rest come to me and make sure you have everything you're packing."

Her look of confusion deepened and she wrinkled her nose as she stared even harder at him. She'd looked at him before but never like this. Like she was actually trying to figure him out. She thought she knew him or rather everything there was to know about him and in her mind he'd abruptly changed the rules.

Wade stood, opening the jacket he wore that had Kevlar inserts between the outer layer and the lining. It wasn't the full protection a vest offered—it was thinner—but it would stop most bullets from mid- to long-range distance and it wasn't obvious he was protected.

As he opened it wider, the two pistols holstered on either side of his ribs where the jacket provided the most disguise came into view. He turned, lifting the jacket to expose a third gun in the band of his pants that had a built-in sleeve to fit the pistol. On each hip, two blades rested in tandem, one larger with a wicked serrated edge designed to inflict maximum damage and the other a smaller, lightweight knife that could be thrown with pinpoint accuracy and slice straight through a man's chest—or any other vital area—or could be used in close combat because its size and sleek design made it easy to be invisible in the right situation.

He hiked his leg up on his abandoned chair and pulled up his pant leg to reveal two more handguns lining the inside of his leg between his ankle and his knee and then he repeated the process to show her matching guns on his other leg.

His pants were loose fitting and designed to look as if they had no pockets. Instead they had flaps that opened from knee to hip and he did so to reveal a variety of explosives that would have to impress even Eliza since his was shit no one outside of the military and no one inside without top secret clearance even knew about much less could get their hands on.

When he was finished with his demonstration, the front door opened and he turned, motioning to the men filing in and he noticed Eliza's eyes widen as she took them in. Yeah, she was impressed. She was also realizing she was in no way dealing with the man she thought she was dealing with.

His arsenal bested hers because he'd ensured it had before tracking her ass down halfway across the country. He knew he'd have to be convincing and, even then, it wasn't as if Eliza was going to say okay you win. Yours is bigger and better than mine so I give up and you can protect me.

He almost snorted at the thought. It was amusing even if unrealistic. But proving he did know somewhat of how her mind worked her reaction didn't surprise him.

Her eyes narrowed as her gaze filtered back to Wade and she

scowled. "What next? Are you all going to whip out your dicks to see whose is bigger?"

He sent her a lazy grin, refusing to rise to her lame attempt at baiting him. "You'll know my dick size soon enough."

"God you're an asshole," she hissed out between clenched teeth.

And she almost looked like his Eliza. So much so that he felt an unexpected jolt of relief and something else altogether.

Something warm. Something that felt good when he had felt nothing but fucked-up shit for the last week. It made what he had to do next suck. Because they'd already fucked away enough time since he'd tagged her at the shithole house she'd been staying in that was so dilapidated and indefensible that even her arsenal wasn't going to help if any heavy shit went down, and he already knew whatever the fuck Eliza was tangled up in, it was *heavy*.

And it was obvious that she sensed the change in his mood and intention, because she paled and all her anger fled, leaving only a stark hollowness that made his already shitty mood even worse.

He dismissed his men with a single motion and when they left to resume their posts, he turned back to the table to release Eliza. Her cuffed hand was curled so tightly around the leg of the table that the tips of her fingers were white. And when he gently unlocked the clasp and her hand fell away, he caught it, felt it tremble in his grasp and he tightened his hand around hers.

Before he even said anything, she closed her eyes and it made the shadows underneath them more pronounced, which in turn made her look even more vulnerable and he hated it all.

"Eliza—"

He was interrupted by his cell phone ringing and he glanced down, pulling it upward from his pocket just enough to see who the incoming call was from.

Fuck. And hell no. Dane was calling. After Wade had told him to step back and that this was his show. Dane had *made* it his show by making the call to Wade and the rules weren't changing now. He hit the button to decline the call, sending it to voicemail and then shoved it back in his pocket. Then his hold on Eliza's hand that had loosened slightly when he'd been distracted by the call tightened again and he fixed her with the full force of his gaze.

"Eliza, it's time we talked," he said in a tone that said he meant business.

This time he didn't flinch at the fear or the shadows that immediately leapt in her eyes. He was prepared for them. It didn't make it any easier to witness, though.

His phone went off again, this time indicating a text.

"You have got to be shitting me," he growled.

Keeping firm hold on her hand, noticing how small it felt in his much larger one, he reached for his phone again, knowing he couldn't afford to ignore any call or text. Or at least ascertain whether he needed to respond.

He yanked the phone up and when he read the text, his blood chilled.

"You have *got* to be shitting me," he repeated, his pulse accelerating.

Situation critical. Check in ASAP.

That was it. Nothing more, which meant it was detailed and it wasn't good.

With a sigh, he gave Eliza's hand a squeeze and guided it back into the cuff, once more securing her wrist to the table.

"I have to make a call, baby," he said softly, giving her a gentle look. "When I get back, we talk. Finish eating. I'll have one of my men come in. There's dessert too."

He caressed the cuffed hand, soothing and ensuring it wasn't causing her any discomfort.

"This won't take long. Then you get me *and* my undivided attention."

Her startled look told him she hadn't missed the inference in his statement. That she wasn't getting his attention. She was getting him. *And* his undivided attention, which meant two separate things entirely.

TWELVE

"I thought I made it clear that I call you. You do not call me," Wade said, his voice enough to lower the outside temperature by another twenty degrees and it was already cold as fuck and drizzling.

He'd stepped out of the house, not wanting to chance Eliza overhearing what was likely to be a very unpleasant conversation with her precious team leader. Or partner. Whatever the fuck they were to one another.

"Tell me you have Eliza," Dane said curtly. "Don't fuck with me, Wade. Tell me you have her."

Wade blinked at the chilling fear in the other man's voice. The first time he'd called he'd sounded merely worried. What the hell had happened to upgrade the status to the terror in Dane's tone? Dane sounded as though he was precariously close to losing his shit. Well, join the crowd and get in line because that made two of them.

"Goddamn it, Sterling, there are things you don't know,"

Dane snarled. "Now is not the time to have a fucking pissing match. Now tell me if Eliza is with you."

"Yes. Currently she's handcuffed to the table I just made her sit down at and eat the first meal she's likely had in days, if not weeks."

"Thank God," Dane whispered and Wade could practically see the man sagging in relief.

"She's safe. She's covered. Now if that's all you wanted?"

"No the fuck it isn't," Dane exploded. "Fuck. Fuck! We've got a huge fucking problem."

Dane went silent as though valiantly trying to pull himself together and Wade frowned at the frenzied, out of control, completely uncharacteristic outburst from DSS's front man. His frown turned to a vicious scowl because there was a hell of a lot he didn't like about this impromptu telephone chat.

Dane was clearly unhinged, worried out of his mind, but it was the last that put Wade on full alert. *We've got a huge fucking problem.* Cold, stark fear vibrated through every single nerve ending until he was battling the very thing Dane Elliot was.

"Since you don't seem inclined to share anything at the moment, perhaps you can start with the cryptic text you sent saying situation critical," Wade snapped. "I need to know what I'm dealing with here because Eliza isn't exactly being cooperative, so if you have intel, particularly information that keeps her alive, then you need to start fucking talking and do it fast. Eliza's reserves are gone, have been gone for a long time, not that you or anyone else noticed," he said in a voice full of derision. "She's currently handcuffed to a table because it was the only way I could force her to eat. She's a fucking mess, Dane. Imagine the worst-case scenario of Eliza falling apart and shattering into a million pieces and then multiply that by a hundred and then you'll start getting close to her current state of mind. Now, I have to have a serious come-to-Jesus meeting with her so I know what the hell has her so fucking afraid when she's never had the goddamn sense to be afraid of anything."

He heard Dane's sudden, vicious intake of air and when he spoke, his words shook and he suddenly sounded a hundred years old.

"She's that scared?" Dane whispered. "You said she fell apart?"

"You have *no* idea," Wade said coldly. "Now start talking."

"Jesus, she's on some kind of goddamn suicide mission," Dane choked out.

And then he outlined in harsh, broken sentences everything in Eliza's letter. Only, Wade wouldn't allow him to paraphrase any of Eliza's words. This was too important. He couldn't take in Dane's biased account so he made Dane read the letter verbatim.

He closed his eyes and swore viciously, sparing none of his anger, fear or torment. When he directed Dane once more, there was no deference in his voice. No acknowledgment that Dane and Eliza's other coworkers had any right to be afraid, to intervene or that they were in any way in control of the situation. Wade was calling the shots.

"You sit on every one of your men, Elliot," Wade ground out. "You do not send off a bunch of half-cocked, pissed off operatives into this situation. Not when Eliza's life is at stake."

"She's ours," Dane said viciously. "Do you honestly believe we're going to sit here and do nothing?"

"She's *mine*," Wade said in a fierce, pissed off tone. "You need to get that and you need to let it sink in. Right the fuck now."

"If anything happens to Lizzie, there will be no safe place for you to hide. I'll devote the rest of my life to hunting you down and taking you apart with my bare hands."

"Nothing is going to happen to Eliza. Second, you're welcome to try and good luck with that." Wade paused a moment and then quietly added, "If something ever happens to her, it will be pointless for you to hunt me down because I'd take care of the matter myself."

After a long moment, and just as quietly, Dane responded, "So it's like that."

"It's exactly like that," Wade said harshly.

He shook off the simmering emotion to clear his head of unwanted images of something terrible happening to the woman he had handcuffed inside the house.

"You sit on your men and you goddamn sit on yourself for at least twenty-four hours," Wade said forcefully. "Give me time to get the story from Eliza and to make my play. After those twenty-four hours, you get your team together, make damn sure they know what's at stake and make very certain they have their heads on straight and then you get your asses to Calvary, Oregon, which is where I found her, and start discreetly poking around and see what you can dig up. In the meantime, I'm going to plant a few seeds. Make it clear that Eliza was there and that she left with me and I'm not going to make it hard for me to be found."

"Jesus," Dane muttered. "You're using her as fucking bait?"

"No, the fuck I'm not!" Wade bellowed. "I'm making myself the goddamn bait. She's made it clear to you and to me that she isn't worried about herself. She's worried about anyone she's associated with. Whatever the fuck is going on with her, she knows enough about the threat to know that she won't be the target. Which is why she's on this goddamn suicide mission. She's sacrificing herself for everyone who matters to her. Don't you think if she were the target, that if she feared for herself, that she would have the sense to confide that in you so her team could have her back? Come on, Elliot. You've worked with her. You call her your friend. She's not stupid. When has she ever been stupid? She's not afraid for herself. She's fucking terrified that everyone she loves is going to die. I'm setting myself up to be an easy target and to draw this son of a bitch to me. And Eliza will not ever have the opportunity to take anything for me."

"I get it," Dane said sharply. "I don't like it, but I get it. We'll check in when we have any intel. I'd appreciate it if you did the same."

"When I know something, I'll clue you in."

With that, Wade ended the call and stood there several long seconds, composing himself for the most difficult hurdle yet. Confronting Eliza. Finding out what godawful demons she's lived with for far too long. And why she's never shared them with anyone.

THIRTEEN

QUIETLY, Wade returned to the table where he'd left Eliza cuffed, to find her staring seemingly a long ways away, her gaze fixed on some distant point. At first, she didn't register his presence, and when she did and brought her gaze level with his, the sadness in her usually vibrant, teasing eyes clutched at his heart.

He thought back to the letter Dane had read to him. Words penned by Eliza. This wasn't a woman on a quest for absolution. She'd already condemned herself and thought herself beyond redemption for whatever sins she carried. Nor was this woman out for revenge. She wasn't angry enough. Not cold enough to be plotting revenge.

He'd seen her in revenge mode, when she'd been so adamant about going after the bastards who'd tortured her and made Ramie, Ari and Gracie's lives hell and taking them down. This was a woman grieving for people she'd already resigned herself to losing, not because they'd die, but because she would.

Which meant she had no illusions about surviving either her

attempt to bring justice against someone who'd escaped it or the punishment for killing a man.

Dane coining this a suicide mission was chillingly accurate.

Doing his best not to succumb to the ice invading his veins, making his blood sluggish and slowing his reaction time down, he went to her and bent to one knee so he could unfasten the cuff from her wrist. When she would have pulled her hand away from him, he caught hold of her wrist, turning it so he could inspect her flesh.

Cursing when he saw the faint red marks, he pressed a gentle kiss to the damage he'd done.

"I'm sorry. It wasn't my intention to hurt you."

She yanked back her hand as if he'd scalded her, clutching her wrist to her chest, covering it with her other hand in a protective measure. Shock rounded her eyes as she stared at him, clearly bewildered by the tender gesture.

"Let's go where we have more privacy," he said, helping her to her feet.

He propelled her toward one of the bedrooms, one that had no windows to the outside and he secured the lock behind them after flipping on the lights. She glanced wildly around as if assessing her escape options and then her shoulders sagged when she realized she had none.

"It's time you told me what's going on, Eliza. I want the whole story. Everything."

She whirled away from him, but not before he saw the panic blazing in her eyes. She put as much space between them as possible, but the room was small and his size overwhelmed it—and her.

He crossed his arms and folded them over his chest, leaning back against the locked door as if to further drive home the point that she couldn't escape him. Not again. Not ever.

Her teeth dug into her bottom lip and it was all he could do not to go to her and thumb away her lip before she broke the skin.

"Eliza?" he prompted, her continued silence only spreading the apprehensiveness already clinging to him like a stubborn vine.

She shuddered violently and just as quickly shut down, shutting him out. She closed her eyes and turned her back, choosing instead to fix her gaze toward the blank wall she now faced.

"Eliza," he said in warning. "My patience is at its fraying point. Don't push me right now."

She whirled back around, eyes wild, hands clenched into tight fists at her sides. Her snarl of rage sent a surge of desire rolling over him like a tidal wave. There she was. His Eliza. His relief was stark as he watched her fury ignite into flames.

"Where the hell do you get off telling me not to push you?" she seethed. "Have you lost your goddamn mind? I didn't ask for you to be here. I didn't ask for you to hunt me down and I damn sure didn't ask for you to handcuff me to your fucking table, told to eat like an errant two-year-old who can't get up from the dinner table until her plate is cleaned."

He shrugged. "If the shoe fits."

She sent him a look that would likely shrivel his dick if it weren't so damn hard for her already. Meek, beaten-down Eliza was not a good look on her. Ever. Fierce, pissed off, magnificent, enraged Eliza was a look guaranteed to make him come in his pants.

"Get out of my life, Sterling," she hissed. "Stop interfering in shit that is not your business to interfere in! If I had wanted you in any way involved, I would have given you a heads-up. Since clearly I didn't, and I just as clearly recall telling you a few nights ago to stay the fuck away from me, it should be very clear to you that I don't want you here."

"Never said I thought you wanted me here, Eliza. You may not want me here or involved, but you need me and that's what pisses you off right now. Is that clear? Since clearly you seem to think using the word *clearly* enough will make it clear to me that you've got everything under control and that you aren't in trouble and you can handle yourself. But after the chat I just had with Dane I'm not going anywhere. So start talking and quit fucking delaying the inevitable. Which, by the way, is me. Here. Involved. Not going away. Now, are we clear?"

He broke off when she went bone white, her eyes so large and wounded against her starkly pale face that for a moment he couldn't breathe. She teetered precariously and he lunged for her, certain she was going to hit the floor in the next second.

But her outburst froze him in mid-action. Her words hit him with the force of a bomb, a shudder rolling over his body until his knees wobbled and he wondered if he wasn't going to be the one who ended up on the floor.

"He killed them!" The words came out in a shriek that made him wince. "He murdered those women in the most horrific manner conceivable and I helped! I killed them! I helped kill them. I have so much blood on my hands that they'll never be clean, Wade. Never!"

Wade hadn't thought anything was left to shock him about the entire situation. Sweet mother of God. He was beyond flabbergasted. There was no way in hell Eliza had ever killed anyone in cold blood. Any kill she'd ever made would have been righteous.

But one had only to look at her to see that she believed her-self to be every bit as guilty as the monster she took responsibil-ity for.

An anguished moan ripped from Eliza's throat and she slid to her knees. She buried her face in her hands as she bowed, forming the smallest, tightest ball possible, rocking back and forth. And then her sobs broke free. Her entire body heaved with the force of her gut-wrenching cries.

Wade had had enough. He reached down and pulled her up and into his arms, hugging her tightly to his body. Tilting her chin upward so he had access, he kissed away the seemingly never-ending trail of silvery tears. He nuzzled his lips at her temple and then rained kisses down her wet cheeks and finally to her lips.

She went utterly still in his arms, like a small, frightened animal in the grasp of a much larger predator, but she didn't fight him. He kissed her lips again, feathery light, gently coaxing her mouth, lapping gently at the corners of her lips and then over the full double arch that drove him crazy every time he imagined that full, perfect bow around his lips.

"Breathe," he whispered against her mouth, coaxing more air inward.

When she complied, her breath escaped on a sigh, giving him the opening he'd been waiting for. He took swift advan-tage and delved inside, nearly groaning at the sweetness of her mouth, the flutter of her tongue over his. So light and delicate, like the touch of a butterfly's wings.

He deepened the kiss, needing it—her—more than he needed to do as he'd instructed her and breathe, and he kept deepening it until he'd tasted every single part of her mouth. She melted into him, as if her strength had been utterly sapped and he was her only barrier to the world, her only protection and he was the shelter she was seeking.

He'd never felt anything sweeter than her soft acquiescence.

Her hands trembled between their bodies as she slowly lifted them, sliding her fingers over his chest to curl into his shirt, forming tight fists as she held on.

"That's right, Eliza. Don't let go. I've got you. I won't let you go. I swear it."

As if something fiercely primitive deep inside her had been unleashed at his soft vow, she began to move urgently against him, hot, wild, like nothing his imagination could have possibly conjured, and he'd spent more than his fair share of time fantasizing about how magnificent she would be.

To his surprise and satisfaction, she took control of the kiss, pushing him back until he was once more pressed against the locked door. Her tongue, so hot and delicious, licked delicately over the contours of his mouth before meeting and dueling with the tip of his in a dance as old as time.

She kissed him with a ferocity and desperation he could not only feel but taste. He surrendered himself to her, allowing her this moment to revel in her control when her entire world had been upended.

He sucked in his breath when she slid her lips from his mouth down his jaw, and then nipping at his earlobe before going lower and grazing her teeth over the side of his neck before following it with a sharp nip that had him growling deep in his throat.

Her fingers loosened, freeing his shirt, and her hands glided across his chest, then lower, yanking his shirt up and sliding her palms over his taut abdomen and then his chest before traveling in a downward path again, this time going much lower.

She dipped into the waistband of his pants, her fingers finding him hot and turgid, shoving with growing urgency against his fly. She fumbled with the button and then he heard the throaty rasp of his zipper and then he was free, his dick thrusting outward into her waiting grasp.

Jesus, but it was like coming home. Sweat broke out on his brow and his breaths grew more rapid as he strained to suck in more air. Never had anything felt as good as her fingers curled around his erection.

"Fuck me, Sterling," she whispered, a plea. "Take me hard and fast. Make me forget. Just for a little while, make me forget."

Wade gently circled both her wrists with his fingers, stilling the pull of her hand on his rigid length, and then he moved her hands outward, away, and then lifted them to press her palms against his chest.

"Eliza, stop," he said quietly. "Breathe for me, baby. Deep breaths and stop for just a minute."

Her eyes dulled, the shadows lengthening, as shame crept into her beautiful, soulful gaze. She turned her face away, presenting only one cheek to his view, her eyes closing as a thin rivulet of moisture slithered down her face.

"I'm sorry," she whispered, so faintly he almost couldn't hear. "I don't blame you for not wanting to be tainted."

Wade cursed savagely and then he cursed even more that she would believe for one moment that she was tainted. That he didn't want her. When he was nearly blinded by his need of her.

She opened her mouth to speak again but he reached for her chin and turned her so she fully faced him once more.

"Shut up," he said fiercely.

And then he kissed her just as fiercely as his outburst had been to stop any further words from her. Words that had already cut him like the sharpest blade.

His fingers tightened around her chin and he softly rubbed his thumb over her swollen lips when he finally dragged his mouth from hers. Though she faced him, her gaze was downcast, refusing to meet his.

"Look at me, Eliza."

She closed her eyes, her nostrils quivering.

"Look at me."

Her eyelids fluttered, unshed tears collecting like gems on her lashes.

"I am not going to fuck you. I'm going to make love to you. I'm going to show you how very beautiful you are to me."

"I'm not beautiful," she said in an aching, pain-filled voice. "God, Wade. You have no idea how ugly I am. On the inside. My soul is so black . . . dead."

Every word that came from her cut him razor sharp to the bone. He couldn't bear to hear a single other one. He silenced her once more with a kiss.

He took over, giving her no chance to speak, to condemn herself even further in her own eyes. Not leaving the silken heat of her mouth for the few seconds it would take him to remove her clothing, he kept his mouth fused to hers and fumbled clumsily with her shirt, unfastened her jeans, yanked downward, leaving them gathered at her knees for now.

As he unhooked her bra and used his fingers to push the thin straps down over her shoulders, he whispered into her mouth, "I'm going to leave your sweet mouth only for as long as it takes me to get you fully undressed, but I don't want to hear a single word out of it unless you're saying my name."

Her only response was the light hiccupping sound of her breath as she sucked it in.

Moving swiftly, he took her hands and placed one over each of his shoulders for her to hang on to while he divested her of her shoes, socks and then her jeans, leaving her to stand before him in only her silky panties.

"I've spent countless sleepless nights dreaming of this," he murmured.

Faint color rose in her cheeks, sweeping upward from her neck. She stared at him in obvious disbelief but there was also a flicker of . . . guilt. As though she'd been caught out on something she'd rather die than have be known. He smiled.

"You too, huh."

"Wade . . ."

"I like hearing my name on your lips. Before a few days ago, you never called me by my first name. Only my last."

Not giving her a chance to respond, he pulled her back against his body, sliding his thumbs down her sides to catch at the lacy band of her underwear. He pushed just enough that when he let go, it slipped the rest of the way down her slender legs and finally she was fully nude.

His bold gaze took in every exquisite inch of her, from her tousled blonde hair to the silky golden tufts between her legs. Her breasts were utter perfection. Gently rounded with just enough bob and sway to make a man's mouth water but they, like the rest of her body, were toned, sleek . . . beautiful. They fit with the rest of her figure. Not so muscled or flat that they were shapeless pads with only nipples to differentiate them from the rest of her body.

Her hips flared enticingly, just crying for a man's hands to palm them, to curl possessively around them while he plunged so deep inside her that they both lost their minds. And her ass. Her ass was to die for. Toned, delicious swells that also begged a man's hands in a variety of ways.

Knowing if he didn't move, didn't get them to the bed soon, he wasn't going to last another minute, he swept her up into his arms, resting his chin atop her head as he stalked over to the bed. He placed her down, ensuring that his gaze was locked with hers and that his shone with approval and desire.

"You're beautiful," he said hoarsely, repeating his earlier assertion.

He kissed her just in case she would deny it again, and he slid his tongue inward, this time forgoing the playful teasing of earlier. He stroked in and out in long, leisurely strokes, giving her a hint of what was to come.

Reluctantly, he pulled away so he could strip out of his own clothing and he made record work of it. As he moved back to her, he saw her staring at him, female appreciation in her sapphire eyes.

He wasn't unused to women liking his body or their many creative ways of expressing their approval. But coming from Eliza it was an altogether new experience. One that made him feel not so certain of himself. But then never had making love to a woman and getting it right been more important than in this moment. With this woman.

He lay down next to her on his side and then turned her so she faced him. Their legs tangled together and one hand slid up the length of her leg, over the curve of her hip, following the indentation of her waistline and then up to cup her breast. He thumbed the firm peak, coaxing it to further rigidity before finally continuing his journey upward.

She emitted a small sigh and turned into his touch the tiniest bit when he cupped and then began caressing her cheek. Almost as if she were enjoying something so simple as his touch. The soft reassurance he was trying so very hard to give her.

"Your face is beautiful," he whispered. "Your eyes. Your mouth," he added, extending his thumb outward to trace her lips. Then he lifted his hand to delve into her hair, tangling his fingers deeply into the tresses. "Your hair is like silk. I could get lost in it. How it smells."

She made a small sound of dismay when he let his hand fall away from her face, but then it turned into another contented sigh when he once more cupped her breast and toyed with the puckered bud.

"Your breasts are fucking perfect, and your nipples are the most mouthwatering shade of pink. I've fantasized about doing nothing for an entire night but sucking and licking them."

Color bloomed again in her cheeks and her eyes grew hazy as if she were entering a different world. A dream world. But he was already there.

"But those things aren't what make you beautiful, Eliza," he said, his tone becoming more serious.

His gaze searched hers, looking for some sign that she understood what he was saying. Or at least understood what he wasn't saying.

"Looks, physical attributes, physical beauty never stay the same in a person's life. They aren't what's important and they aren't what make you beautiful."

He touched her temple, lightly tapping.

"Your mind is beautiful. It's sharp, intelligent. One of your greatest assets. You're funny, witty, always know the right thing to say, always have the answer to any problem."

He lowered his hand and splayed it out over her chest, resting between her breasts.

"This . . . this is what makes you the most beautiful woman I've ever known. Your heart, Eliza."

Her sharp inhale sounded, her nostrils flaring and tears glittered harshly in the light.

"You're warm, funny, kind, compassionate, loyal. You stand for what's right."

Her lips began to tremble and even more moisture welled in her blue eyes. She shook her head but didn't disobey his order not to say anything.

He nodded. "Although I'm certainly not complaining about the way what I have in my arms looks at all. But you're also beautiful where it counts the most. On the inside. And that's rare and so very precious. *You're* rare. *You're* precious. And if you think I'm going to let you throw away rare and precious because you think you did something you aren't even capable of then you're out of your fucking mind."

She wouldn't even meet his gaze any longer so great was the shame reflected in her eyes. Then she closed her eyes and sucked in a deep, stuttering breath that ended on a sob.

"Let it go, Eliza," he said softly. "You don't have to carry your burden alone. Not anymore. Let it go, baby. I'm right here. I'm not going anywhere. Give yourself—and your burden—to me."

FOURTEEN

ELIZA couldn't breathe. Her heart was about to pound right out of her chest. There was simply too much for her to take in and process all at once. She was lying in Wade's arms. Wade was calling her—had called her—beautiful over and over. Wade wanted to make love to her because he thought she was special.

Rare and precious.

You stand for what's right.

His words burned an acid trail through her mind, searing a path straight to her ravaged, already blackened soul. If she stood for what was right, then none of those women would have ever been touched by Thomas's evil.

But most heart-wrenching was his quiet plea for her to put her burden down and share it with him.

If only it were that simple. If only!

Tears burned her swollen eyes. But she'd shed far too many tears and had broken her vow countless times. A vow to never let anyone see her cry again. Ever since Wade had barged into the rented house in Calvary, she'd done nothing but cry.

"Eliza," Wade said gently, tipping her chin upward with one knuckle.

She couldn't look at him. Couldn't bear to look at him.

Then as if understanding how close to becoming completely unhinged she was, he merely lowered his mouth and pressed it to hers in a kiss that was every bit as beautiful as he kept claiming her to be.

"I'm going to make love to you, Eliza," he said, the words rumbling and vibrating from his chest. "I want you with me, baby. Tell me you're with me."

She closed her eyes because just for a while she could pretend. She needed to pretend. For a few moments she wanted to touch something heartrendingly beautiful and poignant.

"I'm with you," she whispered.

At once, his kisses became more masterful, dominant. Aggressive. Shivers of arousal and need erupted but she was anything but cold. For so long she'd existed in ice and now it was as if she'd suddenly been thrust under the sun's rays after a long, harsh winter.

Had she ever lain awake at night fantasizing about being in Wade's arms? She was honest enough with herself to admit she had. He was a gorgeous specimen of alpha male. When she wasn't doing her best to needle him, a self-defense mechanism she'd employed with him from the very start, she was positively shivery at the way he looked at her with naked possession in his eyes.

Even when he seemed to feel the same way about her, that is to say not much at all, and he acted as though she were nothing but a huge thorn in his side, he'd still acted to protect her. Had acted as though what happened to her mattered to him. He'd been furious after she was abducted and tortured. Not just furious. Sick with worry. For her. He'd been the one who'd held her cradled in his arms in the aftermath until she'd realized who held her and then quickly put as much distance between them as possible. Another thing she did often around him.

And then him insisting on accompanying her and her team for the takedown, his fury of her going. Him taking a bullet meant for her. She shivered again as his lips closed over one nipple and she closed her eyes, pushing aside those confusing thoughts and memories. They had no place in the here and now.

As if to confirm every single word he'd given her, beautiful words that brought the sting of tears to her eyes, he lavished kisses over every inch of her body almost as if determined to prove to her how beautiful he found her. Would he feel the same once he knew the full truth?

She shook her head in silent denial. She wouldn't think of that now. Couldn't bear it when his eyes turned condemning and he backed away, judgment shining in those dark eyes. For now, she only wanted this. Him loving her. Nothing mattering except this moment because when it was over, the truth would be revealed and once more she'd be alone to deal with her demons in the only way she knew how.

"Baby, you aren't with me."

Wade's softly chiding voice broke through her thoughts and she glanced down to where his palm splayed possessively over her abdomen and his head was lifted so he could look into her eyes.

"I'm with you," she whispered. "Please, Wade. I need this . . . I need you. Please."

Something stirred in his eyes, something dark and primitive, almost as if her admission sealed her fate. Chill bumps erupted and danced over her body as his hand glided upward over her belly to cup one breast, weighing the slight mound in his palm. His thumb brushed sensuously over her nipple, coaxing it to complete rigidity so it was puckered and straining, begging for his mouth.

Accepting the invitation, he lowered his head and closed his mouth around her nipple, creating a seal as he sucked the point firmly between his teeth. She closed her eyes, arching helplessly upward, wanting more, needing so much more.

"Dreamed of this so many times," he murmured as he pressed gentle kisses around the swell of her breast before moving to the other one and lavishing equal attention on it. "Knew if it ever happened, I was done. Knew that once I claimed you that you were mine and more importantly I was yours. I belong to you. You need to see this for what it is, Eliza. You need to realize the significance of this. You're mine now and I won't let you go. And what is mine I protect with my last breath. You don't stand alone. Not anymore. Not ever again. You have me now and you aren't fighting your battles without me anymore."

"Wade," she protested helplessly, overcome with the enormity of all he'd just confessed. "You can't. You don't understand."

His gaze hardened but there was such tenderness in those dark eyes as he bent his head and licked away the single trail of tears that escaped down her cheek.

"What I understand is that I'll be damned if you cry another tear when I'm not there to hold you and tell you it'll be all right.

You'll never cry alone again, Eliza. You won't cry at all if I can help it. Your tears are killing me, baby. I can't handle seeing you cry. It's the most helpless feeling in the entire goddamn world. If it's the last thing I do, I'll never give you any reason to cry ever again. And I'll kill anyone who puts those tears in your eyes."

She closed her eyes, knowing if she didn't pull herself together that she'd erupt into sobs and this time she wouldn't stop. Wouldn't be able to stop.

"Make love to me," she whispered, for the first time not asking him to fuck her.

She winced inwardly at the crude, thoughtless words. As if she considered him some kind of emotionless machine. It had been an insult, not one she'd meant to hand him. It was herself she had been trying to convince that it was just fucking and nothing more. Nothing deeper or more personal.

Self-preservation ran deep within her. It was the only thing she'd known since leaving Calvary so many years ago.

Wade cupped her face in his hands as he rolled atop her, his hard, muscled body blanketing hers and his heat seeping deep into her bones, warming her as nothing else could. He kissed her long and lingeringly, his tongue lapping ever so slowly over hers as though he were trying to commit her taste and feel to memory. She was doing the same because after this one time, he would go. She'd never see him again. And the memory of his lovemaking would be all she had to hold on to in the coming days.

"Got to get a condom, baby," he whispered against her lips. "Don't move."

She watched as he rolled away from her, leaned down and yanked a condom from the pocket of his jeans where they lay on the floor. Then he was back, sliding back over her, his knee spreading her thighs to him.

He deftly rolled the condom on and then he lifted his hips, one hand holding her hip while the other tangled in her hair holding her head so their gazes locked.

"See me, Eliza. Only me. Don't look away. I want your eyes on mine while I make love to you."

Her eyelids fluttered, the temptation to close her eyes strong because some truths were hard to accept and she was suddenly shy and so very uncertain. He seemed to know the conflicting emotions that ran wildly through her. His expression gentled and went soft. Her chest tightened to the point of pain to see him looking at her with such tenderness in his eyes.

She gasped when he probed at her opening, the blunt head of his penis nudging at her softness. He didn't overpower her or just shove inside her. He very slowly, with infinite patience and care, began to inch forward.

The strain was obvious in his face, lines appearing and his jaw clenched tight. She knew what holding on to his control was costing him. But he was being unselfish and giving. This was for her and she knew it.

She feathered a hand over the rough lines of his face, the first gesture of tenderness and intimacy she'd given him. He went utterly still, staring down at her as his breaths rasped unevenly over his lips.

"Make love to me," she whispered again. "Don't hold back. You won't hurt me, Wade. You'd never hurt me. Please, I need you inside me. I'm so cold. I've been cold for so long. I need your warmth and your strength."

"You'll always have it," he vowed, lowering himself so more of his weight covered her.

He pushed forward with more determination this time and she gasped again when he stopped. Her eyes widened and she looked wildly down at him as her body fizzed in pure delight.

"Why did you stop?" she asked breathlessly. "You aren't all the way in."

Wade cursed and closed his eyes, dropping his head to bury it in her neck where he took several long, steadying breaths before responding. Then he lifted his head again and kissed her, taking her mouth in a wild storm of passion.

"You're so tight," he ground out. "Jesus, baby. I'm not sure you can take anymore and I don't want to hurt you. I'll never hurt you. Do you understand that?"

She shifted, lifting her legs to curl around his waist. She arched her body, sliding downward so the angle of penetration was better. Then she lifted up, biting her lips at the decadent sensations assailing her from a dozen different directions.

"Baby, no," he protested. "You don't have to do that."

She smiled. "But I do. I need all of you, Wade. Finish it. I can take you. You won't hurt me. But please. I need all of you."

He groaned and closed his eyes, sweat forming on his forehead. She leaned up and flicked her tongue over his flat nipple and then followed it with a nip.

He swelled even larger inside her and then cursed all over again.

"Christ what you do to me, Eliza. Never been this aroused in my life. I'm never going to make it all the way inside you at this rate."

She smiled again and then lifted her hips, giving him no choice but to sink farther or withdraw from her completely.

One of his hands slid between them and his thumb delved between her thighs to caress her clitoris. She moaned and her breathing sped up. Her nipples tightened, her breasts swelled in anticipation, and she clenched hotly and wetly around his erection.

He issued a growl of satisfaction. "That's it, baby. Damn you just went all hot and wet on me. That's it. Now I can move."

Thank God.

He withdrew and she whimpered her protest but he shushed her with his mouth in a carnal, possessive kiss that left her completely breathless. Then he plunged forward and she cried out, her arms and legs clamping down around him, holding him as if her life depended on it.

"You okay?" he whispered.

"God yes. Please don't stop."

She knew she was pleading, that she was so far gone that she didn't even know half of what came out of her mouth, but she didn't care. He was her anchor, the only solid, tangible thing in her world to hang on to. And she did. She held him close to her, absorbing his taste and feel, memorizing every inch of him.

He was moving faster and harder now, his thrusts jostling her body and moving them up and down on the bed. Through it all, his gaze remained locked with hers, his eyes searching her very soul.

She'd have to be blind not to see the utter possession his eyes screamed. The possessiveness in his touch, every caress, the way he planted himself as deeply in her body as possible as if he wanted to wipe out the memory of every other man who'd been there before.

There was only him in this moment. Only Wade. The past didn't matter. The future didn't matter. Only now and the utter perfection of being in his arms and being made love to by him.

He dropped his head long enough to nibble and bite at her neck. He nipped and grazed his teeth over the tender skin, marking her, branding her. Then he ran his mouth lower to capture her nipple and he sucked hard, matching the same rhythm of his thrusts.

"Hold on to me, baby," he said. "Don't let go. Come with me. I'm close."

"Me too," she whispered. "I want you to come with me."

"I'll be here."

It was a quietly worded vow with a wealth of meaning. If only she could take that promise he gave and hold it to her heart. If only she could let him move in, take over and protect her as he was so determined to do.

"I'm losing you," Wade murmured, concern firing in his eyes.

"I'm here," she denied.

He gathered her in his arms and crushed her to him, his arms like steel bands around her. So strong and comforting. She leaned on him now when she couldn't any other time. For just a brief moment she allowed herself the fantasy of depending on this man to keep her safe.

Her orgasm swelled, growing bigger and bigger, like an incoming wave off the ocean. She rode it, reveling in the wildness. Her head twisted back and forth against his chest as he held her tightly, his entire body drawn as tight as a bow.

Almost to breaking. Almost . . .

Then the wave broke and it was glorious. Beautiful. Wild. The most intense orgasm of her life. The most wonderful. She screamed into his neck and dug her nails into his shoulders, knowing that like he'd marked her, so too would she mark him.

Wade captured her mouth, forcing her head to still and he breathed into her as they both flew.

She was trembling violently in the aftermath as Wade held her and gently lowered himself the rest of the way down to rest atop her. Her pulse was racing and she felt completely shattered. Naked. Vulnerable. She'd never felt as bare as she did in this moment.

He rolled them to the side and she mourned the loss of his reassuring weight and the loss of him being such an intimate part of her. Then he slipped from inside her and she moaned her protest. But he got rid of the condom and to her shock, he slid back inside her, still hard and so very hot. The shock of feeling him inside her without the barrier of latex was overwhelming. She'd never felt anything to compare.

But he didn't move. He just stayed there, deeply embedded inside her. He just wasn't ready for the moment to be over with. And neither was she. She nuzzled against his chest and buried her face against his male flesh, inhaling sharply and savoring his scent.

Guilt flooded her as did grief and she gripped him even tighter, afraid that if she let go she would fall apart.

"Eliza?" he asked quietly.

Tears burned her eyes and she blinked furiously to keep them away.

"I've just marked you for death, Wade, and I can't bear the thought of losing you," she said, her voice thick with grief.

His voice and touch were so infinitely gentle that it made

her tear up all over again. He stroked over her body and then finally his hand came to rest at her cheek before he tilted her head upward to meet his gaze.

"Don't you think it's time to tell me what's going on?" he asked gently.

FIFTEEN

ELIZA stiffened and would have withdrawn, would have pulled away from Wade's arms, but he tightened his hold on her to prevent her escape. He'd had enough of her putting distance between them and now, when she was lying in his arms after he'd made love to her, there was no way in hell he'd ever let her put any distance between them again.

Her barriers had been down when he made love to her. He could see so clearly the things in her eyes she never wanted anyone to see. Pain, vulnerability . . . fear. And so much grief that it had hurt him to look at her. His heart ached for this woman. This beautiful, brave, fearless woman.

For too long she'd been the protector. Had made it her life's work. Always putting others first. Risking herself so that others would come to no harm. Never had she had anyone willing to do those things for her. Until now. Until Wade. He'd die before ever allowing anyone to hurt her and he'd damn sure die before ever allowing anyone to make her cry again.

"Baby," he whispered, watching as her eyes became cloudy and then shiny with tears when he murmured the endearment. As though she mattered to him. Didn't she understand she was the most important thing in the world to him? No, she didn't. Not yet. But she would. "Lay your burden down. It's time to let someone carry it for you."

He'd said it before but this time it seemed to really register with her and hit home. For a brief moment there was a spark of hope and so much yearning in her eyes that he automatically squeezed her tighter in his arms.

She *wanted* to lean on him. He'd seen that in her eyes right before defeat registered and with it her loss of hope. She truly believed that no one could help her, even if she wanted it. How to make her believe in him? How to make her believe that there was nothing he wouldn't do for her, to alleviate the pain and guilt in her eyes, to permanently remove those bruising shadows? That he would lay waste to any threat to her. To anything that caused her such sadness and grief. Maybe she'd never had that before but that had all changed the moment he'd laid eyes on her in his gallery and wanted nothing more than to kiss her. And a hell of a lot more.

"You make it sound so simple. So easy," she said in a stran-gled tone.

"It's only as difficult as you make it," he said gently.

She closed her eyes and emitted a bone-weary sigh. As though the weight of the entire world was bearing down on her, suffocating the life right out of her. Her eyes were already dead though. Lifeless. Without hope.

He gathered her more tightly in his arms, conveying without words that he was here. Solid. Real. And he wasn't going away. Ever.

"Oh God, Wade. I don't even know where to start."

"At the beginning," he prompted. "We have all night, Eliza. I'll wait. Take as long as you need. I'm here. I'll listen."

Tears slithered like silver strands down her pale, hollow face. She seemed to cave inwardly in defeat and when she opened her eyes again, dull resignation was a shadow in her beautiful gaze.

"It was ten years ago," she began. "I was sixteen."

He cursed under his breath. Ten years she'd suffered the unimaginable, never sharing with anyone the hell she endured on a daily basis. Jesus, she'd been just a *child*.

"I had no one," she went on falteringly. "My parents . . . I never knew them. I don't even know what happened to them. No one ever told me, or maybe I was too young to remember. My earliest memories were of being in the system, shuffled from home to home, never having a permanent place to live or an actual family. I wasn't abused physically. I was just . . . ignored, not there if that makes sense. I wasn't neglected in the sense that I had food and clothing. The bare necessities. But I knew from a very young age that I was merely a source of a check from the state each month and I had no illusions that I ever mattered to the families who took me in. Was never considered a daughter or sister. And that was what I wanted—needed—not material things. Those things didn't matter to me. I wanted to be accepted—loved. To feel like I had a place in the world and was part of something beautiful. A family."

"God," Wade muttered, helpless to do anything but listen to the wretched ache in her voice.

"The longest I was ever with the same family was two years. I was moved often. I never understood why. I never understood why no one ever wanted me. I was a good child. Quiet. Obedi-ent. I would have done anything to please them so they would want me to stay. But no matter how hard I tried, it was never enough. They didn't notice. I excelled in school but they never recognized that. They just didn't care and it took until I was fif-teen that I finally realized that nothing I did would ever be good enough. I didn't want that life until I turned eighteen and would graduate out of the system."

"What happened at fifteen?" Wade asked quietly.

"I left," she said simply, as though it were the most natural thing in the world for a fifteen-year-old girl to just walk away with no means of support, no money or food.

Dear God. The thought of Eliza at fifteen, having nothing or no one and having to make her own way in the world sickened him to his soul.

"What did you do?"

"I picked up a part-time job so I could complete my GED. I worked nights and during the day I haunted the local library doing online courses. As I said I had always excelled in school so I was able to obtain my diploma just before I turned sixteen. Then I hitchhiked to Calvary. It was as far as my ride could take me, and it seemed as good a place as any. I was able to find work in a local diner and even a room at a local boardinghouse owned by an elderly lady. The rent was cheap and it provided breakfast. I ate the rest of my meals at the diner."

She took in a deep shuddering breath, pausing for a mo-ment, seemingly lost in the torment of her past.

"He came in one evening. T-Thomas," she said, stuttering over his name. "He was older, maybe late twenties. Handsome but quiet. There was something about him that, at the time, I couldn't put my finger on. He would always request my section and he always had a friendly smile for me and left great tips."

"I bet," Wade said menacingly, already not liking where her story was headed.

Sixteen and some asshole at least twelve years older—old enough to damn well know better—had cultivated an innocent child whose only crime was wanting to be loved.

"One night I left the diner after two in the morning. I had worked a double and was dead on my feet. I didn't own a car. I didn't even have a driver's license. So I walked everywhere and it was a small town so it wasn't a big deal. Two street punks started harassing me and when I ignored them it turned ugly."

Wade sucked in his breath. "How ugly?"

"Before it got too out of hand, Thomas appeared out of no-where. He wasn't a badass or even that intimidating but for some reason the punks were scared to death of him. He warned them off me, said I was under his protection and anyone touching me would answer to him."

Wade's lips thinned. Some hero. A grown-ass man who damn well should know better than to get involved with a vul-nerable sixteen-year-old girl.

"He walked me home and then every night after that. He was at the diner every single day I worked. I thought it was wildly romantic," Eliza admitted with a flush. "To a sixteen-year-old girl who'd never been loved, who'd never had anyone who cared, Thomas was everything I'd ever dreamed of. He seemed to know all of my secret desires, the things I yearned for and then he made them happen. It wasn't until it was too late that I understood *how* he was able to manipulate me so easily," she whispered.

"What do you mean?" Wade asked in a low voice.

She closed her eyes. "Most people would think I'm crazy, but at least you should have no problem believing me since you know well what Tori, Ramie, Ari and Gracie can do."

A prickle of foreboding snaked up Wade's spine.

"He's psychic," she said baldly. "He can see into someone's mind and pull out every secret thought they ever had. Worse, not only does he have the ability to read minds, much like Gracie, he can also manipulate people into doing his bidding. He can plant a suggestion or an impulse and they are helpless to do anything but obey."

Wade's eyes narrowed. "Is that what he did to you, Eliza? Did he have you under his control?"

She looked on the verge of tears again. Her eyes were swamped with unmistakable guilt.

"He didn't have to," she said, bitterness lacing every word. "I would have done anything for him, *did* do anything."

"You didn't kill those women," Wade said forcefully.

This time the tears not only welled, they fell in endless streaks down her cheeks.

"But I did, Wade. I *did*."

Wade shook his head. "No fucking way. You'll never convince me you killed anyone, least of all innocent women."

"Thomas was—is—obsessed with me. I doubt his years in prison have lessened it to any degree. If anything his obsession has only grown. He loved me or rather his sick, twisted version of love and I believed him. God, I believed him. Worse, I *wanted* to believe it. I didn't want to believe he was a monster capable of such *evil*. I just wanted to be . . . loved."

Her voice cracked with emotion and Wade held her even tighter, shaking with anger and helpless rage.

"He was so gentle and understanding with me. I wanted to make love with him, wanted him to be my first. I was so caught up in the romance of it all. But he told me I was too young, that it would be wrong for him to make love to me until I was older. He told me we had all the time in the world and that he would wait forever. What I didn't realize at the time was that because of his love—obsession—with me he couldn't bring himself to act out his sick perversions on me. So instead he chose other women. Me, he held sacred. His precious love. Too precious to be touched by his evil. So other women died horrible, painful deaths in my stead."

"Baby no," Wade said, his voice aching with sorrow and regret at the horrible guilt she'd carried for far too long. Guilt that was not hers to bear.

"I didn't know," she said painfully. "When the news broke after the first horrific murder, the community was shocked. Thomas was horrified and insisted I never walk to or from work alone. He was with me at all times. Or so I thought. When he wasn't with me, he was raping and torturing those poor women, because he refused to ever touch me with anything other than gentleness and tenderness. With love."

She choked on the last word, shuddering violently as though it made her physically ill.

Wade pressed his lips to her temple and left them there as she trembled in his arms.

"It wasn't until after the third murder that I began to suspect.

Even then I couldn't bring myself to entertain that Thomas could possibly be responsible for committing such reprehensible atrocities on another human being. Not my Thomas. He was so quiet. The epitome of a gentleman. He was liked and well respected in the town. He was a philanthropist. Always willing to lend a hand to someone in need. But then . . ."

She trailed off as a huge, gulping sob overtook her. She buried her face in Wade's chest and wrapped her arms tightly around him, holding on to him like he was the only solid thing in her world to hang on to.

He waited patiently, not pushing her for more. He let her cry, holding and soothing her until finally she quieted and resumed her story.

"And then one day, I asked off from the diner. Told them I was sick. I told Thomas I was feeling unwell and he acted so concerned. He brought me soup to the boardinghouse, fussed over me and told me to stay in bed and rest. I waited until he left and then I followed him."

Wade closed his eyes. Even at sixteen Eliza had possessed a strong sense of justice. She could say what she wanted about being blinded by love and that she had been firmly rooted in denial, but if she hadn't wanted to know the truth, she would have never sought out proof of her suspicions.

"He owned several properties. As I said, he was a wealthy man. A real estate developer and he was well liked by the locals. He'd donated a shelter to the town and quite a bit of money for its operation and upkeep. He told me he'd done so because of me. Because he never wanted a child to know the kind of upbringing I'd been forced to endure. He went to such lengths to perpetuate an elaborate hoax that it's truly mind-boggling.

"I followed him to an older house he was in the process of having renovated. There was a fully intact concrete reinforced basement with soundproof walls. Oh God," she choked out, stopping in midsentence to bury her face in his chest once more.

Wade stroked her hair, pressing kisses to the crown of her head as he murmured soothing words of encouragement.

"While he had a construction crew working on the rest of the house, he held women in the basement and tormented them, delighting in the fact that help was only a short distance away and yet no one could hear them scream. When I saw . . ."

"What did you see, baby?" he prompted gently.

"Hell," she said bleakly. "I saw hell."

"What happened?"

"I snuck down the stairs leading into the basement and the first thing I remember is the smell. Blood. So much of it. And rot. Decomposing human flesh. It made me sick, but I knew I had to be strong and I couldn't give away my presence."

"Smart girl," he murmured.

She ignored him and went on, her eyes locked on some far-away point, lost in her nightmare.

"There was blood everywhere. The floor, the walls. It was as though he purposely splattered it. There was one woman already dead, but she was barely recognizable as a woman or even a human. He'd tortured her so badly that all that remained was . . . pulp," she said in horror. "But there was one who was alive. The one he was playing with and toying with. And what he said to her. God, I'll never forget what he said to her as long as I *live*."

Wade squeezed her but remained silent.

"He apologized to her. Told her he was sorry but that he couldn't ever do these things to his precious love. That I was perfect and he would never touch her—me. He was talking about *me*, Wade! Said he could never touch me with anything but love and tenderness and so he had no choice but to slake his desires on other women. He told her not to worry, though, that he wouldn't keep her much longer. That her torment would end today and she would finally be at peace. Then he asked her to forgive him. Forgive him! I wanted to throw up. I wanted to scream. I wanted to save her, but all I did was stand there where he couldn't see me, so horrified, so terrified and disgusted that I couldn't move.

"She told him to go to hell, that she would never forgive him. That she hoped he rotted in hell. He was so enraged that he killed her right there in front of me."

"Oh baby," Wade whispered, his eyes burning.

He buried his face in her hair and rocked her gently back and forth, holding her as she trembled violently in his arms.

"I got out of there as quickly as I could and went to the police. They called the DA in immediately and questioned me for hours. Asked me if I was certain of what I saw. As if I could forget." She shuddered. "I'll *never* forget. I still see those images when I close my eyes at night. Not a day has passed that I don't remember."

"So what happened then?" Wade asked.

"They arrested him. The dead woman I'd seen was no longer there and neither was the woman he killed while I was there but there was blood everywhere and they found DNA to match the women they'd already found the bodies of as well as DNA to match the as of yet undiscovered bodies."

"You had to testify," Wade said grimly.

She nodded. "It was awful. The defense painted me as a

lovesick teenager with a fixation—obsession—with Thomas and that when he turned me away because of my age that I launched a sick vendetta against him. But the evidence was such that they didn't even need my eyewitness account. He was sentenced to five consecutive lifetimes behind bars."

Wade's brow furrowed. "Then why . . ." His voice trailed off trying to make sense of it all.

"I got a call from the prosecuting DA a few weeks ago," she said bitterly. "He told me that Thomas must have gotten to one of the investigating cops. The cop testified under oath that he'd tampered with evidence in order to make the case a slam dunk. But there was no need and I know the investigator never did any such thing, but if Thomas did indeed get to him then he would have been compelled to carry out Thomas's wishes regardless of whether he was telling the truth or not. As a result, Thomas's conviction was overturned and he'll be a free man in two days."

Wade's blood froze. Now it was all starting to come together and make sense. Why Eliza had severed all ties with the people she loved and why she was on a veritable suicide mission.

Needing confirmation before he jumped to conclusions, although with the arsenal she was packing and the fact she'd sent what amounted to a goodbye letter to Gracie and the others, he knew he was not wrong in his assumption of her plans, he tipped her chin up so she was forced to meet his gaze.

"What exactly are you doing here, Eliza?" he asked in a dangerously quiet voice. "And what did you mean when you said you'd marked me for death? And why is it so fucking important that this guy never know of your association with the people you're close to in Houston? Why the fuck would you go off alone like you have no help, no one to have your back?"

She made a sound of frustration. "Because he will kill anyone I love. Anyone who has had any part of my life. He's obsessed with me and he's irrationally jealous. He would think nothing of removing anyone he viewed as competition for my affection. He wants me to himself. He wants to be the only person in my life. He wants me completely and wholly dependent on him in every way."

Wade processed her statement for a moment. From all she'd told him about this Thomas guy, he didn't find that hard to believe. The guy was one sick fuck, no two ways about it.

"I thought . . ." She broke off as grief washed over her already hollow features. "I thought he would be in prison the rest of his life. That I was free and that I could start over. Do you know that Eliza Cummings isn't even my birth name?"

He knew his face registered the shock he was feeling.

"I had it legally changed. I wanted nothing to do with the life I was leaving. No reminder. I no longer wanted to be that person and so I started over. New name. New identity. New past. And I erased everything that came before. I thought I'd left it all behind. That I was safe to actually lead a normal life. I could make friends. Friends who showed me the true meaning of love and not the sick, twisted thing Thomas professed to be love. If I had known, if I'd had any idea he would go free I would have never allowed myself to get close to anyone. I would have never risked the people I love that way. But now I've made you all targets. He'll see every single one of you as threats and he'll go after every one of you and I can't let that happen, Wade. I can't."

"So you decided to take him out first," Wade surmised, his features grim.

She swallowed and nodded.

"And he would know about the people you cared about and especially that I made love to you by reading your mind."

A spasm of pain rippled across her delicate features. "Yes," she whispered.

He gave her an exasperated look. "Did it ever occur to you to stay the hell away from him? Not to ever give him that opportunity? He wouldn't have found you in Houston and if he had, he would have been taken out and not by you."

She lifted her chin in defiance, a spark lighting her eyes giving him savage satisfaction to see remnants of the Eliza he knew so well lurking there behind the grief and self-recrimination.

"I'm not an idiot, Wade."

"Then stop acting like one."

She shoved up and away from him, glaring ferociously at him. He grinned, which only served to heighten her indignation.

"I couldn't live with myself knowing he was free, that he would kill again. And he would, Wade. He would. The justice system let those women down and I won't let him get away with it. I've got to take him out for those women. For me. And for the people I love. I don't want to live the rest of my life always looking over my shoulder, afraid that he'll hunt me down, and he will. I don't want to be afraid of him going after people I love because I was too weak to do what needs to be done. It's my only choice. The only way I can look at myself in the mirror. I can't bring those women back, but I sure as hell can make sure he never hurts another one. So I'm going to be there when he gets out. He isn't going to have to look for me because I'll find *him*. And then I'm sending him straight to hell and me with him. If I survive taking him down, I won't run. I won't hide. I won't even defend myself because I'll be guilty as sin and if I spend the rest of my life in prison at least he will no longer pose a threat to in-nocent women or the people I love."

"And you don't think you're rare and precious?" he asked softly. "That you don't stand for what's right?"

She looked away, but he nudged her chin back so she looked at him.

"You aren't doing this, Eliza. You are not embarking on some suicide mission to atone for sins that aren't even yours to bear."

"You can't stop me," she hissed.

He arched an eyebrow. "Can't I?"

"I won't be responsible for any more deaths!"

Wade caressed her cheek, feathering his touch over her face and then thumbing her lips as he stared intently at her.

"You weren't responsible."

He gently kissed her, not a passionate, all consuming kiss. One he ached to give her and make love to her all over again. But a tender kiss meant to reassure and comfort her.

"Eliza, you can trust me," he said with absolute sincerity. "You have to know how strong my feelings are for you. You can't be that blind."

Tears glittered like diamonds on her eyelashes as she stared helplessly at him.

"Trusting my instincts is exactly what got me into this mess," she said desperately. "What got me in way over my head with Thomas. I can't trust myself, Wade. I can't afford to ever make that mistake again."

His gaze softened and he kissed her lightly again, still strok-ing her face and then tangling his fingers in her hair, smooth-ing the tresses that hung in disarray. She looked hungry, like a woman who'd been thoroughly made love to and who wanted—

needed—more. He wanted nothing more than to give her just that. Himself. Over and over until he'd solidly pushed everything from her mind except him, the two of them, and nothing else in the world mattered.

"Baby," he whispered in a soft, loving voice he hadn't thought himself capable of. Not ever or with anyone until now—her. Only her. "You were sixteen years old. Just a young, vulnerable girl who had nothing and no one. You only wanted to be loved. That isn't a crime. Everyone wants to love and to be loved. You aren't that person anymore. You haven't been that person in a very long time. You've grown into an exceptional woman with the best instincts and strongest character of anyone—man or woman—I've ever known and that's why I fucking admire you so much."

She looked stunned by his admission. She didn't know what shocked her more, his assessment of her character, or if it was the fact that the words had come from him, a man who until a short time ago had been nothing but an overbearing bastard and a complete asshole.

It was little wonder she would have such a hard time accepting such an abrupt about-face when before, from all appearances, they couldn't stand to be in the same room together. Had she ever wondered *why* he harbored such animosity toward her?

He'd known from day one that she spelled trouble for him. He had known from the start that she was a complete game changer for him and he hadn't liked that one bit. He'd fought it and he'd done plenty of denying, but there was no disputing the fact that she was it for him. He was drawn to her like a magnet, not wanting to be caught in her web but not having any damn choice in the matter.

Wade Sterling, ultimate lone wolf, cold and uncaring, un-feeling, completely unhinged by a petite blonde-haired, green-eyed temptress. Oh yeah, Eliza was his kryptonite. His one and only weakness.

"You think I'm an idiot," she protested. "You think I'm care-less, stupid, trying to get myself killed. You were pissed when I was abducted, pissed that I was tortured and livid when I wanted to be included in the takedown of the monsters who did that to me. Like I was too stupid to live for wanting to get vengeance on the bastards who rendered me powerless instead of sitting on the sidelines like some helpless twit while my big bad cowork-ers took care of business so poor, helpless Eliza could sit on her hands at home and wait for others to seek revenge that was rightly mine to seek. And now you lie here saying you admire me? Is this some kind of bullshit you'll say in order to get me to comply with what you want so I'll tuck myself away and play the hapless damsel in distress and expect others to do my dirty work for me?"

"Did you not hear a word I just said to you, woman?" he roared. "I care about you. I care a hell of a lot! Do you think I was pissed at *you* because you were abducted and fucking water-boarded and God only knows what else because you never shared exactly all you endured? Do you think I was pissed at you because you wanted to get back your own in the takedown? Jesus, you *are* an idiot."

Her mouth gaped open and then shut and he put a finger over her lips before she could say anything further. He leaned in close so that their noses nearly touched.

"I was pissed because someone took you. I was pissed be-cause those bastards put their hands on you. They tortured you.

They hurt you and there wasn't a goddamn thing I could do to stop it. I wasn't pissed that you wanted in on the takedown. I was pissed because you were in no condition to be going anywhere except to bed and I was sick to my soul imagining you being hurt or killed because you'd just gone through hell and had no business going into a high risk op. And I was pissed as hell that you nearly fucking died because a bullet meant for you would have gone right through your pretty neck and if it had hit you there wasn't a goddamn thing anyone could have done except watch you bleed out. And lastly I was pissed because you refused to take any downtime after your abduction and torture or after the op was completed and it was over. You were and have been running on fumes for a fuck of a long time and now I know why. I'm worried about you, Eliza. I'm sick with worry because I care a hell of a lot about you and what happens to you, and if I can prevent anything else from happening to you then by God I'm going to do just that whether you like it or not. Whether you hate me or not. Because at least you'll be alive to hate me."

He took a deep, steadying breath, trying to regain control of his raging emotions. Her eyes were round and wide with absolute shock. Maybe he was finally getting through to her.

"As for admiring you? Jesus Christ, woman. You are the most infuriating, exasperating, brave, tenacious and loyal person I've known in my life. Other people can't hold a candle to you. I don't think there's another person like you on this earth. And by God, you're *mine*. I've laid claim and I'm not letting you go, so get over whatever problem you may have with that because you're stuck with me and I'm not going anywhere except wherever you go. Is that clear?"

He took his finger from her mouth and her lips parted and dropped open as she stared at him in wonder. Her mouth opened and closed repeatedly as if she couldn't get out what she wanted to say. Then finally she spoke, her words hushed, barely above a whisper as she stared at him, raw, conflicting emotions reflected in her eyes.

"You *care* for me?"

"I think I've covered that point," he said dryly.

"But you hate me." Confusion registered and she shook her head in denial of the truth staring her right in the face. "You can't stand to be in the same room as me. You act like I'm the *last* person you want to be around."

He sighed in exasperation. "And why do you think that is, Eliza? Think hard here. Does a man who hates you come for you when you've been abducted and tortured and hold you to reassure himself you're all right? Does a man not even employed by your agency insist on being included in the takedown you insisted on being a part of because he wants to make damn sure you're protected and unharmed? Does a man who despises you take a fucking bullet for you?"

"Oh my God," she breathed.

"*Now* she gets it," he muttered, rolling his eyes heavenward. "Swear to God you are the most hardheaded, stubborn woman in existence and damn if I'm not insanely attracted to every single part of you and that stubborn mind of yours. Do you honest to God think I made love to you out of pity? Or worse, to extort information from you? Got news for you, honey, I would have gotten your story without making love to you."

"I don't know what to say," she said, desperation and bewilderment heavy in her voice.

Once again he put his fingers to her lips. "You don't have to say anything. Only understand. Understand that you are not alone. Never again. That you aren't doing this alone. Over my dead body will you confront this bastard and sacrifice yourself for me, the people you love or anyone else."

SIXTEEN

"TELL me something," Wade said quietly.

Silence had descended in the aftermath of Eliza's emotional outburst and Wade had seemed to sense that she needed time to collect her thoughts and to process the bomb he'd dropped on her. She'd been shocked when he'd declared he had feelings for her. Stunned. It was the very last thing she'd expected him to admit.

Wordlessly, she glanced up at him in question. She was still wrapped solidly in his arms, ensconced in the comforting security and warmth of his embrace. His strength. She wasn't sure she could withstand any more of his unexpected confessions and she mentally braced for what was clearly occupying his thoughts.

He was regarding her intently, but no judgment or disgust was mirrored in his dark gaze. Somehow she found comfort in that when she had so little else to draw reassurance from.

"Did you ever have sex with Thomas? You said you wanted to but he said you were too young, but did you eventually?"

She was pathetically grateful he hadn't asked her if she'd *made love* with Thomas. Especially now when *Wade* had made love to her. Had shown her the difference between sex and making love, even if the thought freaked her out.

"No," she said in a low sorrowful voice.

"You regret that?" he asked in surprise.

"No! God no. But, Wade, I *would* have. I wanted to. I fancied myself in love with him. I already had our future mapped out. We'd consummate our relationship when I was old enough and ready, according to him, but I would have had sex with him regardless of whether I was eighteen or not and that shames me. I was envisioning home, heart, babies, all the things a young girl dreams of when she's been deprived of the hope of ever having those things."

"You have to stop holding yourself accountable for things you felt when you were still a child," he said gently. "How many have there been?"

She blinked, uncertain as to where this line of questioning was going. What he was leading up to. Surely he couldn't be jealous of other men or rather man she'd had sex with. She'd rather forget the entire embarrassing episode.

Heat burned her cheeks and she tried to look away, but Wade wouldn't let her. He simply stared at her, again with no judgment or accusation in his eyes. Just patient understanding as though he simply wanted to know everything there was to know about her. Her secrets, things she'd shared with no one. Things he wanted her to share—and trust—with him.

"Just one," she choked out. "And it took me years to work up the courage. Years to stop feeling guilt that I was in some way betraying a man who in no way deserved my loyalty or fidelity and also because after him, I didn't trust myself, my instincts, my choice in men. Because obviously my instincts had been all wrong. God, I was so stupid."

"Stop," he said harshly. "Just stop it, Eliza. Stop beating yourself up over the past. You can't change it. It's done and over with. But you can change the future. It's not written in stone, no matter that you refuse to believe that and you believe that you've already set the course for your destiny and have no choice but to see it through to the bitter end. Your end. And I will not allow that. Not now. Not ever."

"Why do you ask?" she asked defensively. "Why does it matter how many men I've slept with?"

"It matters because if you've only ever had sex with one other man, then I'd like to know why me. It's obvious sex is not casual to you. Was I just someone you wanted to fuck you to make you forget? Was I a convenient dick? Would any man in the right place at the right time have done? Would he have satisfied you?"

She looked at him in horror, mortified by having her crass words thrown back at her, much the way she'd thrown them at him. It was no less than she deserved after the way she'd treated him. Like he had been a convenient dick and that she'd been using him as some sort of emotional crutch, but it hadn't been that way. Not with Wade and she was at a loss as to explain why it had been different. Why he made her feel different. The way he made her feel scared her and made her feel vulnerable and open, as though he was the first person she'd ever let past her carefully constructed barriers. He *was* the first.

Seeming to sense her hesitation, Wade spoke. "You mean something to *me*, Eliza. I'm merely trying to ascertain whether I'm flying solo here or if maybe, just maybe, you aren't as immune to me as you'd like me to think. That maybe you have feelings for me buried under all that animosity we both use as a shield, protecting ourselves from the truth of just how much we mean to one another."

She froze, shoving her hands beneath the covers so he wouldn't see how badly shaken she was. How his words gave her a ridiculous thrill, and worse, allowed her the forbidden comfort of hope. But he wasn't fooled. He wasn't a man to ever be easily fooled. His eyes softened with so much tenderness and under-standing that it was all she could do not to dive into his arms and burrow as deeply beneath him as possible and hide from the world. Lean on him. Borrow his strength and invincibility because Eliza felt anything but invincible right now.

"Is it so hard to admit you feel something—anything—for me?" he asked with gentle patience she hadn't thought him ca-pable of.

She could swear she heard hurt and uncertainty in his voice, but that was impossible. Wade was made of stone. Impenetrable and at times so icy that he could make her shiver with one look. And he was nothing if not ultimately confident. He wore arro-gance like others wore clothing. Why would he *care* how she felt about him? Why was he acting like it mattered and why did she feel as though so much hinged on her answering him honestly and that if she chose wrong, she stood to lose more than she ever imagined?

Because he cared for her.

She was still shaken by his admission, because he wasn't a man to ever express his feelings and open himself up to rejection. How could she reject him when he'd put everything on the line for her?

He'd laid bare his soul and she'd given him nothing in return. Nothing at all. Not even her trust. He'd risked everything to come after her. Risked his life by refusing to back down and leave before Thomas discovered his presence. And Wade was not a man to ever put himself in a position of vulnerability. He was cloaked in shadows, much like herself. His past was nebulous and questionable. So was his present. And yet he'd opened himself to her in a way she'd never imagined him opening himself to another living soul. That more than anything told her that she meant something to him. Not something. Everything.

"I feel *too* much!" she nearly shouted, the words bursting free before she could call them back. "There, are you happy? Are you satisfied? Haven't you taken enough pieces from me? Will you not be finished until there's nothing left of me at all?"

He gathered her tightly in his arms, ignoring her angry protests, her attempts to push him away, her struggles and her tears of helpless rage and frustration. "Was that so hard?" he asked gruffly. "Baby, I don't want to take you apart piece by piece. I don't want to take until there's nothing left. Never that, my love. I want to give you everything in my power to give. I want to put all those pieces back together so you can be whole again. So you can be mine. My Eliza. Not this shell of her lying in my arms right now. I won't rest until I have *all* of her back."

"She isn't there," she said sadly. "She's never been there. She isn't even *real*. She's a role I've played for years while I've hidden like a coward from who and what I really am."

"No baby," he denied. "You became who you weren't *meant* to be. And just so you know, you sealed your fate when you told me you didn't hate me and that you cared for me. When you thought to protect me because I'm important to you. I'm not a patient man in any sense of the word. Except when it comes to something I want and something that is worth waiting for. I'll wait for fucking ever if that's what it takes, but you're mine, Eliza. *Mine.* And I don't give up what is mine without one hell of a fight. So prepare yourself for fucking war. Fair warning, I fight dirty and I don't fight fair. I'll do whatever I have to in order to make you mine."

"I'm not yours!" she said in desperation. "I don't belong to anyone."

The last was said with sadness heavy in her heart. Once she would have given anything to have belonged to someone. To be cared about, cherished, loved. But she'd given up those fanciful, unrealistic dreams a lifetime ago because they weren't real. Would never be real. No matter how hard she wished otherwise.

His gaze swept hotly over her naked body, possession glittering in his eyes.

"No?" he asked in a dangerously low voice that should have sent her bolting from the bed as fast as possible. But the steel bands around her body held her firmly in place. "I think perhaps another demonstration is in order."

Panic swept through her, but before she could react to his sultry statement and the glittering determination in his eyes that told her she was in way over her head, his mouth descended on hers. Hot, passionate and oh God, loving and so very tender that it brought the sting of tears to her eyes.

His tongue swept inside her mouth, delving deep until he tasted her and he was all she could taste. She tried to insert her hands between them, to push him away, but he merely held her more firmly, telling her without words that she wasn't escaping.

She let out a moan that was part desire and part despair. His kiss gentled and then he feathered his lips over her cheek, down her jawbone and then upward, pressing his mouth tenderly over both eyelids. He licked away the tiny evidence of moisture at the corners of her eyes even as his arms fully enveloped her, anchoring her body to his.

"You matter, Eliza," he whispered against her skin. "You matter to a lot of people, but you matter to me. To *me*. And I'm not letting you go now that I've finally gotten you where I want you."

He rotated, rolling until he was solidly atop her, his warmth and strength seeping into her very bones. When was the last time she truly felt safe? When was the last time she felt free to just . . . be? He overwhelmed her. Made her feel all the things he'd attributed to her. In his arms she truly felt precious. Important. Loved . . .

She shook her head in silent denial. She wouldn't—couldn't—go there. No one could ever love her. Find her worthy. How could they when she knew the truth? When she bore the sins of a lifetime and there would never be absolution for her. But God, he made her want. Just for a few precious moments, he made her dream of what could have been if she hadn't made so many mistakes.

"Whatever you're thinking, get it out of your head," Wade said fiercely. "Look at me, Eliza. Look only at me and see me."

Reluctantly she lifted her gaze to his, so afraid of what he'd see. Of the evil lurking beyond the façade she'd perfected over so many years. A knot formed in her throat, robbing her of the ability to speak, because there was only understanding. Gentleness and such tenderness that it made her want to weep all over again.

"You're so beautiful," he whispered, his lips hovering just above hers. "Inside and out. Never have I met a woman as fierce, loyal, loving and vulnerable as you. You break my heart, baby. And as God as my witness I'm going to piece every part of you back together so that one day you'll look in the mirror and see exactly what I see. A woman who stands for good. A woman who won't back down at the first sign of adversity. Someone who will go to the wall for those she loves. A protector of the innocent and bringer of justice. And you're mine."

Satisfaction was a savage light in his eyes as he announced his claim. He didn't wait for a response, not that she could have given him one anyway. He ravaged her mouth in a hungry kiss as if he were starved for her. As if he'd waited forever for this moment. It bewildered her. He bewildered her.

His mouth swept down her throat, his teeth grazing her sensitive skin, alternately sucking and nipping his way down to her breasts. Her hands fluttered to his shoulders but he quickly captured her wrists and pinned them above her head, holding her in place while he took possession of every inch of her flesh.

For a moment she struggled, not liking that she felt so helpless, but he raised his mouth to hers again, shushing her with a deep, spine-tingling kiss.

"You know I won't hurt you, baby," he said, his eyes full of tenderness. "But this is my show. I've waited for fucking ever to have you beneath me, mine to do with as I wish, and I'm going to savor every minute of it."

The lump in her throat grew larger. He couldn't possibly mean it. His words, his expression, the way he looked at her. It wasn't real. It couldn't be real. No one could ever love her. Not after knowing all she'd done.

"Stop," he said in a forceful voice. "Stop thinking and just feel. If you won't believe my words then I'll have to show you what you mean to me."

She stared at him with all the fear and vulnerability she felt. He had the power to destroy her. She, who admitted no weakness, no vulnerability, had realized that he held the key to her ultimate destruction. If he turned away from her after making her believe . . . She closed her eyes, unwilling to even think it. He could destroy her when nothing else had. He could do what even Thomas had been unable to accomplish and she hated being so powerless against Wade.

"Baby."

Just one word. So filled with the one thing she'd never allowed herself to even entertain. The one thing she had craved above all else. He kissed her again. And again. Then he began working his way once more down her body, lavishing so much caring in every kiss, every caress.

He pressed a kiss to her navel and then flicked his tongue into the shallow indention, causing an immediate eruption of chill bumps over her belly. He went lower still, gently parting her thighs, patiently waiting when she immediately went rigid. He merely waited, lifting his gaze to hers as though silently willing her to trust him. And oh God, she did. She did trust him.

Gradually she relaxed and he spread her legs, running the tip of his finger through the net of curls between her thighs. He grew bolder, parting the soft folds and then caressing the sensitive bundle of nerves at the very heart of her.

She cried out when his mouth followed suit and he carefully licked and then sucked the taut bud into his mouth. He licked his way downward, leaving no part of her most intimate flesh unattended. The tip of his tongue circled her opening and then delved within. Her back bowed off the bed in an unconscious plea for more. She wanted all of him.

"Wade, please," she cried.

Her outburst seemed to wrest his carefully wrought control from him as though he'd been using great restraint until now. Suddenly he was dominant and forceful, his body moving over hers, his eyes glittering with harsh need that matched her own.

Once again he pinned her wrists above her head, holding them tightly against the mattress so she was helpless to move. His big body covered hers in a blatant show of dominance as he fed ravenously from her mouth, her neck, bending lower to ravage her breasts.

No longer did he take things slow and sweet. He was showing her his ownership, that he'd never let her go now, and God, but she didn't even care. She wanted—needed—was desperate for release. Need clawed at her insides. Never had she felt anything to match this. Never had she even imagined needing someone the way she needed Wade.

He kneed her thighs apart, his turgid erection prodding urgently at her opening. In one thrust he was so deep inside her that she couldn't differentiate between the two of them. In that moment they were one person. One body. She gasped at the fullness but then he withdrew and hammered forward again, wringing a desperate cry from her.

She wanted to touch him, to caress him as he'd done her, but her arms were firmly captured against the bed, his hands wrapped around her wrists as he pounded into her over and over. And suddenly he yanked himself from her body and she whimpered her protest, suddenly bereft of his warmth, his comfort, his strength.

Before she could ask him what was wrong, he flipped her over onto her stomach and once more placed her arms above her head with a gruff command not to move them. Then he slid one strong arm underneath her belly and lifted her to her knees. When she would have raised her head, he gently placed his palm over her hair and pushed her head back to the pillow.

With her ass in the air, head down and arms above her, she felt . . . captured. Deliciously so. Arousal thrummed hotly in her veins. Wade wasn't finished with his show of ownership.

His fingers dug into her hips and then feathered over her behind. She felt the brush of his lips at the small of her back and she closed her eyes as her thighs were once again parted. Then he was on her, inside her, plunging so deep that she gasped and balled the sheets with her fingers into tight fists to stave off her impending orgasm. Not yet. Oh God, not yet. She closed her eyes as her body rocked forward with the force of Wade's thrusts.

He set a relentless pace, hard, deep, planting himself into her very soul. And yet through it all, his hands and mouth were gentle on her skin. So tender and sweet her heart ached. It was as if he were sending her a message, one she'd refused to hear verbally.

"How close are you, Eliza?" he asked hoarsely. "I want you with me, baby. Always with me."

"Close," she choked out. "Please don't stop, Wade. Please."

He pressed his lips between her shoulder blades and whispered against her skin. "You'll never have to ask me for anything that is within my power to give you."

As brutal and commanding as his pace had been earlier, he

slowed now, stroking leisurely, prolonging both their releases. And when it came, it was nothing like Eliza had ever experienced in her life. It was so beautiful and heartrending that she couldn't have spoken if she wanted.

Wade lowered his body to hers, following her down flat on the bed. He rolled to his side so she didn't bear his weight, still embedded deeply within her. He wrapped his arms solidly around her and held her tightly against his thudding chest. He buried his face in her neck and remained so for several long moments.

Emotion overwhelmed Eliza. As did regret. Tears streaked down her cheeks as she clutched at the arms wrapped firmly around her.

"Eliza?"

Wade sounded worried and unsure. He lifted one hand to wipe at her cheek.

"Baby, what is it? Did I hurt you?"

She shook her head mutely and then closed her eyes, her heart shattering into a million pieces.

"Oh God, Wade. What have I done? I can't let you fight my battles for me. I can't risk you. I can't lose you. It would destroy me," she said tearfully.

His grip tightened around her and he kissed her temple. "And you don't think it would destroy me if I lost you?"

SEVENTEEN

WADE woke, instinctively knowing that Eliza was no longer asleep beside him. She was sitting up, distance between them on the bed, her knees drawn to her chest, a pensive expression marring her beautiful features. She was miles away, her thoughts not pleasant judging by the slight frown and the sorrow in her eyes.

He shifted quietly so as not to disturb her and then sat up, closing the distance as he scooted toward her, not wanting any space between them. He wrapped his arms around her, pulling her side to his chest. She surprised him by laying her head on his chest and emitting a soft sigh that told him he'd been correct that her thoughts were not happy ones.

"What are you thinking?" he asked quietly, brushing a kiss over the top of her head.

"What a mess I've gotten you into," she said in a low tone filled with regret.

"I don't remember giving you a choice," he said dryly.

"He has to be taken out, Wade," she said earnestly. "I can't—won't—just let it go. You can't ask me to do that."

"He needs to be taken down," he agreed. "But you will have nothing to do with it. I will not let you face that bastard again. Ever."

"Then we have to come up with a plan that will work," she said, for the first time giving him any indication that she was accepting his help.

He tightened his hold on her, shaken by her quiet acceptance and humbled by her trust, even if she hadn't given him those exact words.

"We will."

"I have an idea," she began.

"Do I want to hear this?" he asked, his tone one of clear warning.

"You can't barge into that town and let it be known you're looking for him or that you have any interest whatsoever in him. He'll know, Wade. And then whatever plan you've come up with will be useless. It has to be me."

He was already shaking his head. No way. No fucking way was he putting her in harm's way.

"Just listen to me, please. I've given this a lot of thought."

"All right," he said grudgingly. "I'll listen but that's all I can promise you."

"I've already announced my presence in town. Not in so many words, but I've been seen. Made certain I was seen and that people knew who I was. They know I'm back and I've seen the disdain and disgust in their eyes. They blame me every bit as much as they blame Thomas. Maybe more so because they believe I should have been punished too and in their eyes I got away with murder, my role in those murders, and I went free while Thomas was sentenced to jail time."

Wade's jaw tightened and he was filled with murderous rage.

"He goes free tomorrow so I only have one more day and I need to make the most of it. I need to go back into town. Let it slip that I'm waiting. Let it be known where I am, wherever here is. Bait the trap. Because he'll come for me. He won't be able to control himself. We set a trap for him and when he shows, then we take him down."

"I take him down," Wade said firmly.

She shrugged. "You, me, as long as it's done but I won't let you take the rap for me, Wade. I won't. I'll claim full responsibility and nothing you can say will make me change my mind."

He wanted to shake some sense into her stubborn head. God, but the woman infuriated him even as he admired her sense of justice.

"Your team is headed to Calvary today," he said, bracing for her reaction.

"*What?*"

She paled and began to tremble, her eyes wide with fear and panic.

"Baby, do you honestly think they'd just sit on their hands when someone as important to them as you is in danger? When you wrote what amounted to a fucking goodbye letter and scared the ever living fuck out of them? Dane was completely unhinged. Lost his shit. It took everything I had and all manner of threats to make them sit on their hands for at least twenty-four hours until I could talk to you and we could come up with a plan of action. You matter to them, Eliza. Every bit as much as they matter to you and if you don't think so then you must not have a very high opinion of the people you work with."

"They can't be here," Eliza said, her voice shaking, tears welling in her eyes. "Oh God, Wade, I can't lose them. I can't lose you. Can't you understand that? It would kill me if anything happened to *any* of you."

"And you think you're expendable? You're wrong. Dead wrong. You matter a hell of a lot to a lot of people and there is no way in hell any of us are going to stand back and let you take the fall for something you hold no responsibility for."

She buried her face in his chest and wrapped her arms around his neck, clinging desperately to him.

"What do we do?"

"Now that I have a better handle on the situation, I'm going to call Dane and tell him to be very fucking discreet and not to barge into town asking a bunch of questions that will raise suspicion. Their job will be to shadow Harrington once he's released from jail and monitor his movements. They're the best. He won't know he's being watched. But I want to know what he's doing, where he's going, so we're prepared for any eventuality.

"As much as I fucking hate the idea of you going into town, you're right in that it will be you he goes after and if he knows you're with me then he's not going to think you're an easy target and that's precisely what we want him to think. So you lay the seeds, leave a trail so you are not hard to find and with DSS trailing him plus my own team here for your protection then he'll be walking right into our hands, which is exactly what we want. But you will not face him. You will not confront him. He's mine, Eliza.

"But you aren't going anywhere alone. I'll be there, you just won't see me. My men will be there but you won't see them either. They're the best at what they do and no one will ever see them unless they want to be seen. That's all I'm willing to compromise on. If you can't deal with that, then we go with plan B."

"What's plan B?" Eliza asked fearfully.

"Plan B is me handcuffing you to this bed and me leaving my men to protect you while I go into town and make it known that you're with me and making sure Harrington gets wind of it."

"Not much of a choice," she muttered against his chest.

He smiled. "No, but it's the only two choices you get."

She sighed. "Then we'll go with plan A. I need to get up and get into town early. The diner is crowded for breakfast and with Thomas being released in a day, the town is a flurry of activity. All the locals are out. Most know I'm back and they don't want to miss any drama unfolding. The media will be rolling in as well. It's going to be a circus."

Wade scowled because the very last thing he wanted was that kind of exposure for Eliza. She'd suffered the judgment of others for far too long and they'd crucify her, not only in town but in the media as well. It went against every grain for him to allow his woman to be hurt and tormented like that, but he also knew he had no choice if he wanted to permanently remove the threat of Thomas Harrington so Eliza could finally achieve the peace she so greatly deserved.

"I need to check in with Dane and make damn sure he knows what he and his team are to do and nothing more. They'll be on the move shortly. I expect them to arrive by this afternoon and I need them in place. You want coffee?"

Her face softened at his offer but shook her head. "I'll just shower and get dressed and head to the diner and have breakfast and coffee there. Go ahead and make your call and then let me know what's going down."

She paused a second, sorrow flashing in her eyes.

"Tell Dane . . . tell him I'm sorry I let him down."

"You didn't let anyone down," Wade said fiercely. "They aren't angry with you, Eliza. They're worried sick about you."

She nodded but the sadness didn't leave her eyes as she gently extricated herself from his arms and got up to head for the shower. Wade didn't waste any time placing the call to Dane.

After outlining everything Eliza had shared and listening to Dane curse long and hard, Wade outlined the plan and what he wanted Dane and his operatives to do. It clearly didn't sit well with Dane not to take action and to be low-key but Wade was firm and reinforced his instructions with the fact that if they didn't follow them to the letter, they could get not only members of Dane's team killed but also Eliza.

"I need your best on this, Elliot," Wade said with utter gravity. "Their job is to not be seen or noticed and to go absolutely undetected. Their only assignment is to tag Harrington the minute he's released from custody and to shadow his every movement undetected. One wrong move and people die. And if anything happens to Eliza because one of your men fucks up, I'll have his head and *yours*. We clear?"

"We don't fuck up," Dane said, ice dripping from every word. "We'll shadow him and when he makes his move, we'll be there when this all goes down. You just make sure that Eliza is safe at all times. *You* get her killed and I'll have your balls."

"Understood," Wade said smoothly. "Now, how soon can you get up here?"

"We're already on our way."

There was a brief pause and then Dane grew quiet.

"You take care of her, Sterling. Make sure *you* don't fuck up. I'm trusting you with one of the most important people in my life. And tell her . . . tell her I'll always have her back and that isn't ever going to change. I don't profess to know what's going on in her head right now other than she's a goddamn mess, but you make damn sure she knows that nothing changes between us or anyone at DSS. She's ours and she will always be ours."

EIGHTEEN

TRUE to his word, Wade was not visible, nor did she spot any of his men, and he'd introduced her to them before she'd left the safe house to go into town. But she could *feel* his gaze and how she could discern his from the many other stares she was receiving mystified her, but she *knew* it was him. His interference and determination to protect her should annoy her—had annoyed her in the beginning—but now she drew comfort knowing he was so close even if she couldn't actually see him.

Knowing—feeling—that he was watching her, never taking his eyes off her warmed her all the way through and made her feel . . . safe. More than safe. Cherished.

Rare and precious.

Those words he'd said with absolute sincerity, words she hadn't put much stock in at the time, now meant something because he made her believe them, or at least made her believe that he believed them. He made her feel all of those things. Safe. Cherished. Rare and precious. And it was a heady, foreign sensation. Never before had she been made to feel so important to someone.

Oh sure, at sixteen she'd convinced herself that Thomas made her feel special but after learning of his abilities and the fact that the moment he was no longer able to manipulate her, her true feelings for him had emerged. He'd made her feel what he wanted her to feel. He'd wanted her to be as obsessed with him as he was with her, but it wasn't real and it had taken her far too long to recognize that.

Never would she forget leaving the courthouse, Thomas's hold on her no longer existing, and the veritable storm of emotions that had swamped her. Anger, humiliation, sorrow but most of all . . . hatred. In that moment she'd hated him with every bit as much passion as she'd once loved him. The realization that she had never truly loved him at all had ripped the few remaining vestiges of her soul into irreparable shreds. Because she'd allowed him to make her feel things she hadn't ever truly felt for him. It had all been a carefully orchestrated deception, her choices taken, leaving her powerless to his control. She'd felt violated. Raped. Not physically but emotionally because he'd raped her mind, had taken everything from her and left her with nothing.

She hated him for giving her false hopes and dreams. For making her believe for a brief time that all the things she'd longed for her entire life were finally hers and leaving her crushed beyond repair because where she *had* nothing before, now she *was* nothing. Unworthy, unloved without the ability to ever dream of better again. She didn't deserve better and never would. And damn Wade Sterling for giving her the first stirring of hope when she'd refused to ever travel down a path that only led to heartbreak and shattered dreams.

Rare and precious? It was a lie. The idea that he had made love to her was a lie. It was sex. Nothing more and she was a fool for pretending even for a few beautiful, stolen hours.

She exited the diner after an hour-long breakfast where she'd suffered the scrutiny of countless gawkers. It seemed that the entire damn town suddenly descended on the diner to the point it was standing room only, all tables filled and no space available at the long bar by the register where people usually sat when they were only having coffee or just eating alone.

Some didn't even make the pretense of being there to eat. They walked by her table at the window, staring shamelessly, judgment in their eyes, disapproval twisting their lips. Some openly sneered. A few bolder than the ones who looked and judged in silence made no secret of their contempt and had no issue voicing it loudly enough to be heard in the crowded diner.

Eliza never responded, never said a word. She ate in silence, not giving anyone the satisfaction of getting a reaction from her.

Her shoulders sagged as soon as she was down the block and out of sight of the prying eyes from the diner. Her eyes briefly closed and the courage and bravado she'd clung to like a shield for the last hour seeped from her bones like a deflating balloon. Her hands shook and she stuffed them into the pockets of her jacket, refusing to allow anyone to see her outward show of weakness.

And then she felt it again. A warm prickle of awareness that immediately melted the ice forming in her soul. Wade. She didn't even bother turning to look for him. She knew she wouldn't find him. Just knowing he was there bolstered her flagging reserves. It comforted her and terrified her in equal parts.

When had she ever depended on anyone except herself?

Yeah, she depended on Dane, her team, but in a professional capacity and they depended on her every bit as much as she depended on them. They had to in order to keep each other alive. There was no such reciprocity when it came to Wade and there was nothing professional about her sudden dependency. It was personal and she had no idea how the hell it happened or when.

Or why she wasn't fighting it. Why was she accepting it? Had she not just moments before chided herself for being stupid and for believing the lies that both she and Wade were guilty of believing?

Had she turned into the very thing that had gotten her into this horrific mess to start with? A needy, clingy woman wanting to be loved, equating sex with something more and becoming emotionally attached to a man who until a few days ago she had loathed the very sight of and expecting more and reading more into the situation because it reopened an old wound and reawakened the fierce longing to love and be loved?

Or had she become so adept at hiding her emotions, closing herself off to others and lying to herself that she hadn't recognized the simple truth that she'd been fiercely attracted to Wade Sterling from the very first time she'd gotten into his face and snarled at him?

It's a lie, Eliza. It's all a lie. Stop doing this to yourself.

Movement in her periphery diverted her attention from the disastrous direction her thoughts were headed and she gratefully turned, welcoming the reprieve, even knowing it was temporary because now that she'd finally been honest with herself and acknowledged what had been staring her in the face for months, she knew that those thoughts—and Wade—weren't simply going away.

Her brow furrowed and she frowned as she viewed the convoy of media vans driving down Main Street, stopping, to her dismay, directly in front of the diner and parking alongside the grassy knoll in front of the courthouse.

People poured out of the diner and Eliza shrank back, taking refuge in the tight space between two buildings where she could see but not be easily seen by others. Camera crews got out and began setting up equipment on the grass while reporters and their cameramen did a check of their mics. One even began rolling footage with the reporter looking into the camera, a serious expression on her face as she gave her report.

What the hell was going on? Surely Thomas's release wouldn't cause *this* kind of uproar. Local coverage, yeah. Eliza would have expected that. But there was a CNN crew as well as media personnel from Fox News. In addition to the national media, there were also crews from news stations in Portland and Salem. Hell, even California and Washington state had crews here, San Francisco and Seattle being the most prominent.

What the ever loving fuck?

A prickle of apprehension chased away the awareness of Wade's vigilant gaze as she took in the hubbub and the ever growing crowd gathering at the now roped off area between the street and the grassy area where the media had set up camp. Damn it, she needed to get closer so she could find out what was up. The last thing she needed was *this* much focus and awareness.

This could well fuck up her one and only chance at taking Thomas down for good and there was no way in hell she was letting the bastard slip through her fingers, enabling him to pick up where he left off. Torturing, raping and killing women who were powerless once he had them in his thrall.

As she stepped from her hiding place, she could actually feel the heat of Wade's angry stare. Could hear him in her mind telling her to get the fuck away and not take unnecessary risks. She was only doing what she'd set out to do and what she and Wade had agreed that she would do. Make sure her presence was noted and not be discreet about where she was staying.

With that in mind, she strode swiftly toward the crowd, half afraid Wade would suddenly appear and haul her away. When she reached the edge of the crowd where a dozen or so people hung back more loosely, choosing to observe from a distance, she stopped, pretending interest in the goings-on in front of her.

But she took in the people closest to her from the corner of her eye, looking for her best option to approach. Only two seemed not to have noticed her yet, so hoping to catch one of them off guard and not give them time to recognize her, judge and then dismiss her, she skirted around behind the others and approached the older of the two men who hadn't appeared to have noticed her presence yet.

"What on earth is going on?" Eliza asked in a breathy, excited sounding voice.

She had positioned herself slightly to the left but behind the man so he would have to turn to see her fully.

"Big press conference happening tomorrow," the man muttered as he began turning.

Eliza braced, curling her hands still stuffed in her pockets into tight fists as she waited for the inevitable.

He stared at her a long moment, regarding her thoughtfully. "You're her, aren't you? That girl who turned that sadistic bastard in to the police and then testified against him at his trial."

To Eliza's complete surprise there was no disgust or

condemnation in his eyes or expression. It was such an over-whelming pleasant surprise that she found herself dropping the act of the lovesick fool who'd come back for her man when he was released.

"Yes," she whispered.

"It was a brave thing you did, young lady. You were only a child. Not many would have had the guts to do what you did."

There was honest to God sincerity and admiration in his tone and his eyes were kind but she also saw pity.

"Why is there going to be a press conference?" she asked, pressing her momentary advantage and the fact he hadn't already turned away in disgust. She needed all the intel she could gather because this had not been expected and it could put a serious kink in the meticulous, cold-blooded vengeance plan she'd spent days and weeks putting together.

Now disgust blatantly chased away the softness to his features, but it wasn't directed at her. He shook his head, anger flashing in his eyes. He jabbed his thumb over his back in the direction of the media crews setting up on the lawn of the courthouse.

"There's going to be some huge, nationally televised press conference when that spawn of Satan gets out of jail tomorrow."

Eliza's brow furrowed in genuine confusion and it took every bit of her will to control her growing agitation. "Why on earth would this gain the attention of networks like CNN and Fox News?"

"He asked for one. You didn't know? It's all everyone is talking about."

Eliza smiled, or tried, but even she knew it was a pathetic attempt. "No one here speaks to me, or rather some do, but they don't exactly strike up a conversation. They tell me exactly what they think about me and then go on their way. So no, I didn't know."

Pity once again flashed in the older man's eyes, this time more pronounced, and it made Eliza inwardly flinch. She wasn't sure which was worse. The obvious hatred directed at her or pity. Neither was welcome or pleasant.

"Not right the way they're treating you," he muttered. Then he paused a moment and cocked his head, studying her until she was almost twitching with discomfort. "If you didn't know about the press conference, then why are you here? Why would you come back to a place where you're treated like garbage and people make no secret of their hatred? Word is you're still in love with him and you're here for him, but I don't buy that. It's been a long time. If you were that in love with him and willing to take him back after what he did, then you would have never turned him in and faced him in a courtroom and named him for what he was."

Eliza clenched her jaw and inhaled rapidly, vowing to fight the sudden sting of tears that threatened to well.

"I didn't believe it," she said softly, telling a half truth. "I couldn't believe they could set him free after what he did. I had to know, to see for myself."

"Going to give you some advice, girl. Get out of town and get as far away as possible and do it now while you have the chance. He's got something up his sleeve. Most people in his position where everyone knows he's guilty as hell and got off because of some ridiculous loophole and a dumb-as-a-brick cop not doing his job worth a damn would get out quietly. They'd leave quietly and they wouldn't want to garner attention or notice. They'd move somewhere they could blend so no one would ever know who he was and what he did. But him? The arrogant bastard had his lawyer call up every network they could think of to set up a press conference on the lawn of the court-house where he was convicted and he's going straight to that press conference the minute he's released."

Jesus. This was not good news. Not good at all. It was a fuck-ing nightmare with the potential to be more horrifying than anything he'd previously done.

"You need to go," the man said gently. "People are starting to stare. They're talking and they're angry and just looking for someone to blame and to take their anger out on. But the biggest reason you need to leave right away is because that man will be looking for revenge and you are the only reason he spent the last ten years in prison. He's had a lot of time to think on that and to dream about getting his revenge. You aren't safe here. The people in this town hate you, blame you. Thomas Harrington hates you and blames you as well. It shames me to say this because I've lived here all my life and most of the people who live here are good people, but not many would be sorry to see you suf-fer. And just as many would celebrate if Harrington does get to you. So go now. Get out of here while you can and may God be with you."

"Thank you," Eliza said, barely able to get the words out. "Your kindness means more than you'll ever know. I'll never for-get you or your kindness."

"You can thank me by staying alive. Get out, girl. Do it now and do it fast and never look back. There's nothing here for you but judgment, pain and misery. You deserve better than that."

Impulsively, Eliza reached out and grabbed the wrinkled,

work-worn hand, squeezing it, her fingers trembling with emotion. Then she withdrew her hand and turned away, not trusting herself to say anything further. She left the crowd, ignoring the looks, the comments, and she kept walking, pulling her jacket around her, a barrier, not to the cold, but to the condemnation thrown at her from every direction.

One more day. Less than twenty-four hours now and she had only that much time to reassess her options and adapt because she would not fail this time. She would succeed at any cost and no one, especially not Wade, would die because of her.

Because she could call what she felt for Wade a lie for an eternity and exist in the same state of denial that got her in over her head years ago, but she knew the truth. It was raw and it was painful, as only the truth can be, but what she felt for Wade, what he made her feel for him and the fact that he gave her a taste of the forbidden—hope—and one night of feeling loved was no lie.

It was real. Too real. And it scared the ever loving hell out of her because she could not allow her deepest secrets, the hopes and dreams she'd never shared with anyone or the longing for what Wade offered to be real and not just a hopeless dream interfere with her objective, distract her or sway her from her mission.

Too many lives depended on her having the strength to carry out and execute her plan. A mission that had consumed her very existence the moment she'd received that horrifying phone call telling her Thomas would become a free man in a couple short weeks.

She lived the mission. She ate, breathed and slept—the few times she could sleep—the mission and nothing, not even the promise of experiencing the beauty she'd never had and had once wanted more than anything in the world, would interfere with her destiny.

Some would call it revenge. Others would call it retaliation. Few would say justice had been served. But to Eliza, it was none of those things. They didn't even factor in.

For her, this was love. The love she'd been denied for most of her life but had finally seen it, witnessed it, experienced it for what it truly was. Love was sacrifice. Love was being willing to do anything to protect someone you loved. Love was making the hardest decision you would ever face in a lifetime and then when it was done, knowing you'd do it all over again with no hesitation, no regrets.

Not many would understand Eliza's reasoning or what it meant to her. But for her, it was simple and uncomplicated. Her task, her mission, the necessary evil she had undertaken without a second thought, no hesitation and no regret was for love.

And there was no sacrifice too great for love.

For Wade.

Oh God. She couldn't lie to herself anymore. This wasn't her. She'd always been nothing but honest with herself. Too honest at times. Wade meant something to her. And she was so mixed up, confused and conflicted but above all else, for the first time she felt hope. And damn it, but it felt good. Better than good. And it was Wade who'd given her that gift. It was Wade who put himself out there, made himself vulnerable while she'd held back, refusing to give him back what he gave to her.

He'd told her she mattered. That she was important to him. He cared. About her! God only knew she'd done nothing to merit his regard, the patience and tenderness he displayed.

She'd treated him reprehensibly, and worse, she'd tried to use him. Like he wasn't human and didn't have feelings or emotions. She'd erected a concrete wall between them so he couldn't get in, couldn't see past the façade she'd spent a decade perfecting. And yet somehow, he'd slipped right past her barriers, had dug deep below the surface of the caustic camouflage she wore like she was born with it and had found the real Eliza beneath all the anger, fear, bullshit and the dozen other roles she donned out of self-preservation and he'd handled the real Eliza with care and so much tenderness and understanding that she ached just remembering it all.

Wade was dark and broodingly handsome, a lethal combination that made women throw themselves at him whenever he walked into a room. He was wealthy with a dangerous edge that only added to his already considerable appeal. He could have any woman he wanted with no more effort than a crook of his finger, so why the hell had he chosen her?

Was he a masochist? What man in their right mind would even consider a woman with so many issues that it would take hours to list them all? He should be running as fast and as far away as possible now that he knew the real Eliza, but he'd done none of those things.

He was still here. Watching over her with a careful, attentive eye. Taking her back, protecting her. Laying the law down about her having no part in a face-to-face meeting with Thomas. He didn't want her within a mile of Thomas at any time.

Eliza had never been in love. She'd seen it, had experienced the beauty and selflessness of it through the eyes of others, but she had no personal experience with it at all.

But what were the feelings she had for Wade if not love?

How could he make her feel so much and how could she be so overwhelmed by even the simplest tender gesture if it wasn't love? Did she love Wade? Was this what love really felt like? How would she even know when nothing about her "love" for Thomas had been real. Not a single damn part of it.

As a result, she didn't trust herself anymore when it came to her emotions. Never again did she want to willingly hand someone so much power over her. It scared her, but at the same time, there was a yearning so deep within her that had never been filled, a fanciful dream that she had resigned herself to never achieving, never living.

Those things were for other people. Deserving people. Good people. Like the people she worked with. They weren't for the likes of her. This was her penance for her sins. To live her life without such beauty that it hurt to look at two people who loved each other with everything they had.

Did she love Wade? Did she experience that beauty when she was in his arms? She couldn't answer that. Yet. She was too afraid to dig any deeper than she already had because she was terrified of what she might discover and she couldn't afford any distractions at this stage of the endgame.

If she survived and if a second miracle occurred and she didn't spend the rest of her life in jail, then she would try to solve the mystery of Wade Sterling and why she was so off balance with him. And why she had no defense against him when her defenses were impenetrable and no one got by them unless she allowed it.

Wade had stormed into her life as though concrete barriers didn't even faze him. It was embarrassing just how easily he saw past her guard, how he slipped right by her and was there right in the heart of her before she even realized he was there.

Love. Beauty. Hope.

Three things she'd been denied and were forbidden to her. Three things that in a matter of a few days she'd finally experienced firsthand and not through the eyes of others. Three things that she now knew she could no longer live without, yet she very much feared that she would have no choice and it would devastate her to lose them now that she knew how very wonderful they were.

She would have rather never touched the sun and experienced the beauty that Wade had so unselfishly given her than to have been shown what she'd been missing all her life only to have it cruelly yanked away.

You don't miss what you never had. But you mourn what you had and lost forever.

An old saying came to mind, one she'd never paid much attention to. Until now and she realized she didn't at all agree with the sentiment.

It's better to have loved and lost than to have never loved at all.

Because if she allowed herself to love Wade and lost him, it would destroy her in a way that Thomas never could.

NINETEEN

ELIZA winced when the door opened and slammed with enough force to shake the walls just seconds after she herself had entered the safe house. Slowly she turned to face a very furious Wade. His expression was black and ominous as he stalked toward her.

"What part of me telling you that you were to follow my instructions to the letter did you not understand?" he barked, fury blazing in his eyes.

Her eyes narrowed and she refused to be cowed or to back down even if he was a seething mass of pissed off alpha male.

"And what instructions did I supposedly not follow to the letter, oh lord and master," she said sweetly, sarcasm dripping from every word.

"Damn it, Eliza! You could have been hurt," he roared. "That entire crowd was in a feeding frenzy and just looking for someone to take out their anger on. They would have turned on you in a heartbeat and I could be visiting you in the hospital right now or identifying your body in the fucking morgue."

Some of her annoyance faded and she relaxed her stance, recognizing he wasn't as angry with her as he'd been worried. Very worried. She softened her tone, losing the sarcasm.

"I had to find out what was going on, Wade. We have a big problem and we now have less than twenty-four hours to make adjustments to our plan of action because the arrogant son of a bitch called a goddamn *press* conference, and whatever he fed the news sources must have been of major interest because in addition to local coverage, there are stations from San Francisco and Seattle and there's a fucking CNN and a Fox News crew setting up to cover the event."

Wade's lips tightened and his jaw bulged and then he swore viciously.

"He's up to something," Eliza said quietly. "And whatever it is, it isn't good. He's setting up his play and God only knows what he has up his sleeve."

"That much is obvious. You think he's made us or any of your people?"

Eliza shrugged. "I don't see how he could have. He's not free yet. He may have eyes and ears on the ground here, but my guys are good. You and your men are good. No way Thomas could know anything except that I'm here."

Wade's expression grew savage. She knew he realized the implications of her last statement. That she was here meant whatever he had planned definitely involved her. Then in direct contrast to the anger vibrating his entire body, he gently cupped her cheek and caressed her chin and lips with the pad of his thumb.

"What did the old man say to you?"

There was concern and a distinct edge of protectiveness in his voice.

A knot formed in her throat and, against her will, tears burned the edges of her eyelids.

"What the fuck did he say to you?" Wade demanded fiercely.

She shook her head to let him know he had no reason to be angry with the man who'd spoken to her because he looked as though he was about to go hunt the guy down and mete out serious retribution for causing her upset.

"He was nice," Eliza choked. "He's the only person in this entire town who not only was nice but expressed concern for me. He warned me and told me I needed to get out now and go as far away as possible, as quickly as possible."

"Is that all?" Wade asked gently.

She shook her head again. "He told me that what I did took a lot of courage. That what I did was brave." The last came out strangled, conveying that the idea of being called brave when she'd been anything but appalled her.

"He was absolutely right," Wade said, giving her a look that dared her to argue.

"He said everyone thought I was here now because I'm still in love with Thomas and that I came so we could be together when Thomas was released but that he didn't believe that for a minute. Then he asked me *why* I was here."

"And what did you say?"

"I told him that I couldn't believe it. Couldn't believe they would let him go free after what he did and that I had to see for myself."

She finished in a whisper and then Wade wrapped his arms around her, holding her tightly as he soothingly ran his fingers through her hair. She closed her eyes and related everything the man had said to her and his warning that Thomas would seek revenge.

Wade's hold around her went still and his body coiled, his muscles going rigid. She could feel the fury simmering within him, emanating from him in waves. Eliza knew what she had to tell him, what she had to do could very well shatter the control he was barely clinging to.

But she'd save that for last. He needed to know the first before and then maybe he'd take what she said next a little better. Or so she hoped.

"He won't hurt me," she whispered. "He's obsessed with me. Has always been obsessed with me. He's sick, twisted and a complete monster, but he treated me like a princess. Like I was the most precious thing in the world."

When Wade grew even more rigid, she hurried to explain.

"I'm not defending him, Wade. I'm trying to explain him, how he was, how demented he was. How could he have treated me like a queen while torturing and raping and murdering other women? It sickened me to know that I was spared that treatment because he loved me, put me on a fucking pedestal convinced I was perfect and couldn't bring himself to ever hurt me and so he slaked his perversions on others."

Wade pressed his lips to the top of her head and simply held her as she continued the painful recount.

"He will want me back, yes. But he won't use violence. He won't seek revenge or hurt me. He'll attempt to manipulate me like he used to. Nothing I felt for him then was real. My feelings for him weren't my own. They were his. He planted the thoughts, feelings, emotions he wanted me to have for him and he manipulated every aspect of my life. My actions. I thought it was all real, that what I felt for him was my choice, my decision. It wasn't until I walked out of that courtroom and his connection to me was finally severed that my real feelings emerged and, God, I was sick to my soul over what I allowed him to do. What I allowed myself to become. And how pathetically weak and needy I was that I was such an easy conquest for him. I have never hated like I hated him in that moment. *That* was real. *That* was me. Finally myself and capable of having feelings not orchestrated by Thomas. Hatred and revulsion were my true feelings. Because God help me, Wade, even when I discovered what he was, what he'd done, even when I went to the police and when I testified against him, I loved him. I was heartbroken and felt like I was betraying him for turning against him. I still loved him and I can never forget that. Can never forgive myself."

"Oh baby," Wade said, his voice aching with sorrow and regret.

"And that's what he'll try to do again," she said, forging ahead, needing to get everything out. There was so much to do before tomorrow and it was going to take everything she had to convince Wade to go along with her plan.

"He'll be convinced that all he'll have to do is plant feelings for him, make me think I love him and then he'll sweep in and take me away so we can finally be together."

"Can he?" Wade asked, worry giving his words an edge. "Can he still do that?"

"He'll think he can," Eliza said grimly. "And that's all that matters. But no. *Never* again. I've spent years working to strengthen my mental barriers. I researched endlessly, reading every article, study, book I could get my hands on dealing with psychic powers and strengthening mental barriers that make people susceptible to psychic influence."

She pulled slightly away from Wade, returning the gesture he'd made moments before. She cupped his face, staring earnestly into his eyes.

"I didn't know any better then. I didn't know what love or hate was. So it was easy for him to convince me that what I felt for him was love and that it was real. But then I felt hate when he was no longer manipulating my thoughts and feelings. And the hate was so much stronger, so much more powerful than the love I was made to feel for Thomas because that love wasn't real," she said fiercely. "But my hate was. It was very real and it was mine. It belonged to me and wasn't controlled by anyone else. That was when I understood the difference between what was real and what was merely a manifestation of childish fantasies and hopeless wishes and that I was a naïve idiot for believing in dreams coming true."

"Will he know he can no longer control you?" Wade asked, his brows drawn together in concern. "And how certain are you that you can block him now?"

There was a hint of fear in his tone, one that made Eliza realize that Wade feared losing her to the man who'd once controlled every aspect of her life. A man she had freely admitted she'd once loved and would have done anything for. A man she'd planned forever with.

"No one will *ever* control me again," she said through clenched teeth. "I'll have to be careful to keep my emotions in control because he's as adept at reading emotion as he is thoughts. He will recognize that I am different. That he won't be able to have me under his thumb with minimal effort. But the advantage is mine. He won't hurt me, but I'll kill the son of a bitch without a second thought."

"No the hell you will not," Wade growled. "We've been over this, baby. You aren't even getting close to him."

Eliza took a small step back, steeling herself for the explosion that was about to erupt.

"I have to be at that press conference tomorrow," she said quietly.

Wade's eyes darkened, black like a midnight storm. It was obvious he was making a concerted effort not to completely lose it right then and there. He swallowed hard, his lips parting and then snapping shut as if thinking better of what he'd been about to say.

"Fuck no," he finally said, his breaths coming in rapid spurts, his nostrils flaring with the force of each inhale as he fought for control. "Have you lost your goddamn mind? Forget for a moment the threat of Thomas and the fact that everyone in this goddamn town has it out for you and let's focus on the fact that the media will be crawling all over the place. They'll eat you alive. You'll be on every television in the fucking country and they'll crucify you. They'll vilify and condemn you with or without actual facts. The plan is for Thomas to come to you where I'll be waiting for him."

"I don't plan to stay the entire time," Eliza said calmly. "Just long enough for him to see me. I *want* him to see me. And I want him to think I'm there for him and waiting. As soon as I've made certain he's seen me, I'll leave and then we proceed as we planned. Dane and his team will monitor Thomas at all times and track his movements. Your men will maintain a tight perimeter around the safe house. He's not invincible, Wade. He won't be hard to take out."

"It's never a good idea to underestimate one's opponent," Wade warned. "Damn it, Eliza, you don't need to be there. I don't want you there. You've suffered enough. Why put yourself through hell all over again by showing up at a press conference everyone in town will be at where your presence will only confirm what they think they already know? I don't want that for you. Haven't you suffered enough?"

She closed the distance she'd put between them and wrapped her arms around Wade's waist and hugged him fiercely, laying her cheek against the solid reassurance of his heartbeat.

"This is something I have to do for me," she said quietly, pleading with him to understand. To know that she had to do this and couldn't just stand idly by while someone else solved all her problems for her. "For so long I felt helpless and hopeless. Then I felt hatred and bitterness but also guilt, grief and overwhelming sorrow. The guilt was the worst. I saw those women every single night when I closed my eyes. They haunted me for years. Things got a little better when I met Dane and he recruited me for DSS. I grew up and learned to be more self-reliant. The nightmares became less frequent but they never went completely away. I thought that Thomas was completely behind me, at least in the sense that I'd never again have to see him and I drew comfort from the knowledge that I was finally free. I had a good life. Good friends. People I cared about and who cared about me. They taught me so much. And I drew comfort from knowing that Thomas would be spending the rest of his life in prison paying for his sins and that while I was finally living free and happy, he would never have those things.

"I won't lie. I used to lie awake at night and wish that I could face him one last time. So he would know that he didn't own me, that he never had *me*. So I could tell him that hell was too good for him. I dreamed of killing him. And not quickly or mercifully. In those moments I was no better than him," she said painfully. "Because I imagined doing to him exactly what he'd done to the women he tortured and killed. I imagined him suffering until he begged for death. I wanted him to feel what those women felt. I wanted him to hurt. And I wanted to be the last face he saw before he took his final breath. I wanted him to see me smiling, victorious, and for him to know that I beat him and that I'm stronger than he is. Worse than the fact that it makes me no better than him, I feel no shame, no remorse and no regret for wishing with all my heart that somehow I could make that dream a reality."

She lifted her head, dread heavy in her heart as she slowly lifted her gaze to Wade's.

"*That's* who I am, Wade. I'm not special. I don't stand for what's right. And I'm not rare or precious. The woman I just described? That's who and what I am. Can you honestly stand there and tell me that's the kind of woman you'd want any part of? The kind of woman you'd want in your life?"

"Eliza?"

She swallowed and glanced up again fearfully. In agony over what she'd see in his eyes. Bracing herself for the inevitable rejection and judgment she found in the eyes of so many others.

"Don't say another goddamn word," Wade said in a clearly pissed off tone. "Jesus, woman. You still don't get it."

Her gaze turned to bewilderment as she searched his face for some clue of what he was thinking. And what was it she still didn't get? She opened her mouth to ask but he growled low in his throat and framed her face between his hands. His gaze was piercing but no longer angry. There was frustration, worry and something else she was afraid to examine too closely because it did funny things to her heart and she had the sudden urge to run, to hide. To do what she was best at and avoid allowing people in. That something in his eyes that suddenly made her question her assessment of herself scared her and thrilled her all at the same time as she waited, not even breathing, for what he was going to say next.

"Not. Another. Fucking. Word. I've had enough of the shit that isn't even close to being true coming out of your mouth. You're going to have to give me a minute because I'm so pissed off right now I don't even know how or where to begin responding to that load of garbage you just spouted. The *only* thing keeping me from losing my shit and turning you over my knee and spanking your ass is the fact that you actually believe every single word you said, and I don't know how to make you see it for the utter nonsense it is and that really pisses me off because it hurts you and goddamn it, it hurts me to watch you judge yourself, condemn yourself and stand there saying that you're no better than that piece of shit pathetic excuse for a human being while I have to stand here and watch you bleed right in front of me. But as God as my witness, baby, I'm going to make you see the truth. And not your fucked up version of the truth. If it's the last thing I do, I'm going to find a way to make you see the Eliza that I see when I look at you. To know the Eliza that I know and admire and have more respect for than I do any other living person."

She stared wordlessly at him, too overwhelmed to say anything. What could she say to that? He was staring at her like she was the only person in the world—his world. His words, each and every one of them, she committed to memory, savoring and holding them close to her heart where they'd all remain safe and untainted, touched by no one. No one could ever take them away from her. They were hers, given to her, and they meant everything to her.

No one had ever looked at her with so much caring and fierceness, with so much possession and protectiveness there in their eyes for the world to see. No attempt to disguise it, pretend it didn't mean anything or that he hadn't meant any of the things he'd said.

"I can see that maybe I'm finally getting through," Wade said gruffly. "Maybe now you're getting it. You mean something to me. *You*. And that means all of you, not just the parts you want me to see while you hide the parts you're so determined to be ashamed of and feel guilt over. You're mine, Eliza. All of you. Every inch of you, body and soul. And it wasn't just your body that I claimed when I made love to you and was inside you so deep that there will never be a time you don't feel me. I also claimed your heart, your soul, your mind and everything that makes you the person you are and what you were meant to be. And what you were meant to be is *mine*."

Tears made him go blurry in her vision as she stared at him in wonder, afraid to believe. Afraid not to believe. Wanting so much and yet so scared that she'd never have what she wanted most. That this was all just a dream. The most beautiful dream she'd ever had.

"Wade, I have to do this," she choked out. "Please believe me. I'm not trying to be a vigilante or a lone wolf, determined to go it by myself so I don't involve the people I love. You're already involved. I'm not walking blind into a situation nor am I planning to do anything stupid. But I need to do this. For me, Wade. For *me*. Not for him or anyone else. Not even for the women who died because of his sick obsession with me. I have to get something back that he took from me because until I have it, I can never give all of me to anyone else. I need you to understand and more than anything I need your support and the knowledge that you'll have my back so I can walk into that press conference with my head held high and then look him in the eye so he knows he no longer has me. I can accept not being the one to take him down. I can accept not dispensing justice that is rightfully mine to dispense. But I cannot accept not being able to at least face the monster who has controlled me for so fucking long because I *let* him. Even after he no longer had the ability to manipulate, I still let him affect my choices, my decisions and my happiness. I shut myself off and never allowed anyone in because of him. Because he taught me that I couldn't trust anyone. He was fucking wrong and I will never be able to put him completely behind me and heal until I can look him in the eye and let him know he did not win."

"I'm sorry," Wade said, sorrow brimming in his eyes.

She stared at him, stunned. What on earth was he sorry for? It was the very last thing she'd expected him to say.

He caressed her face, holding it in his hands as he stared down at her, fierce pride replacing the sorrow.

"I was wrong," he said simply. "And I was being no better than the bastard who took your choices from you all those years ago. I was doing the same goddamn thing and I'm sorry, Eliza. I didn't realize how important this is to you. I couldn't see past my blinding need to keep you safe. My fear of something happening to you. I didn't recognize that he did so much damage to you. Damage that you're still healing from. And you need closure. You need to know you beat him. I get that. I do. I don't want you there. I'd much rather you be where I know you're safe, where I can keep you from ever being hurt again. But I understand why you need to do this and I support you, baby. And for the record, I will *always* have your back."

She threw her arms around him again and hugged him, trembling and shaking from head to toe with emotion. He rubbed his hands up and down her back and simply let her hold on, let her take what she needed while he held her just as tightly as she held him.

After a while, Wade bent and brushed his lips across hers in a tender kiss. "Plans have to change. I need to call Dane and apprise him of the newest developments. I want them on you tomorrow watching you every fucking second. And then you get your ass back here to me where you belong."

Belong. Such a simple word and yet it hit her like a ton of bricks. She'd never belonged to anyone. She'd never belonged anywhere. Wade said she belonged to and with him, and she'd never felt anything sweeter than knowing that, finally, she actually felt a sense of true belonging.

TWENTY

ELIZA purposely arrived at the site of the press conference early so she could select a place directly in front of the podium so there was no chance of Thomas not seeing her. She hadn't shared this with Wade, but she'd only given him one of her reasons for insisting on being here when Thomas had his day in the spotlight. She hadn't lied. Every single thing she'd told him about needing to face Thomas was absolutely true. But there was another reason, one she hadn't dared impart to Wade or he would have shut her down so fast her head would have spun.

She wanted to be as close to Thomas as possible because she knew once he spotted her, once he knew she was there, almost in touching distance, he would attempt to begin his manipulation. And now that she understood the difference between thoughts and feelings psychically implanted and those that were solely her own, she knew she was no longer that starry-eyed teenager living without hope with only her daydreams and fantasies to make life bearable.

She would know immediately if Thomas was able to break through the mental barriers she'd spent years strengthening. And she needed to know, because if he could still manipulate her, then she was a danger to every single person important to her. Thomas could use her to turn against people absolutely loyal to her, betray them, destroy them and herself in the process.

It was a test. The most important test of her life with *everything* riding on the outcome. Whatever the result, she would still walk away once Thomas registered her presence. It was only a matter of whether she would return to Wade, confident in her ability to withstand a mental assault, or ... if her barriers were breached then she'd run and she'd keep running. Forever. Whatever it took to ensure she would never be under Thomas's control again and used to destroy the lives of the people who meant the most to her.

She checked her watch, casually turning ever so slightly so she could view the growing crowd. Though she had yet to speak to Dane since the last time she'd seen him when she'd requested vacation time, it heartened her to know he was out there. Watching over her, taking her back like always, and with him the other DSS operatives. Zack. Newly married or not, she knew he would have insisted on being here. Next to Dane, Zack was closest to her of everyone she worked with.

She had the utmost confidence in her team. Knew they were watching, taking in every detail, any sign of danger, protecting her and then, when she left, they would shadow Thomas's every move and even Thomas with his psychic abilities would never know he was being watched. Her pride in the people she worked with was well deserved, absolute and unwavering. They'd proven themselves time and time again. Even when she'd been abducted and subjected to grueling torture, she'd never once lost faith that they would find her and get her out alive.

More and more people gathered until the entire street between the grassy circle and the businesses behind them was clogged with bystanders making it impassable to vehicles. The businesses had all closed for the press conference. No one would be anywhere but here. Afterward, they'd reopen and likely do a booming business as the locals gathered to gossip and offer their opinions on Thomas's statement. And Eliza's presence of course.

As safe as she knew she was in the hands of her teammates watching over her, she wished Wade was here, even just doing what her team was doing. Watching, invisible, ghosts. But Wade had good reason not to leave the safe house. With so many people, media, cameras and filming, he couldn't risk being seen by anyone.

If he was the one taking Thomas down—and he was adamant that it was his mission and his alone—then he couldn't be linked in any way to the town or the media, and he could not be seen by anyone who could place him in the vicinity of Thomas.

It still made her sick to her soul to have Wade take someone's life for her. It was her risk to take, her fall to take, her right to finally bring him to final justice. She shook off the unwanted thoughts and images of Wade risking all for her and did another quick scan of the now massive crowd. The many media crews were already set up, some giving a preliminary live report with cameras panning the huge gathering while the reporter chirped her spiel as if this was something good and exciting.

Her lips curled in disgust and then she froze, all her breath leaving her lungs in one forceful exhale. She stared, nearly paralyzed with panic and anxiety as she watched a procession of police cars flanking a four-door sedan pull up to the cordoned-off and guarded section of street directly in front of the courthouse on the opposite side of the grassy area from where the press conference was set up.

She stared in horror as the driver stepped out, doing a quick scan of his immediate surroundings before opening the door to the backseat. A half dozen police officers converged as Thomas stepped from the vehicle, surrounding him as they began walking slowly across the grass to where the platform and podium had been set up.

Even spending years in prison, Thomas looked as though time and age had been good to him. Even in his twenties, he'd possessed a timeless look, making it hard to accurately judge his age. And now, he looked only slightly older than he had at twenty-eight. Even more unbelievable, he had grown more handsome over the years.

He'd always possessed a quiet, distinguished air that drew people to him like a magnet and that look had only intensified. Anger and bitter hatred boiled in her veins. It wasn't fair! He'd viciously murdered women with no remorse or regret. He felt nothing at all. They were dead, their lives cut short and he was now a free man whose looks and appeal had only heightened during the time he served, and he still had a long life to look forward to. The women he killed had nothing, their young lives ending in terror and unspeakable agony. Her only consolation was that if all went according to plan, his life would end just when he thought it would begin again.

Her hands shook when she saw Thomas smile at the cop nearest him and the two shared a laugh. Thomas looked happy. Satisfied. Like he didn't have a care in the world. How could he be smiling or laughing when he was about to appear on live television to presumably proclaim his innocence and express his gratitude for the cop who'd supposedly tampered with evidence coming forward and admitting his part in sending an innocent man to prison?

Innocent my ass.

She was seething with fury and she quickly got a handle on her rage and forced herself to calm her rioting emotions before Thomas stepped up to the podium. She couldn't blow it now. She only had one shot at this and she had to pull it off before Thomas selected his first victim. She would not let that happen to another woman. Never again.

She sucked in several steadying breaths, purposely focusing on more pleasant, bland and nondescript thoughts. She immediately shut down the most pleasant thought that crept into her mind. Thomas dead, no longer wearing that smug smile, no longer laughing, never being able to hurt another person again and boarding a one-way trip straight to hell for his appointment with the devil.

He didn't immediately see her when he stepped to the microphone, his police entourage strategically placing themselves to ensure his protection. She quickly swallowed back the bile rising in her throat at the knowledge that the soulless bastard was being protected by men sworn to bring men like Thomas to justice.

He smiled broadly at the crowd, as though greeting long-lost friends and as if he were expecting a hero's welcome home. Strangely, the crowd was completely silent. Eerily so. It was as if time stopped as everyone anticipated the purpose of Thomas calling the press conference.

"It is with great joy and relief that I stand before you here today. A travesty of justice has been corrected and I am grateful to the officer who came forward to right the wrong committed against me."

She was going to be sick. He dared to speak of travesties of justice when he stood there, a free man, exonerated of crimes he was guilty of? It was hard but she forced blankness to her face, an expression of disinterest as if it didn't matter to her whether or not he was guilty and was here for one reason and one reason only.

She knew the instant he saw her. Felt the sudden intensity of his gaze. He paused in his speech, his chin lifted as if looking beyond her so his gaze encompassed the majority of the crowd. But his eyes were fixed solidly on her. She felt a peculiar sensation, a flutter of awareness in her mind as if he were probing to find his way in.

And as suddenly as it happened, it was gone, and a slight frown marred Thomas's face before he quickly recovered and once again resumed his speech.

Relief and a keen sense of victory fizzed through her body like a bottle of champagne having the cork popped and the contents bubbling out and over. He hadn't been able to push past her barriers! She'd felt his attempt, something she'd never even been aware of before. She'd never felt or sensed anything at all when he'd accessed her mind all those years ago.

She was careful not to let her jubilation show and to temper her thoughts of victory and immense satisfaction. He would try again. Of that she had no doubt. And she'd give him that attempt. One more and then she was done here. She'd accomplished what she'd set out to do and she'd baited the trap. All she had to do now was hope he fell neatly into it.

She went rigid when she tuned back into his polished, very practiced recitation of expressing his thanks to everyone who supported him and who fought for him and believed in him blah blah. She'd zoned out until she heard her name. Or rather what used to be her name.

Her gaze caught his and for the first time she looked directly into his eyes, boldly, refusing to look away. And as he spoke, once again she felt that odd fluttering sensation in her head, sharper, more forceful than before. Pain sizzled through her head and she clenched her jaw against the nearly unbearable strain, but her thought patterns never changed, didn't deviate from what she was focusing on and none of her hatred for the man now saying her name had diminished in the least.

"It was with a heavy heart that I learned that Melissa Caldwell has been the recipient of so much ill will and has been treated poorly by the citizens of this town. I harbor no animosity for Miss Caldwell. I pity her, as you all should too, and she should be granted more understanding. You see, she was but a child then. A mixed-up, confused child who had no family, no home of her own and had been on her own with only herself to rely on since she was fifteen."

Nausea welled in Eliza's stomach and it took every ounce of willpower she possessed not to vomit right there on the ground. She was shaking and this time, no attempt at controlling it was successful. She had to keep it together. She should leave now. Her objective had been achieved. But she was frozen to the spot where she stood, unable to turn away without hearing the rest.

Thomas sighed dramatically and affected a pained, sympathetic look of regret.

"She convinced herself she was in love with me," he said, as if admitting to some heinous crime. "I fear I carry partial blame for that, though that was never my intention or desire. She was attacked on her way home from work very late at night and I happened on the scene and managed to fend off her attackers. I felt responsible for her in a way that an older brother would feel responsibility for his younger sister. I would walk her home because I couldn't in good conscience allow her to come to harm when she had no one else to look out for her."

He ran his hand through his hair in faked regret.

"She mistook my kindness for something more and as a result she became obsessed with me. I tried very hard to let her down gently. I didn't want to hurt her or embarrass her in any way. I explained that even if I felt for her the way she thought she felt for me, it wouldn't be appropriate. She was far too young and I was much too old for her. I told her that she was too young to be thinking about the kind of relationship she wanted. With me," he added with a grimace. "That she had all the time in the world and that one day she would meet the man meant for her but that I wasn't—could never be—him."

He paused for dramatic affect and once more flickered his eyes in her direction, a thoughtful, puzzled look on his face. She had to act fast. No, she didn't want him fucking around in her head and yes, she wanted him to know he could no longer control her, but she didn't want to come across as hating him. She was here to convince him that she came for him. That she still loved him and wanted to be with him. The thought nearly made her gag, but she quickly swallowed and sent a slow smile aimed directly at Thomas, one she put everything she had into making sincere, welcoming, loving and hopeful.

Then, as had been his custom in the past, she made a fist and slowly raised it to her chest and then pressed it against her heart, knowing he would recognize the gesture immediately. And its meaning.

He blinked in surprise and then his eyes brightened and what looked like delight flashed momentarily. He didn't smile back. He couldn't be that obvious. But he sent her a smoldering look, one that was filled with hunger, want and need. Oh God. She couldn't take this a minute longer.

Thomas broke off in midsentence, and she got the distinct impression that what he said next was not what he'd originally planned or rehearsed. Originally he'd thought to crucify and vilify her despite his claim to wanting just the opposite. But whether it was the silent invitation in her eyes and the intimate gesture known only to the two of them or he in some way saw a glimpse of the girl he'd known as Melissa Caldwell, he changed his direction completely and did a complete one-eighty in his portrayal of her.

"I don't blame or fault Miss Caldwell for what she did. She did what was right, and she should be commended for having such courage when she was only a child. She saw a crime and she reported it and then she testified in court in her attempt to see justice served. Without a doubt, she had the best of intentions, and she should be admired for that. Unfortunately, she misidentified me as the man who committed those horrific and barbaric atrocities against those poor women. It is my belief that in her shock at witnessing the gruesome scene she inadvertently came upon that she identified someone who likely *resembled* me, honestly thinking and believing that it was me she saw that day. It was an unfortunate mistake, but an honest one. I do not believe for one minute that she maliciously launched her accusation at me out of spite or to seek revenge for my rejection of her romantically. I have forgiven her just as I have forgiven the police officer who tampered with evidence in order to make it impossible for me to receive a fair trial and so was subsequently convicted. It is my desire to put this entire ordeal behind me and move on with my life. Quietly and peacefully. I would respectfully request my privacy not to be disturbed. I think I am owed that much and it is all I ask. I have turned down the state's offer of restitution for wrongful imprisonment. I am not a vengeful man. My only desire is to start my new life as a free man and not have my privacy or life intruded upon."

Eliza could stomach no more, and she needed to leave, *now*, before he concluded his nauseating play for sympathy and his brazen effort at manipulating the entire assembled crowd into changing their minds about him. He'd solidly put the blame on her shoulders and had blatantly insinuated that she was an obsessed, psycho, scorned woman out for revenge and because of her, an innocent man had been jailed while the real killer was still out there, free.

He'd reversed his position and changed his story after the odd exchange between them, but the damage had already been done, the seeds already planted. She needed to get out ahead of the crowd while they were still absorbed in his humble victim speech and he had them eating out of his hand. Otherwise, it could get ugly very quickly for her. It only took one person bold enough to decide she needed to be taught a lesson and the rest would follow like sheep. And if that happened, her team would be forced out of surveillance to save her ass, thus sending a huge, blazing neon sign to Thomas that she wasn't alone and she had badass backup.

She moved slowly to the side, edging cautiously, careful not to draw undue attention, halting her progress when there was a momentary lapse in Thomas's speech and then moving again when all attention was riveted on Thomas once more, his every word being hung on to by men and women, old and young alike.

She wasn't the only one who'd spent years honing her skills. While she'd been working diligently to strengthen her mental barriers so they were impenetrable and not vulnerable to a psychic attack, Thomas had evidently been honing his powers, making him more powerful than before and an even bigger threat. He held the entire crowd in his thrall, had them all eating out of his hand. They looked at him like he was a God. They gasped in horror when he brought up any injustice to him and frowned, glared and even booed when he mentioned anyone responsible for his being sent to prison.

When she was finally clear of the crowd lining the very front of the gathering, she expelled a sigh of relief but didn't make the mistake of letting her guard down or thinking she was out of the woods yet. She still had to make it to where she'd parked her car and that was a quarter mile away.

Head down, the hood of her jacket pulled over her hair, she strode in a straight line toward her vehicle. She should have felt jubilant and wildly victorious but her victory was hollow. She'd held her own against a master at bending people to his will and compelling them to do his bidding. He'd tried twice to slide into her mind and he'd failed both times. The second time, he'd used a hell of a lot more power and had doubled the intensity of his attempted assault. Her head ached vilely from the strain of fend-ing him off and from the sheer force of his second attack.

But she'd won. She'd defeated him. She was no longer a weak, powerless pawn he used with little effort. Never again would she be anyone's puppet. She'd die before ever allowing anyone so much control over her every dream, thought or action.

TWENTY-ONE

THE door opened before Eliza was close enough to put her hand on the handle to let herself in. Wade was there, his gaze fixed intently on her, worry reflected openly in his eyes. Without a word, he pulled her into his arms, wrapping them firmly around her, fully encompassing her in his warmth and strength. Before she even registered them moving, he had maneuvered them through the doorway, shutting the door behind them and then lifted her so her feet dangled inches from the floor so he could carry her farther into the house.

When they were in the middle of the living room, he eased her down until her feet were planted on the floor and he palmed her chin, tilting it upward so their gazes met.

"You okay?" he asked quietly.

She closed her eyes, holding them closed for a long moment as she fought the multitude of conflicting emotions and tried to process and prioritize the information to give to Wade.

"Baby?" he prompted, stroking his thumb down her lips.

She forced her eyelids open and stared up at him, drawing strength from the silent support so visible in his eyes. Then she took a deep breath.

"There's so much," she said wearily. "I'm not even sure where to begin."

"Wherever you want," he said softly. "However you want. I'm here. I'm listening. Whatever you need, I'll give."

She leaned her forehead into his chest, resting it there as she simply absorbed everything about him. The way he felt. His scent. The thud of his heartbeat. How safe she felt in his arms. How she wished she'd never gotten that damn phone call weeks ago.

"I told you that I needed to be there today. And why I needed to be there. I told you the truth. I just didn't tell you the other reason it was so important for me to be there," she admitted in a whisper.

She held her breath, waiting for his reaction, wondering if he'd be angry because he'd been nothing but honest and blunt with her. Brutally so at times.

To her surprise, he swept her up into his arms in an effortless motion and carried her to the couch. He turned his back and then simply sat down, her cradled on his lap as he leaned back, pulling her with him.

"If we're going to talk, you're going to be comfortable and you're going to be in my arms when you're talking," Wade said.

Then he simply arranged her to his liking, tucking her shoulder underneath his so that the top of her head was nestled under the line of his jaw, pressed to the side of his neck.

The fact that his body language, the tone of his voice, hadn't registered the slightest change after her confession that she'd kept something from him gave her a strong measure of relief and the courage to forge ahead and not fear his reaction.

When had his approval become so important to her? When had it ever mattered to her whether she pissed him off or not? She was still struggling with the abrupt about-face their relationship had experienced and, in the back of her mind, there was a nagging worry that when this was over and she was no longer in danger, things would go back to the way they'd been before when they practiced reluctant tolerance of one another for the sake of their mutual friend.

But then she was far guiltier of being an ungrateful, childish bitch than he was of being an overbearing asshole. She'd never even *thanked* him for taking a bullet for her. For saving her life. Instead she'd avoided him when at all possible, and when avoidance wasn't a possibility, she'd been snarky, sarcastic and purposely needled him at every opportunity.

It hadn't bothered her then. She'd given it little thought. But now it ate at her. Her actions, her behavior and her treatment of this man *deeply* shamed her.

"You going to share, baby?" Wade asked, interrupting her self-castigation. "Not that I'm complaining about sitting here and just holding you, but you're obviously upset, and from what I saw and heard, you have cause to be."

"You watched it?" she asked in a low voice.

"Yeah. Hated that I couldn't be there watching over my girl so I looked for her by tuning in to the broadcast."

She curled her fingers into his shirt, wanting, needing to just hold on to him.

"I explained that I've worked endlessly to strengthen my mental barriers. And when I told you how he manipulated my mind, you asked if he could still do that. And I said no."

He gave her a comforting squeeze.

"But I didn't know that for certain," she whispered shakily. "How could I? I had once thought to have Gracie try to read my mind to see if I could successfully shut her out, but Thomas was in prison and I thought he would never be a threat to me again and if I asked that of Gracie then I would have had to explain things I'd never shared with anyone and never *intended* to, so I just let it go but kept working at it. In a way, I think it was a part of my healing process. I was weak and easily manipulated and so desperate to be loved and to belong, and I hated myself for that for a very long time. I still do at times," she admitted.

"I blamed myself for so many years. So taking steps to make myself *believe* that I was overcoming what I considered a weakness gave me back some of the power I'd lost. It made me feel protected whether it was true or complete bullshit."

"Baby, if it gave you even a measure of security, made you feel safer, and especially if it gave you back anything that bastard took from you, then not only is it real, but it obviously provided something you needed. Who gives a shit if it can be scientifically proven? You and I have both witnessed the extraordinary. More than once and in more than one person. Do you think Ramie's, Ari's or Gracie's abilities could ever be scientifically proven? Do you think there is a way to measure their abilities? Ever reproduce them in a lab or an experiment?"

"But it *did* work," Eliza breathed, her fingers tightening into a ball, wadding his shirt in her grasp, pulling it taut across his chest.

Wade went still and then he gently pried her hand from his shirt and circled her wrist with his fingers, pulling her from the crook of his shoulder and positioning her so she straddled his lap facing him.

"What do you mean by that?" he asked, his brows drawing together in a mixture of confusion and concern.

"I purposely positioned myself in front of the podium so Thomas would see me. Because I knew that when he saw me, he would attempt to manipulate me. He would want to reestablish my love and adoration for him and the desire to go anywhere with him. And I had to know, before this mission went any further, if I was strong enough to block him. I was so afraid, Wade," she admitted painfully. "I was terrified that I have been fooling myself so I didn't have to admit how weak and powerless I was."

The ache in her head, the residual effects of Thomas's forceful attack, intensified just remembering it. She went silent and leaned in to Wade, resting her forehead against his lips, needing that contact, needing the soothing comfort and unconditional support he gave so readily.

His hand went to the back of her head and gently massaged, nearly making her moan at the brief respite from the pain the simple stroke of his hand gave her.

He gave her another few moments, as if realizing how much she needed them. Just a few to collect herself before she continued. Finally, she lifted her head and met his gaze, suddenly bereft and hollow at the loss of that contact.

"So he tried," Wade said grimly.

"He didn't see me right away. He'd begun his ridiculous spiel, but I knew the instant he noticed me. I *felt* his eyes on me."

She shuddered, chill bumps appearing on her arms. Wade

slid his hands over her arms, chasing the chill away as he rubbed up and down.

"And then I felt an odd flutter in my head. A probing sensation. It was painful, like an actual physical attack, but nothing like the second time."

Wade's expression darkened, his eyes glittering fiercely.

"I watched him the entire time and kept my thoughts and emotions in check. And then I saw his shock when he wasn't able to get in, wasn't able to read me. He even frowned and paused in his speech but then looked away and continued on. I knew he'd try again and I was going to give him that one last chance and then I was getting out of there."

Wade frowned as he watched her closely.

"The second time he came at me hard and fast, striking without warning. I was stunned by how painful it was. My head felt like it was going to explode. Like something was going to pop or burst. But again, I warded him off and he couldn't get in. And then I realized my mistake or rather the mistake I nearly made."

Wade's eyebrow went up in question.

"Yes, I wanted him to see me and, yes, I wanted him to know that he could no longer control me, that he no longer had any power over me, but I needed him to think that even though he was no longer manipulating my actions and emotions that I still loved him and *chose* to be with him. I wanted him to think that I was there because of him, so that we could be together and live happily ever after and all that other bullshit I thought I wanted when I was sixteen," she said with an edge of bitterness she couldn't suppress.

"So I looked directly into his eyes, and I smiled at him. I

put on the act of my life by faking joy, desire, love and need and pouring all of that into my eyes and my smile. And then, so he couldn't possibly misunderstand, I made a gesture that he used for me when we were together."

She balled her fist and demonstrated the gesture for Wade so he would see instead of relying on her description.

"I swear I saw delight flash in his eyes and then he sent me this smoldering look that was a mixture of desire and need and oh God, Wade. It made me sick to my soul. Even though I already knew that I'd beat him, that he could no longer control me psychically, it was then that it really sank in, because if he had been able to exert his will then I would not have reacted to him looking at me the way I did. If he had been controlling me, I would have been delirious with joy for him to have looked at me that way. My feelings, my reactions to him were *mine*. Not his."

Wade leaned forward and kissed her long and so very sweet, his tongue brushing over the seam of her lips as he lightly tasted her. When he leaned back again, pride and fierce satisfaction blazed in his eyes.

"Proud of you, baby."

He reinforced his words of praise by gathering her hands between them and squeezing them and then lacing their fingers together before lowering their joined hands to his lap.

"Before that moment, he'd vilified me and ripped me to shreds and then suddenly he did a complete one-eighty and defended me."

"Yeah, I heard that," Wade muttered.

She lowered her gaze to their linked hands, staring at something that seemed so ordinary and yet it was symbolic to her in a way she couldn't fully explain.

She wasn't alone.

She had someone to lean on.

She had someone she trusted.

She had someone she . . .

"He's going to come after you, baby," Wade said in a grim tone.

"Yeah, I know," she quietly acknowledged. "But I'll be ready this time."

"No, *we'll* be ready," Wade said forcefully. "You will not face this bastard. Not now. Not ever. He shows his face, he's a dead man. He's already voiced his wish to disappear and be left in peace, and in doing so, he unwittingly played right into my hands. Because I plan to give him exactly what he asked for. No one will ever find his body. No one will ever know—or care— what happened to him. He will have simply disappeared like he already stated he planned to do."

It wasn't as though she hadn't known of Wade's intentions. It wasn't the first time he'd stated his mission. But somehow hearing it now, when Thomas was free and within reach, Eliza was seized with absolute panic and paralyzing fear.

"I don't want you to do this for me," she said fiercely, des-peration heavy in her voice. "Please don't do this, Wade. I could never live with myself if you killed a man because of me. *For* me."

Wade slowly brought their joined hands up and turned one of hers so it was pressed to his mouth. Then he looked at her, utter gravity etched in every part of his expression.

"You still don't get it yet, do you Eliza? I fucking love you. You're *mine*. There is nothing I wouldn't do to ensure your safety and happiness and you'll never be either as long as that bastard breathes."

All the breath was squeezed painfully from her lungs, and it was physically impossible for her to draw in more air. She stared at him in complete bewilderment, shock splintering and ricocheting up and down her spine. Her lungs burned, her chest was on fire and tears burned like acid at the corners of her eyes.

"You love me?" she whispered in a nearly inaudible voice.

She finally managed to drag in a shuddering ragged breath. She was trembling so hard that her hands shook in Wade's firm grasp.

He shook his head but his smile was achingly tender. "Do you honestly think I don't? Do you doubt it? Baby, when this is over and done with and a threat no longer exists to you, you're marrying me. I'm never letting you go. And I'll love and protect you and do everything I can to make you happy until I draw my very last breath."

The tears she'd tried so hard to suppress ran freely down her cheeks in endless streaks as she stared back at him in wonder. In awe. She was so overwhelmed that her throat knotted and closed. She couldn't have spoken in that moment if her life depended on it.

He loved her. He'd given her the most precious words she'd ever been gifted with. She tried to speak. To say something, anything, but the knot only grew larger until she freed one of her hands from Wade's hold and held it to the front of her throat, rubbing in an effort to alleviate the aching obstruction.

Hadn't she battled with herself endlessly over her feelings for Wade? Questioned them. At times, nearly admitting it, as recently as just moments ago when she'd marveled at what she was to Wade. But before she had actually formed the word *love* Wade had spoken, taking the conversation in a different direction.

How long had it been there? Unrecognized, denied even, yet there all the same. Did it matter when or how long or even why? She couldn't pinpoint an exact moment she'd fallen in love with Wade. Maybe the seed had been there from the start only to be fought, resented, even feared or perhaps she'd felt undeserving. She'd spent so much of her life believing that she was unworthy of being loved and as a result hadn't ever allowed herself to love. Self-preservation. A defense mechanism she was only all too well acquainted with.

She'd spent her young life wanting what so many others took for granted. And she'd thought that her ultimate dream had come true, only to realize how hopelessly naïve and desperate not to mention weak, brainless and foolish she'd been. Then she'd veered to the opposite extreme, never allowing anyone close, never allowing herself to become emotionally involved or attached to anyone and never trusting anyone with her most shameful secrets.

Not until she'd met Dane and gone to work for DSS had she finally begun to open up to others, but it hadn't been overnight or even soon. It had been a gradual process and it had taken time for Eliza not only to want or demand trust from the people she worked with but for her to have faith enough in her judgment to finally place her trust in even those closest to her.

The people she worked with taught her about love. What love really was and what it wasn't, but Eliza had always been an observer. On the outside looking in. Wade hadn't just taught her how to let herself love and be loved. He'd shown her with his actions far more than with his words.

For the first time in her life, Eliza loved. Deeply. Passionately. Unconditionally. Limitless. With a fierceness she hadn't known existed when loving someone.

She knew Wade was watching her, waiting, observing the parade of mixed emotions and thoughts that had to be obvious due to her ever-changing expressions and the sheer awe and wonder that coursed through her blood like the most potent drug. She owed him the same honesty and commitment he'd given her but she was terrified to make herself so vulnerable when she'd sworn that she would never let herself be as exposed and fragile as she'd been when Melissa Caldwell still existed.

At the thought of that name, a person who no longer existed, Eliza stopped cold in her tracks, going utterly still as her face and eyes filled with wonder and revelation. Dear God, how could she have been so blind? So deeply rooted in the past of a person who didn't even exist that she'd never allowed herself to live. And be free.

Wade's brow furrowed and where before he'd seemed content to regard her with tender amusement, watching the myriad of emotions during Eliza's self-demanded come-to-Jesus meeting, now he looked worried and uncertain.

Then Eliza smiled. Really smiled. So wide and big that the corners of her mouth stretched to the point of discomfort. She could feel herself glowing. Radiating joy like she'd never experienced or felt in her life. She reached out to palm Wade's face, cupping it between her hands as she stared lovingly into his eyes, for once unafraid to be vulnerable, to open herself up and allow someone into places in her heart and soul that no one had ever had access to. She was safe. And she was loved.

"I'm not her," she whispered in awe.

And then she promptly burst into tears, sending Wade into complete panic, his eyes wild and frantic. She wrapped her arms around his shoulders, holding on to him for dear life. She clung to him like a burr and wept noisily into his neck, huge gulping sobs welling from the deepest recesses of her soul. A soul she thought she'd lost a lifetime ago, but Wade had restored it, healed it and her. With his love.

She cried, not because she was unhappy but because she was finally releasing pent-up emotions she'd suppressed for a decade. She was letting go of all the grief, the guilt and so much pain that she no longer felt.

She was free. Finally free of the bonds she'd placed on herself after being freed of the bonds Thomas had imprisoned her with.

You don't have to carry your burden alone, Eliza.

Let it go, baby.

I'm right here.

I'm not going anywhere.

Give yourself—and your burden—to me.

Wade's words drifted to her on the most beautiful wave, rolling over her and washing her clean. How could she have ever doubted he loved her? How could she have even questioned it? He may not have given her the words until just now, but he'd shown her in every possible way how much she mattered to him. The evidence, the proof, had been staring her right in the face almost from the very start, but she'd been too bent on protecting herself from the pain of briefly touching the sun only to have a storm roll in and cover it with black clouds, never to be revealed to her again.

What she hadn't realized was that Wade *was* the sun.

Her sun. And even the fiercest storm could never suppress his warmth, his light, his love.

Her sobs quieted, leaving only soft hiccups in their wake. She lay limply against Wade, her face buried in his neck as she clung desperately to him, afraid that if she so much as blinked, he would be gone.

Wade ran his fingers over her face, wiping the last of her tears from her cheeks and then he carefully tucked the tousled strands of hair stuck to her face and partially covering her eyes behind her ears and smoothing the rest away, leaving no way-ward strands behind.

He pressed a kiss to her forehead and sighed softly. "Baby, what happened just now? Have to say, that wasn't exactly the reaction I was expecting to me telling you I love you and that you're marrying me. Is the idea of me loving you so terrible? Or is it the marrying part that freaked you out?"

He carefully maneuvered her face from his neck to look at him. There was such a look of vulnerability in his eyes, some-thing she'd never seen in this hard man who rarely let his emo-tions out from behind the impenetrable mask that was such a permanent fixture on him.

Seeing that naked, raw uncertainty so clearly reflected in his expression made her tear up all over again.

Wade's expression immediately became frantic, agitation radiating from him in waves.

"Baby, don't cry. Please don't cry anymore. You're breaking my heart. Whatever it is, we'll fix it, I swear. I won't rush you. I'll wait forever if I have to. I'll give you all the time in the world you need and when you're ready, I'll be right here, waiting."

"Oh God, Wade," she said tearfully. "I love you too. So much.

And it scares me to death. I'm terrified. I haven't allowed myself to love anyone except the few people I call friends—family," she corrected. "But even them I keep at arm's length, never letting them too deep inside me, because it's so ugly and I'd never let them see that part of me. I can't lose you, Wade. Not you. It would destroy me. I don't know how to love. I've never loved the way I love you and have never *been* loved like you love me.

"I thought I was in love, but I was so wrong. You've shown me what love is, how beautiful and selfless it is and I want it more than I want to breathe, but I'm so scared, because I don't know how to love someone the way you deserve to be loved. It terrifies me to care so much about someone. To have so much—all—of my happiness depend on one person."

For a moment Wade didn't respond. He didn't seem capable. He closed his eyes, his relief a living, breathing entity, and it was then she noticed that he was trembling just as she had been shaking a short time ago. When he reopened his eyes, they were so full of love and understanding that they looked near to bursting and they were lighter than she'd ever seen them before.

"Now you understand how I feel," he said gruffly. "I've never loved anyone in my life, Eliza. Never even knew what love *was*, what it felt like, what it meant. It's beautiful and scary as hell all at the same time. You think you have ugliness? You have nothing on me. I'm not a good man. I've done things you can't even imagine and I've never suffered a single regret. But that's over with now because I would never risk you that way. I will never let anything ugly touch you again and if that means me going straight and becoming legitimate then I'm more than willing to do that if it means I have you. You are everything to me, which is why I'm not letting you risk yourself to take this maniac down.

I will always stand in front of you and anything that puts you in harm's way. You need to understand that and deal, Eliza. Life with me won't be easy. I'm an overbearing, controlling bastard and I will never allow you to take risks with your safety."

He framed her face and looked fiercely into her eyes as if willing every bit of his impassioned statement to be permanently engraved in her mind, her heart and her soul.

"But, baby, I can promise you this. If you take a chance on me. If you stand with me and by me and never give up on us, and if you're willing to risk it all for a man who isn't nearly good enough for you but loves you and wants you with every beat of his heart, then I will always do anything to make you happy. There is no sacrifice I won't make. No dream you have that will go unfulfilled. No wish that will not come true. And you will be the most treasured, cherished, pampered, spoiled, loved and adored woman who ever lived. I vow it on my life."

"Not good enough for me?" she whispered incredulously.

She stared at him in utter stupefaction. Not good enough? Was he insane?

"Wade, do you even realize what you're taking on? How much baggage comes with me? You deserve so much more than I'll ever be able to give you," she choked out, stifling the sob that lodged in her throat. "But I'll make you a promise as well. If you're willing to risk so much for someone as damaged and unworthy as I am then I will spend every single day doing everything I can to make sure you don't ever regret taking a chance on me."

"I love you," he said. Just that. Nothing more. But it was enough. It would always be enough. It was all she'd ever dreamed of, wished for, hoped for and it was what she'd never thought she'd have.

"I love you too," she whispered.

She closed her eyes, savoring these few stolen moments, knowing that all too soon reality would once more intrude and they would be forced back into the real world where evil was far too prevalent.

"What do we do now?" she asked quietly, her heart clenching, filled with dread for what was to come.

Wade shrugged. "We wait for him to make his move. But, in the meantime, I'm going to take you to bed and spend the rest of the afternoon making love to you."

TWENTY-TWO

DUSK had fallen, casting shadows across the bedroom where Eliza lay nestled in Wade's arms, both on their sides, facing one another, legs tangled, their bodies molded tightly together. She purposely cleared her mind to everything but the intimacy that blanketed the entire room and the sensation of lying next to the man she loved and who loved her.

Wade had made love to her, drawing out her pleasure until she'd been mindless with want and need, her desire for him the most desperate, urgent sensation she'd ever experienced. He'd given her the words over and over, but he'd also shown her his love by touching, caressing, kissing, licking and sucking every inch of her body from head to toe, spending extra time on the parts in between.

He'd been in no hurry. No rush to orgasm. No quick slaking of lust and desire. He'd taken his time, bringing her to the brink of release only to back off and give her just enough time for the edge to not be as sharp and then he began all over, taking her up the peak again and again delaying her release until she was in complete freefall. Weightless and floating in a sea of indescribable pleasure.

When he finally brought her to completion, she'd fallen apart in his arms, utterly shattered by the beauty of having a man who loved her without measure make sweet love to her. Tears had slid down her cheeks, joy filling every place deeply hidden that had been barren and devoid of any feeling for so long. He reached every one of those dark places and brought light and life to them all.

And afterward, he'd held her while she cried, this time overwhelmed by the realization that she was finally home. She finally belonged. She was finally loved and wholly accepted without conditions, reservations or judgment.

Then he'd made love to her again. And again, until they'd fallen into a light sleep, content to rest in each other's arms and soak up every minute of the start of something new and special, the first day of their future together and the promise of many tomorrows.

Eliza had awakened first and lay quiet and unmoving as she studied Wade's handsome features at rest. His face lost the natural harshness that was such a part of his personality and he looked younger, more relaxed and at peace. She could spend hours simply watching him, smug in the knowledge that this beautiful man was hers.

She was loose and limber, completely sated and content. Her eyelids were slowly closing as she surrendered once again to the lure of sleep when the peel of Wade's cell phone startled her, making her flinch.

Wade came instantly awake, rotating to his other side to reach down and snag his phone.

"Sterling," he said shortly.

There was a pause as Wade listened to whatever the other person was saying and then Wade's next words froze her to the bone.

"No. He's mine. Sit on him. Do not let him out of your sight, and make sure he goes nowhere until I get there. My men will remain here to protect Eliza. I'll be there as soon as possible."

He sat up, swinging his legs over the side of the bed and then swiveled, turning to look at Eliza. She saw the inevitable in his eyes. She'd only heard his side of the conversation, but it was clear what was about to happen. She pushed herself up to her knees, staring at him pleadingly, her heart in her throat.

"Please don't go, Wade. Don't do this. Not for me. Let's just leave. He can't control me anymore. He is no threat to me. Let's just go. I'll go anywhere you want, do anything you ask. I don't want to lose you," she said brokenly.

"Come here," he said quietly.

She scrambled over the bed, launching herself into his arms, clinging desperately to his neck, biting into her lip to staunch the scream that echoed over and over in her heart. He pulled her into his lap and then turned so he was perched on the edge of the mattress, his feet planted on the floor.

He cupped her face and kissed her hard. Fierce. His tongue tangling wildly with hers until his chest heaved from lack of oxygen. Then he pulled away, cradling her face in his hands as he stared intently into her eyes.

"Baby, I can't let it go," he said gently. "I'll never breathe easy if he's alive and out there. I'll never allow a threat to you to exist. He damaged you. He hurt you. He made you doubt yourself. For that alone he dies. He took something from you and I'll be damned if he ever takes you from *me*. I have to do this, Eliza. I need you to understand that. You know who I am, the kind of man I am. You've accepted that part of me that I hope to God never touches you. And after this, nothing ever will. You did what you had to do. I didn't like it but I understood. It was important to you. Baby, this is everything to me and this is something I have to do. Don't make me choose between loving and protecting you with my every breath or losing you anyway because you can't forgive what I have to do."

She closed her eyes and leaned her forehead against his, emitting a sigh she knew he would recognize as her acquiescence.

"I love you," she whispered. "Promise me you'll come back to me. Swear it, Wade. I can't lose you. Not when I've finally found myself *and* a man who knows every ugly secret I have and loves me anyway. How can I not do the same for you? Swear to me this doesn't touch you, doesn't lead back to you or implicate you in any way because I will not let you take the fall for me," she said fiercely. "I swear to you, Wade, if this falls back on you I will make a full confession and I will plead guilty and swear under oath that I was the one who killed him."

Wade's eyes went soft with so much love that she felt shattered. He stroked her cheek and kissed her lovingly.

"Baby, I don't say this to freak you out, and after this, I will never talk about anything like this with you again because you're going to live free and you're going to live in the light, never in the shadows and I'll break my back to make you happy and to make sure you live free and in the sun. But I am good at what

I do. Not saying I'm proud and I'm not bragging. It just is. I've done a lot of shit in my life, shit I will never share with you and I hope that doesn't hurt you but this is me protecting you and busting my ass to make you happy every day. I will never be implicated, suspected or even considered in the matter of Thomas Harrington's death. I need you to trust me and I need you to have faith in what I'm telling you. I would never do anything that made it so I'm not with you or that I'm not the man making you smile and laugh and live free. So when I tell you that I'll be back and that neither me or you will have any suspicions cast our way, I need you to tell me you believe in that."

There was no way she would ever send the man she loved off on a mission that could get him killed, hurt or jailed worried that she would never be able to accept him for who and what he was. He'd done that for her with no hesitation, no reservations and she could do no less for him.

"I believe in you, Wade," she said, her voice serious and grave. "I'll always believe in you. Just be safe and hurry back to me. I'll be waiting."

He rose, lifting her from his lap and then setting her back down onto the bed. Then he leaned down and kissed her one last time.

"Love you, baby. This will be over soon and you'll be free and you'll never have to worry about him again. I want you looking ahead. Focus on the future. Our future. Let me take care of the present."

TWENTY-THREE

WADE had only been gone half an hour and Eliza had settled in for a long night. She was tense and anxiety consumed her. She was sick at heart, sick to the depths of her soul over Wade doing what amounted to her dirty work. It was her fault he was on his way to kill a man. For her. She was the one who'd begun the quest for justice. Vengeance. Wade wouldn't be here if she hadn't taken it upon herself to play God and dispense justice as she demanded it.

He hadn't even known what she was planning to do. He'd tracked her down because he was worried, knew she was in trouble and was determined not only to protect her but to shield her from any repercussions of a choice made solely by her.

He was stepping in to clean up her mess. To prevent her from suffering the consequences of her decision. A decision she'd made when she'd been in no state of mind to be making such a drastic resolution. And now Wade would pay the ultimate price. Not her.

Even if he did escape implication, suspicion or God... arrest and conviction, he'd still have to live with the knowledge that he'd killed a man in a premeditated act of murder for the rest of his life. And he'd forever have Thomas Harrington's blood on his hands. Would he eventually come to hate her? Would he later be consumed with regret and guilt. Would he blame her and eventually resent her for putting him in this position to begin with?

She didn't even make the attempt to go back to sleep though she'd nearly been just that when Wade had gotten the phone call. She was wired for sound and so rigid and tense with fear that her muscles already ached from the strain.

With a resigned sigh, knowing she was facing a long night, she shuffled into the kitchen after pulling on one of Wade's shirts. It was warm like he was and his scent was all over it. It wasn't even close to having the real thing, but wearing his shirt, feeling his warmth and smelling him on her gave her a small measure of comfort.

Knowing the last thing she needed was caffeine when she was already so worked up, she opted for a glass of juice and rummaged in the fridge for something to eat, more out of the need to have something to do than any real hunger. After dumping several of the items she'd pulled from the fridge onto the counter, she reached back to shut the fridge just as her cell phone rang.

She stared at the phone laying next to the sink, a sense of dread settling into the pit of her stomach. Wade had now been gone thirty-five minutes. It was too soon to be hearing from him or any of her guys on surveillance. What if something had gone terribly wrong?

Then realizing she was standing there staring while the phone continued to ring, she lunged for it, not even checking to see who the incoming call was from.

"Hello?" she said, her voice trembling.

"Hello my darling. It's been far too long since I last heard your voice. I've missed it."

Eliza felt the blood drain rapidly from her face and she felt blindly for one of the barstools behind her, sinking down before her knees buckled and gave out.

"Thomas," she whispered.

Something wasn't right. Something was very, very wrong. Dane had called Wade because they'd tagged Thomas and had the residence he was staying in or at least using surrounded and were only waiting for Wade's arrival before they went in to take Thomas out.

If all of that was so, then how on earth was he on the phone with her and how had he gotten her number?

Or maybe he was calling her from the house Dane and his team were watching. If Wade hadn't yet arrived or if they simply hadn't swarmed in and apprehended Thomas then all she had to do was keep him talking, distracted, so it would make Wade's and Dane's jobs that much easier.

"I was very disappointed that you didn't stay to see me after the press conference ended," Thomas said, annoyance vibrating his voice.

"They hate me," Eliza said, tempering her voice so she sounded more like the meek, obedient teenager he once knew and nothing like a highly trained security specialist who kicked people's asses for a living. Trying to sound embarrassed and even sad, she said, "I had to leave while they were absorbed in your wonderful speech. It was risky for me to even go. They've made no secret of their hatred and disdain for me since I returned. But I had to see you, Thomas. I had to be there to see you when you were released. I wanted to reassure myself that you were well."

"I've already chosen my next victim," he said as casually as if they were discussing the weather and completely ignoring or dismissing her response.

She went completely still, her heart thudding painfully against the wall of her chest. She gripped the phone so tightly that her fingertips were as bloodless as her face.

"She's here with me now," he continued in a cheerful voice. "You can save her, you know."

"H-How?"

Eliza began to fervently pray that Thomas was where Dane thought him to be and that at any moment, they would bust in, take Thomas down and save the woman from certain death.

"I'll trade her for you," Thomas said, his tone suddenly going completely serious. "All you have to do is come to me and I'll let her go. I give you my word."

She wanted to scream at him, to unleash her fury and hatred and wish him to hell. But she couldn't do anything to risk his ire. If he killed yet another woman because of Eliza, she would well and truly lose her sanity.

"Where?" Eliza choked out. "Tell me where and I'll come immediately. And, Thomas, if you hurt that woman, I'll never forgive you." She injected hurt into her voice, hopefully masking the rage and hatred that boiled and burned like acid in her veins. "I had hoped you had changed during your time in prison," she added quietly. "That's why I came. Because I wanted my Thomas back. I can forgive you the past if you swear you'll never hurt another woman.

"I'm yours, Thomas. I've always been yours. But you betrayed me and you hurt me. I need to know I can love you and trust you again. So promise me."

Thomas was silent but she'd heard his sudden intake of breath, as if she'd completely surprised him and he hadn't expected her to say any of what she'd said to him.

"I'm sorry, my darling girl," Thomas said, his tone becoming loving and even contrite. "Please say you'll come. I've changed. I swear to you I have and I'll make it up to you. I never meant to hurt you. You were the one person I would have never hurt, Melissa. Come to me and I'll let the woman go. I promise. She means nothing to me but you are my world. You and I will leave this place and go somewhere far away where we can start over. We'll have a new beginning and be together forever as we were meant to be."

Eliza shivered because his statement though earnestly voiced sounded ominous and threatening.

"Where?" she asked again, because trepidation had firmly set in along with a sense of impending doom. It had been too long and wherever Dane and Wade were, Thomas was not, which meant Thomas had likely made one of the DSS agents.

"I'll text you the address," he said smoothly. "Get here soon, Melissa. I don't like to be kept waiting."

"I need a few minutes before I leave," she said softly. "I want to look nice for you, Thomas. I'm in my nightshirt."

"You have half an hour."

The call went dead as he abruptly ended it. Panic and despair hit her like a tidal wave. She stumbled to her feet, barely able to make it into the bedroom. Oh God, she had so little time and she had no idea what she was walking into.

She grabbed clothing from one of the drawers and then selected what weapons she could. Only a few were small enough to be undetectable with what she'd chosen to wear. She slipped them into place and raced back to the kitchen. She couldn't just take off without leaving Wade a way to find her. Thomas knew more than he was letting on. He'd purposely not given her the address over the phone and had set a time limit that gave her next to no time to do anything but make the drive and she had to figure out how to get past Wade's men without them knowing.

Helplessness gripped her. She couldn't call Wade and tell him the situation because if she did, he'd have his men lock her down so fast she wouldn't know what hit her and then an innocent woman would die. There was no guessing or ifs, ands or buts about it. Thomas had proven many times over that killing was second nature to him. He got off on it, thrived on it.

All she could do was write notes to Wade. And to Dane, just in case she didn't make it out alive. And then she had to get the hell over to wherever Thomas was holding his victim and pray that Wade would find her in time.

TWENTY-FOUR

WADE slid through the night to where Dane was waiting, anticipation and a keen sense of vengeance racing through his veins.
Finally, the bastard would be taken down and Eliza would never
have to worry about him again or torture herself over the knowledge that now free, he would resume his sadistic practices.

Most importantly, he would pay for hurting Eliza and putting her through hell for so long.

"Sterling?"

The whisper came from the dark and then Dane appeared,
his face set in stone, his stance one of anticipation, mirroring
Wade's own.

"Has he moved?" Wade demanded shortly.

"No. As soon as we followed him here, I set a perimeter
around the house and called you. Every man I have is on this. He
won't get past us. What's your plan?"

"Go in. Take him out. Permanently," Wade clipped out.

Dane didn't react to the fact that Wade was going in to kill a man.

"Is Eliza safe?" he asked.

"Yes. My men are guarding her. She's in a safe house, and like you, I set a tight perimeter around it so no one gets close to her."

Relief flared in Dane's eyes. "You ready to get this over with? Your call. We'll cover. You do what you need to do."

There was no judgment or condemnation in Dane's eyes. In fact, he looked disappointed that he would have no part in taking Harrington out, but he didn't argue and Wade respected him for that.

"Appreciate that," Wade said quietly. "Let's roll. Have your men converge and when we have all potential exit points covered, I'm going in. I'd like you to go in with me and have my back."

Dane nodded. "Done. No question."

They moved stealthily toward the house. The lights were on in seemingly every room. Arrogant bastard. But it would make Wade's job easier and the sooner he took care of the problem, the sooner he could get back to Eliza and take her home.

They paused at one of the side entrances that opened into the kitchen until Dane received confirmation that all his men were in place.

"Go time," Dane said grimly. "Let's do this."

Wade tried the knob and to his surprise the door was unlocked. He and Dane slipped inside, weapons up as they scanned the interior and listened for any betraying noise that would give away Harrington's location.

The distant sound of a television was the only discernible noise. Wade motioned for Dane to take one side while Wade took the other as they slowly moved through the house. The kitchen was empty and they checked the small laundry room off the kitchen before moving quietly into the dining room.

The house wasn't huge and Dane's recon had reported two bedrooms, a living room, dining room and kitchen so the only places Harrington could be were the living room or one of the bedrooms.

They paused just outside the living room, pressed to the wall next to the open doorway. Carefully, Wade eased around, taking in every inch of space in the living room where the television was on.

There was a couch and two chairs but otherwise unfurnished. It was an open space with no areas someone could hide, which meant he had to be in one of the bedrooms. Wade's pulse accelerated as he closed in on his prey.

I've got you, you bastard. You will pay for all the hurt and damage done to Eliza.

The first bedroom was obviously a guest room as it was small and like the living room unfurnished. There wasn't even a closet or a bathroom someone could hide in. There was only one remaining place, the master bedroom, and he had to temper his urge to burst in and make Harrington suffer like he'd made Eliza suffer and those women he'd brutally murdered. Never again. His reign of terror ended tonight.

The master bedroom was closed so he and Dane stood on either side of the door and Wade held up his fingers to count to three. When he reached three, Dane kicked the door open, shattering the wood, while Wade dropped low so all bases would be covered. They swarmed into the room doing a sweep with their guns only to find the room . . . empty.

Wade stormed into the bathroom but as with the rest of the house, no one was there. His stomach clenched and sweat formed on his forehead. Something wasn't right about this entire situation.

"Radio your men. Have them report in. They had to have seen something. He couldn't have vanished into thin air."

Dane barked orders and demands into his mouthpiece, his expression growing darker and darker with every passing second. Fury blazed in his eyes but worse, Wade saw abject fear reflected in the other man's gaze.

"Tell me," Wade barked.

"Goddamn it!" Dane roared. "Nothing! We have nothing. We followed him here, watched him go inside. His vehicle is still here but that's the last anyone has seen of him. Not a single one of my men detected movement, saw him leave, and, Sterling, regardless of what you may think, my men are the best. They don't fuck up. Especially when it comes to safeguarding one of our own. He had to have had an escape route and he had to have planned this well in advance because he did not just walk out of here or we would have known it."

"Shit," Wade hissed. "Shit, shit, shit!"

Then he went rigid, terror seizing his heart.

"It was a fucking setup. It was a goddamn fucking setup. Somehow he tagged one of us or maybe he's just a paranoid, cautious motherfucker. But he planned this well in advance and took into account every possibility and then made certain he had a solution."

He yanked his phone from his pocket and dialed Eliza's number.

Please be there, baby. Please answer. Please be okay.

But it went straight to voicemail, which meant she either didn't have service, it was powered down or had been destroyed.

His hands shaking so badly that he could barely manage to operate his phone, he hit the contact button for his team leader. Jones answered on the first ring.

"Where's Eliza?" Wade demanded.

"She's still in the house, sir. We have every angle covered and every possible vantage point. We'd know if she left."

Yeah, yeah. He'd heard that just minutes ago when Dane had made the same assurances.

"I want a visible confirmation," Wade said in an icy tone. "Get the hell in the house now. I want you to be looking at her when you tell me she's still in the house."

"On it," Jones said shortly.

Wade held the phone to his ear, each second an eternity as he waited for his man to tell him Eliza was safe and accounted for. He heard the door open, heard Jones's footsteps. Then they stopped. Then they began again. What the fuck was taking so long? The house wasn't that big.

"Fuck!" Jones said explosively.

Wade's heart bottomed out and he closed his eyes, dreading what Jones would say next.

"Tell me," Wade said lifelessly, dread encompassing his soul.

"She's not here, man," Jones said, worry and anger edging his voice. "I have no idea how the fuck she got by us. She left two sealed envelopes on the counter. One with your name and one with Dane's name."

"You have got to be shitting me!" Wade exploded. "How the fuck could you let this happen?"

"We had the entire house cased," Jones said grimly. "But your girl is good. You know that. She's trained."

"Get the goddamn letters and meet us in town. Now!" Wade barked.

"Tell me where and we'll be there double time."

Wade thought a moment and then chose the most central location, one that would hopefully not put them too far from finding Eliza, wherever the fuck she was, and barked his order for where Jones was to meet them.

When he ended the call, Dane stared him down, fury and worry that went bone deep etched into his every feature.

"Tell me she hasn't disappeared," Dane said in a pissed off voice. "Goddamn it, Sterling. You swore to keep her safe!"

"If your men hadn't fucked up and let Harrington give you the slip, we wouldn't be having this goddamn conversation," Wade bit out. "We've got to move out now. Get your men so we can meet with Jones."

Dane flinched and then briefly closed his eyes, his grief evident. But then Wade didn't blame him considering the last letter she'd left that amounted to little more than a goodbye before embarking on a suicide mission.

"We can't afford to wait to read the letters to act," Wade said grimly. "We need every man you've got on this. I need to know everything about Thomas Harrington we can unearth. Any houses or property in his name. Anyone affiliated with him. Eliza told me one of the Devereaux brothers is a computer whiz and can hack into just about anything. We need to get him on Harrington and leave no stone unturned. Pay particular attention to the time he spent in prison and find out if he had visitors, contact with the outside world and if anything seems suspicious or if he received any special treatment while in prison. We already know he got to one of the police officers who investigated the case and was instrumental in gathering the evidence that put Harrington away for life. Look for any other irregularities. Anything. We're operating blind here and we need every piece of intel on the bastard we can get. He has Eliza. I know it. He purposely lured us here so he'd have a clear path to Eliza and we took the bait, hook, line and sinker."

"Let's roll," Dane said harshly.

Wade didn't wait around for Dane to gather his men. He ran to his SUV, threw himself behind the steering wheel and pushed the vehicle to its very limits, knowing every precious minute counted.

He roared into town, screeching to a halt just as his men pulled to the back of the diner in a convoy of three vehicles. Wade was out of the seat before the SUV came to a complete halt, killing the engine and causing the vehicle to rock violently with the force applied to the brakes. He wasted no time stalking over to Jones and yanking the envelopes from his grasp.

Just seeing Eliza's hastily scrawled address, his name, on the paper filled him with anguish. His hands shook violently as he tore it open to reveal the contents. As he pulled the single piece of paper from the envelope, headlights illuminated the area and bounced erratically as Dane and his crew roared up.

Dane got out and rushed over, taking the envelope Jones extended. Wade paid no attention to the others as he unfolded the letter and sucked in a deep breath as he began to read.

Wade, I know you'll be angry that I snuck away and broke my promise to you to stay at the safe house and let you take care of Thomas. I'm sorry, but I had no choice. He called me. I have no idea how he knew my number but he obviously set up a diversion to lead you and Dane in the wrong direction. He told me he had already chosen his next victim and that she was with him now but that I could save her by trading myself for her, that he would let her go if I would come to him. He knows about you or Dane, maybe both, because he wouldn't tell me the address over the phone. He told me to leave and he'd text me the address. I couldn't call you for two reasons. You would have had your men lock me down and you would have gone instead of me. And when I didn't show, he would have killed her. I had no other option. And I couldn't live with myself if another woman dies because of me. I just can't. Please understand that I can't sit back and do nothing. I don't want to die. I have too much to live for now. I will do everything I can to survive, to take him down. I'll do whatever it takes to make it back to you. I love you. You taught me the true beauty of love and the difference between love and obsession. For the first time in my life, I was loved, truly loved, and I felt loved. You gave me the most precious gift anyone has ever given me. I have to try to save her, Wade, and I hope you'll forgive me if I live to beg for your forgiveness. Always and forever. Eliza.

Tears burned like acid, blurring his vision. His chest ached. His heart hurt so damn much and he was sick to his soul. His beautiful, courageous, brave, compassionate Eliza. A woman who had no idea of her worth or how very loved she was, how very deserving of love she was. Dear God. He couldn't lose her. He wouldn't survive it. He had to find her fast.

He glanced up to see that Dane fared no better, the letter Eliza had written him shaking like a leaf in his trembling grasp. Sorrow and grief were so evident on his face that it was as if she'd already died, as though the letters were notifying them of her death.

Fuck that. He would *not* lose her. Not now. Not ever.

"If everyone doesn't get that fucking look off their faces right the fuck now, swear to God, I'll kill every damn one of you," Wade said furiously. "We have not lost her. I have not lost her. Now snap the fuck out of it and give me anything you've got and you better have something, Elliot."

Dane's expression lost the despair and fiery determination ignited in his eyes.

"I have a list of houses, a few businesses and property he owns in a fifty-mile radius. Given the short amount of time between when he entered the house we had under surveillance and when Eliza disappeared, they have to be somewhere close. We divide up, divvy out the locations and hit them as quickly as possible."

Zack Covington stepped forward, his expression grim, anger billowing from him in waves.

"Beau and I will partner up. Give us some locations and we're out of here."

Dane nodded then looked to the rest of his assembled men. "Isaac, you take Shadow and Knight. Eric, you take Dex and Zeke. Capshaw and Brent, you two work together, and I want all of you to be on your toes at all goddamn times. There has never been a more important mission than this one. One of our own is on the line. You make damn sure she's not caught in the line of fire and that you protect her with your lives. Take Harrington out any way you can, as soon as you can, but make damn sure Eliza doesn't end up as collateral damage or I'll have your balls."

Dane took out his phone and then looked to Wade. "You want north end of town or south?"

"I'll take north. My men and I will spread out and cover as many locations as possible so give us an entire sector. You and your men see to the rest."

"I'm forwarding the locations Quinn texted me so check your phones for your assignments. Now get moving so we can take Eliza home where she belongs."

"Something's not right. It's too easy, too obvious," Wade growled into the phone as soon as the call connected to Dane. "We're missing something here. He's not stupid and he's had a long time to plan this. He wouldn't bring a victim or lure Eliza to a place that a public record links him to."

Dane's voice was urgent and tense when he broke in.

"I was in the process of calling you when you buzzed me. Quinn found something and I think it's the only logical answer."

"Spit it out then. We've wasted enough goddamn time," Wade said, his body rigid as he waited, hoping, praying that Quinn had come through in a big way.

"Quinn accessed Harrington's prison records. Visitor logs, correspondence. His every move or anyone he had any contact with. The cop who testified that he tampered with evidence had visited Thomas in prison just a week before the cop made his confession. Here's the interesting part. When Quinn accessed records of all correspondence Harrington received while in prison, he discovered that the cop's wife had been writing to Harrington for a long period of time before the cop visited Harrington in jail and then subsequently confessed to a crime. The cop disappeared right after testifying and most assumed he did so to avoid sanctions and possible jail time. The wife, however, remained in Calvary and owns a house just north of town. Not far from where you currently are. Now, the woman may or may not be a victim. She may be in league with Thomas and helped lure Eliza to her house, but it's the only logical conclusion. We've come up with jack shit on every other lead."

"Give me the address," Wade demanded. "I can be there before you. Get there as fast as you can, but I'm not waiting."

TWENTY-FIVE

ELIZA pulled to a stop in front of a modest ranch-style home in the vehicle she'd hot-wired and stolen as soon as she'd slipped past Wade's men. The closest neighbor had been a five-minute walk. Eliza had made it in two at a dead run. Since Thomas likely assumed she was in Calvary, he'd given her a deadline that forced her to drive like a demon possessed the entire way, praying she wouldn't be seen by a cop.

She wiped her damp palms down the jeans she'd chosen, and glanced quickly at her top, praying it would be nice enough for Thomas not to call her out on her lie about wanting to look nice for him. She'd quickly brushed out her hair and fluffed it out by bending over and tousling it with her fingers because Thomas like it that way. Thank God he wasn't a fan of makeup, in fact he considered women who "painted their faces" whores, which saved Eliza time by not having to apply it.

Opening the door, she got out and sucked in several breaths to compose herself. This was it. This was everything. The biggest test of her strength she'd ever face. One she couldn't afford to fail. A woman's life depended on Eliza pulling off the ultimate deception. Eliza's life depended on it. And no doubt countless other women's lives depended on Eliza succeeding.

She walked slowly toward the porch and when she reached the first step, the door opened and Thomas appeared, a welcoming smile on his face.

"Melissa, darling, you have no idea how long I've hoped for this day. How many nights I spent dreaming of us being together again as we were always meant to be."

Eliza swallowed and met Thomas's gaze, careful to keep any hint of anger or disgust from her expression.

"I'm here now, let the woman go," she said quietly. "I won't set foot in that house until I see that she's alive and is allowed to go free."

In a daring, calculating move, praying she wasn't making a huge mistake, she sent him a challenging stare, her words an obvious taunt.

"It's not as though you should have any worry over letting her go free. You can manipulate people so easily without them ever knowing. You can make them do your bidding. All you have to do is make her leave and plant a false memory or simply command her to forget all about you."

Thomas smiled and Eliza could swear he looked as though he were proud of her. "And yet you seem immune to my powers now. You're much stronger now. I can't read you like I could before."

"I was a vulnerable, mixed-up teenager who only wanted to be loved. I'm not that girl anymore, Thomas. You're right. I am stronger now, and I don't want us to be together because you *make* me feel things that aren't real. Is that really what you want? A puppet you control, knowing the entire time that her feelings for you are manufactured by you? Don't you want to be wanted for who you are? Isn't that what we all want?"

Thomas stared at her, shock reflected in his gaze. But also a glimmer of hope, as though she'd hit the nail on the head and had exposed a vulnerability he'd refused to acknowledge until now. His features softened and then he abruptly turned, stepping just inside the doorway and called for the woman.

A moment later, a pale woman in her forties stepped onto the porch next to Thomas, looking up at him as though awaiting instruction.

Thomas stared hard into her eyes, holding her gaze in a fixed manner. The woman's eyes glazed and she swayed as though she were in a complete daze. A puppet awaiting its master's manipulation. But then that was what Thomas cultivated. Mindless followers incapable of making independent decisions.

"Get out," he said sharply. "Leave and don't return until tomorrow."

As if in a trance, the woman started down the steps, barefooted and only dressed in a nightgown, her gait jerky and stilted. She walked straight to a vehicle parked a short distance away, got in and then simply drove away, disappearing down the drive.

Panic swamped Eliza and she lifted her chin in determination, staring Thomas down.

"If you planted a compulsion for her to commit suicide, I'll never forgive you."

In a sickeningly sweet and soothing tone he said, "You have no need to worry about the woman. No harm will come to her.

She'll return to her home tomorrow and resume her pathetic existence. Now we need to hurry. We are also leaving this house and this town."

"I didn't pack a bag," Eliza murmured, her tone regretful and apologetic. "I wasn't sure what you wanted, what your plans were or if you even still wanted me."

Thomas's eyes glittered, triumph and victory gleaming brightly. "You don't need anything, my love. I will provide every-thing you need. I only have one task for you before we depart."

Eliza sent him an innocent, puzzled look. "You know I'll do whatever you want."

Thomas nodded approvingly. "You will write a letter explain-ing that you are leaving with me and that you only want a quiet life with me away from the prying eyes of those who would judge and scorn you."

"But why bother?" she asked. "No one would care. Everyone here hates me. They won't care that I'm gone. In fact, they'll be happy."

Thomas made a sound of impatience. "If we both disappear, it will raise suspicion and we will never have the life I want for us. It will be suspected that I killed you in revenge so you have to convince the public that you willingly chose to go away with me."

A chill slithered down Eliza's spine. She had been wrong about Thomas's obsession with her and her certainty that he would never harm her, only those he saw as a threat for her love. He was lying about the reasons for wanting her to write the letter. He had no intention of taking her anywhere. The letter would only serve to exonerate him when he killed her and she disappeared, leaving him free to also disappear and everyone would assume she went willingly with him. No one would even look for her body or blink an eye over her sudden disappearance.

Except Wade and Dane.

They'd never buy anything she wrote about loving Thomas and going away with him. But would they find the letter—or her—too late to save her? Did Thomas plan to kill her here or would he take her somewhere so he could make her suffer for as long as possible before finally killing her?

Thank God he couldn't read her now or he'd know everything. Everyone she loved would be a target. And because he couldn't read her he didn't know about her ace in the hole. Wade. She just had to buy enough time for him to find her. He wouldn't rest, sleep or eat until he found her. She knew that. She just had to pray that he found her in time.

"Of course I'll write a letter. Is there anyone specific you want me to address it to?"

She purposely injected excitement into her voice and then asked, "Where are we going Thomas? Where will we live? I can't believe we are finally free to be together. You have no idea how long I've waited for this moment."

His smile was smug and victorious. He thought he had her right where he wanted her and he was positively gleeful over the idea of retribution and escaping justice yet again.

"You don't need to worry about a single thing. I'll take care of you just like I always did."

She smiled despite the fact she was screaming on the inside. She had to hold it together. She couldn't fall apart. Everything was riding on her being able to deceive Thomas and buy enough time to either catch him off guard and take him down herself or for Wade to track her down and swoop in like an avenging angel and mete out his own brand of retribution.

"I know," she said softly, her tone dreamy. "You always took care of me, Thomas. You always protected me. You've always been my hero."

"Come," he said, extending his hand to take hers. "We need to get you inside so you can write the letter and then we'll leave immediately."

Eliza let him take her hand and managed not to shudder or recoil. She even leaned into him as they entered the house, but the entire time she was fervently praying that she would live to tell Wade how much she loved him again.

Thomas urged her to the kitchen table where pen and paper were already laid out. He directed her to sit, forgoing any attempt to be tender and loving as he'd been earlier.

He stood over her, dictating word for word what she was to write and he watched closely, ensuring she did as commanded. It took all of Eliza's hard-won and practiced self-discipline to maintain her composure and calmly write exactly what Thomas recited without her hands shaking or her handwriting being illegible.

She made a mental sigh of relief when she completed the letter without giving herself away. She signed her name and dated it and then tilted her head up to look at Thomas and smiled.

"So do we leave now? Where are we going? I'm so excited, Thomas. You have no idea how much I've longed for this. It's like a dream come true."

Thomas reached over and snatched the paper, folding it neatly and then laying it aside.

"Stand up," he said coldly.

She adopted a hurt, confused look as she rose from the chair. "What's wrong, Thomas? Did I do something wrong? I wrote the letter verbatim as you told me to."

His hand slid inside his jacket and he pulled out a handgun, aiming it directly at her. Her heart sank. She'd known this was going to happen but a secret part of her had hoped she was wrong. Was he going to kill her right now? How could she buy time? Time had run out for her.

"What are you doing?" she whispered. "I don't understand."

His eyes glittered with rage. "Did you honestly think that I would just forget and forgive what you did? I loved you. I would have done anything in the world for you. There is nothing I wouldn't have given you. And you betrayed me. You are a lying, deceitful whore. I've spent the last ten years dreaming of this moment. To return the pain and suffering you caused me. I lost years of my life because of *you*. You ungrateful bitch. I gave you everything and you gave me lies. Now it's my turn to make you suffer. To cause you unspeakable pain and I'm going to enjoy every minute of it."

TWENTY-SIX

WADE tore recklessly down the bumpy dirt road leading to the residence belonging to the wife of the cop who'd been responsible for Harrington's release, his heart pounding with fear and praying the entire way that he would get there in time. That he wouldn't be too late. God, please don't let him be too late. He'd sworn to protect Eliza, that nothing would happen to her and he'd fallen neatly into Harrington's trap.

As he rounded the bend, he was blinded by oncoming headlights and then yanked the steering wheel to the right to avoid a head-on collision. The other vehicle veered to the left, losing control and spinning in a complete three hundred and sixty-degree circle before skidding to a stop, hitting a large tree that lined the road.

Fuck! He didn't have time for this shit!

He slammed on the brakes and bolted from the SUV, running to check on the driver, hoping no serious injury had been incurred. All he could do was call 911 because he couldn't stick around when Eliza was in the hands of a madman and every minute counted. Every second he was delayed could mean the difference in Eliza living or dying.

He yanked open the driver's side door and blinked in confusion. A woman was sitting stock-still, her gaze fixed through the windshield as if she had no awareness of the situation. Even more alarming was the fact that she was dressed only in a nightgown and her feet were bare.

"Ma'am, are you okay?" he asked sharply.

Slowly she turned her head and an eerie sensation slithered over Wade's skin, raising chill bumps as he stared into vacant, lifeless eyes.

"I have to leave," she murmured. "He told me to leave and not to return to my house until tomorrow. But where will I go?"

Oh sweet Jesus. In a flash, he knew this was the cop's wife. And that it was Harrington who had compelled her to leave. She was the victim he had used to lure Eliza to come to him. A bargain. Her for the victim. Harrington got to Eliza in the one way she would never refuse. He would have known all too well the guilt and grief that had crippled her. He'd used her compassion and inherent goodness against her, knowing she would never refuse to save the life of another woman.

Wade grasped her shoulders and gave her a gentle shake, desperate to break through the fog. "Was anyone else there? A woman? Did he tell you to leave after she arrived?"

Confusion clouded her eyes and her brow puckered as if she were trying to recall what exactly had happened.

"Think!" Wade said forcefully. "I need you to focus. *Fight* him. I need your help. *She* needs your help."

The woman's hand fluttered to her forehead, pressing in as

she closed her eyes in concentration. Then her expression crumpled and she brought both hands to cover her face as a sound of utter despair seemed ripped from the deepest part of her soul.

"He said he loved me. That we would be together. But then she came and he told me to leave."

Assured that she had sustained no physical injuries, he guided her back into her vehicle and issued a harsh command for her to stay there until help arrived. Then he ran to his SUV and roared down the road, every muscle in his body tense and coiled, preparing to fight the most important battle of his life. To save the woman he loved.

As soon as the house came into view, Wade doused the headlights and pulled as close as he dared before shutting down the engine. He grabbed the Glock laying in the passenger seat and quickly popped in a thirteen-round clip as he jumped out and ran the remaining distance to the house.

Two vehicles were parked in front and the house was illuminated with light, nearly every window reflecting lights on in the residence. He skirted around the front, pressing himself against the brick exterior of the side, peering into each window before he ducked and moved on.

When he reached a window toward the back of the home, he saw that it was the kitchen and he halted in his tracks, his relief so profound that his knees buckled and he nearly went down.

Eliza was seated at the table and Thomas stood a few feet away. Wade gripped the pistol resting in his palm tighter, quickly assessing his entry options. Eliza handed him a piece of paper and after Thomas snatched it from her fingers, Eliza rose from her seat. Then Wade's heart stuttered and nearly stopped when

Thomas suddenly pulled a gun from the inside of his jacket and aimed it directly at her head.

Eliza stood frozen as she stared down the barrel of the pistol Thomas pointed at her. It was akin to an out of body experience. She stepped outside of herself, a passive observer to the goings on. Where before there had been a multitude of emotions reflected in Thomas's eyes, now only one stared malevolently back at her. Hatred. His features were twisted in a sinister expression. His aim was steady. He appeared completely calm as if killing her was just an item to check off on his to-do list. But then she supposed it was.

"You won't get away with this," Eliza said softly.

"People are easily manipulated and controlled. You should know," he said mockingly. "I can command people's will. No one can stop me."

"Is that why you went to prison?" she mocked back.

His hand dipped the slightest of inches before steadying, the pistol leveling at her head once more. He opened his mouth to speak but a crash sounded and Wade barged into the room, gun in hand, pointing it straight at Thomas.

Oh God. No. This wasn't happening. She'd prayed for Wade to find her, but not now, not when Thomas was armed. She couldn't lose him—wouldn't lose him. She'd never survive knowing he died for her. It had to be her that Thomas chose to kill. Choking fear paralyzed her, freezing her blood in her veins as her heart plummeted, her stomach bottoming out. Her mouth went dry and tears burned the edges of her eyelids.

"Drop it now," Wade said in a savage tone.

Oddly, Thomas showed no fear at all. There was a sense of

triumph in his eyes as he stared thoughtfully at Eliza. Then he smiled, and that frightened her more than the fact he had a gun pointed at her head. Wade moved closer to her, moving to shield her, to form a barrier between her and Thomas.

Thomas's smile became sinister. "You're much stronger now. I hadn't been able to read you at all, couldn't forge a pathway into your mind. Until now. But love is stronger than you are and now I know. I would have never hurt you back then. Never killed you. But you betrayed me and so you became my target, not the people you care about as you assumed. Now I know how to hurt you the most, how to make you suffer far more than ending your miserable existence. Yes, my darling Melissa. You're much stronger now, but not as strong as love, and now you will suffer for an eternity for betraying me."

In a swift move, he moved his hand so the gun was now pointed at Wade and not her. And she knew exactly what he was going to do. Her love for Wade and her overwhelming fear for his life had weakened the barriers she'd spent so long strengthening and now she was an open book. He was going to kill Wade because he knew it would utterly destroy her. Far more than killing her.

"No!" she screamed, and she flung her body in front of Wade's just as Thomas shot. Fire exploded through her chest and her mouth opened in a soundless cry just as another shot sounded.

As she slid to the floor, she saw the neat hole form right between Thomas's eyes and then he was flung back, falling lifelessly onto his back.

Thank God.

She closed her eyes, her relief so profound that for a moment she didn't feel the horrific pain tearing through her chest. Wade was safe. That was all that mattered. Then another sound, a terrible, guttural cry of heart-wrenching pain registered close to her ears. Oh God, had Wade been hurt after all?

She felt hands on her face and strangely, wetness as well. She struggled to open her eyes and saw Wade's head hovering over hers, his eyes awash with tears.

"Stay with me, Eliza," he said hoarsely. "Oh God, baby, why? Why did you do it? You have to stay with me. Don't you dare close your fucking eyes."

She watched hazily as he yanked his phone to his ear and began yelling that he needed an ambulance and the situation was critical. For some reason the room was growing darker, but she knew the lights were on. Why was it getting so dark?

Then Wade's face loomed over hers again but she could barely make out his features. His hand feathered over her cheek and he looked . . . terrified. That was odd. Wade didn't get scared. Her eyelids grew heavier and then the room went completely black.

"Don't you give up!" Wade yelled hoarsely. "Don't let go. You're free now, baby. He can't hurt you anymore. Please don't give up. I love you so much. I've been in love with you ever since you got into my face the first time we met in my art gallery. Why the hell do you think I spent so much time pissed off at you? You always seemed so determined to get yourself killed. Why would I have taken a bullet for you?"

He went quiet, making a choking sound and she struggled against the darkness to pry her eyelids halfway open, trying to focus on him, to do as he demanded. More noise erupted as people poured into the kitchen. She heard her name from seemingly a dozen directions, but she was only focused on Wade. She was afraid if she lost sight of him, he would be gone forever.

His eyes had gone all watery again and he continued stroking her cheek. Sirens echoed in the distance, becoming louder by the second.

"Lizzie, my God, Lizzie, are you okay?"

Dane was here? Her muddled mind struggled to make sense of the chaos around her. She attempted to look in the direction of his voice, wanting to tell him she was sorry, but when she tried to move, a spasm of pain overtook her and warm, metallic liquid coated her tongue and then slid from the corner of her mouth.

A weird sound that mimicked stabs of pain confused her and then Wade's lips were on her forehead, pressing tenderly against her skin.

"Be still, baby. Try to stay still for me. I need you to hang on." He was stroking upward over her forehead, smoothing her hair in a repetitive motion. "In here!" he yelled to some distant person.

She blinked but her eyelids felt so heavy. Wade grew fuzzier and she felt cold. He looked at her with such torture in his eyes.

"Why did you take a bullet meant for me?" he asked brokenly.

She smiled faintly and struggled to respond, battling against the lure of unconsciousness. She licked her lips, trying to rid herself of the odd slickness slithering over her tongue. She couldn't breathe right, and she wasn't sure she could respond to his question, but it was too important. He had to know.

"Because I love you and if you died, it would destroy me, kill me anyway. You're a good man, Wade. The very best. I thought

I'd learned what love was. I saw it. It was beautiful. Worth dying for. But you taught me how to love and be loved. It's all I've ever wanted and you gave that to me."

Her voice became fainter, more somber as she drifted further and further away. A sense of peace settled over her, the most wonderful feeling she'd ever experienced. She smiled, tears sliding hotly down her temples.

"I'm free," she whispered. "I'm finally free."

"Eliza!"

The world faded rapidly as more faces pushed in, one barking orders while another pressed on her chest. The last image that registered was of Wade roaring at her not to leave him and of Dane and Zack physically restraining Wade as he tried to lunge for her.

TWENTY-SEVEN

WADE stood in the surgical waiting room, staring broodingly out the window, Eliza's blood still bright on his clothing, his hands. His team and hers were assembled, all tensely waiting for word. He could feel the weight of Dane's stare, but there was no judgment, only worry and grief.

He glanced at the rest of her team from his periphery, and they were little better. Their expressions were drawn tight, hopelessness evident in their posture and stance.

Eliza had been in surgery for hours. She'd coded as the EMS personnel had arrived and were attempting to stabilize her. They'd left performing CPR in a load-and-go situation. That had been the last time Wade had seen her.

Eyes closed, lifeless, after saying she was finally free.

Grief welled within him once more and he curled his fingers into tight fists. If only he'd gotten there a few minutes earlier. If only Eliza hadn't thrown herself in front of him to take the bullet meant for him.

Never had anyone cared enough about him to put themselves between him and death. No one had ever loved him until Eliza, and God, he couldn't lose her now. He cursed the time wasted, the time he had spent fighting the inevitable. She'd barreled into his life, upending his carefully ordered existence, and for the first time in a lifetime he'd felt alive. And now she lay on an operating table fighting for her life. Because she'd saved his.

Don't leave me, Eliza. Fight, baby. Please fight. I can't live without you. Please don't leave me alone.

He bowed his head, emotion knotting his chest and throat until he couldn't breathe. All he could see and hear was Eliza screaming *no* and then launching herself in front of him just as Thomas had fired. Her body jerking, then him shooting Thomas and Eliza sagging to the floor in a pool of blood. He'd never forget that sight. Never get it out of his mind. For the rest of his life, that image would haunt his dreams. He only prayed that she would be lying in bed next to him so when he woke she was there, alive, whole, loving him.

The phones of Beau and Zack went off every half hour. Their wives, demanding updates, sick with worry for Eliza. Caleb, the only DSS member to remain behind, had also been a constant caller, his furious voice audible in the quiet waiting room.

He couldn't do this. He couldn't stand here while a surgeon came out and told them that Eliza hadn't made it. That they'd been unable to save her. He wouldn't survive it. He wouldn't want to survive it.

She was his. Had been his since that very first day. He should have staked his claim earlier, made it evident to her that she belonged to him. It had been obvious to everyone else, but Eliza had closed herself off to the possibility of any sort of relationship and had been oblivious. Well maybe not oblivious, but he'd frightened her, had shaken her routine every bit as much as she'd shaken his, and he should have pressed his advantage instead of backing off the way he'd done and waiting. Watching, protecting from a distance.

After her abduction and torture, he should have moved in and taken over. He hadn't. He'd been furious when she had declared she was in on the mission to take down the sick bastards who'd caused so much damage to the DSS wives—and to Eliza. But he hadn't shut her down as he should have. And then, when she'd damn near been killed in that op and he'd taken the bullet meant for her, the one that would have killed her, he sure as hell should have made certain that she was in his bed every single night.

None of this would have happened if he hadn't been so . . . *afraid*. He closed his eyes as the painful admission settled over him. She scared him to death. She made him vulnerable. Because for the first time, there was someone who meant everything to him, and the risks she took terrified him. More than that, however, she scared him merely for the depth of what she made him feel, and he'd been determined to maintain careful distance so that when he did make his move, it would be on his terms. So he wouldn't have been so vulnerable or need her as much as he did.

What a fool he'd been. Stupid, stupid, stupid. By denying the depth of his caring, his love for her, he'd denied her the protection she'd so desperately needed. The support, both physical and emotional. She wouldn't have ever left to face Thomas alone. That wouldn't have even been an option because Wade would have been there. Every goddamn day. He would have known something was wrong, unlike her team who thought she was still recovering from the trauma she'd experienced.

If Dane hadn't called him, would Wade have even known what Eliza was up to until it was too late? Would he have received the news after the fact like her team would have? That she died alone, no backup, no protection, no one to stand for her and all because she was desperately trying to protect the people she loved—including him?

He hadn't seen it then, but God, he saw it now. He'd been so blind, so determined that he'd have Eliza on his terms and his terms only. He had seen the same things he felt reflected in her eyes, the same fears he felt, the same vulnerability. He'd scared her every bit as much as she'd scared him, but she'd cared enough to distance—or try to distance—herself from Wade so Thomas would never know of his existence.

"Sterling," Dane's quiet voice sounded next to him.

Wade jerked, thinking that perhaps the doctor had come in while he'd been lost in thought and self-recrimination. But the waiting room was as it had been for the last hours, only now Dane stood at his side, the first time anyone had approached him.

"You can't do this to yourself, man," Dane said in a low tone, meant only to be heard by Wade. "You can't tear yourself apart and blame yourself or grieve prematurely. Eliza is a fighter. She won't go down easy. She knows Thomas is dead now. She will never worry about him coming after her or the people she cares about."

"She *took*. A *bullet*. For *me*," Wade hissed, his fists clenching tighter.

He wanted to tear the waiting room apart. Wanted to punch

the walls until his hands bled. Anything to release the overwhelming pain and despair. Never had he felt this kind of agony. Such a sense of loss. Like half of him had been cut away, like he'd lost the other half of his soul.

"I know she did," Dane said somberly. "She would have done it for anyone she cared about. Hell, she would have taken it for a stranger. That's just who she is. She'd likely deny that Thomas in fact made her a better person, made her into the selfless, beautiful person she is today, one who fights for justice no matter the cost. But the truth is, what happened to her when she was sixteen shaped her. She walked away from that life, became someone else because she refused to allow him to continue controlling her. She wrongly took the blame for the deaths of every single one of his victims and that fucks with you."

"She had nothing to do with their deaths," Wade exploded. "She had *no* right to carry that burden for ten goddamn years. She was only sixteen. *Sixteen*. And she insists on looking at the choices and emotions of a young girl who had nothing, no one to love her, no one who cared, through the eyes of an adult, with an adult's knowledge."

Dane nodded. "You and I know that, but she doesn't. Maybe she never will. Or maybe she'll finally be at peace now that justice has been rightfully served."

"Not at the expense of her life," Wade said fiercely. "I'll never accept that she has to die in order to find peace. I sure as hell won't. I'll never know another goddamn day's peace knowing she sacrificed her life for mine."

"She'll pull through," Dane said simply. "Eliza simply doesn't know how to quit."

But Wade could see the worry and despair, reflections of

his own, in Dane's eyes. Could see it in every single one of her teammates' expressions. None of them would ever know peace again if Eliza died.

Wade turned back to the window, staring blindly at the sky as the first soft light of dawn appeared on the horizon. He didn't want to face another sunrise without her. He wanted her to be the last thing he saw when he went to sleep at night and the first thing he saw when he woke the next morning.

She held his heart in the palm of her hands, held his future, his destiny. It all belonged to her, was wrapped up solidly in her and he waited with growing resignation to know her—and his—fate.

The sun rose steadily, dousing the waiting room with bright sunshine, a direct contrast to the black storm of emotions held within. The quiet was driving Wade out of his mind. He was going to go insane if someone didn't tell him something soon.

But he feared the appearance of hospital personnel even as he waited, on edge, for someone to come. Because if they told him the worst, his heart and soul would die in that moment.

Exhaustion and worry had taken its toll on him, and he finally sank into a chair, leaning forward to bury his face in his hands. He had to hold it together. If he broke, if he let even the first wave of emotion get the better of him, he'd never stop. And so he held rigid in his vigil, mind numb, sorrow wrapped solidly around his battered heart and soul.

Still more hours passed and with it the threads holding Wade's sanity together grew thinner. No one had moved. No one had eaten or even gotten up to go to the bathroom. No one stood down for a single moment.

Close to noon, a haggard looking man in scrubs appeared in

the doorway, exhaustion pronounced in his eyes. When he called for those here for Eliza Cummings, Wade surged to his feet, as did every single other occupant of the room.

Wade was there first, pushing by the others so he stood squarely in front of the surgeon.

"Tell me," Wade muttered fiercely.

"She made it through surgery," the doctor said, though there was no real joy or relief in his statement. "I have no idea how the hell she made it. When they brought her in, I gave her less than a five percent chance of surviving the first hour. But she hung on, refusing to give up."

"Can I see her?" Wade asked hoarsely, afraid to feel hope.

"She isn't out of the woods yet," the doctor said grimly. "I don't want to give you false hope. She could still die. Her condition is critical and she's on life support. As soon as she's out of recovery, she'll be moved to ICU. You can see her then. We'll just have to take it day by day, but for now, she's alive."

No. Surely he wouldn't be given such hope only to have it snatched from him in the cruelest way possible. His heart pounded and he felt light-headed as relief poured over him. He hadn't lost her yet. She'd made it through surgery. No way she'd go down after surviving the worst. All she had to do now was recover. Get better. And he'd ensure she did exactly that. He wouldn't leave her side.

"I'll have someone come get you when she's been moved to ICU," the doctor said before taking his leave.

Wade took several steps back and then numbly sank into one of the chairs, his hands shaking. He closed his eyes and swallowed visibly, knowing that when he did see Eliza, it wouldn't be good. But he had to be as strong for her as she'd been for him.

TWENTY-EIGHT

FOR four of the longest days of Wade's life, he kept vigil in the ICU, never leaving Eliza's bedside. The nurses had tried to make him leave, citing strict visitor hours. Wade had dug in and told them over his fucking dead body would he leave her. There had been a tense standoff until the charge nurse had intervened, taken one long, hard look at Wade and then had told the other nurses to let him stay.

Maybe she'd seen just how close he was to losing it. It didn't matter. All that mattered was that he was with her, holding her hand, talking to her. He slept for short intervals, awakening to once more encourage her, bully her, demand that she wake up.

Her team came in, one at a time, at regular intervals. The nurses had already allowed one breach of the rules. Allowing more than two people in Eliza's room at the same time was where they put their foot down solidly. Wade hadn't cared about that either. As long as he was with her, he didn't care who else got to see her.

On the fifth day, Wade had dozed off, leaned over the rail of her bed, his fingers wrapped around hers when he was awakened by a small movement. His eyes snapped open and he glanced down, unable to determine whether he'd dreamed it or if she had really moved her hand.

And then she moved again. Just one tiny clench of her fingers around his. Almost as if to let him know she was there, with him, that she wasn't going anywhere.

Excitedly he leaned forward, talking urgently to her, telling her he was here, that she was okay and he begged her to open her eyes. He begged for half an hour when, finally, he saw it. The slightest movement of her eyelids as if she were straining to open her eyes.

Suddenly remembering the tube down her throat and the fact that if she came around, she'd likely panic, he quickly pushed the button for the nurse with his free hand, all the while continuing his steady encouragement for Eliza to open her eyes.

The nurse came in, looking sharply at Wade.

"She's coming around," he said hoarsely. "She's been moving her hand for the last half hour and I just saw her eyelids twitch. She's coming out of it."

The nurse sprang into action and soon the room was filled with other medical personnel as they prepared to extubate her. An ICU doctor stood by, prepared to re-intubate her if she was unable to breathe on her own. Through it all, Wade continued to remain at her side, holding tightly to her hand, and no one argued with him as they worked around him.

He found himself holding his breath when the tube had been removed from Eliza's throat and held it through the tense seconds following as they waited to see if she would breathe on her own.

Her vitals were checked every minute and then finally, the most beautiful words he'd ever heard came from the doctor.

"Her vitals are good and improving. She should wake soon."

Wade's knees buckled and nearly gave out. He gripped the railing with his free hand and stood there shaking, tears swimming in his eyes. Then he leaned over to kiss her forehead and whispered against her skin.

"Come back to me, baby. You're going to be just fine. Open your eyes and look at me. Let me know you're all right."

Again he saw her eyelids twitch and her eyes moving beneath the closed lids and he caught his breath when he saw the first tiny glimpse of the whites of her eyes.

"That's it," he said urgently. "You can do this, Eliza. Wake up, baby. Wake up so I can tell you how much I love you and that I'm going to spend the rest of my life taking care of you."

Her eyelids fluttered and then blinked, her gaze slowly tracking upward to his face. Then they remained open as she stared at him with recognition and awareness.

"Hi," she whispered hoarsely, nearly inaudible.

It was too much for him to bear any longer. Tears streamed down his cheeks as he pressed his forehead to hers, holding on to her hand while she held on to his.

"Hi yourself," he choked out when he was capable of speech. "Welcome back, beautiful. You scared the ever-loving hell out of me. How about we agree you never do that again?"

Her lips quivered into a semblance of a smile and her eyelids drooped as though it was taking all her strength to remain awake. He pulled his forehead from hers and then stroked her brow lovingly with his hand.

"Go back to sleep, baby. I'll be here when you wake up. I swear it."

"Wade?"

Wade roused instantly when Eliza's voice reached his ears. It was a low, husky whisper, but nothing had ever sounded sweeter.

"I'm here, baby. How you feeling? Are you in pain? Do you want me to call the nurse?"

After regaining consciousness the initial time, Eliza had roused a few more times, but hadn't had the strength to do much more than direct her determined stare at Wade and squeeze his hand. She'd held his hand while her team filtered through, often falling back asleep after only the first few had gotten to talk to her. Wade didn't know how aware of them she had been or if she would even remember their presence.

Carefully, Eliza shook her head. Then she pursed her lips and Wade leaned forward, knowing there was something she wanted to say. He pulled her hand to his lips and simply pressed it against his mouth as he gazed at her with so much love in his heart that it was a physical ache.

"Thomas?" she rasped out.

Wade's expression tightened. "Dead."

Relief washed through her eyes and for a moment she closed them and he thought he'd lost her again to unconsciousness. But then she reopened them, tears turning the beautiful green glossy.

"Good," she whispered.

"Not happy about you taking a bullet for me," he said in a tense voice that still reflected his vivid memory of the event.

She half-smiled. "Didn't figure you would be."

God, she seemed stronger now. After several days of drifting in and out, not even speaking after her first whispered, "Hi," she seemed more determined to remain awake this time.

"Swear to me you'll never do anything so stupid again," he demanded, or rather he intended it to be a command. It came out as a fervent plea, him begging her to never frighten him the way she'd frightened him again.

Her smile was crooked now and she squeezed the hand he'd never once let go. "Can't promise that."

Her words were labored and raspy and she sounded as though she were in pain. He leaned forward in concern.

"Do you need the nurse?" he asked again. "You're hurting, baby."

"No," she said. "Need you to talk to me. Don't want to sleep anymore. I hate sleeping. I feel so alone. It's so dark."

She shivered as she spoke, and it nearly undid him.

"You aren't alone, baby. Never again. Do you understand that? I'm here. I'll always be here. I'm not going anywhere so don't get any ideas of getting rid of me. I'll give you the moon, and there isn't a damn thing I won't do to make you happy, but what I will *not* do is ever leave you."

A tear trickled down her cheek and he tenderly wiped it away.

"I couldn't let him take you away from me," she said painfully. "When you burst in, the last thing I was thinking about was guarding against his mental intrusion. I was so terrified. I wouldn't have survived losing you and he got in because I lost focus, because I panicked and allowed him to see what you meant to me. He wanted to punish me, hurt me, by killing you and I couldn't let him do that."

"Do you think I would have been any happier if you had died?" Wade asked, his voice cracking with emotion. "Do you not have even a clue how much I love you? How much I need you? That I am and have nothing without you? You are the only person I have ever loved, Eliza. The only person who has ever loved *me*. That kind of beauty can't be lost once experienced. You couldn't expect me to survive losing you. I *wouldn't* have survived it."

"And I couldn't have survived losing *you*," she whispered.

He sighed. "Don't we make a fine pair. Bitching about not taking bullets for the other when we've both done exactly that because we love one another and can't even begin to fathom our lives without one another. That's rare, Eliza. That's rare and precious. Just like you."

Her eyes shimmered with emotion at hearing the words he'd given her what seemed a lifetime ago. Words he'd meant absolutely.

"I guess what we have *is* pretty special," she murmured.

"Bet your ass it is," he said around the knot in his throat. "What do you think we should do about it?"

She went pensive, exhaustion creeping in to her features. He thought she might fade away but she seemed to rouse herself and once more directed her full focus on him.

"Are you going to demand that I quit my job?" she asked after a hesitation.

He softened all over with love for his badass, justice-minded woman.

"Not unless you continue with these suicide missions."

The corner of her mouth turned upward and relief flickered in her eyes. He kissed her hand again and became utterly serious when he said his next words.

"I once told you that you stood for what's right. That's who you are, Eliza. And I wouldn't change one single damn thing about you. Will I worry about you and bitch over some of the missions you take? Hell yeah. But I'll never stand in your way or demand that you choose between me and something that is one of the biggest reasons I love you so much. I will, however, expect you to allow me to help when I need to help."

Eliza's eyes were warm as she gazed back at him. "We do make a pretty good team, don't we?"

"Bet your ass," he said again. "And speaking of team, they're all here. I don't know how much you remember, or if you remember them being here at all, but they've been camped out in the waiting room ever since you were brought into surgery. Dane has been worried sick. He loves you, Eliza, and he feels guilty for not doing more to shut you down before you took off for Oregon."

Eliza sighed, pain replacing the warmth in her eyes. "I'd like to see him. I need to apologize. What I did wasn't cool. It was selfish. I made a lot of people who care about me worry. I was too focused on my own pain, fear and vengeance to realize that I was the one hurting the people I love."

"You were *protecting* the people you loved," he gently corrected. "And yes, he's here. I expect he'll be in at the top of the hour when they allow the next visitor back."

She swallowed nervously and he squeezed her hand, kissing her knuckles.

"Baby, he isn't angry with you. None of them are. They just

want to know you're going to be okay. That's all any of them want, especially Dane. Well, and I think he'd very much like to have his partner back. As long as he understands that you are no longer exclusively his."

He smiled as he said the last and delighted in her returning smile.

"I think he already gets that," she said ruefully.

"So, are you going to put me out of my misery and make an honest man out of me?"

She stared inquiringly at him. "Was that a rhetorical question? Because I'm pretty sure this is the first time the subject has been mentioned, or at least an actual question has been asked."

Damn but that was his Eliza. Sassy and sharp-tongued. Never missing a beat or an opportunity to bait him.

"You know damn well I want forever," he said gruffly. "And that means you and me having a ceremony with everyone who means anything to us in attendance that will make me want to crawl out of my skin in discomfort but will suffer through because the end result is you. You being mine in every way possible. Forever."

"I want forever too," she said, an ache to her voice. "I love you so much, Wade. I think I've loved you for a long time, but you scared me. I was scared to love you."

"Me too, baby. Me too. We can be scared together."

"And yeah, I'm going to make an honest man out of you. In more ways than one," she said, her eyes narrowing. "Don't think I don't know about some of your 'business practices.' You're about to clean up your act, Wade Sterling."

He threw back his head and laughed. God, it felt so damn good when he thought he'd never laugh again. Never have reason to be happy. When the most precious thing in the world to him had nearly been taken from him.

When he stopped laughing, he leaned over and brushed his lips over hers, tasting her sweetness, inhaling it, absorbing it into every part of him. So she became the air he breathed.

"As soon as you're out of this place, I'm taking you home and we're getting married. I don't care if I have to carry you down the aisle. I'm not waiting."

She lifted one brow. "You in a hurry?"

"Hell yes, I'm in a hurry. I don't want to give you any time to change your mind and back out. The sooner I get my ring on your finger the better I'll feel."

"In that case, I guess I better set my mind to getting out of this damn hospital as fast as I can," she said teasingly. "That way *you* don't have time to get cold feet and change your mind."

"That will never happen," he said fiercely. "You're stuck with me forever. Every rotten, bad tempered, impatient part of me."

Her smile lit up the entire room and she slowly pulled his hand to her mouth so she could kiss his palm.

"Guess it's lucky for you that I'm wildly in love with rotten, bad tempered and impatient."

ELIZA eased down in the comfortable chair, careful not to wrinkle her wedding gown. She still wasn't fully recovered and had only been out of the hospital for four weeks, four weeks where Wade hovered and refused to allow her to lift so much as a finger. As adamant as he had been in the hospital that they marry the moment she was released, he'd done a complete one eighty and argued that they should wait until she was stronger.

She was just as determined they marry as soon as possible. She belonged. She was loved. And she was deathly afraid that one morning she would wake up and it would have been just a dream.

She gazed at her reflection in the mirror, stunned that the pretty, feminine face looking back at her was really *her*. She'd asked Gracie, Ari, Ramie and Tori to give her a moment alone. The women had overwhelmed her, sharing in the excitement and joy of the day. Gracie had teased her and said that only Eliza ever had a hope of taming Wade while Ari had dryly commented that only a man like Wade ever had a hope of taming Eliza.

The preparations had exhausted her, though she'd never admit to it. Wade would have called off the wedding, or worse, he would have had her in bed and brought in a justice of the peace to marry them so Eliza wouldn't overexert herself. This was her wedding day. A day she'd dreamed of since she was a little girl fantasizing about a fairy tale ceremony and marrying her knight in shining armor. There was no way she was forgoing something she'd resigned herself to never having.

A soft knock sounded at the door and she called out a come in. She slowly turned, surprised to see Dane enter the bridal chamber. She swallowed hard. She and Dane hadn't had the opportunity to really talk since she'd been shot a month ago. Wade had surrounded her, ensuring her every comfort and need and any visits from her coworkers were light and brief.

She couldn't bring herself to meet his gaze, guilt heavy in her heart.

"You look beautiful, Lizzie," Dane said quietly. "Just as a bride should."

She lifted her head, tears obscuring her vision. "I'm so sorry, Dane."

His expression immediately became one of concern. He crossed the distance and sat down in the chair across from her. He collected her hands in his, squeezing in a comforting manner.

"Why are you sorry?"

"For deceiving you. For lying to you. For not trusting you and coming to you from the start. For not being honest with you from the start. You are my dearest friend, but I haven't been a friend to you."

"Lizzie," he said gently.

She refused to look at him.

He cupped her chin and forced her to look at him. "Lizzie, look at me."

Reluctantly she once more met his gaze and her heart squeezed when she saw the camaraderie, the unconditional support, the friendship reflected in his eyes.

"Do I wish you had come to me? Do I wish you had told me about your past when we started working together? Absolutely. But I understand. You need to know something, though. Never. Never have I thought less of you. You are one of the strongest persons I've ever met. And there is no one I'd rather have at my back than you and nothing will ever change that."

He leaned forward, gathering both her hands in his. "Know this, Lizzie. I will always have your back. If you ever need a friend, help or just a shoulder to cry on, I'll always be there."

"Damn it, Dane, if you make me cry and ruin my makeup, I'll kick your ass."

"Hate to tell you but you're hardly in any condition to kick a toddler's ass."

She glared at him and he scowled in response.

"You should still be in bed recovering. Stubborn fool woman. No idea what you're thinking getting married so soon after getting out of the hospital. You'll be lucky if you make it down the aisle. Wade should have damn well handcuffed you to your sick bed."

"One overbearing alpha male is quite enough," she muttered.

"You aren't walking down that aisle alone, Lizzie."

Her eyes widened in surprise. "What?"

"I know you planned to walk the aisle by yourself because

you don't have a father to give you away. Not going to happen. I'm giving you away and it's not open to negotiation."

A knot formed in Eliza's throat and she tried in vain to swallow the obstruction. The tears she'd tried so hard to keep at bay trickled down her cheeks. Makeup be damned.

"You truly are my dearest friend," she whispered. "There's no one I'd rather walk me down the aisle than you."

To Eliza's shock, she saw a glimmer of moisture in Dane's eyes. His hold on her hands tightened.

"He's a good man, Lizzie. I admit we had our differences but we have one thing in common. The most important thing. We both care very much for you. I know he'll take care of you and protect you when I'm not doing it on the job."

Another knock on the door sounded and Tori peeked her head in. She flushed in embarrassment when she saw Dane was inside with Eliza.

"I'm sorry to interrupt," she said nervously. "But it's time, Eliza. Gracie, Ari and Ramie are lined up and I have to hurry back so I don't hold up the ceremony. You've got two minutes."

"Thank you, Tori," Eliza said with a smile. "And thank you for standing up for me."

Tori smiled back. "You're important to us all, Eliza. You've done so much for us all. How could we not be present on your big day?"

With another quick glance at Dane, she hastily ducked from the doorway, shutting it behind her.

Dane stood and then assisted Eliza to her feet. "You ready, Lizzie?"

She smiled. "I've never been more ready in my life."

He walked her slowly out of the bridal chamber, the same

room Gracie had waited in when she married Zack. Who would have thought that Eliza would follow suit? If someone would have told her she would be getting married so soon after Gracie she would have laughed herself silly.

Eliza paced herself, hating the lingering weakness and how quickly she fatigued. It seemed to take forever to get into the vestibule and to the closed doors leading into the sanctuary.

"Take your time," Dane murmured. "Whether you want to admit it or not, you shouldn't even be on your feet much less going through a ceremony and reception."

She bared her teeth, impatience gnawing at her. She wanted the doors to open so she could see Wade and assure herself he hadn't changed his mind. Just as she was getting positively jittery, music swelled and reverberated through the church. The doors opened and she realized she'd been holding her breath. Her gaze immediately locked onto Wade and all the air escaped her lungs leaving her shaken.

He was here. He loved her. He was marrying her.

She paid no heed to the tears streaming down her cheeks as she made her first haltering step on Dane's arm. She had eyes for no one but Wade.

Wade stared, utterly transfixed by the vision of his bride slowly making her way toward him, Dane hovering close by to ensure she didn't fall. Damn it but she hadn't sufficiently healed enough to even be out of bed much less endure a wedding ceremony. Wait, the plan was for her to walk by herself down the aisle, a plan he'd been vehemently opposed to. Apparently Dane hadn't been any fonder of the idea than Wade had been. He grudgingly gave the man credit for looking out for Eliza when she was being too stubborn for her own good. The fool woman was convinced that Wade would change his mind and no longer want to marry her. As if!

Good intentions or not, no way in hell another man was walking his bride down the aisle. Wade strode down the aisle, ignoring the sounds of surprise and laughter as he closed in on Dane and Eliza. He stopped in front of them, ignoring the confused look on Eliza's face.

"Thank you for seeing after Eliza," Wade said to Dane. "But that is my duty, my honor and my pleasure."

Without another word, he swept the open-mouthed bride into his arms, ever mindful of her still-healing injury, and carried her the rest of the way to the floral arch where the pastor stood, trying—and failing—to suppress his amusement.

"Wade," Eliza hissed. "Put me down!"

"I like you just where you are," he said firmly. He looked at the preacher, indicating with a nod for him to proceed.

Nestled securely in his arms, her cheek resting against his chest, Eliza married her knight in shining armor. Never once did his hold waver. They recited their vows, gazes locked. It was as if the pastor didn't exist. Those gathered faded into the background and there were only the two of them.

When it came time to recite their vows, Wade had a surprise for Eliza. Forgoing the traditional vows, he instead looked deeply into her eyes and in a gruff, emotional voice, he said, "Never did I imagine finding the other half of my heart and soul. Never did I believe in the concept of soul mates or there being only one able to complete another. I'm not worthy of you, Eliza. You are everything I'm not. You stand for what's right. You're rare and precious. And you have the most loving, loyal heart of anyone I've ever known. Though I'll never be worthy of your love, your goodness and your heart, know this. No one will ever love you more than I will. Never will there be a more precious, spoiled and pampered woman. Every single day of my life will be spent doing whatever it takes to make you happy and I'll spend the rest of my life trying to be worthy of you. I love you, Eliza. Yesterday, today, tomorrow, forever, eternity. There will never be another I love as I love you. I know it's traditional to say until death do us part, but I refuse to let you go even in death. Long after our lives here are done, our love will live on. Strong, enduring, everlasting. In sickness and in health, in good times and bad. I will always be at your side."

Eliza wasn't the only one who cried at her wedding. There wasn't a dry eye in the entire church. Even Eliza's male teammates were seen discreetly wiping at the corners of their eyes.

And since he'd already defied convention by carrying his bride up the aisle, as soon as Wade and Eliza were pronounced man and wife, he kissed her until even the pastor grew fidgety and then he promptly carried his new wife back down the aisle and into the waiting limousine.

Wade had already told Dane not to expect Eliza back to work for three months, as he was taking her on an extended honeymoon. A very extended honeymoon.

He just hadn't yet informed his new bride of that minor detail, and it caused much amusement in the DSS offices as to Eliza's reaction when she learned she was on an extended leave of absence.

BOOKS BY #1 *NEW YORK TIMES* BESTSELLER MAYA BANKS

WITH EVERY BREATH
A Slow Burn Novel

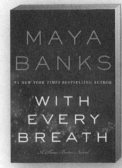

Wade Sterling has always lived by his own rules, a law unto himself who answers to no one. He's never professed to be a good man, and he's definitely not hero material. Wade never allows anyone close enough to see the man behind the impenetrable mask—but one woman threatens his carefully leashed control. She was under his skin and nothing he did rid himself of the woman with the courage of a warrior and who thinks nothing of putting her life before others.

SAFE AT LAST
A Slow Burn Novel

They say young love doesn't last, but a girl from the wrong side of the tracks with unique abilities and the hometown golden boy were determined to defy the odds. For Zack Covington, Anna-Grace—his "Gracie"—was the one. Until one night forever alters the course of their future, when a devastated Gracie disappears without a trace, leaving Zack to agonize over what happened to the girl he loved.

IN HIS KEEPING
A Slow Burn Novel

Abandoned as a baby to a young wealthy couple and raised in a world of privilege, Arial has no hint of her past or who she belonged to. Her only link lies in the one thing that sets her apart from everyone else—telekinetic powers. Protected by her adoptive parents and hidden from the public to keep her gift secret, Ari is raised in the lap of luxury, and isolation. That is, until someone begins threatening her life.

KEEP ME SAFE
A Slow Burn Novel

When Caleb Devereaux's younger sister is kidnapped, the scion of a powerful and wealthy family turns to an unlikely source for help: a beautiful and sensitive woman with a gift for finding answers others cannot. While Ramie can connect to victims and locate them by feeling their pain, her ability comes with a price. Every time she uses it, it costs her a piece of herself. Helping Caleb successfully find his sister nearly destroys her.